"Figure a smooth spar, fifty-five feet long, sloping at a height of as many feet to the water's surface, the said surface not being a mill-pond, but a sheet of foam; figure a pitch dark night, a line stretched along the yard, down which you must slide to the extremity, a sail weighing half a dozen tons banging at your head and your feet, and doing its utmost to throw you; then, having reached the extremity of the yard, figure your legs thrown across it as you might bestride a horse, beneath you the foaming sea, almost at right angles the inclined deck of the ship, a long stone's throw distant — a deep darkness everywhere, save where a wave, breaking massively, flings out a phosphorescent light and deepens the blackness of its own chasm — whilst the gale yells about your ears, and blinds you with spray that stings like hail!"

It is with such magnetic, intense colour that W. Clark Russell consistently entertained his legions of readers and established a formidable reputation as a writer of the sea.

I0680346

JOHN HOLDSWORTH,
CHIEF MATE

JOHN HOLDSWORTH,

CHIEF MATE

by

W. CLARK RUSSELL

ADELAIDE

MICHAEL WALMER

2013

John Holdsworth, Chief Mate first published 1875
This edition published 2013

by

Michael Walmer
49 Second Street
Gawler South
South Australia 5118

ISBN 978-0-9874835-5-3 paperback
ISBN 978-0-9874835-6-0 ebook

TO

MY ONLY TWO BROTHERS

The Rev. Lloyd Russell

and

John Russell, Kimberley, S.A.

and to the

MEMORY OF MY MOTHER

(née Isabella Lloyd)

who died November 14, 1887

CONTENTS.

———◆———

CHAPTER I.

JOHN HOLDSWORTH, CHIEF MATE.

CHAPTER I.

SOUTHBOURNE.

IN a period of English history which graybeards call
the good old times—the fine old times; that is to say,
when Parliament was horribly corrupt, and the Poor
Laws as barbarous as the Inquisition; when it took
fifteen hours to go from London to Dover; and when at
least one-half of the conveniences which we now very
reasonably call the necessities of life had no existence—
Southbourne was a small straggling village, and, by
reason of the quaint and primitive aspect of its houses,
something, even in those good old times, like an
anachronism on the face of the land. What is now a
well-looking street, fairly paved, and decorated with a
number of showy shop-windows, was then an uneven
road, with great spaces of grassy land, dusty and closely
nibbled by goats, between the houses; whilst the houses
themselves were mostly gable-roofed, with latticed windows, which served excellently to exclude the light, and
which gave a blank and lack-lustre look to the edifices,
as though they were weary to death of the view over
the way.

B

Yet, in spite of its architectural deformities, South-bourne was such a place as would weave its homely interests about a man's heart, and be present to his mind when gay and splendid scenes were forgotten. At the very entrance of the village, as you went into the street out of the dusty London Road, stood the King's Arms Inn, a long, low-built, white-faced tavern, with a great sign-board hung flagwise over the doorway, which, when the wind was fresh, would swing with hoarse out-cries, as though urging the distant wayfarer to make haste and enjoy the welcome that was to be obtained, for a few pence, from the stout, well-fed host who pre-sided within. Opposite this tavern stood a decent farm-house, its thatched roof black with time, begirt with walls and palings, within which, when the harvest moon was high, great stacks of hay would rear their gold-coloured sides, and make the air as sweet as the smell of new milk. And all about this pleasant farmhouse were apple and cherry trees, under whose shadows a vast family of cocks and hens held the day eternally busy with their voices; while pigs in unseen sties grunted their hungry discord, and did their lazy best to drown the mournful cooing of doves in wicker cages, and the cheerful notes of the birds, who were attracted in count-less numbers to the farmyard.

Between these two houses ran what the villagers called the High Street; and the eye followed the road, patched here and there with dark-coloured grass, for nearly a third of a mile, noting the gable-roofed houses that looked at each other from either side; the black-smith's shed, where the bellows were always roaring; the flat-roofed baker's shop, standing importunately forwards, away from the little house in which the baker lived ; the butcher's hard by ; the apothecary's next to that ; and the linendraper's shop, which had absorbed the frontage of no less than two solemn-looking houses —noting these and other details contributing to the carnal or frivolous interests of the place, until it settled upon a small building, which, standing in the centre of the road, narrowed it into a large and a small lane, and thus marked the extent and importance of the High Street.

Our story opens on a summer's evening. The daylight is still abroad upon the distant hill-tops, but the twilight has fallen like an inaudible hush upon Southbourne, and the farmyards are tranquil, save when, now and again, some uncomfortable hen seeking a resting-place near to her sovereign cock hops for his perch, but in hopping falls and awakens the sleepers with her fluttering scrambles and keen notes of distress, echoed by a hundred wondering throats.

The evening is warm, and many of the house doors are open ; and at these open doors sit, here and there, men in their shirt-sleeves, or in homely smocks, smoking long pipes, and addressing each other from across the road with voices bespeaking laborious thought, which demands many reflective puffs to clarify and adjust. Now the apothecary's boy comes out and lights the coloured lamp over the door, while the apothecary within sets two wax candles against his brilliant globes of lustrous dyes and illuminates the darksome roadway with a crimson and a yellow gleam. Now the linendraper's assistant steps forth and puts up the shutters to his master's windows, whilst the master himself struts along the floor, flapping his counter with a dust-brush, and inhaling the appetising perfume which streams from an

inner room, and which is the best assurance he could
demand that his supper is preparing.   Anon comes a
lame man, armed with a ladder, a lanthorn, and a can
of oil at his girdle ; he sets the ladder against a lamp-
post, and in five minutes' time succeeds in kindling a
faint uncertain light in the darkling air.   Thrice does
he perform this laborious duty, and then, lo ! the High
Street is illuminated.

These lights seem to act as signals for sundry groups
of gossips, standing here and there along the dusty road,
to disperse.   The small cackle of talk, like the click of
wheels driven against springs, ceases ; the old hobble
towards the houses, the young follow yet more leisurely ;
the gloom deepens ; one by one the doors are closed
and little yellow lights twinkle mistily upon the latticed
windows.   And now, though the clock of St. George's
Church has not yet tolled the half-hour past eight, one
may easily see that the good village of Southbourne,
with one eye upon the candles, costly at sixteenpence
the pound, and another eye upon the early hour that is
to expel it from its slumbers into the fields and the work-
shops, is making what haste it can to creep with heavy
eyelids into bed.

In the house that looks askant down the road and
breaks the thoroughfare into lanes, there is a sorrow at
work that should seem absolutely inconsistent with the
serenity and peace of the summer evening outside.

Three persons are seated in a cosy room ; a tall lamp
on a table sheds a soft light upon the walls ; the window
is open, and the large tremulous stars look in through
the branches of the elms which front the little building.
How sweet is the smell of the clematis about the win-

dow! and see, a great black moth whirrs towards the lamp and occupies the silence with its vigorous slaps against the ceiling.

The old woman in the high-backed chair, looking down upon her placid hands, is a perfect picture of handsome old age : hair white as snow ; a sunken cheek touched with a hectic that passes well for, if indeed it be not, the bloom of health ; a garrulous under lip ; a mild and benevolent expression. She is dressed in an antique satin gown, and a fine red silk handkerchief, as large as a shawl, is pinned about her shoulders.

Facing her sits a young man, broad-shouldered and bronzed, with large lustrous black eyes and dark wavy hair. He wears a pilot cloth coat and black trousers, bell-mouthed at the feet, and a plain silver ring upon his left hand.

Close beside him, on a low chair, sits a young girl, with a sweet and modest face, and bright yellow hair which shines in the lamplight like gold, and blue eyes filled now with tears.

So they sit, so they have sat, for many minutes in silence, and nothing is heard but the ticking of the clock on the mantelpiece, or the awkward moth that hits the ceiling, or now and again the melancholy plaint of some dreaming or belated bird from the dark country that stretches outside like a vision under the throbbing starlight.

Presently the old lady, lifting her head, says :

"I don't think it pleases God that people's hearts should be sorrowful. Nothing should grieve us but the fear of His anger ; and if there be truth in religion, and any wisdom in human experience, there is nothing in this world that should make us sad."

The girl presses her hand to her eyes, and answers in a broken voice :

"John and I have never really been parted before."

"We never can be parted, Dolly, my sweet little wife," says the young man. "There was a fear of parting before, but none now, dear one. I am only leaving you for awhile—and that is not parting, is it, grandmother? Parting is separation, and those whom God has joined cannot be parted, cannot be parted, my Dolly!"

"Ay, that is right!" exclaims the old lady. "John is only leaving you for awhile—you cannot be parted—remember that."

"But it is to be a long while, and my heart will be so lonely without him, granny."

The old lady gives her head a dispirited shake.

"It is all going and coming in this world," says she. "To-day here, to-morrow there : 'tis like breathing on a mirror."

"No, no!" cries the young fellow, "that is a melancholy simile. Life is something more than a breath. I would be content to know nothing but its sorrows, rather than think it the hollow illusion people call it. Oh, Dolly, you must cheer up and help to give me heart. I want all the courage I can get. After this voyage we needn't be separated any more. Remember, next year I shall be skipper, and then I can take you to sea with me."

"If next year had only come !" the poor little girl sobs, and lets her face fall upon her husband's hand.

"Nay, nay," the old lady chides, gently, "'tis thy business to help and support thy husband, Dolly. Will tears help him? Resolution is softened by them, and made weak and womanish. Your mother before you, my child, knew what it was to part from your father. He once went to Spain, and for many months we knew not whether he was living or dead. You were a little child then. What came to her, came to me, and must come to you as it comes to all women who will needs transplant their own hearts into men's. Know this, Dolly, that no love is purely sweet that has not known trials and afflictions."

"Hear that, my little one," says the young husband, stooping his head until his lips touch his wife's ears. "Let us seek a blessing in our grief, and we shall find one. It teaches me to know my love for you—our love for each other. Is not such knowledge blessed ?"

"See here, Dolly," continued the grandmother, battling with the tears provoked by the influx of hurrying memories which followed her reference to her own child, Dolly's mother. "When John is gone, we will put up a calendar against the wall in your bedroom ; and every night, after we have worshipped God, we will prick off a day, and you shall see how quickly the calendar grows small under our hands. I am seventy years old, and it was but the other day that I was dancing your mother in my arms, and I was a young woman, and your grandfather a hearty man, with brown hair under his wig, and bright big eyes like yours. Why, that was fifty years ago, and it seems but yesterday ! Many's the bitter tear I have shed, and the grief I have borne ; but the times *I* mourn cannot come back to me, they are gone for ever—my life is but an empty chamber now ; there is no fire in the grate, and the chairs are vacant, and I feel so lonely that I sometimes wish I was dead. But what is your grief ? It is but a few months' separation, and every day that dies will give you happiness. It is not so with others, nor with me—no! no!"

As the old grandmother spoke, with some perception, perhaps, of that rather discreditable characteristic of human nature which finds the best solace for its own trouble in the consolation that is wrought out of the griefs of others, the girl gradually raised her head and fixed her eyes wistfully on her husband's, then laid her cheek against his shoulder, as a child would whom its tears have worn out.

"Grandmother," said the young man, "I leave my Dolly to your care, and I know you will love and cherish her as though you were sure that any ill that came to her would break my heart."

"She cannot be dearer to me than she always was," answered the old lady, solemnly; "but be sure, John, that I'll take extra care of her, since her preciousness is doubled by being dear to you and having your life bound up in hers."

"And you will keep her heart up with happy thoughts of me, grandmother," continued the young fellow, his dark eyes made infinitely tender by the shadow of tears, "and bid her remember that when the wind blows here it may be a summer calm where I am, and blue sky when there are thunderstorms here. You'll remember this, Dolly?"

"Yes, John."

"The calendar is a good thought of grandmother's. Or you may watch the flowers, Dolly; you'll see them fade away and leave the ground bare. By-and-by they'll spring up again, and they will be a promise that I am coming back to you—coming quickly—quick as the wind will blow me—back to my little wife, to my sweet wife, Dolly."

She sobbed quickly with renewed passion, and clasped his hand.

There was a childlike beauty in her face that made her sorrow infinitely touching for him, who loved her with all the strength of his great heart, to behold. He looked wistfully at the old grandmother; but she, more powerless than he, was brooding over the to-morrows which were to come when he should have gone away and left her alone with Dolly's grief.

"I have a mind," she said at last, "to send for Mr. Newcome, the rector. He should be able to point out to Dolly better than either of us can, that there is something unrighteous in suffering our hearts to be overcome by any dispensations God in His wise providence may choose to ordain."

"No, I don't want Mr. Newcome," sobbed Dolly. "I must cry, granny. When John is gone, I'll dry my eyes, and think of nothing but the time when he is to come back to me. But whilst I see him, and know that this time to-morrow he will be gone, I can't help crying, indeed I can't, granny."

"Ay, my dear, but if your tears could bind him to you, and take the place of his duties which summon him away, they would be very well. But it is your place to help him in his troubles, as it is his to help you in yours; and see what a lonesome air his face has as he watches you, because he feels himself away from you by your refusing to listen to the words he tries to comfort you with."

"I would give my right hand to save Dolly from these tears, grandmother," said John, "but it is her love that frets. By-and-by her eyes will grow bright, for she will know that every hour which passes after I have left her is bringing us nearer to next summer, when we shall be together again."

"But a year is such a long time," wailed Dolly. "It is four times over again the months we have been together, and it seems ages ago since you came home, John. And granny doesn't know the dangers of the sea. You have never talked to her as you have to me. Haven't you told me of shipwrecks, and how men fall overboard, and how some ships catch fire and not a creature saved of all a great ship's crew?"

"Yes, Dolly," he answered, smoothing her bright hair; "but I have always said that the sea isn't more dangerous than the land. There's danger everywhere for the matter of that, isn't there, grandmother?"

"Oh dear yes," groaned the old lady; "there are deaths going on all about us, on the dry land, quick as our pulses beat."

"Ay, true enough, grandmother," rejoined John; "more deaths are going on ashore than are going on at sea. But why do we talk of death? People part and meet again—why shouldn't we? There is no end to trouble if once we begin to think of what *may* happen. A man should put his trust in God"——

"Yes, that first, that chiefly," interrupted the grandmother.

"And fight his way onward with as much courage and hope and resolution to win as though there were no such thing as death in the world at all. When I bid you good-bye, Dolly, I shan't say good-bye, *perhaps for ever;* no! no! I will say good-bye till next summer. Summer is sure to come, and why shouldn't it bring me back?"

"We will pray God that it will," exclaimed the grandmother.

Thus these honest hearts talked and hoped; but, in truth, the parting was more bitter than Dolly could bear.

On this, the eve of her husband's leaving her, she could see no promise in time, no sunshine in the long and dismal blank that stretched before her. She was quite a young bride, had been married only three months; but his presence had already become a habit to her, a portion of her life, a condition of her happiness.

She had engaged herself to him eighteen months since, not many weeks before he sailed on his last voyage; but though she had learnt to love him tenderly as her sweetheart, his going did not then afflict her as it now did. He was only her lover then, but now he was her husband. She was ardent when she became his wife, flushed with the sweet and gracious emotions of her new state, and because the thought of the approaching time threw a shadow upon her happiness, she drove it deep down in her heart, out of sight almost, and so unfitted herself for bravely encountering the certain trouble that was to come.

It had come now; its full weight was upon her; she thought it must break her heart.

When we found them, they had not long returned from the last walk they were to take together for many a weary month; and it was so bitterly sad to them both, that no words can express its pathos. They were surrounded by familiar and beloved objects; and every detail that had heretofore made up the colour and life of their married love now came, each with its special pang of sorrow, to tell them that their dream was dissolved, and that their embraces, their whispers—indeed their very hopes—must be postponed until a period so far off, that it seemed as if no time would ever bring it to them. The poor fellow did his utmost to inspirit her; all the unsubstantial comfort he strove to lay to his own heart he gave to her; but his broken voice made his cheery assurances more sad even than her tears; and down by the little river, when the evening had gathered, and the soft stars were looking upon them, he had given way to his grief, and wept over her as if the form he pressed to him were lifeless.

The story of his courtship and marriage was as simple as the pastoral life of the village in which it occurred.

He had been called to Southbourne by his aunt, who lived there, and who felt herself dying. He had then just returned from a ten months' voyage. He was fond of his aunt, as the only living relative he had, and came to her at once. At her house—indeed, by her bedside —he met Mrs. Flemming, Dolly's grandmother. Mrs. Flemming took a fancy to him, admired his handsome face, his honest character, the cordial tenderness of his nature, which he illustrated by his devotion to his sick aunt, and asked him to her house, where he met Dolly.

He fell in love with her; and then, but not till then, he found that Southbourne was an infinitely better place to live in than the neighbourhood of the West India Docks.

Dolly was an innocent little creature, and hardly knew at first what to make of the love she had inspired in her grandmother's young friend; but by degrees the old story was read through between them, and the last chapter found them betrothed with Mrs. Flemming's full consent.

Meanwhile the aunt had died and left her little savings to her nephew, who gave the money to Mrs. Flemming to take care of for him until he came home. He was then chief mate, aged twenty-eight. When thirty he was to command a ship, his employers promised. So when he returned, twenty-nine years old, with only another year before him to serve out as a subordinate, he claimed Mrs. Flemming's leave to marry Dolly; and within three weeks from the time of his arrival they were man and wife.

There could be no hitch: there was nobody's leave but Mrs. Flemming's to get. He and Dolly were both of them orphans. Her parents had died when she was a little girl; his, some years before this story begins. His father had been skipper in the service John belonged to, and the shipowners' favourite captain. Indeed, Captain Holdsworth had served his employers well, and as a token of their gratitude, they kept their eyes on his son; which meant that he was appointed the moment he had passed his examination as first mate, and was to be skipper at an age when a good many in the service were just entering upon their duties as second in command. But this only really argued that the owners knew a smart seaman when they saw him. Young Holdsworth was that; and critical as was the jealousy his quick promotion excited, there was not a man who could be got to say that Jack Holdsworth wasn't as good a sailor as ever trod upon shipboard.

The first thing he did, when he had the banns put up at St. George's, was to rent the little house that turned its shoulder upon the Southbourne main road, and furnish it with the money his aunt had left him. That was to be Dolly's and grandmother's home. Old Mrs. Flemming had some furniture of her own and an annuity; this last she was to club with John's pay, which Dolly was to draw every month, and so they would have money enough to keep them as ladies. But the old grandmother's furniture was very crazy: she of course thought it beautiful and elegant; but this did not prevent the chairs from breaking when John sat on them, nor the legs of the tables from coming off when they were handed through the doors. Such of these relics as did not go to pieces were put into hèr bedroom, at her particular request, because they enabled her to realise old times; the rest vanished in a cloud of dust into a distant auction-room, and were never heard of more.

The young people's life was an idyl until the time approached for Holdsworth to sail. They went away for a week after they were married, and Dolly saw life: that is, she saw London, which frightened her, and she was very glad to get home. They had pretty nearly three months before them, and that seemed to give them plenty of time to enjoy themselves in. To be sure, the little cloud upon the horizon grew bigger and bigger every day, and Dolly saw it, and knew that in three months' time it would have overspread the heavens, and filled the earth with its leaden shadow; but she shrank from looking in that direction, and fixed her eyes on the blue sky overhead, and was as gay under its brightness as if it were never to know an eclipse.

Mrs. Flemming and Dolly had several friends in Southbourne, and during these months tea-parties were pretty frequent. Even the rector asked them to tea, and went to drink tea at their house; and this occasion was a celebrated one, for the rector was a kind, whimsical old gentleman, and insisted on a game of forfeits being played. There were three girls besides Dolly present, so kissing was practicable; and loud was the laughter when it fell to the rector's lot to kiss Mrs. Flemming, which he did with such a courtier-like air, that, under its influence, the grandmother's memory unfolded itself; and she instructed the company, in a tremulous voice, and with a lean, underscoring forefinger, in the behaviour of the men of *her* day, when men *were* men, etc. etc. Hunt the slipper followed the forfeits, and the evening was closed with portnegus, October ale, and dishes of fruit, sandwiches, and sweetmeats.

Hours so spent would make just such a memory as would keep a man's heart warm in his bosom under any skies, in any climes, in calm or in storm. Years after the very inscriptions on the tombs of the rector and Mrs. Flemming were scarcely to be read amid the encrusting moss and the toothmarks of time, John Holdsworth remembered that evening: how, flushed as the two Miss Lavernes were into positive prettiness by laughter and Mr. Jackson the curate's discreet kisses, Dolly looked a queen to them; how her sweet eyes had peeped at him over the rector's shoulder, as the worthy clergyman claimed his forfeit; how she hung about him and sported, as any infant might, at his side, with her laughter never so ringing and melodious as when her hand was in his. How the kindly grandmother had hobbled about the room, with rusty squeaks of laughter in her mouth, to elude the rector's reluctant pursuit;

how Miss Nelly Laverne blushed, and giggled, and tossed her head about when Mr. Jackson kissed her. . . .

The curtain was falling, the lights were dimming, and now tears and sighs and heartrending yearnings were making a cruel ending of the pleasant summer holiday.

CHAPTER II.

THE "Meteor" was a full-rigged ship of eleven hundred tons, with painted ports and a somewhat low freeboard, which gave her a rakish look. Her figure-head represented a woman, naked to the waist, emerging from a cloud, and was really a sweet piece of carving. She was a ship of the old school, with big stern windows, and a quaint cuddy front and heavy spars. Yet, built after the old-fashioned model, her lines were as clean as those of an Aberdeen clipper.

She made a glorious picture, as she lay off Gravesend, the clear summer sky tinting the water of the river a pale blue, and converting it into a mirror for an ideal representation of the graceful vessel. Many boats were clustered about her side, and up and down her canvased gangway went hurrying figures. The ensign was at the peak, and at the fore floated the blue-peter, signal to those who took concern in her that she would be soon under weigh.

She was bound to New York, whence she was to carry another cargo south, ultimately touching at Callao before she spread her wings for the old country.

There were a few first-class passengers on board, and some of them stood near the gangway in low and earnest talk with friends, while others were on the poop, gazing at the shore with wistful eyes. One of these was a widow, whose husband had been buried a few weeks before in the churchyard of a little Kentish town. She was taking her boy back with her to New York, where her friends were; and there they stood, hand in hand, the child with wondering eyes everywhere, the mother with a fixed gaze upon the land which was consecrated for ever to her heart by the beloved form it held.

The river was brilliant and busy with vessels at anchor or passing to and fro, with boats pulling from shore to shore, with the gay sunshine deepening and brightening the colours of flags, or flashing white upon the outstretched canvas, and trembling in silver flakes upon the water. Sailors hung over the forecastle of the "Meteor," bandying jokes full of pathos, or exchanging farewells with wives and sweethearts, or male friends in boats grouped, with outstretched oars, around the bows of the ship. Some of the hands were aloft casting off the yard-arm gaskets, ready to sheet home when the boatswain's pipe should sound. The wind—a light breeze—was north, a soldier's wind that would take them clear of the river, and make a fair passage for them down Channel; and now they were only waiting for the captain to come on board with the pilot to start.

By eleven o'clock the ship was to be under weigh; and even as the clear chimes of the clock striking the hour floated across the river from the land, a boat pulled by three men swept alongside, and the captain, followed by the pilot, sprang up the ladder.

A tall, broad-shouldered young man stood at the gangway to receive them, and touched his cap as the captain came on board.

" All ready, Mr. Holdsworth ?"

" All ready, sir."

" Man the windlass then."

" Ay, ay, sir."

He was on the forecastle in a jiffy, and the thunder of his voice went along the deck and brought all hands to the windlass as if a line had pulled each man to his place. The boatswain's pipe shrilled, the pilot's face, coloured like mahogany, took an anxious expression; and then clank! clank! clank! went the windlass, followed in a moment by a hoarse song, which at regular intervals burst into a chorus :—

> " And when you come to the dockyard gates,
> Yo, boys, yo !
> You'll find that Sal for her true love waits,
> Heave, my bully-boys, heave !
> Then, heave my boys, oh, heave together !
> Yo, boys, yo !
> And get her out o' the stormy weather !
> Heave, my bully-boys, heave !"

Then came such cries as these :—

" Sheer off you boats there !"

" Get the gangway ladder in-board."

" Loose the inner jib, one of you !"

" A hand aft to the wheel !"

To see young Holdsworth now was to see a sailor, with a voice like a gale of wind, the whole great ship and her thousand complications of spars, ropes, sails, packed, so to speak, like a toy in the palm of his hand.

The skipper was below; the pilot was lord and master now, and Holdsworth watched his face for orders.

Soon the cable was up and down, the anchor lifted, and some hands left the windlass to make sail. The tide had got the ship, and she was floating almost imper-

ceptibly past a large American vessel that had brought-
up the evening before. A few boats followed; some
turned and made for Gravesend, the inmates standing
up and waving their hats and handkerchiefs.

By this time the anchor was catted, and all hands
quitted the forecastle to make sail. Then you might hear
cries of "Sheet home!" from the air; down fell great
spaces of canvas like avalanches of snow; chains rattled
through blocks; fore and aft songs and choruses were
raised and continued until silenced by the order "Belay!"
The yards rose slowly up the polished masts and stretched
the canvas tight as drum-skins. The men on board the
Yankee crowded her forecastle and gave the Britisher a
cheer as she passed. Amid the songs of the men, the
piping of the boatswain and his mates, and the noisy
commands of the pilot, the "Meteor" burst into a cloud
of canvas, chipped a white wave out of the blue river,
and went ahead like a yacht in a racing match.

The breeze freshened as the river widened. The
decks were quiet now, the ropes coiled down clear for
running, and everything hauled taut and snug. At
two o'clock she was foaming along under royals and
flying-jib, whisking past colliers dragging their main
channels through the water as if they were drowning
flies struggling for the land; overhauling smart
schooners and ships as big as herself, and making the
land on either side of her dwindle down and down into
flat marshy country.

The pilot, pompous to the last extremity, with bow
legs and moist eyes, strutted fore and aft the poop, sometimes calling an order to the man at the wheel, and
constantly looking aloft, ahead, and around him. The
passengers lounged about the deck or hung over the

side, watching the foaming water rush past them, and almost losing—those of them, at least, who were leaving their homes—their sadness in the sense of exhilaration begotten by the swift speeding of the vessel through the glory and freshness of the summer afternoon.

Forward, the men were industrious in the forecastle, rigging up their hammocks, or preparing their bunks for the night, or overhauling their sea-chests, or the canvas bags which, among seamen, often answer the purpose of sea-chests. It was a queer sight to see their busy figures in the twilight of the forecastle—here the black face of a negro; there the broad features of a Dutchman; here a mulatto; there a lantern-jawed Yankee, peak-bearded and narrow-hipped—a world in miniature, something after the nature of a menagerie, all talking in English, with accents which made the effect indescribable gibberish to the unaccustomed ear. They were most of them friends already; some had sailed in company before; and now they would suspend their work to offer one another a chew of tobacco, to beg the loan of a " draw," meaning a pipe; while the air grew insufferable to all but a seaman's digestion, with the smell of black cavendish and the inexpressible odour of bilge-water, tar, hemp, and the ship's cargo generally, which rose directly through the fore-hatch, and was blown into the forecastle by the draught under the foresail.

At eight o'clock the "Meteor" was off Margate, all sails but royals set; one of the noblest spectacles of beauty, grace, and majesty the world has to offer—a full-rigged ship—a leaning mountain of canvas rushing under the sky, with a whirl of foam bursting like two gigantic white arms from her sides.

But the North Foreland brings you to a sharp turn, and the wind had drawn three or four points to the west, and was blowing fresh in Mid Channel as the pilot saw by the distant Goodwin Sands on the port bow, which lay upon the horizon in a long streak of foam, like the Milky-way in the sky.

This was a pity, because, unless they were disposed to stand for the French shore, and so make Folkestone by a long board, they would have to bring-up in the Downs.

However, there was no help for it; for, though the vessel's yards were braced hard up against the lee rigging, she continued to fall off half a point by half a point, and, by the time she was off Ramsgate, her head was south. But the "Meteor" could sail to windward like a yacht. They furled the mainsail, took a single reef in the topsails, and then all hands stood by to put the ship about. Standing-by is sailors' English for being ready. The men went forward, and the ship, with two hands at the wheel, made straight for the South Sand Head—the southernmost portion of the formidable Goodwin Sands.

The Channel was a glorious scene. The sun had sunk behind the land, bequeathing a broad red glare to the heavens, over which some great clouds were unfurling themselves—livid promontories with flaring crimson headlands. Astern rose the solid white cliffs, looking phantasmal upon the dark-coloured water. On the right the land swept into a bay, hugging the water flatly as far as Deal, then rising into a great front of frowning cliffs, which stood black against the background of the red sky. The gloom of the gathering evening had paled the outlines of the houses into the shadowy land ; but here and there you could see small vessels riding close in shore, or smacks with red sails creeping round the various points, whilst all between was the quick-running sea, coloured by the different depths of sand into an aspect of wild and multiform beauty. Away on the left the water, quivering with hurrying waves polished like oil, stretched to a dim and desolate horizon. Here and there a brig, or a barque, ploughed laboriously for the Downs, shipping seas like columns of snow and lurching like a drunkard that must presently fall. The " Meteor " overtook and passed many of these vessels as if they were buoys, sometimes running so close along-side as to take the wind out of their sails and set them upright on an even keel. It was strange to look down upon their decks, lying close to the water, and see the steersmen gazing upwards, the masters walking to and fro and not deigning to notice anything but their own ships, a head or two peering over the bulwarks ; to hear the groaning and grunting of the timbers, the yelling of the wind in the masts ; and then, in a moment, to see them pitching and tumbling astern, dwindling into toys and scarcely perceptible among the lead-coloured waves.

But now the crimson had faded out from over the land, and where it had vanished burned a strong and steady light, topping the summit of the highest and outermost cliff. The night fell, and all about the expanse of water innumerable lights started into life : lanterns of vessels in the Downs, of passing ships, of the Goodwin beacons. The clouds which had looked slate-coloured against the sunset were now white, and rolled like great volumes of steam across the stars.

Then right ahead of the ship rose a pale white line—
a quick, spectral play of froth, and a great, red star
shining like an arrested meteor, and which a few minutes
before seemed to be many miles distant, grew big and
lurid and dangerous.

A deep voice sounded along the "Meteor"—"All
hands about ship!"

A rush of feet and then a silence; round flew the
wheel like a firework; the red light ahead swept away
giddily to the left.

"Helm's alee!"

The canvas shook like thunder, and the passengers
crowded aft, wondering to find the ship upright.

"Mainsail haul!"

And at this signal forth burst a loud chorus; the
released braces allowed the yards to fly round, the decks
echoed to the tramping of feet and to the cries of men;
the vessel lay over as though she must capsize; there
was a rush of inexperienced passengers to windward;
another hoarse command; round flew the foreyards, and
in a few minutes the "Meteor" was darting through the
water with her head for Deal, and the pale phosphorescent gleam of the Goodwin Sands dying out upon the
sea on her weather quarter.

The ship tacked three times during the next hour;
and at half-past nine the wind lulled, and the moon
came out of the sea, a broad, yellow shield. There was
something indescribably solemn in the rising of this orb
as she climbed in a haze over the edge of the horizon,
and flashed a wedge of quivering light into the tumbling
waters. The sails of the "Meteor" caught the radiance
presently, and her long wake glittered in the light like
a trail of silver spangles.

She was in the Downs now, and in a dead calm, and within half-an-hour she was riding at anchor, everything furled aloft, and taut and snug as a man-of-war, with many ships about her, resting like phantom vessels on the surface of the water.

An anchor-watch was set, and the crew after smoking, and yarning and lounging about the forecastle, went below, and a deep repose fell upon the erewhile busy labouring ship. The silence was unbroken, save by the murmur of some of the passengers talking in a group around the cuddy skylight, or by the sound of a fiddle played in some one of the nearer-lying vessels, or by the faint, melodious murmur of the breakers boiling upon the pebbly strand of Deal.

A breathless summer night! with big shooting-stars chasing the heavens, and a moon growing smaller and brighter each moment, and the dim tracery of the tapering masts and rigging of the "Meteor" pointing from the deep and vanishing in the gloom. Away on the left, for the tide had swung the ship round and pointed her bowsprit up Channel, glittered the lights of Deal, suggestions of home life which riveted many eyes and made many hearts thoughtful and sad—none more so than Holdsworth's, whose watch it was, and who, now that his active duties were over, could surrender himself to the bitter luxury of thought.

He paced to and fro athwart the poop, his heart far away in the little village he had quitted. The face of his child-wife rose before him, and he lived again in the hard parting that had wrenched his heart and sent him sobbing from his home. He felt her clinging arms about his neck; he looked down into her swollen eyes;

he repeated again and again, in broken tones, his fond and last entreaty that she would keep her heart up, pray for him, and think only of the joyous summer that would come to bless and bring them together once more.

The music ceased in the distance; the tinkling of bells, announcing the half-hour past ten, came stealing across the water, and was echoed by five ringing strokes upon the bell on the "Meteor's" quarter-deck.

Half-past ten! Was Dolly sleeping now? Had her grief and her tears wearied her into repose? How long, how very long, it seemed since he saw her last! The time was to be counted in hours, but it appeared days and weeks to him.

He leaned with his arms upon the poop rails, and stood lost in thought. A question asked in a soft voice made him turn.

"Do all those lights there belong to ships?"

The speaker was the widow to whom Holdsworth's attention had been several times attracted during the day by the air of sadness her face wore, and her devotion to her bright-haired little boy, whose sweet wondering eyes, as he cast them round, had reminded him of Dolly's, and drawn his heart to him.

"Yes, they belong to ships at anchor like ours."

"How beautiful is this night! I have left my boy asleep and stolen from the cabin to breathe the fresh air."

"I daresay the dear little fellow sleeps well after the excitement he has gone through. I noticed that his wondering eyes were very busy when we were in the river."

Hearing this, she grew frank and cordial at once.

Her woman's heart was as sure of him as if she had known him all his life.

"Did you notice my child? I should have thought you were too much occupied. He was tired out, God bless him! when I put him to bed; too tired even to say his prayers. He has no father now to love him, so I must give him a double share of my love."

"Ah, you will not find that hard. He is a manly little fellow, and he and I will become great friends, I hope."

"I trust you will. . . . You are Mr. Holdsworth? I heard the captain call you by that name. And you are the chief mate?"

"Yes, madam."

"I admire your profession, Mr. Holdsworth, and have a good excuse for doing so, for both my father and brother were sailors. But I don't think I could ever let my boy go to sea; I could never bear to part with him. And I sometimes wonder how the wives of sailors can endure to be separated from their husbands."

"That is the hardest part of our profession," answered Holdsworth quickly. "I never understood it before this voyage. I have had to leave my young wife; may God protect her until I come back."

"Is she very young?"

"Nineteen."

"Poor girl!" exclaimed the widow, with deep sympathy in her voice. She added, cheerfully, "But this separation will only make you dearer to each other. You are sure to meet again. Time flies quickly, and all these weary days will seem no more than a dream to you when you are together."

She sighed and glanced down at the deep crape on

her dress. The moonlight enabled Holdsworth to notice the glance, and the pathos of it silenced him. In the presence of such an experience as *her* parting was—he knew whom she had lost by her reference to her fatherless boy—his own sorrow appeared light.

"There is always hope, there is always the promise of happiness in store while there is life," she continued gently. "Do not be down-hearted, Mr. Holdsworth. This parting is but a temporary interruption of your happiness. Be sure that God will protect your young wife while you are away, and do not doubt that He will lead you back to her." She smiled softly at him, and adding, "I must go to my little one now," bowed cordially and went away.

He could have blessed her for an assurance which, having no better foundation than a woman's sympathy, cheered him as no thoughts of his own could have done. "That is a true heart," he said to himself, and resumed his walk, repeating her words over and over again, and drawing a comfort from them that made his step elastic and his eyes bright.

CHAPTER III.

DOWN CHANNEL.

AT six o'clock next morning the sleeping passengers were awakened by cries and trampings which, to some of them at least, were novel disturbers of their slumbers. They might have told the reason of all this noise without going on deck; for those who slept in cots found the deck making an angle with their beds, and the lee portholes veiled with rushing green water, and all the movables crowded together at any distance from where they had been deposited the night before. And hoarse cries sounded, and the clanking of massive chains, and the strange groaning a ship makes when she heels over to a weight of canvas.

Yes! the "Meteor" was under weigh, with a spanking breeze on the starboard quarter, which she would haul round abeam—her best point of sailing—when she had cleared the South Foreland. If this breeze held, the pilot said, he would be out of the ship and toasting her in rum and water at Plymouth before the sun went down next day.

Some of the passengers came on deck when the ship was off Folkestone, and then they saw as fair a sight as the world has to offer—the great white English cliffs topped with swelling tracts of green, with here and there

small bays with spaces of yellow sand between ; houses
thickly grouped—so it seemed in beholding them from
the sea—upon the very margin of the cliff; slate-coloured
hills paling far, far away with visionary clouds upon
them ; and between the ship and the shore many
pleasure-boats and other craft, with white or ochre-
coloured sails and bright flags, lending spots of red and
blue to the perspective of the chalky cliff.

The pilot hugged the wind, rightly apprehensive that
it might draw ahead and cripple him for sea room ;
and the "Meteor" hereabouts was so close to the land
that those on board her could see the people walking
on shore—man's majesty illustrated by dots of black
upon the beach or the heights. Overhead was a bril-
liantly blue sky, with small wool-white clouds driving
over it ; the sea laughed in dimples and shivered the
white sunlight far and wide, so that every crest gleamed
with a diamond spark of its own ; and away on the left,
a pale faint cloud floating upon the horizon, was the
French coast.

The gay panorama swept by and new scenes opened
—stretches of barren coast with ungainly Coastguards'
huts for their sole decoration ; spaces of vivid green
ruled off with lines of soft brown sand, and low black
rocks mirrored in the lake-like surface of the water
under the lee ; whitewashed villages with wreaths of
blue smoke curling from their midst, and broad expanses
of trees darkening the lightlier-coloured landscape with
delicate shadows. Sturdy vessels, the dray-horses of
the Channel, slow, deep laden, and wafting, many of
them, the scent of pine and other woods across the water,
were overtaken and passed, often amid the laughter
of the crew on the "Meteor's" forecastle, and "chaff,"

which even the grave Captain Steel, the "Meteor's" skipper, condescended to smile at. How picturesque these vessels! Here a Dutch barque painted white, with square-faced men staring over the bulwarks, a red-capped commander in sea boots and vast inexpressibles, and a steersman who sometimes looked at the "Meteor" and sometimes at the sails of his own ship, mixing duty and curiosity in a manner delightful to behold ; there a North-country brig with dirty patched sails and black rigging, and a crew with smoked faces and a grinning head at the galley door; sometimes a French smack with as many hands on board as would man a Black Ball Liner, women among them in red petticoats and handkerchiefs around their faces, some gutting fish, some mending nets, some peeling potatoes, and all talking and gesticulating at once, but suspending both their work and their talk to crowd to the smack's side and stare at the noble English vessel ; and sometimes a little open boat at anchor, with a man in her fishing with deep gravity, and paying no more heed to the ship in whose wake his cockle-shell would bob like a cork float, than were he the only tenant of the great glittering surface of water.

But soon the coast sank low in the horizon. The "Meteor" was standing for the deeper water of the Middle Channel, and close hauled, but with all sails set, she had paled old England into a thin blue cloud, and was heading straight for the great Atlantic Ocean.

The night passed ; the morning broke ; but the "Meteor" was not out of the Channel yet. The pilot grumbled as he cast his groggy eyes aloft and saw the weather-leaches lifting. He would have to go about to fetch Plymouth, unless he had a mind to cross the Atlantic, and this was certainly not his intention.

All the passengers came on deck after breakfast; the ladies brought out their work, the gentlemen lighted cigars, and those who had made a voyage before looked knowing as they cast their eyes about and asked nautical questions of the captain.

As to the pilot, he was ungetatable. Moreover, his language was so clouded with marine expletives that his lightest answer was generally a shock to the sensibilities.

Every boatman from Margate to Penzance calls himself a pilot nowadays; but the genuine pilot—such a man as this who was taking the "Meteor" down Channel —stands out upon the marine canvas with an individuality that makes him unique among seafaring human kind. Figure a square, bow-legged man, in a suit of heavy pilot cloth, a red shawl round his neck, a tall hat on his head, a throat the colour of an uncooked beefsteak, and a face of a complexion like new mahogany, small moist rolling eyes, a voice resembling the tones of a man with the bronchitis calling through a tin trumpet, and an undying affection for Jamaica rum. Such was Mr. Dumling, the "Meteor's" pilot, a man to whom the gaunt sea-battered posts, the tall skeleton buoys, the fat wallowing beacons, and the endless variety of lights ashore and at sea, from the North Foreland to the Land's End, were as familiar and intelligible as the alphabet is to you; who was so profoundly acquainted with the Channel that he boasted his power to tell you within a quarter of a mile of where he was, by the mere faculty of smell! A man who could look over a ship's side and say, "Here are four fathoms of water, and yonder are nine," "And where the shadow of the cloud rests the water is twelve fathoms deep;" and so on, every inch of the road, for miles and miles—a miracle of memory ! To appreciate the value of such a man you should be with him in the Channel in a pitch-dark night, blowing great guns from the north-east, with the roar of the Goodwin on the lee bow, and a sea so heavy that every blow the ship receives communicates the impression that she has struck the ground, while the black air is hoarse with the gale and fogged with stinging spray.

The wind is nowhere more capricious than in the English Channel. At one o'clock the spanking breeze swept round to the south-east ; the watch went to work at the braces; up went the foretopmast-stun'sail, and the " Meteor " rushed ahead at twelve knots an hour.

"We shall be off Plymouth at eight o'clock," says the pilot, and went below to lunch with a serene face.

He was right. At eight o'clock the " Meteor " was lying with her main yards backed, dipping her nose in a lively sea, with a signal for a boat streaming at her mast-head.

The passengers might take their last look at old England then, whilst the glorious sunset bathed the land in gold, and made the wooded shores beautiful with colour and shadow. And now, dancing over the waters, came a white sail, which dimmed slowly into an ashen hue as the crimson in the skies faded and the waters darkened.

" Any letters for shore ?" says Captain Steel, moving among the passengers, and soon his hand grows full. Many of the men come forward and deliver missives for the wife, for Sue, for Poll, to the skipper, who gives them to the pilot. The boat, glistening with the sea-water she has shipped, sweeps alongside, ducks her sail, and is brought up by a line flung from the main chains.

" Good-bye, cap'n," says the gruff pilot ; "wish you

a pleasant voyage, I'm sure, gen'l'men and ladies;"
drops into the main chains, and from the main chains
drops into the boat; the sail is hoisted, a hat waved, a
cheer given from the ship's forecastle, and away bounds
the lugger in a cloud of spray.

Now bawls Captain Steel from the break of the
poop; round swing the main yards; the noble ship
heels over, trembles, and starts forward, and, with the
expiring gleam of the sunset upon her highest sails, the
"Meteor" heads for the broad Atlantic, and glides into
the gloom and space of the infinite, windy night.

CHAPTER IV.

IN THE ATLANTIC.

THERE were eight passengers and twenty-seven hands, counting captain and officers, on board the "Meteor;" in all, thirty-five souls.

In these days half that number of men would be thought ample to handle a ship of eleven hundred tons. Taking fourteen men as a ship's company, we find— one, the cook, who is useless aloft; five ordinary seamen, equal to two able-bodied men; four ill and unable to leave their bunks; the remainder consist of the captain, two mates, and the carpenter. So that a summons for all hands to shorten sail, for example, brings forth about enough men to do the work of one yard—one yard, when there are twelve, exclusive of trysails, jibs, stun'sails, spanker, and staysails. This modern system of undermanning ships is an evil next in magnitude to that of sending crazy and leaky vessels to sea; and as many ships are lost for want of hands to work them on occasions which demand promptitude and muscle, as are lost by rotten planks and overcharged cargoes.

The passengers on board the "Meteor" consisted of four gentlemen, two ladies, a little boy, and a female servant. Of the gentlemen, one was a young man named Holland, who was going to America for no other purpose than to see Niagara; another was a merchant, who was to represent a London house in New York. He was accompanied by his wife and her maid. The third was a General in the United States Army, a fine old man with a chivalrous courtesy of manner and a handsome honest face, who had been picking up what professional hints he could find by a year's sojourn in the military depôts of Great Britain. The fourth male passenger was an actor, magnificently named Gerald Fitzmaurice St. Aubyn, in quest of more appreciative audiences in the New Country than his genius had encountered in the Old. The widow and her son completed the list.

It took these good people a very short time to settle down to their new life and adjust themselves to the novel conditions of existence that surrounded them. The ladies lay hidden at the first going off; and, although Mr. St. Aubyn put in a punctual appearance at meals and smoked a great quantity of cheroots, it must be admitted that he was peculiarly pensive for a comedian, whose genius, he affirmed, was chiefly at home in genteel farce, though he had enacted tragedy with applause.

The "Meteor" met with adverse winds, but brilliant weather, during the first few days. She tacked north and south, and crowded canvas to make headway, but, though her speed was great through the water, her actual progress was small.

"No matter," said Captain Steel, patiently; "we may get a gale astern of us some of these hours, and then we'll make up for lost time."

But whilst the weather remained so beautiful, the wind brisk and the sea smooth, the passengers could hardly regret the delay. It was like yacht sailing—dry decks, steady motion, and always the pleasurable sense of swiftness inspired by the beaded foam crisping by and stretching like a tape astern. Now and again they signalled a ship homeward bound or journeying south. The widow's little boy clapped his hands to see the bright flags flying at the mizzen-peak, and the ladies were lost in wonderment to think that those gay colours were a language as intelligible to those concerned in their interpretation as "How do you do?" and "Very well, thank you."

The "Meteor" had a snug cuddy; and a hospitable sight was the dinner-table, with the white cloth covering the long board, the gleaming silver and glass, the fine claret jug (testimonial by former passengers to the captain), the colours of wines in decanters, the grinning negro always colliding with the steward, and the skipper's rubicund face, relieved by soft white hair, at the head of the table, backed by the polished mizzen-mast. Overhead was the skylight, through which you might see the great sails towering to the heavens; and over the dinner table swung a globe of gold-fish between two baskets of ferns. There was a piano lashed abaft the mizzen-mast; and all around the cuddy were the cabins occupied by the passengers, the captain, the mates, with highly-varnished doors and white panels relieved with edgings of gold.

Everybody took an interest in the widow's little boy, both because he was a pretty child, and because it was whispered about that he had lost his father but a few weeks ago. He and Holdsworth became great friends, as Holdsworth had said they would. Whenever it was the first mate's watch on deck, the little fellow would paddle away from his mother's side and come to him, and ask him to tell him stories, and show him the ship's compass, at which he was never weary of looking. Then you might see Holdsworth on a hencoop, or the skylight, with the child upon his knee, coining nautical fairy-yarns of people who live under the sea, and ride in chariots composed of coral, to which fish with scales shining like precious stones are harnessed.

Sometimes the widow, whose name was Tennent, would come on deck and find them together, when she would sit beside them and listen with a smile to Holdsworth, whose stories the little boy Louis would on no account suffer his mamma to interrupt. And to repay him for his kindness to the child, and not more for that than because she admired his honest nature, and was won by his gentle and tender simplicity, she would lead him on, with a world of feminine tact, to talk of his wife, and comfort and make him happy with her sympathy, her interest, and her assurances.

She was a calm, gentle-faced woman, with a settled sorrow in the expression of her eyes that made her look older than she was, but her age would scarcely exceed thirty-six. She showed little inclination to converse with the other passengers, and would retire early at night, and in the daytime sit in quiet places about the deck, always with her boy beside her.

The merchant's wife, on the other hand, Mrs. Ashton, was a gay, talkative woman, a showy dresser, and fond of a quiet boast, which her husband, a short man with a yellow beard, took care never to contradict. Mr. Holland began to pay her attention straightway, and then Mr. St. Aubyn stepped in with theatrical emphasis and smooth observations, like the speeches in comedies.

Captain Steel, though very polite to this lady, inclined to Mrs. Tennent,—his sailor's heart appreciating her defencelessness, and propounding all kinds of problems how best to amuse, please, and cheer her. But though she could not fail to like the honest skipper, she evidently preferred Holdsworth, who would go and talk to her for an hour at a time about Dolly, and then listen, with a face of kindliest sympathy, to little passages out of her own life.

And so a week went by, and the ship strove with the baffling winds, which blew directly from the quarter to which her bowsprit should have pointed, and captain and men began to chafe, finding the job of putting the ship about tiresome at last.

On the seventh day, about the hour of sunset, the wind fell, and the surface of the sea became polished as glass, though from the north-east there came, through the mighty expanse of water, a long and regular swell, which made the ship rise and fall as regularly as the breath of a sleeper.

"We shall have the wind from that quarter, I think, sir," said Holdsworth to the skipper.

"Or is this an after-swell, Mr. Holdsworth?" suggested the skipper, sending his keen gaze across the sea to the horizon, where the sky was as blue as it was overhead.

There was no telling. This long and regular swell might be the precursor of a gale, or the effects of one that had passed. The barometer had fallen, but this might only indicate a southerly wind, not necessarily dirty weather. The heavens were perfectly tranquil; the day was fading into a serene and gloriously beautiful evening, with no hint in all its benign aspect to suggest the need of the slightest precaution.

Mrs. Ashton was at the piano, accompanying Mr. St
Aubyn to a song, which he sang so affectedly that some
of the hands forward mimicked him, and the forecastle
seemed full of guinea-pigs.

Her husband popped his head over the skylight and
called to her to come and view the sunset. Up she
came, escorted by Mr. Holland and the actor, flounced
showily into a chair, and fell into a rapture.

"Oh, how beautiful! The sea looks like gold! doesn't
it, Captain Steel? See how red the sails are! Ah, if
I could only paint! what fame such a picture as this
would bring me."

True; but then what manner of pigments was needful to reproduce the glory, the colour, the calm, the
infinity of that wonderful scene!

The sun was sinking down a cloudless horizon, and
was now a vast crimson ball, throbbing and quivering
with his lower limb upon the sea-line. There was something overwhelming in the unspeakable majesty of his
unattended descent. As the huge crimson body appeared to hang for some moments above the sea before
dipping, even Mrs. Ashton held her tongue, and seemed
impressed with the tremendous spectacle of loneliness
submitted by the globe of fire sinking away from the
sky with the vast solitude of the deep in the foreground.
Far into the measureless ocean he had sunk a cone of
fire, while the heights above and around him were dim
with burning haze. The sails of the "Meteor" were
yellow in the expiring light; her topmasts seemed veined
with lines of flame; and the brass-work about her decks
reflected innumerable suns, each with threads of glory
about it, that blinded the eyes to encounter.

But even while they gazed the sun vanished, and

darkness came with long strides across the deep, kindling the stars and transforming the masts and yards of the ship into phantom tracery as delicate as frostwork to look at.

"Upon my word!" exclaimed Mr. Holland in a tone of rapture, "that's as fine a sight as I must hope to see anywhere."

"If you could introduce a scene like that, Mr. St. Aubyn, on the stage, eh?" laughed the General.

"Why, as to that," replied Mr. St. Aubyn, "let me tell you, General, that there are some very fine scenes to be found in the large theatres in London. In the second act of 'Pizarro,' as I saw it the other night at Drury Lane, there's a scene representing the Temple of the Sun; the sun is setting—and God knows how they managed it, but the sun *did* sink, not like yonder one, but very finely in clouds, just as 'Ataliba' exclaims, drawing his sword, 'Now, my brethren, my sons, my friends, I know your valour. Should ill success assail us.'" . . .

"Yes, yes," interrupted Mr. Holland impatiently; "but I always considered 'Pizarro,' as a play, to be full of very poor rant. Who talks in real life like the fellows in that piece are made to talk?"

"My dear sir!" exclaimed Mr. St. Aubyn with a smile of contempt, "the stage is the arena of poetry; we are idealists." . . .

"Because you never mean what you say," said Mr. Ashton, lighting a cigar.

"Oh, excuse me," rejoined Mr. St. Aubyn; "true actors are always in earnest. Siddons was."

"I once met Sarah Siddons," said Mrs. Ashton. "Do you remember, dear, at Lord Shortlands?" addressing her husband.

"I was only once at a theatre in my life," observed
Captain Steel, who had been listening to the conversation with an impressed face. "That was at Plymouth.
They gave us our money's worth. There was plenty of
fighting and love-making, and two traitors, both of
whom died game and covered with blood. There was
a little too much gunpowder at the end; but I rather
think they raised smoke to hide the acting, which fell
off as the piece made headway. The best part of the
entertainment, to my thinking, was a fight between two
sailors in a private box. Mr. St. Aubyn, where do you
gentlemen, when you are run through the body, stow
all the blood you lose? That's often puzzled me to
think."

"Oh, don't let me hear," cried Mrs. Ashton. "I hate
to be told such secrets."

"Captain," said the General, "how long is this calm
going to last?"

"All night, I am afraid. How's her head?" sang
out the captain.

"East-south-east, sir," responded the man at the
wheel.

"We're homeward bound," said the captain laughing;
"the old girl wants to get back again."

He walked away from the group, and stood near the
wheel, gazing aloft and around. The passengers continued talking and laughing, their voices sounding unreal
when listened to at a distance, and with the great,
desolate, silent sea breathing around. The sails flapped
lazily aloft, and the wheel-chains clanked from time to
time as the vessel rose and fell. Mrs. Tennent came
on deck, the captain joined her, and they walked up
and down. On the other side of the deck paced the

second mate. Forward were the dark shadows of some of the hands upon the forecastle, smoking pipes and talking in low voices.

The night had fallen darkly; there was no moon, but the stars were large and brilliant, and glittered in flakes of white light in the sea. Presently a fiddle was played in the forecastle, and a voice sang a mournful tune that sounded weirdly in the gloom, and with a muffled note. The air and voice were not without sweetness, but there was the melancholy in it which many songs popular among sailors have, and the wailing cadence was helped out by the ghostly sails rearing their glimmering spaces, and the subdued plash of the water about the bows, as the ship sank into the hollows of the swell.

Mrs. Tennent stopped, with the captain, at the poop-rail to listen.

"What odd music!" cried Mrs. Ashton. "It sounds as if some one were playing out in the sea there."

"Let's have the fiddler here," said Mr. Holland. "I like to enlarge my mind by observation, and have never yet heard a real Jack Tar sing."

"Oh yes! oh yes!" exclaimed Mrs. Ashton, while Mr. St. Aubyn called out, "I'll go and fetch him."

"Better stop where you are, sir," said the skipper, drily; "the forecastle's a dangerous hold for landsmen to put their heads into. Mr. Thompson," he called to the second mate, "just go and send that fiddler aft here."

Presently came the man, followed at a respectful distance by a crowd of his mates, who drew to the capstan on the quarterdeck, and waited for what was to follow.

The fiddler and vocalist was a stumpy seaman, with black whiskers, a hooked nose, and keen black eyes, dressed in loose canvas breeches, well smeared with tar, and a canvas shirt, with a belt about his middle, in which was a sheath - knife. He hailed from Southampton, but had gone so many voyages in every species of ships—Danish, French, Spanish, American—that he might fairly claim to belong to the whole world.

He scraped with his left foot, and stood bashfully awaiting orders, his glittering eyes travelling over the group of gentlemen and ladies.

"You're wanted to sing a song, Daniels," said Captain Steel.

"Ay, ay, sir. What might it be?"

"Something wild and plaintive," suggested Mrs. Ashton.

"Give us a song about a sweetheart," said Mr. Holland.

This was English to the sailor; so, after a few moments' reflection, he screwed his fiddle into his neck, scraped a few bars, and then sang.

He did his best, and murmurs from time to time about the capstan illustrated enthusiastic appreciation in one portion of his audience at least. Those on the poop were more quiet, impressed by the peculiar wildness of the song, and the rough, uncouth melody of the tune.

The song was about a woman whose husband was a sailor. The sailor went away to sea, and did not come home, and she thought he had deserted her; so she put on man's clothes, shipped on board a vessel as a " hand," and went in search of him. One night she is on the forecastle, on the look-out. The watch are asleep; there's not a breath of air:

> When, looking over the starboard side,
> She sees a face as pale
> As snow upon a mountain top,
> Or moonlight on a sail.

The figure attached to the face rises, waist high, out of the water, and extends his hands.

> " O God !" she screams, " is this my love?
> Can this my Joey be?"
> And then she casts her eyes above
> And jumps into the sea.

And sure enough the phantom *was* Joey, who had not deserted her, as she had cruelly thought, but had been drowned in the very spot where the vessel she was on board of was becalmed. The song wound up with an injunction to all wives or sweethearts of sailors never to think that their Joes have played them false because they do not return to their homes.

The passengers thanked the man for his song, and Mrs. Ashton wanted another; but Captain Steel, holding that enough condescension had been exhibited, bade the singer go to the steward and get a " tot of grog."

Much criticism followed; but all, with the exception of Mr. St. Aubyn, owned themselves impressed by the rough simplicity and tragical theme of the forecastle ballad.

"Pshaw !" cried the actor; " put the man on a stage before an audience, and he'd be hissed off. It's the queer scratching of the catgut and the picturesque costume of the fellow that have pleased you. His voice isn't good enough to get him the post of call-boy at a theatre."

A warm argument followed this decision, and lasted nearly half an hour, during which the General and Mr. Ashton left the group; then the steward's bell rang, and the passengers went below to their nightly potations and to munch sweet biscuits.

CHAPTER V.

A GALE OF WIND.

AT midnight Holdsworth came on deck to relieve the second mate. A man out of the port watch came to the wheel, and stood yawning, scarcely awake. The night was dark—a hazy atmosphere through which the stars gleamed sparely, and the sea like ebony. The rise and fall of the ship flapped the sails against the masts and drove eddies of air about the decks, but in reality there was not a breath of wind.

There was something stupendous in the black, profound, and breathless placidity of the night. The compass swung round in the binnacle anywhere, but the swell made the rudder kick heavily now and again, and gave the wheel a twist that flung the spokes out of the man's hand and woke him up.

This prolonged inactivity was galling. One longed to hear the rush of parting water and the singing of the wind in the shrouds.

The mainsail flapped so heavily that Holdsworth ordered it to be furled. The song of the men brought the captain on deck. He flitted, shadow-like, about the binnacle, sniffed at the night impatiently, and then went to Holdsworth.

"The glass has fallen half an inch since eight bells," said he.

" Yes, sir ; there'll be a change before morning."

" Better stow the royals and mizzen-top gall'ns'l."

" Ay, ay, sir."

These, the topmost sails of the ship, were just discernible from the deck. In a few moments their dim
outlines melted, and some dark figures went up into the
gloom and vanished.

The captain returned to his cabin, and Holdsworth
strolled the deck. At two bells (one o'clock) the haze
went out of the sky and the stars shone fiercely. Holdsworth, standing on the starboard side of the poop, felt
a light air creeping about his face, and the sound of the
flapping sails ceased.

" How's her head ?"

" North-a-quarter-west, sir."

He sang out an order, and a crowd of figures came
tumbling out of the forecastle and manned the port
braces. The air died away, but presently came a quick
puff which made the water bubble around the ship.

Holdsworth's eyes were upon the weather-horizon.
The stars burned purely, but away upon the water-line
was a thick shadow.

Again the wind died out and there was a breathless
stillness, amid which you might hear a sound—vague,
murmurous, indescribable — a distant echo it might
seem of something infinitely distant.

" Stand by the topgallant halliards !"

A sense of expectation seemed to pervade the very
ship herself as she stood upright with her dim canvas
flapping in the darkness above.

The distant murmur grew more defined, and took
such a tone as you may hear in small sharp rain falling
at a distance upon leaves. Then, out of the murky

horizon some clouds came rolling—long, attenuated shadows, resembling visionary arms clutching at the stars. The murmur approached; the clouds, swinging along the sky, formed into compact groups. Hark to the quick hissing of the water lashed by the wind!

In a moment the sails were round and hard, the ship with her port-chains under water, and the wind screeching fiercely over the ebony surface of the sea, and whitening it with foam.

The captain was on the poop, holding on to the main-topgallant backstay, and shrieking orders like one possessed. It was indeed briefly a case of "Let go everything!" Under full topsail, foresail, staysails, and jibs, the ship was too heavily weighted for the surprising violence of the wind, and was powerless to right herself. But every order given was the right one. And now you heard the deep tones of Holdsworth's powerful voice mingling with the agitated commands of the skipper, while yards came rushing down upon the caps, and sails banged and roared aloft, and men shouted lustily about the decks, and the sea fled in cataracts of foam under the vessel's bows.

A time of deep excitement, but scarcely of suspense —there was too much hurrying for that.

There would have been something incredible to an inexperienced landsman in the sight of the dark figures swarming up the shrouds to give battle to the wild array of canvas which groaned and bellowed like a dozen thunderstorms in the sky—a spectacle of human pluck not to be realised, or in the faintest degree appreciated, by those who have not beheld it. The night black— the yards slanting so that the extremity of the main-yard touched the water; the footing upon those yards a thin

line which must be felt for by the feet; the canvas,
loosened by the lowering of the yard, bellied by the
force of the wind many feet above the heads of the
reefers, and presenting to their hands a surface of iron;
and the three masts quivering under the shocks and
convulsions of the sails!

All hands were at work now, and there were men
enough to reef both big topsails at once, whilst others
over their heads furled the topgallant sails. Holdsworth
had been one of the first to spring up the main rigging;
he knew the value of every pair of hands in that
moment of danger; and away — active, daring, his
hands and arms like steel—he clambered for the weather-
earing. But the boatswain was before him, so he made
for the lee yard-arm.

Figure a smooth spar, fifty-five feet long, sloping at
a height of as many feet to the water's surface, the said
surface not being a mill pond, but a sheet of foam;
figure a pitch dark night, a line stretched along the yard,
down which you must slide to the extremity, a sail
weighing half a dozen tons banging at your head and
your feet, and doing its utmost to throw you; then,
having reached the extremity of the yard, figure your
legs thrown across it as you might bestride a horse,
beneath you the foaming sea, almost at right angles the
inclined deck of the ship, a long stone's throw distant—
a deep darkness everywhere, save where a wave, breaking massively, flings out a phosphorescent light and
deepens the blackness of its own chasm—whilst the
gale yells about your ears, and blinds you with spray
that stings like hail!

Figure this, and you will then very faintly realise
what " taking the lee-earing " in a gale at sea means.

The cries of the men aloft, and the beating of the canvas, sounded like an unearthly contest in mid-air; but they ceased presently, and then the hands came hurrying down the rigging and fell to the halliards. Holdsworth sprang on to the poop, his cap gone, his hair blown about his eyes, and roared out orders, while the captain, more easy in his mind about his spars, went aft and hung about the binnacle, watching the compass often.

The ship was now under double-reefed topsails, and reeling through the darkness almost bare of sail. The wind was increasing in violence every five minutes, and an ugly Atlantic sea was running right athwart the ship's course, hurling great waves against her starboard beam, which ran in waterspouts of foam as high as the main-top, and was blown in big hissing flakes through the rigging to leeward. It was soon deemed expedient to close-reef the topsails; but even under these mere streaks of canvas the "Meteor" lay over to the gale down to her water-ways, and the water bubbling in her lee scuppers. But luckily the gale was right abeam, and the vessel could hold her course; but her speed was comparatively small, and she laboured heavily.

So passed the darkest hours of the night. At four o'clock the gale was at its worst. They had rigged up a hurricane-house in the mizzen rigging—a square of tarpaulin, which the wind flattened hard against the shrouds—and under this shelter sat Holdsworth and the captain, scarce able to hear their own voices, pitched in the loudest key, amid the howling of the tempest. Once Holdsworth went below to look at the glass, and came back saying it was steady. The skipper roared that he never before remembered so sudden a gale, and

Holdsworth owned that only once was he so caught—
in the Pacific, when they lost their fore-topmast.

There was nothing more to be done, unless they
hove the ship to; but this was not needful. The dawn
broke at five, and the pale cheerless light illuminated a
wild and dreary scene of tumbling desolate waters
billowing in mountains to the horizon. The "Meteor,"
almost under bare poles, her yards pointed to the gale,
her ropes and lines blown in semicircles to leeward,
laboured heavily, caught now by a sea that threw her
on her beam-ends, and now swooping into a chasm
walled with boiling green water, making the gale screech
like a million steam-whistles through her rigging, as she
drove up against it, while coiling tongues of water ran
in cataracts up her glistening sides and fell in dead
weights upon her decks. The sky, from horizon to
horizon, was a dark lead colour, along which under-
clouds, in appearance resembling volumes of smoke,
were swept along, torn and rent, and discharging at
intervals quick, biting showers of rain.

Some of the passengers came on deck—the General,
Mr. Holland, and Mr. St. Aubyn. The General turned
about when he had advanced a few feet, and disappeared;
Mr. Holland in a very short time followed his example;
but the actor, with manifest looks of terror in his pallid
face, pushed onwards with outstretched hands for the
hurricane house. The captain advised him to go below;
but at that moment the ship, rolling suddenly to windward, shipped a shower of spray, which soaked the poor
actor through and through; a moment after, the vessel
heeled heavily over to leeward; away rolled the actor,
impelled both by the wind and the unerring law of
gravitation, and was flung against the lee mizzen rigging,

to which he was pinned by the violence of the gale as effectually as if he had been lashed to the shrouds. He screamed for help, on which Holdsworth went over to him, took him by the arm, and dragged him against the wind to the companion-hatchway. As Mr. St. Aubyn staggered below, clinging like a kitten to whatever he could lay hands on, he was heard to implore Holdsworth to tell him if there was any danger; but, before the words were out of his mouth, Holdsworth was clinging to the weather-rigging and calling the captain's attention to a brig, which had risen out of the sea like an apparition, and was tearing before the gale with full topsails and topgallant-sails set.

"A Yankee, by her build!" said the captain. "It's only a Yankee who would carry that sail in such a wind."

It was a sight to see her flying along, sinking her hull sometimes out of sight, then poised on the giddy summit of a huge wave, whose crest broke under her bows, her copper bottom glistening like red gold against the slate-coloured water. She passed within a quarter of a mile of the "Meteor's" weather-beam, and up flew the stripes and stars and stood like a painted board at her peak. The second mate answered the salutation by bending on the small ensign and running it up. Any further signalling was out of the question in that gale. The men on board the brig could just be made out. She was a smart vessel, black-hulled, with bows like a knife, and skysail poles, which gave her masts an aspect of perfect symmetry; and she was splendidly handled. She went like a swan over the seething billows, streaming a foaming wake, and in a very few moments was lost in the haze and gloom of the near horizon.

As the morning advanced the gale decreased, but a terrible sea was up, which made the ship labour so furiously that to steady her in some degree they set the trysail and foresail. There was, however, the comfort of daylight abroad, and the men could see what they were about. Both Holdsworth and the captain went below to get a little sleep, and the vessel was left in command of the second mate, a young man named Thompson. There were two hands at the wheel, and two on the look-out on the forecastle, glittering in oil-skins, and ducking now and again to the seas which swept over the ship's bows.

The fore and main hatches were battened down, and the main-deck was a foot deep in water, which washed to and fro as the ship rolled, and which, as fast as it ran through the scupper-holes, was replaced by fresh and heavy inroads of the sea.

But all this was trifling; the vessel was snug, the gale was moderating, and the extra sail that had been made was driving the ship through the water in fine style.

Meanwhile, the passengers below, having been reassured by the captain, were making what breakfast they could off the rolls, tea, and rashers of ham which clattered about the table, and tumbled into their laps. The trays swung wildly from the deck, and it demanded great vigilance and close attention to their convulsive movements to repossess oneself of the cup or plate one placed upon them for safety. The negro steward shambled round the table, halting every moment to make a grasp at anything that came in his road, to steady himself. Now and again you heard the smash of crockery. Some conversation was attempted; and the General invited Mr. Holland to go up on deck and witness a scene which would probably exceed in majesty Niagara Falls; but Mr. Holland said he would wait until the vessel was steadier. Mr. St. Aubyn had changed his clothes and sat holding on to the table, looking the part of fear infinitely better than he could hope to impersonate it before the footlights. The ladies remained in their cabins. Mrs. Ashton, overcome with sickness and the fear of drowning, was driving her maid distracted with orders, which it was out of the poor wretch's power to execute. In truth, the maid's legs were perfectly useless to her, which Mrs. Ashton, lying on her back, refused to understand. Cries were repeatedly coming from the direction of her cabin for " Harry ! Harry !" which received no attention, owing to Harry's—in other words, to Mr. Ashton's—utter incapacity to move a step without being flung upon the deck.

A somewhat different scene was presented by the interior of the forecastle, where both watches were having breakfast. Men holding tin pannikins stepped easily round to the galley, where the cook was dispensing a milkless, sugarless black fluid called tea, and retreated into the twilight of the forecastle, carrying the steaming beverage. There sat the sailors, some swinging in hammocks with their legs dangling down, some on sea-chests, some on canvas bags, drinking from pannikins, swallowing lumps of biscuit hard as iron, or hacking with the knives they wore in their belts at bits of cold pork or beef, floating in vinegar, in tin dishes held between their knees ; some smoking, some making ready to "turn in," and all jabbering away as gaily as if they were comfortably seated in a Liverpool or Poplar singing-house—the mariner's earthly paradise—and each with his Sue or his Betsey at his side. Here, more than in any other part of the ship, you felt her motion—the mighty lifting of her bows, and the long sweeping fall as she pitched nose under, while the heavy seas boomed against her outside as though at any moment the timbers must dispart and the green waves rush in.

At twelve o'clock the gale had decreased to such a degree that they were able to shake two reefs out of the main top-sail and set the topgallant sail. The action of the sea, moreover, was much less violent. The weather had cleared, the pale blue sky could be seen shining through the white mist that fled along it, and the sun stood round and clean and coppery in the heavens, throwing a dark red lustre upon the quick, passionate play of the sea beneath.

Some of the passengers crawled upon deck and gazed with wonderment around them. Certainly the panorama was a somewhat different one from what had been unrolled to their eyes the day before. The ship had a fagged and jaded look with her drenched decks, her ropes blown slack with the violence of the wind, and the canvas made unequal to the eye by the reefs in the topsails. It was again Holdsworth's watch on deck. The captain walked up and down chuckling over the improved aspect of the weather and on the wind, which was drawing more easterly, and therefore more favourable.

"You can shake out the reefs, Mr. Holdsworth. She'll bear it now," he called out.

Out reefs it was : the ship felt the increased pressure, and rushed forward like a liberated racehorse.

"This is capital!" exclaimed the old General, tottering about with outstretched hands, ever on the alert for a special roll. "A week of this, captain, will carry us a good way on our road."

" Ay, sir, and we must make up for lost time."

And then presently he gave orders to set the mainsail and the other two topgallant sails.

" The glass still keeps low, sir," said Holdsworth.

" But let's take advantage of the daylight, Mr. Holdsworth. We mustn't lose an opportunity."

The sky had now cleared, the sun shone cheerily; the wind, having drawn aft, was now no more than what sailors would call a main-royal breeze. The foretopmast stun'sail was set. The passengers regained their spirits, and though the ship still rolled pretty freely, Mr. St. Aubyn and Mr. Holland, to show that they were now masters of their legs, walked up and down the deck, diversifying their conversation with sundry stumbles, and now and then by falling against each other. But the bright sunshine made such *contretemps* a source of merriment. Moreover, the ladies were on deck now, Mrs. Ashton having been pushed up the companion-ladder by her husband, who, in his turn, had met with great assistance behind from the kindly hands of the negro steward, who was anxious to get them both out of the cuddy, that he might show his teeth to the maid-servant. Captain Steel seeing Mrs. Ashton attended by the other gentlemen, who were industrious in their inquiries after her nerves, gallantly gave his arm to the widow, whilst her little boy ran to Holdsworth, who took his hand, kissed and began to talk to him, finding endless pleasure in looking into his eyes and humouring the suggestions of home-life, of flowers, of women's love, of his own wife, which were somehow conveyed to him by the boy's prattle and wise child-smiles and perfect innocence.

CHAPTER VI.

TAKEN ABACK!

AT five o'clock the wind was south-east; a fresh breeze, with a lively sea and a cloudy sky. The wind being aft, the ship sailed on an even keel, to the great comfort of the passengers, who found the inclined decks intolerable.

From the aspect of the sea, it was evident that the ship had got into water which had not been touched by the gale of the morning—of such narrow proportions sometimes are the tempests which sweep the ocean. Away northwards, whither the clouds were rolling, there loomed a long, low, smoke-coloured bank of cloud or fog, so exactly resembling a coast seen from a distance that the passengers were deceived, and some of them called out that yonder was land!

"Tell us now, captain," cried Mrs. Ashton; "it *is* land, isn't it?"

"Why, madam," rejoined the captain, "for anything I can tell, it may be Laputa."

"Or Utopia," suggested the General, "the land of idealisms and paradisaical institutions."

Mrs. Ashton laughed, seeing the joke, but Mr. St. Aubyn, conceiving that they were talking of real countries, proposed that the captain should head the vessel for the shore.

"No, no ! too far out of my course," answered the skipper, with a wise shake of the head. "It would make a Flying Dutchman of the ship were we once to set to work to reach that land."

"If I really thought it Utopia," said the General, stroking his moustache, "I would beg you to land me at once, so eager am I to witness the condition of a people living under a form of government the like of which, for wisdom, humanity, and availability, is not to be met with in any other part of the world. But it *may* be Laputa, as you suggested."

"Or Lilliput," said Mr. Holland ; whereupon the actor, perceiving that a joke was playing at his expense, scowled dramatically at the bank of cloud, and muttered, that, for his part, when he asked a civil question he usually looked for a truthful answer.

Just then a voice forward shouted out, "A sail on the lee bow !"

There is always something exciting in this cry at sea. Storms and calms grow wearisome after a bit, but the interest that clusters about a vessel met on the broad deep never loses its freshness. The captain went for his telescope, and, after a brief inspection, announced the vessel to be a large barque going the same road as themselves. Mrs. Ashton asked leave to look through the telescope, and a good deal of coquettish bye-play took place ; for, first she shut both eyes, and then she couldn't see at all ; and then she shut the eye that looked through the telescope, and, keeping the other open, declared that she could see better without the glass. Then the telescope wouldn't keep steady ; so Mr. St. Aubyn went upon his knees and begged her to use his shoulder for a rest. At last, after an infinity of trouble,

and when the cramp was just beginning to seize the
actor's legs, she obtained a glimpse of the barque as it
swept through the field of the glass, and owned herself
delighted and satisfied.

The "Meteor" came up with the stranger hand
over fist, keeping to windward of her; and soon she
was no farther than a mile off, a big hull high in the
water, bare and black, with round bows and a square
stern.   They hoisted the ensign on board the "Meteor,"
but the barque showed no colours.

"Some sour North Countryman, I reckon," said
Captain Steel.   "She has a Sunderland cut."

She was under full sail, but just when the "Meteor"
got abreast of her, she clewed her royals up, down came
the flying and outer jibs, and the topgallant yards.

"What is she afraid of?" exclaimed Captain Steel,
gazing at her curiously.

You could see the pigmy figures of the men clambering up the rigging, and presently down fell the topsail
yards and up went more figures, and the spars were
dotted with heads.   Anything more picturesque than
this vessel—her black hull rolling majestically, her
white sails vanishing even as you watched them, her
rigging marked against the cloudy sky, the sense of the
noisy activity on board of her, of which no faintest echo
stole across the water, and all between, the tumbling
cloud-coloured waters—cannot be imagined.   The crew
of the "Meteor" watched her with curiosity; but she
now fell rapidly astern, and in a short time could be
seen clearly only by the telescope, which Captain Steel
held to his eye, speculating upon her movements.

The dinner-bell rang.   It was now the first dog-watch.
Thompson, the second mate, came on deck, and the

passengers went to dinner. The sunlight had a watery gleam in it as the lengthening rays fell upon the skylight, and Holdsworth's eyes constantly wandered to the sails, which were visible through the glass. The skipper was in high humour, and during dinner laughed at the barque they had passed for shortening sail under a blue sky.

"I'll wager a hat," he exclaimed, "that she's commanded by a Scotchman, even if she don't hail from a North British port. I don't mean to say that your Scotchman's a timid man, but he's unco' thoughtful. My first skipper was a Sawney, and every night, as regularly as the second dog-watch came round, it was 'In royals and flying-jib, and a single reef in the mizzen-top-sail.'"

"But there must be some reason for the barque furling her sails," said the General.

"From his point of view, no doubt, sir. You have seen what the weather has been all the afternoon?"

"The wind is dropping, sir," said Holdsworth, looking through the skylight.

He had an uneasy expression in his eyes, and he frequently glanced at the skipper; but etiquette of a very severe kind prohibited him from imparting his misgivings of a change, in the face of the skipper's manifest sense of security.

"It may freshen after sunset," rejoined the skipper. "Mr. Holland, the pleasure of a glass of wine."

The conversation drifted into other channels. Mrs. Ashton gave an account of a country ball she had attended a week or two before she left England, and described the dress she wore on that occasion, appealing often to her husband to aid her memory, and riveting the attention of Mr. St. Aubyn. Then the General talked of the garrison-towns he had visited, and paid some handsome compliments to the British army, and to English society in general. Mrs. Tennent, seated on the captain's right hand, with her boy at her side, listened to without joining in the conversation.

Holdsworth's eyes roamed incessantly through the skylight.

It happened presently that the General, in speaking of the beauty of English inland scenery, mentioned the county in which Southbourne was situated, and instanced in particular the country around Hanwitch, a town lying not half a dozen miles from Southbourne. Holdsworth pricked his ears, and joined in the conversation. He had reason to remember Hanwitch. One of the happiest days he had spent, during the three months he had been ashore, was that in which he had driven Dolly over to that town, and dined in the queer little hotel that fronted a piece of river-scenery as beautiful as any that is to be found up the Thames.

Whilst he and the General talked, the skipper argued with Mr. St. Aubyn on the merits of the English as a paying people. St. Aubyn declared that the English public, taken in the aggregate, was a mean public, rarely liberal, and then liberal in wrong directions, supporting quack institutions, responding to quack appeals, and ignoring true excellence, especially histrionic excellence. Both grew warm; then Mr. Holland joined in. He sent the discussion wandering from the point, and in stepped Mr. Ashton.

Meanwhile the decanters went round, the cuddy grew dark, and the negro was looking at the steward for orders to light the swinging lamps.

Hark!

A loud cry from the deck, followed by a sudden rush of feet, and the ship heeled over—over—yet over!

The women shrieked; the skylight turned black; plates, decanters, cutlery, glass, rolled from the table and fell with quick crashes. The decks fore and aft echoed with loud calls. You could hear the water gurgling in the lee port-holes. A keen blue gleam flashed upon the skylight; but if thunder followed the lightning it was inaudible amid the wild and continuous shrieking of the wind.

The skipper and Holdsworth scrambled to the companion-ladder and gained the deck. In a trice they saw what had happened. The ship, with all sails set, had been taken aback.

Away to windward, in the direction directly contrary to where the wind had been blowing before dinner, the sky was livid, flinging an early night upon the sea, and sending forth a tempest of wind that tore the water into shreds of foam. The whole force of the hurricane was upon the ship's canvas, which lay backed against the masts, and the vessel lay on her beam-ends, her masts making an angle of forty degrees with the horizon.

The confusion was indescribable. Every halliard had been let go; but the yards were jammed by the sails, and would not descend. The clew-lines were manned, but the sheets would not stir an inch through the blocks. Nor was the worst of the squall, tempest, hurricane, whatever it might be, upon them yet; that livid pall of cloud which the lightning was seaming with zigzag fire was still to come, and with it the full fury its scowling aspect portended.

"My God!" thundered the skipper to the second

mate, who stood white, cowed, and apparently helpless, "what have you brought us into?"

The wheel was jammed hard a-starboard, but the ship lay like a log, broadside on to the wind, her masts bowed almost on a level with the water.

"Haul! for your lives, men! haul!" shrieked the skipper frantically to the men, who appeared paralysed by the sudden catastrophe, and stood idly with the clewlines and reef tackles passed along them.

Holdsworth, half-way up the weather-poop ladder, his head above the bulwarks, saw sooner than the captain what was about to happen.

"Crowd to windward, all hands!" he roared. There was no time to say more; the great broad, livid cloud was upon them even whilst Holdsworth sang out the command; the men held their breath—unless the masts went the vessel was doomed.

Crash! A noise of wood shivered into splinters, of flogging ropes and sails thundering their tatters upon the wind; the fore and main masts went as you would break a clay-pipe stem across your knee—the first, just below the top, the other clean off at the deck; and the huge mass of spars, ropes, and sails lay quivering and rolling alongside—a portion on deck, but the greater bulk of them in the water—grinding into the vessel's side as if she had grounded upon a shoal of rocks.

The ship righted, and then another crash; away went the mizzen-topmast, leaving the spanker and cross-jack set. The wind caught these sails and swept the ship's head round right in the eye of the storm, and off she drove to leeward, disabled, helpless—dragging her shattered spars with her, like something living its torn and mangled limbs.

There was no situation in the whole range of the misfortunes which may befall a ship at sea more critical than the one the "Meteor" was now in. The sea was rising quickly and leaping high over the ship's bows, pouring tons of water in upon the decks (the weight of the wreck alongside preventing the vessel from rising to the waves), and carrying whatever had become un-lashed—casks, spare spars, and the like—aft to the cuddy front, against which they were launched with a violence that broke the windows, and soon promised to demolish the woodwork.

But the worst part of the business was—the action of the sea set the spars in the water and the hull of the ship rolling against each other, and the thump, thump, thump of the bristly wreck against the vessel's side sent a hollow undertone through the hooting of the tempest that was awful to hear.

Though the mizzen-mast still stood, the weight of the other masts in falling had severely wrenched it, and it literally rocked in its bed to the swaying of the great spanker-boom. Add to all this the midnight darkness in the air, which the flashes of lightning only served to deepen by the momentary and ghastly illumination they cast.

Yet, if the ship was not to be dragged to destruction, it was imperative that she should be freed, and freed at once, from the ponderous incumbrance of the wreck that ground against her side. The captain had shouted him-self hoarse, and was no longer to be heard. But now Holdsworth made himself audible in tones that rose above the gale like trumpet-blasts.

"We must clear the wreck or founder! All hands out with their knives and cut away everything!"

A comprehensive order that must be literally obeyed.
"Carpenter!" he roared.

"Here, sir," came a voice from the main-deck.

Holdsworth sprang in the direction of the voice: shouted again, and the man was at his side.

"Quick! Where's your tool chest? Bear a hand, now!"

The two men fought their way through the water that came drenching and flying over the forecastle, to the boatswain's berth, which the carpenter shared; and in a few moments returned staggering aft with their arms full of tools, which they thrust into the hands of the men. Holdsworth seized an adze; the carpenter another; and to it fell all hands, feeling for the ropes and then letting drive at them.

The mere occupation heartened the men, who worked with a will, bursting into encouraging cheers from time to time and calling to each other incessantly. The lightning was so far useful that it enabled them to obtain glimpses of the progress they made. The starboard shrouds lay across the deck, from bulwark to bulwark, like bridges; these were the first that were dealt with. They kept the wreck close alongside, and the strain upon them was enormous. Whilst Holdsworth and the carpenter hacked, they repeatedly called to a few of the men whose zeal kept them working on the lee side, though their figures could not be seen, to stand clear, wisely guessing that after a few of the shrouds had been severed, the whole would part like a rope-yarn: and this happened. One final blow divided a shroud and left the weight upon a few others, which were unequal to support it; and as they flew a loud shriek rose; a man had been caught by the flying shrouds round the body and whirled overboard like dust. But in the darkness none could tell who the messmate was that had lost his life.

The parting of these shrouds released the wreck from the ship's side, and it drifted some fathoms away. The horrible grinding sounds ceased ; but still the masts and yards, which the lightning disclosed seething in the water, black, ugly, and as dangerous as a lee-shore, were attached to the hull by a network of rope, all which must be severed. The knives of the men cut and hacked in all directions ; and first here and then there, and sometimes as if crashing in half-a-dozen places at once, the adze wielded by Holdsworth was to be heard.

The last shroud was at length severed, the last rope parted ; the hull, drifting faster than the dead weight of wreck, fell astern of the horrible incumbrance, and the next flash of lightning showed the water boiling round the black spars ahead.

"Hurrah !" shouted Holdsworth ; but the men, wearied and faint after their long and great struggle, and sickened by the shriek of their perishing comrade, whose cry still sounded in their ears, answered the encouraging shout faint-heartedly.

The ocean was still a black and howling wilderness, and the vessel plunged and rolled, and trembled in the jumping seas, with her head right in the wind's eye, and the water pouring over her in sheets of undulating fire. The water had stove in the cuddy front, and was washing in tons down into the steerage. What they had now to do was to furl the cross-jack ; aft came the men and clewed the sail up ; on which the vessel fell broadside to the wind and rolled her bulwarks under water.

To furl the cross-jack was a job full of peril ; but, if

the thing was to be done at all, it was to be done by a *coup de main*. Holdsworth, crying to the hands to follow him, sprang up the port mizzen rigging. Half-a-dozen went up after him, the rest skulked in the darkness, and stood holding their breath, expecting every moment the crash that should fling the men aloft into the sea. No glimpse of the brave fellows was to be obtained; nothing but the flapping outline of the white sail could be seen; the mast creaked harshly; but from time to time the men's voices could be heard even above the roar of the tempest, the groaning of the ship, and the rolling of spare casks, a sheep-pen which had become unlashed, and other things about the waist and quarter-deck; and slowly the faint spaces of thundering canvas vanished in the darkness, and were securely stowed.

Meanwhile, the hands about the poop had been sent to man the pumps. The carpenter had sounded the well and reported three feet of water in the hold.

"She must be tight, sir! I am sure she is tight, sir! She has shipped the water that's in her through the mast-coat of the main-mast!" the skipper shouted to Holdsworth, who stood, panting from his exertions aloft, close against the mizzen-mast, that he might judge what chance there was of its standing.

Meanwhile, the wheel was hard a-starboard, and the gale was now upon the ship's quarter, the huge waves breaking under her counter and sending her wildly yawing forward. Had there been daylight, they could have rigged up a jury foresail on the stump of the fore-mast, which would have served to keep her before the wind; but nothing could be done in the overwhelming darkness except to keep the pumps at work.

But she was riding more easily now, and shipping

fewer seas; the port bulwark just abaft the gangway
had been crushed to a level with the deck by the fall
of the main-mast, and offered a wide aperture for the
escape of the water, so that the main-deck, where the
hands worked the pumps, was practicable.

Furiously as it still blew, it was evident that the
storm was abating; there were rifts in the clouds,
through which, here and there, a pale star glimmered
for an instant, and was then swallowed up.

It was now five bells (half-past ten); the skipper
ordered rum to be served out to the men, who were
wet through to the skin, and fagged to death by their
extraordinary exertions. The carpenter sounded the
well again, and reported an increase of three inches in
the depth of water. This was a terrible announcement,
and proved beyond a doubt that the ship was leaking,
though the crew were kept in ignorance of the report,
that they might not be disheartened.

At six bells the clouds had broken into huge black
groups, with spaces of clear sky between, and the wind
was lulling as rapidly as it had risen.

The ship was still buoyant enough to rise easily over
the seas; but anything more forlorn than her appearance, as it was disclosed by the dim light that fell from
the rifts among the clouds, cannot be imagined.

The fore-mast stood like a black and lightning-
shattered tree; the jib-boom hung in two pieces from
the bowsprit; where the main-mast had stood were
some huge jagged splinters; and aft towered the
mizzen-mast, with the cross-jack swinging to the roll of
the ship, the spanker with its peak halliards gone, and
the whole picture of it completing the unutterable air
of desolation presented by the storm-shattered vessel.

At eight bells the carpenter reported no increase of the water in the hold, which cheering intimation the captain delivered to the men from the break of the poop, who received it with a faint cheer.

The pumps had been relieved three times, and now the port watch was at them, making the water bubble on to the deck, where it was washed to and fro, and poured in streams through the scupper-holes.

At one o'clock, Holdsworth, who had been on deck since a quarter to seven, went below to put on dry clothes; and as he was leaving his cabin to return on deck he met Mrs. Tennent. Her face was very pale in the light of the swinging lamp, and she stood at her cabin door, by the handle of which she supported herself.

"Are we not in great danger, Mr. Holdsworth?" she whispered, in a tone of deep excitement.

"The worst is passed, I hope," answered Holdsworth cheerfully.

"Do not be afraid of telling me the truth. I can be brave for my child's sake. If real danger should come, Mr. Holdsworth, will you remember him? Will you be near him in that moment?"

"We won't talk of danger yet, Mrs. Tennent. We have had an ugly bout of it, but the daylight is coming, and then we shall be more comfortable."

"Many times," she exclaimed, "I thought we were sinking! O God! what a horrible night this has been! I heard the water rushing past the cabin door, and I tried to reach the deck, but was too faint to carry my child, and I could not leave him."

"Well, you see we are still afloat," Holdsworth answered cheerily. "Depend upon it, we will do our best to save the ship. Take my advice and lie down and get some sleep. This water here," pointing to the cuddy-deck, "means nothing; a swab will put that to rights. The morning is coming, and you are sailing under a skipper who knows what he is about."

He waved his hand cordially, and left her.

All through that long night the hands stuck to the pumps, but the water gained upon them inch by inch, and when the morning broke at last, the vessel was deep and heavy, rolling sluggishly, and leaking fast.

The sun was a welcome sight to the poor fagged seamen. Up he sprang, flushing the universe with a pink splendour, and dispersing the heavy clouds which hung in clusters about his rising-point.

Up to that time there had been a fresh breeze blowing, the dregs, so to speak, of the storm that had dismantled the ship; but this lulled as the sun rose, the sea smoothed out its turbulent waves, and a day filled with the promise of calm and beauty broke on a scene as desolate as any the heart can conceive.

One of the watches was in the forecastle; half the other watch on dock was at the pumps, the monotonous sounds of which had been echoing many hours, together with the gushing of water surging over the decks, and pouring in streams from the ship's sides.

The vessel was now no more than a log on the water; not a shred of canvas, with the exception of the mutilated spanker upon her, her port bulwarks crushed, her fore-mast a stump, her decks exhibiting a scene of wild disorder—loose spars that had been washed from forward encumbering the entrance of the cuddy; the cuddy front battered to pieces, spare casks piled tumultuously about the poop-ladders, and the long-boat, lashed between the galley and the fore-mast, and which had held some of the live stock, full of water and drowned sheep. On the port side, the severed shrouds, which had supported the masts, trailed their black lengths in the sea; and all about the starboard side were the fragments of ropes and stays hacked and torn to pieces; while the port main-chains had received a wrench that had torn the bolts out of the ship's side, and left the irons standing out.

As yet none of the passengers had made their appearance. The captain had brought a chart from his cabin and unrolled it upon the skylight, and stood with his finger upon it, calculating his whereabouts by yesterday's reckoning, and waiting for Holdsworth to return from the hold, which he and the carpenter were exploring for the leak.

The swell, which was heavy, surged against the ship's sides; but her buoyancy was gone, she hardly moved to the pressure.

Presently Holdsworth came out of the hold, wet and exhausted, followed by the carpenter in worse plight.

"Well?" exclaimed the captain, in a subdued but eager voice.

"I am afraid it is a hopeless case, sir. She's leaking in a dozen different places."

"The worst leak is just amidships," said the carpenter. "It's under the water in the hold. You can hear it bubbling, but there's no getting at it."

"What soundings have you got?"

"Eleven feet, sir!"

"Good God!" cried the skipper; "that's an increase of a foot and a half since seven bells."

"We had better look to the boats, sir," said Holdsworth, scanning the horizon.

"Don't talk of the boats yet, sir!" panted the skipper. "Clap some backstays on to the fore-mast and turn to and rig up the spare staysail."

"Ay, ay, sir," answered Holdsworth, and went forward to call all hands and make what sail they could upon the stump of the fore-mast, whilst the skipper walked passionately to and fro, perfectly conscious of the hopelessness of their situation, but determined to blind his eyes to it.

The first among the passengers to come on deck was the General, who stood transfixed by the spectacle of the wreck. He and some of the others had attempted during the night to leave their berths and find out the reason of the uproar that was going on over their heads, but had been literally blown back again the moment they showed their noses above the hatchway; and none of them, with the exception of Mrs. Tennent, having had an opportunity of speaking to either the captain or Holdsworth, they were all in perfect ignorance that the vessel was actually a wreck.

Whilst the General stood gasping and staring up aloft in search of the majestic masts and sails that had reared their graceful heights when he was last on deck, he was joined by Mr. St. Aubyn and Mr. Holland, both of whom turned pale with amazement and fear.

Then all three of them ran up to the captain.

"Oh, tell us what has happened? What will become of us? Are we sinking?" cried the actor.

"Where are the masts gone? Is it possible that we can ever reach America in this condition?" gasped Mr. Holland.

"Captain, we seem to be in a frightful mess! Why, we are foundering, sir!" exclaimed the General, rolling his eyes over the sea and then fixing them upon the captain.

"Gentlemen! gentlemen!" returned the skipper, extending his hands, "pray leave me! You distract me by your questions."

"Are we in danger?" implored Mr. St. Aubyn.

"Yes, sir; can't you see?" answered the skipper fiercely.

"Is it possible?" stammered Mr. St. Aubyn, turning deadly pale.

"It is possible!" cried the skipper scornfully. "But I hope you are not going to be afraid, sir. Look over the break of the poop and you'll see the men pumping for their lives. Danger is one thing, and drowning is another. I beg, sir, that you will control your fears. Panics are easily created, and you will remember, please, that we have women among us."

Saying which he walked some paces away. Mr. St. Aubyn burst into tears; Mr. Holland gazed around him with an air of stupefaction; the General followed the skipper.

"Is our position really serious?"

"Yes, General; the ship's bottom is leaky fore and aft."

"What do you mean to do?"

"Keep her afloat as long as I can. And now will you do me a service? Go and clap that snivelling actor on the back and put some heart in him. One coward makes many, and this is no time for any man on board my ship who values his life at one farthing to lose his pluck."

By this time the hands forward had lashed a block on the stump of the fore-mast, and run up a spare staysail. Holdsworth then came aft to the poop. The captain called him to the skylight, and they hung together over the chart, calculating their neighbourhood, and devising expedients in subdued tones. The men who were far enough forward to see them as they stood together on the poop eyed them curiously, and held muttering conversations together, some of them going to the ship's side and looking over.

It was felt by every man among them that the vessel was sinking ; and those who worked the pumps plied them languidly, as though understanding the fruitlessness of their labour.

Mrs. Tennent came on deck with her boy and stood near Holdsworth, asking no questions, but with an expression on her face that plainly showed her conscious of the danger and prepared for the worst. Soon afterwards came Mrs. Ashton, who shrieked out when she beheld the dismasted hull, and clung convulsively to her husband. Her maid followed her, shivering, cowed, with big eyes staring everywhere like a madwoman's.

Then a dead silence fell upon the ship, disturbed only by the languid clanking of the pumps and the fall of the continuous streams of water over the ship's sides.

It was now half-past eight o'clock. Not a breath of air rippled the surface of the sea, which rose and sank to a deep and voluminous under-swell. Some heavy clouds hung motionless in the blue sky, from one of which a shower of rain was falling about a mile off, arching a little brilliant rainbow upon the water.

Presently Holdsworth advanced to the poop-rail and sang out to the carpenter to sound the well. This was done, and the report showed that the leak was gaining fast upon the pumps.

On this announcement all heart went out of the captain like a flash, and left him silent and spiritless.

He rallied, went to Holdsworth's side and called out: "Belay that pumping there! Boatswain, send all hands aft to the quarter-deck."

The sound of the pumping ceased, the men came aft in groups and stood in a crowd.

Some of them were bearded, some quite young; their attire was various but always picturesque: here a red shirt, there white, here blue serge, there coarse canvas, many with bare brown arms ringed with tattoo-marks; some in sea-boots, some with naked feet. The bright sun gleamed upon their upturned faces, pale for want of sleep and with the intense weariness of their long and heavy labours. There was no want of respect suggested by any of them; but, on the contrary, there was a rough and sympathetic deference in their manner and gaze as they fixed their eyes on their white-haired skipper and listened to his speech, which he delivered in a voice that now and then faltered.

"My men, I had hoped to keep our poor old hooker afloat by manning the pumps day and night and head for home, which, with a breeze astern of us, we might have reached even in the trim the gale last night has put us in. But I find that the water is gaining upon us faster than we can pump it out, and it's not my intention to fag you with useless work. But in this sea the hull is likely to float for some hours yet; so we shall have plenty of time to get the boats out and do the best we can for our lives. You are most of you Englishmen, and those who are not are all brave fellows, and no man can be better than that, let him hail from what port he may: so I can depend upon you turning to and obeying orders quietly. There are thirty-four souls aboard of us and four boats; there's room for thirteen in the long-boat, and for seven apiece in the quarter-boats. I'll take charge of the long-boat, your chief mate of the pinnace, and the second mate and boatswain will take the others. There's no hurry, and there must be no confusion. Let a dozen hands man the pumps, the rest go to breakfast and then relieve the pumps. Then tumble aft, get the long-boat launched, and do the best we can for ourselves; and may God preserve us! Amen."

At the conclusion of this speech the men raised a cheer, the boatswain's pipe shrilled, clang went the pumps again, and the quarter-deck was deserted.

The captain turned to the passengers.

"Ladies and gentlemen, these are ugly straits for me to have brought you into, and I would that God in His mercy had ordained it otherwise. I have been forty years at sea, and the like of this has never befallen me before. But that's no matter. I'll take care to do my duty by you to the last. We have got enough boats to accommodate us all comfortably; the weather promises fair, and it's odds if every one of us isn't snug and safe on board some ship before to-night; for we're right in the track of homeward-bound ships from the United States. Some of you will come with me, and some go along with my chief officer, who has worked nobly for us all, and who'll work as nobly right away through for those who are with him whilst the life is in his body. Ladies, keep up your courage; for a sinking ship is a small matter when you've got good boats, and are with men who know how to handle 'em. We'll go below now and make as good a breakfast as we can; we'll then

provision the boats and put off, as sure as our hearts
can make us that God's eye, which is everywhere, will
not lose sight of us."

There were some murmurs, and then a silence, which
Mrs. Ashton broke by bursting into a passion of tears.
When she was in some measure calmed, the General
said :

"Fellow-passengers, will you unite with me in a
prayer to our merciful God for His protection?"

The men took off their hats, but the captain exclaimed :

"General, there are hands for'ard who might like to
join us. We should give them the chance."

Holdsworth went to the forecastle, and presently
returned with the whole ship's company following him.
The hands at the pump ceased their work to gather
round the capstan, and the passengers attended the
skipper in a body to the quarter-deck. The old General
stood in the midst of the crowd and knelt—an example
followed by the rest.

There was something too sacred in the nature of the
extemporaneous prayer offered up by the General to
make it proper for me to write it down here ; but its
effect was deeply impressive. Noble, beyond the power
of words to describe, was the spectacle of the fine old
American, bare-headed and kneeling, his trembling hands
clasped, his kindly, honest face upturned to the skies,
breathing forth in broken tones an earnest entreaty that
God, in His infinite mercy, would look down upon His
servants now and grant them His all-powerful protection
in this their hour of danger and suffering. Equally
affecting was the spectacle of the men—some with hands
clasped before their faces, some kneeling with reverently-

bowed heads, some gazing with earnest eyes upon the petitioner, and some even weeping—not unmanly tears —those who wept were among the bravest. The widow knelt with her arms about her child's neck, in an attitude both shielding and imploring. The husband and wife prayed hand-in-hand.

Overhead shone the joyous sun; the long and polished swell surged against the sluggish vessel's side; and amidst the tones of the old General and the solemn murmur of those who followed his words, you might hear the gurgling of the water in the hold, and feel the ship's growing weight and helplessness in the heavy and weary rolls she gave to the movement of the sea.

CHAPTER VII.

IN THE BOATS.

By twelve o'clock they had baled the long-boat out and got her over the ship's side, a task of no small difficulty, since, the main-mast being gone, they had no means of slinging her. The other boats were also lowered, each with a hand in her, and hung in a group about the port side of the ship, where the bulwarks were smashed.

Each boat was properly supplied with mast, sail, and oars; also with water, biscuits, some rum in bottles, etc. They looked mere cockle-shells alongside the great hull, and it seemed difficult to realise that they would sustain among them the weight of the crowd of men who stood by ready to jump into them.

The ship was settling fast. They had left off pumping her some time since, and she had now sunk a great hole under her port fore-chains to a level with the water, which gushed in like a cascade.

Mrs. Ashton was the first to be handed out of the ship. She screamed and hung back, and threw her hands out to her husband; but the men, raising her firmly in their arms, offering her the while certain rough and hearty encouragements, passed her over the ship's side to the sailors in the boats, who deposited her in the long-boat. The widow, at her own request, was assigned to Holdsworth's boat. They handed her boy over first, and then she followed and seated herself in the stern-sheets, holding her child tightly.

Then rose a cry of "Bear a hand! the ship will founder!"

Mrs. Ashton's maid was passed out quickly, and then the passengers; the actor and the General getting into Holdsworth's boat, the others into the long-boat. After this, the seamen, feeling the imminence of the danger, tumbled rapidly into the boats; and then Holdsworth quitted the ship, followed by the captain.

"Shove off!" shouted the boatswain, who commanded one of the quarter-boats.

Out flashed the oars; the boats parted and stood aloof from the hull at a distance of about three hundred feet.

It is impossible to describe the mingled emotions of dismay, curiosity, and breathless suspense with which the men awaited the sinking of the hull. There was not a soul among them who felt privileged to depart until the vessel, so noble once, so desolate and broken now, had sunk to her long home in the deep Atlantic. Something absolutely of human pathos that appealed to the heart, as the distress of a living thing might, seemed mixed up in the aspect of unutterable desolation she presented, the more defined and keen because of the mocking joyousness of the sunlight that streamed over her, and the fair and azure surface of the sea on which she rested. Her figure-head, uninjured by the gale—as perfect a piece of workmanship as ever graced a vessel's bows—might, by no violent fantasy, have been deemed the spirit of the ship poising herself an instant ere she soared towards the sky. The two sails upon her flapped hollowly to her roll, and once there came from her silent deck a sound as of a bell being struck, which filled the listening sailors with awe, and set them bending superstitious glances in search of the Shadow that was tolling the ship's funeral knell.

All on a sudden the hull lurched in the direction of the boats and exposed her sloping decks. "She's going now!" cried one of the men. This was true. Down sank her stern slowly, so slowly that many seconds passed ere her stern-windows were on a level with the water. She righted, and her bows, high raised, pointed the shattered jib-boom aloft, as though in her last agony she raised her mangled limbs to heaven. She then sank stern foremost, the deepest tragical dignity attending her descent: the silence unbroken, save by the sullen gurgling and bubbling of the water forcing itself through her decks. Her stern disappeared; then her bows stood black on the water; they vanished, and the fore-mast with the sail upon it alone remained visible. Lower and lower these crept, but still it was possible to trace the undulating outline of the hull in the clear water. The sponge-like sail sucked up the water quicker than it sank, and arched a brown shadow upon its snow; then the jagged top of the fore-mast only was to be seen; this vanished, and the boats were left alone upon the mighty surface of the deep.

A deep silence prevailed among the men while she was sinking; and not for some moments after she had disappeared did the spell upon them break, and a long and tremulous sigh escaped them.

Then the captain's voice in the long-boat was heard:

"Mr. Holdsworth, our course is east-north-east. Every

boat has a compass aboard of her. Now, my men, up
with your masts ; we may get a breeze before sun-down.
And, meanwhile, out with your oars and make what
way we can towards the old country !"

The stout-hearted fellows answered with a cheer ; in
all four boats they shipped the masts ; out went the
oars, and the water bubbled round the stems.

The men were right to cheer. God knows they
needed what encouragement each other's voice could
give them.

What pen shall describe the overwhelming sense of
the immensity of the sea, now that its surface could be
touched by the hand—its huge presence so close !
That sense alone was a weight that oppressed the hearts
of the passengers like death. The height of a large
ship from the edge of the water implanted a habit of
security ; but here, they overhung the deep by an arm's
length, and near enough to see their own pale faces
mirrored in the green abyss from which they were
separated by planks not much stouter than the sole of
a boot.

There were in Holdsworth's boat : himself, Mrs.
Tennent and her boy, Mr. St. Aubyn, the General,
and two seamen—Winyard and Johnson ; in all, seven
souls. The long-boat, in the distance, looked crowded ;
but then she was the largest of the boats. Astern of
her rowed the boat commanded by the boatswain ;
astern of Holdsworth's, the boat commanded by Mr.
Thompson, the second mate.

There could be no purpose gained by rowing, for,
let them ply the oars as hard as they would, they could
not urge the heavy boats faster than three miles an
hour. Holdsworth steered for the long-boat, and pro-

posed to the captain that they should lay their oars in
and wait for a breeze ; which was agreed to.   The sun
shone hot upon the glassy sea, and the boats hoisted
their sails as a protection against the rays.   And for ever
the men bent earnest and anxious glances round the
bare and polished horizon for a sail.

In Holdsworth's boat the two seamen sat forward,
talking together in low voices ; Mr. St. Aubyn reclined
with his back against the mast, glancing incessantly
about him with quick, scared eyes, but quite silent, as
though the novelty and horror of the situation was
more than his mind could receive, and he was labouring
to master it.   The General's face was placid, and even
hopeful.   The widow, holding her son at her side, kept
her eyes bent downwards, and often her lips moved.

In the other boats the men talked, and often called
to one another.   Their voices sounded forced and unreal
as the tones floated across the water, and in a strange
manner heightened the unspeakable sense of solitude
inspired by the boundless and tenantless deep.

For some time the little boy appeared to share in
the feelings which held all but the two sailors in
Holdsworth's boat silent ; but he presently grew restless, and pulling his mother by the skirt, asked her in
a whisper when the ship was coming back to take them
on board again.

"Another ship will come and take us soon, pray
God, Louis," answered the mother.

"But where is our ship, mamma ?"

Holdsworth overheard the question, and answered in
his hearty, cheery manner :

"Look well about you, Louis, and, by-and-by, you
will see a tiny spot of white rise somewhere on that

clear circle," pointing round the horizon, " and that will be our ship coming to take us home."

"Oh, Mr. Holdsworth!" said the actor, in a faint voice, "if the wind rises, will not the water get into our boat and sink it?"

"Not if I can help it, sir. I am waiting for the wind to rise. There is no chance of a rescue in this calm."

"Though we should be grateful for this calm," exclaimed the General, "for it has enabled us all to leave the sinking ship in safety."

"I have lost my all in that ship—all the money I had in the world, and my clothes, and things that were priceless to me," moaned Mr. St. Aubyn.

The widow raised her head, and exclaimed, "I too have lost much that was precious, and which no money could ever purchase. But, so far, God has watched over us and preserved our lives, and I can well spare all else—all else—if He will but leave me this treasure." She wept as she bowed her head over her child.

"Let us not murmur, Mr. St. Aubyn," said the General softly, "but call upon Him who rebuked the winds and waves in the sea of Galilee, and calmed them. Have not we His disciples' faith? He is in our midst, watching over us, even as we sit now. This ocean is but the symbol of His majesty and might: His servant who will bear us safely on its bosom at its Lord's command. Our Saviour sleeps not, neither will He forsake us. We forget Him when we yield to our fears."

"Thank you for those words, sir," said the man named Johnson. "God don't forget those who are at sea any more than those who stop on shore. I have been worse off nor this, sir, lashed to a raft for forty-eight hours, and here I am to tell the story. Begging your pardon, sir," he added, touching his cap, and drawing back respectfully.

By this time the boats had drifted some distance apart; but the voices talking in them could still be heard with the utmost clearness, so exquisite a vehicle of sound is the smooth surface of water.

It was one o'clock by Holdsworth's watch when they beheld the horizon in the east darkening under what resembled the shadow of a cloud, and the voice of a man in the long-boat came across the water, crying, " A breeze at last, my boys !"

It was a light breeze, and moved very slowly, but it filled the sails and sent the boats rippling gently through the water. As it came foul of the course the skipper meant to take, they lay as close to it as they could ; and eyes were strained in its direction for the welcome sail, some of them whispered, it might bring along with it. Some white clouds came up, and as they soared about the horizon, they so closely resembled the sails of ships that even Holdsworth's experienced eye was deceived, and he gazed intently with a beating heart.

The breeze freshened, and the unequal sailing qualities of the boats manifested themselves. The long-boat drew ahead rapidly ; Holdsworth's came next ; the other two fell astern. The wind, though in reality light, seemed tolerably strong, owing to the boats sailing close to it. Holdsworth's boat lay over, which terrified St. Aubyn, and made him cling to the weather-gunwale.

" You're afeard rather early, sir," said one of the seamen—Winyard—sarcastically.

" The boat will turn over !" gasped the actor.

Indeed his fear and despair were pitiable, and had

not only dulled his eyes, but pinched and thinned his face as though he were fresh from a sick bed.

"Take a pull at this," said Holdsworth, offering him some rum, and heartily commiserating the man's sufferings. But St. Aubyn shook his head, and gazed with distended eyes at the water, shivering repeatedly, and sometimes talking to himself.

In order to let the hinder boats come up, the long-boat ahead from time to time stopped her way by putting her helm down, which example Holdsworth regularly followed ; and so they sailed throughout the whole afternoon, the breeze remaining steady and the sea smooth.

The boat commanded by Holdsworth was about twenty-seven feet long, with seven feet or thereabouts of beam. There was a locker aft, which had been filled with small bags of bread, as they call biscuits at sea ; and forward were one small and two large kegs of water, and a tin pannikin to serve out the allowances with. At the bottom of the boat was a set of gratings, meant to keep the feet clear of any water that might be shipped, with a well convenient to get at, and half a cocoa-nut-shell with a handle let into it, to bale the boat with. The boat was new, stoutly built, and rigged with a lug-sail. A small compass had been put in her, and Holdsworth had lashed it carefully to a thwart. This was the only nautical instrument they had with them, and unless they could guess their whereabouts, it would not, after a time, be of much service.

They had during the afternoon ascertained the quantity of provisions and water they carried, and discovered that there was enough to last for about ten days, providing each person had no more than two biscuits, and a quarter full of the pannikin of water, a day. They

had also three bottles of rum.   The first allowance was
served out by Holdsworth at five o'clock in the afternoon.
A biscuit was handed to each person ; the little boy and
the two seamen ate theirs hungrily : the General and
Holdsworth nibbled only a portion of theirs : but Mrs.
Tennent and the actor ate nothing.   The mother gave
half her biscuit to her boy, and put the other half in
her pocket for him to eat during the night.   The actor
refused his allowance altogether, and Holdsworth returned it to the bag he had taken it from.

All the other boats remained in sight ; the long-boat
ahead, and the other two at unequal distances astern.
From time to time they encouraged each other by waving
their hats ; and just before sunset some of the men in
the long-boat struck up a hymn, the chorus of which
stole faintly across the breeze, and mingled with the
bubbling play of the water round the boat's bows.

The sun went down, branding the great ocean with
an angry glare ; but nothing was visible upon either
horizon but the deceptive tail-ends of clouds rising or
dwindling.   The breeze grew stronger as the darkness
crept on, and they lowered the sail and took a couple of
reefs in it, whilst there was light enough abroad for
them to see what they were about.   They soon lost
sight of the other boats, and Holdsworth finding the
wind drawing ahead, put the boat round, judging that
the others would do so likewise.

Now, if at no other time, was the sense of the profound helplessness of their position forced upon them.
It is easy to write and read of an open boat far out in
the Atlantic Ocean, and darkness around ; but none save
those who have experienced the situation can realise all
the horror of it.   Waves which would scarcely more

than ripple against the sides of a ship, make a dangerous sea for an open boat, and arch their seething heads over her with a threat in every one of them of destruction.

But *the* overpowering sensation is the near presence of the sea. Your feet are below its surface; your head but an arm's length above it. And you hear the quick splash of the boat's bows as she jumps awkwardly into the hollows of the waves, wobbling as she goes forward with jerks and many stoppages, while now and again the sea chucks a handful of spray into your eyes as an earnest of the way it means to deal with you presently, when the wind has made it more angry.

The stars came out and shone placidly among the clouds which were rolling away to the north-west. There was a short quick sea, which made the boat dip uncomfortably, and now and again whisked a sheet of spray over the seamen who sat forward. But there was more south than east in the breeze, which kept the temperature of the night mild. The little boy fell asleep in his mother's arms; Mr. St. Aubyn reclined against the mast, his arms folded, and his head drooping on his breast, starting at intervals as the spray fell like a shower of rain in the boat, but speedily relapsing again into the sluggish or semi-unconscious state into which he had fallen shortly after the sun had gone down. The General and Holdsworth sometimes conversed. Presently Winyard, turning his coat collar over his ears, slipped under the thwart, where he coiled himself like a cat, and went to sleep.

"I wish I could induce you to lie down, Mrs. Tennent," said Holdsworth. "My coat will make you a capital pillow. I don't want it indeed. I have slept on deck in my shirt-sleeves in colder nights than this. I shan't put the boat about again to-night if this wind holds, and you will lie with your boy alongside of you as snugly as possible on this seat."

She thanked him, but said it would be useless for her to lie down; she should not be able to sleep.

"You have eaten nothing all day," said the General; "you must not allow your strength to fail you. Pray try to eat a little biscuit."

Holdsworth handed her a biscuit, and she broke a piece of it off and appeared to munch it; but in the darkness they could not tell how little she ate.

No sign was to be seen of the other boats, although once Holdsworth imagined he heard a voice halloing a long way to windward. The boat's head was now pointing east-north-east; but she lay close to the wind and made scarcely more than four knots an hour. The jump of the sea deadened her way materially; but this jump decreased as the night wore on, for the waves grew longer, with steadier intermissions. At twelve o'clock, Holdsworth, who was worn out by his long spell at the helm, called to Johnson to awaken Winyard. Up jumped the seaman from the bottom of the boat and came aft. Holdsworth gave him the yoke-lines, and bidding Johnson lie down and get some rest, seated himself on the lee-side of the mast and scanned the sea to right and left of him. The old General had fallen asleep right along the thwart on which he sat, his face buried in his arm. The boy slept soundly in his mother's arms, but whether she slumbered or not, Holdsworth could not tell. Once Mr. St. Aubyn started up as from a nightmare, muttered some broken sentences, and was silent again.

"Keep her close," said Holdsworth to Winyard, "and watch the seas."

"You had best take some rest, sir. I can handle the boat whilst you're down."

"No. I'll wait until Johnson has had his nap."

So passed two hours.

It was drawing near half-past two in the morning when Winyard called, in a loud whisper:

"Master, isn't that a ship to windward, there?"

No one in the boat heard him but Holdsworth. He jumped up and peered into the starlit gloom ahead, where, sure enough, the outline of a dark shadow could be traced, though only by looking on one side of it.

"Yes, that's a ship!" he answered hoarsely; "but she's too far to windward to hear our shouts. Have we any lights aboard of us? Quick!"

He pulled the General, who leaped up, rubbing his eyes.

"Have you any matches about you?"

"No—what is it?"

"There's a ship yonder! I could souse my handkerchief in rum and set fire to it. Hi! Mr. St. Aubyn! feel if you have a match in your pockets." But the actor answered with a stupefied stare, whereupon Holdsworth searched his pockets without avail.

Johnson was awake, standing up in the bows, with his arms lifted.

"Ship ahoy!" roared Holdsworth. One might have thought the voice deep and powerful enough to have carried twice the distance of that gliding shadow.

They waited breathlessly; but no sound was returned.

"Altogether, now!" shouted Holdsworth; "one, two, three—ship ahoy!"

The united voices sounded like a shriek of death-agony rising out of the ebony-coloured deep; but no response was brought back by the wind.

"O God!" raved Winyard. "they'd see us if we could only show a light!"

"She is running before the wind," cried Johnson; "she's passing us!"

"Put your helm up!" roared Holdsworth. "We'll follow her. She may hear us when we get her to leeward."

They let go the halliards, shook the reefs out of the sail, and set it again, slackening the sheet far out. The boat headed for the visionary shadow, which was fast fading in the universal gloom, and the foam boiled under and alongside of her.

"Altogether again!" sang out Holdsworth.

Once more went forth the loud, despairing chorus, to be followed by silence. They might as well have attempted to chase a cloud. Keen as the sailors' eyes were, they could no longer perceive the shadow.

"Never mind!" exclaimed Holdsworth, cheerily, "there may be others near us; we'll keep a sharp look-out."

"She may fall in with one of the other boats," said Johnson, "and, maybe, she'll cruise about to find us."

The chill of disappointment passed, and they grew hopeful. The mere fact of having sighted a ship imparted a new encouragement.

"We should be in the track of outward-bounders," said Holdsworth. "Give us a hand here, Johnson, to take these reefs in. Bring her close again, Winyard. Pray God we shall be talking of this night on a ship's deck by noon to-morrow."

The little boy, who had been awakened by the hallo-ing of the men, shivered, crept closer to his mother's side, and fell asleep again.

CHAPTER VIII.

"Mr. Holdsworth," said the General, "will you not
let me watch whilst you get some sleep? You have
been up now for nearly three nights running, and I beg
you to consider the preciousness of your life to us all."

"I am much obliged to you, General. I'll do as you
ask me. Johnson, come aft and relieve Winyard here.
Keep a sharp look-out, my lads, and wake me up if the
breeze freshens." He seated himself in the bottom of
the boat, rested his head upon a thwart, and in a few
moments was fast asleep.

A hush fell upon the boat which nothing broke but
the quick angry sousing of the bows as the boat fell
with her short length into the trough of the sea. The
widow had fallen asleep at last, and leaned against
Johnson, who steered, whilst her boy slumbered with
his head on her lap. The sailor sat motionless for fear
of waking her, calling once in a whisper to Winyard to
come aft and look at the little 'un, and tell him if he
thought that God would let such innocence be drowned.

"He's the image of my little Bill," answered Winyard, stooping his bearded face low that he might see
the child's features. "I'm glad the poor lady's sleeping. Keep steady, Dick, or you'll wake her. She ain't

tasted a mossil of food all this blessed day, and it 'ud cut me to the heart to see the little 'un left without a mother."

"Ay, and so it would me, Harry. May be we'll sight a ship to-morrow. I've got my old woman to keep ashore, and I guess, when rent-time comes, she won't know what to do, unless I get back."

"I wish I had some 'baccy with me. Ain't got a bit in all my pockets. I wonder where t'other boats have got to?"

The conversation, which had been carried on in hoarse whispers, was at this point interrupted by a movement of the little boy. Johnson raised his hand and Winyard crept forward, where he sat like a bronze statue, watching the horizon.

It was about four o'clock, as the seamen guessed, when the wind, which had been pretty steady from the south-east, lulled, and then veering northward came on to blow freshly. The men awakened Holdsworth, who went to the helm. Mrs. Tennent, who had been aroused by the withdrawal of the sailor's shoulder, shivered with the cold and crouched down to hug herself in her clothes. Indeed, the north wind was cold enough; but Holdsworth, observing the woman's condition, whipped off his coat without a word and buttoned it over her shoulders, silencing her protests by kindly laughter and encouraging words.

The change of wind produced a cross sea which drenched the boat and made her movements horribly uncomfortable. The wind increased, bringing up large clouds, each of which was charged with a small rain-loaded squall of its own. The sea rose, and matters began to wear an ugly look. The men close-reefed the sail, and Holdsworth finding that the boat shipped water when on the wind, let her go free; and away they scudded with a breeze growing in force every five minutes astern of them. The utmost vigilance was now needful in steering the boat. The waves were quick and irritable, and broke in noisy surfaces of foam on either gunwale, and from time to time it seemed inevitable that their curling crests must arch themselves clean into the boat and swamp her. Holdsworth parried them with the rudder like a fencer with a foil. His eye was marvellously quick, the movements of his hands delicate and unerring. What the waves were to that small open boat, the seas of the Pacific under a westerly gale are to a full-rigged ship. She sank into hollows half-mast deep, where the air was stagnant, behind and before her black walls of illuminated water, the hinder ones of which, catching her under the stern, raised her with irresistible force to a height that turned her inmates giddy and sick; and there, exposed to the wind, her sail blew out to cracking limits and hurled her madly forward—to sink into a new abysm, to experience another interval of breathless, deadly calm.

"May God have mercy upon us!" exclaimed the General, in one of these awful intervals, folding his arms tightly and fixing his eyes on a towering sea rearing astern of them like a hill.

But Holdsworth's voice echoed cheerily: "She is a brave boat, General; and it's not my intention to let such ripples as these" . . . the rest of the sentence was drowned in the hooting of the wind, as one of these "ripples" swung the boat high in the full face of it, and the "ripple" itself broke into an acre of foam under the boat's bows.

The two sailors sat like logs, ready for the worst; yet with a supreme confidence in Holdsworth's skill as a steersman, which he had already illustrated in a hundred subtle ways, appreciable to none but them. St. Aubyn lay in the bottom of the boat, motionless. The General, holding on to the mast, was seated amidships, commending his soul, and the souls of his comrades, to God, in inaudible prayers. The widow crouched with her boy, who still slept, in the stern-sheets; and beside her towered the form of Holdsworth, a yoke-line in each hand, his body inclined forward, his shirt-sleeves rolled above his elbows, every nerve, every muscle in him strung to the tension of steel, his glittering eyes fixed upon the seas ahead, his whole attitude resembling a sculptured personation of audacity, skill, and the finest British courage.

The dawn broke and found them swinging over an ugly sea, with the wind moderating. As the pallid light spread over the bleak surface of gray and moving waters, the weary shipwrecked men turned their eyes about in search of a vessel; but the ocean was tenantless save by its own leaping seas, which played around in an eternal mockery of a fluctuating hilly horizon.

They were now sailing due south. Holdsworth steered the boat, and Winyard baled her out; but, thanks to the wonderful skill with which the rudder was used, no single sea had been shipped, and what water there was consisted of the spray that had been blown into the boat off the crests of the waves when she was in their hollows.

The sun rose and diffused an exquisite pink through the ribbed clouds that barred the sky. His glorious light flashed jewels upon the water, and sent a message of hope among the inmates of the tiny boat striving amid the wild and throbbing wilderness of the deep.

The General stood up, and arching his hand over his eyes, gazed slowly and intently around the whole circumference of the water-line.

"We are alone," he said; but instantly corrected himself. "No, I speak thoughtlessly. We have God with us. He has been with us all night. We thank Thee, O God," he murmured, folding his hands and reverently lifting his face to the sky, "for Thy protection; and we humbly implore Thee not to abandon us, but to be with us in our anguish and desolation, and in Thine own good time to snatch us from the perils that encompass us."

They all cried Amen!

"The wind's lulling, master," said Johnson to Holdsworth. "We'll have the sea smooth before long."

"Oh, Mr. Holdsworth!" exclaimed Mrs. Tennent, starting up suddenly and hurriedly removing his coat from her shoulders, "how cruelly selfish I have been to deprive you of this covering throughout the long cold night."

"I'm better without it," cried Holdsworth. "Even my shirt-sleeves were too heavy for me—you see I have had to turn them up. Winyard, rouse up Mr. St. Aubyn. We shall be none the worse, any of us, for a mouthful of biscuit."

He patted the little boy with his left hand, with his right kept the boat's head straight as a line.

"Come, sir, wake up, please. Biscuit's going to be served out," said Winyard, pulling the actor somewhat unceremoniously by the arm.

Both seamen thought him a white-livered gentleman, and despised him accordingly.

The poor man lay athwart the boat, his legs doubled up and his arms hiding his face. He shook his head, without raising it, when Winyard pulled him, but did not speak. The man, thinking him numbed or cramped, raised him up ; whereupon St. Aubyn struggled to his feet, and looked about him with a fixed smile. That smile made his face terrible to behold, for he was deadly white, and a wild fire, with no more merriment in it than a madman's laugh, shone in his eyes, which looked unnaturally large, and his lips were blue and thin, and laid his teeth almost bare.

" You fellows may shrug your shoulders, and some of you may hiss," he muttered, never remitting his fixed smile, but speaking through his teeth and bringing his clenched fist upon his knee, " but you shan't starve me, because you don't understand what true acting means. Do you think I can't tell what this hollowness, this sinking is, here !" laying his hand upon his stomach and sending his lustrous eyes travelling over the others, who watched him in silence. " You are starving me, you fiends, and driving a poor actor to death. But do you think you will force him into the workhouse ? No, by God ! He has spirit, and will seek a new home, a new country, a new world, rather ! Who tells me I cannot act ? Try me in farce, in comedy, in tragedy ! See now—shall I play you Tony Lumpkin ?" He began to sing :

> " ' Then, come, put the jorum about,
>   And let us be merry and clever !
> Our hearts and our liquor are stout,
>   Here's the three Jolly Pigeons for ever.'

" Or shall I give you Lear?" He stretched out his hands to the sea :—

> " ' Blow, winds, and crack your cheeks ! rage ! blow !
>   You cataracts and hurricanoes, spout
>   Till you have drench'd our steeples, drown'd the cocks !
>   You sulphurous and thought-executing fires,
>   Vaunt-couriers to oak-cleaving thunderbolts,
>   Singe my white head ! '

Is not that fine, gentlemen ? Now turn about with more shrugs, and drive me mad with your cant. Ha ! ha ! ha !"

His laughter was shocking. The seamen shrank away from him.

" He has gone mad with terror !" whispered the General.

The widow hid her face in her hands.

" Johnson," said Holdsworth, " mix some rum and water in that pannikin and give it to him with a biscuit."

The actor took both, staring first at the pannikin, then at the biscuit.

" Gentlemen !" he cried, with his wild smile, " I am Timon of Athens, sour, crusty, and " . . . he stopped with a laugh. " But before his mind went, he pledged his friends, standing thus :—' Here's to you—dogs !'" He flung the contents of the pannikin at Holdsworth, and dashed the vessel into the boat; " and with this, I feed the winds !" and he hurled the biscuit into the sea.

" Seize him !" shrieked Holdsworth, noticing a quick movement on the actor's part. The men sprang forward, but too late to catch him. He leaped on to the thwart and bounded overboard with a peal of laughter, ere you could have cried " Hold !" and vanished under the crest

of a wave that was breaking at the moment under the
boat.

"See!" cried the General; "he has come to the surface! There is his head! He may be saved yet!"

But the boat was foaming through the water at six
or seven knots an hour; the sea was still so lively that
to broach her to would have been to capsize her in an
instant.

"We cannot save him!" exclaimed Holdsworth,
bitterly, grasping the situation at once; and kept the
boat's head doggedly away.

Those who watched the drowning man, saw him, a
mere dot, on the tumbling waters, heaved high on the
summit of a wave, with both his arms upraised; then
down he sank into the trough of the sea, the next wave
boiled over him, and they beheld him no more.

The General covered his face with his hands and
wept aloud. The widow was so sick and faint with the
horror of the scene, that she leaned back, white and
motionless, with her eyes closed. Johnson came aft
and put some rum to her lips, which revived her, and
then she began to weep silently, casting shuddering
backward glances at the sea, and hugging her boy to
her passionately. She had become, during the night,
the very ghost of her former self; her complexion was
ashen, her eyes hollow, her countenance gaunt with a
hard, weird look of old age upon it. Holdsworth
noticed that her dress was wet with salt water and
clung to her legs; but this it was impossible to remedy.
Infinite pity smote him as he gazed from her to her
child, and he handed her a biscuit, entreating her to eat
it. The boy ate his allowance quickly; but even out
of him something of the youthfulness and freshness of

his infancy had passed ; a perception of their danger and misery appeared to have visited him ; and he clung to his mother's side, holding her dress with one hand whilst he ate the biscuit, and gazing about him with puzzled eyes, in which was mixed up a strong expression of terror.

The impression produced by the sudden and tragical death of the actor was more lasting on the widow and the General than on the sailors, who were too sensible of their own peril to find more than a passing occasion of horror in the scene they had witnessed. They and Holdsworth ate a biscuit apiece and drank their allowance of water mixed with rum ; but the General turned, with an expression of loathing in his face, from the food, and Mrs. Tennent could not be induced to eat more than a few mouthfuls. Both drank of the water.

The waves were still lively enough to demand the utmost care in the steering of the boat ; but Winyard had proved himself a smart steersman, and Holdsworth, whose hands were cramped and blue with long grasping of the yoke-lines, gladly surrendered his place to the sailor.

"Strange," muttered the General, " that we sight no ships !"

"Our course is east," said Holdsworth. " If the wind would haul round a few points to the west, I'd out reefs and bear up."

The breeze held until twelve o'clock, when it slackened. The sea having grown smoother during the morning, Holdsworth hauled the sheet of the sail aft and steered south-east by the compass, which was as close to the sea as he deemed it advisable to sail the boat. The sun now shone hot overhead, which greatly comforted Mrs. Tennent and revived the spirits of her boy, who pulled a piece of string from his pocket, to which he fastened a crooked pin, and began to fish. As the afternoon advanced, the wind gradually died away, and a thin haze settled upon the southern horizon, portending both heat and calm. The water's surface turned to an aspect of polished steel; the boat rose and sank to the swell, easily and with a soothing motion, and the sail flapped idly against the mast.

During the afternoon, some porpoises came to the surface of the water, about a stone's throw from the boat, rolling their gleaming black bodies in a southerly direction.

"They always make for the quarter the wind's coming from," said Winyard.

"I am afraid we shall have no wind to-night," answered Holdsworth; "the weather looks too settled."

They watched the fish turning their solemn somer-saults until they were out of sight, and then, as though to meet hope half-way, Holdsworth swarmed up the boat's mast and swept the horizon with piercing eyes, but saw nothing but the boundless water-line paling away against the sky.

The sun went down in glorious majesty, burnishing the deep, and dazzling the eye with a splendour of small radiant clouds, pierced with threads of glory, and momentarily changing their brilliant hues until the orb was under the sea, when they turned a bright red colour. The twilight followed fast, the stars came out, and the darkness of night fell upon the lonely deep.

CHAPTER IX.

THE THIRD DAY.

As no object could be served by keeping the sail hoisted, they hauled it down and spread a portion of it over the widow and her child. Holdsworth kept watch till ten, and then awakened Winyard, who watched till twelve; afterwards Johnson watched; and so the three men took turn and turn about, all through the long and breathless night, until daybreak, which found Winyard awake in the stern-sheets, watching the pale dawn breaking in the east.

Its approach at first was imperceptible. A faint gray mingled in the prevailing darkness, and gradually grew more defined; the stars languished, and those in the extreme east hid themselves. Then a clearer light broke stealthily about the eastern horizon; the sea caught the glimmering dawn, and mirrored a pale and sickly illumination, infinitely vague, as would be the reflection in a looking-glass of a faint light. But soon the lustre broadened, and streaks of horizontal silver floated above the deep, and stood in layers of crystalline clearness, awaiting a more ardent transformation. Then a delicate pink flushed a wide space in the eastern sky, which spread and spread until the farthermost heavens shook off the heavy curtains of the night and melted into a pale and visionary blue. Anon, upon the eastern water-line, stood a mere speck of white and exceedingly brilliant light—a pure silver point of glory—which, as the eye watched it, increased in size, flinging flake upon flake of glittering icy splendour upon the water, until, as with a sudden bound, it soared in sun-like shape and flooded the heavens and the sea with strong rejoicing light.

It awoke Holdsworth, who started up and stared around him.

"Look, sir!" said Winyard, in a whisper that sounded fierce with excitement, pointing towards the south-east, where, upon the remote horizon, stood a white speck clearly defined by the sunshine.

Holdsworth hollowed his hands tube-wise, gazed intently for some moments, and then cried, "A sail!"

"Becalmed, master, as we are!" shouted Winyard; whereat the sleepers in the boat stirred and opened their eyes.

"Out oars, my men!" sang out Holdsworth. "A sail, General! Do you see her? Look, Mrs. Tennent; follow the direction of my finger! She is becalmed! She cannot escape us! Hurrah, my lads!"

In less time than it takes me to write it, both seamen were bending to the oars like madmen, making the water break in clear lines of ripple against the boat's bows, which headed directly for the distant sail. Language is powerless to describe the excitement of the poor creatures. Mrs. Tennent shed tears; the General, upon whose constitution, debilitated by old age, their perilous situation and the mental sufferings which accompanied it were beginning seriously to tell, stood clutching the mast, his eyes riveted upon the white speck, and his attenuated face flushed with eagerness and hope. The men, stretching to the long oars, looked from time to time over their shoulders to remark the progress they were making, and encouraged each other with cheerful cries.

They had but two oars, and the boat was heavy and moved reluctantly to the pressure of the blades; moreover, the men were weakened by exposure and want of nourishing food. Still they urged the boat through the water at pretty nearly three miles an hour; and Holdsworth repeatedly encouraged them by representing that every stroke of the oars brought the boat nearer within the range of the vision of those on board the vessel, and increased the likelihood, under God's providence, of their rescue.

When the vessel was first sighted, she could not have been less than ten miles distant; this was made manifest by the circumstance of their continuing to row a full hour before they had exposed her large sails, and even then her hull was invisible. The ocean, meanwhile, remained perfectly polished, without a shadow anywhere upon its vast bosom to indicate the passage of wind.

The seamen presently showing symptoms of distress, Holdsworth took an oar, and bade Winyard, whom he replaced, to drink some rum, and hand a draught to Johnson. The General begged to take Johnson's place for a time while the man rested himself; but the poor old gentleman, after rowing a few strokes, found himself utterly unequal to the weight of the oar, and he returned to his seat covered with perspiration, and breathing with difficulty and pain.

It was seven o'clock by Holdsworth's watch before

the hull of the vessel grew discernible; and then
Johnson, whose sight was very keen, pronounced her to
be a large three-masted brigantine. She had all her
sails set, but she was still so remote as scarcely to be
distinguished by an inexperienced eye from a cloud.

Winyard, who steered, asked Mrs. Tennent for her
black shawl, with which he climbed up the mast and
made it fast, flagwise. The motion of the boat hardly
created draught enough to unfurl it; but, drooping as
it did, it could scarcely fail to serve as a signal. The
calm which would have disheartened them under other
circumstances, as suspending all prospect of a rescue
whilst it lasted, was now deeply welcome to them as a
guarantee of their speedy release from the horrors of
their situation. As the vessel grew in dimensions under
the desperate exertions of the rowers, Mrs. Tennent became hysterical, laughed and wept at the same moment,
and hugged her boy passionately to her. The old
General stood up waving his handkerchief, and talking
to himself, even wildly at times.

Holdsworth was now steering, and he bent eager
glances in search of some signal, some flag whose spot
of colour would surely be visible even at that distance,
to tell them they were seen.

Suddenly he cried out:

"Johnson—Winyard! Look! tell me what you can
see?"

The men rested on their oars simultaneously and
turned their heads towards the vessel. A silence ensued, lasting some moments. Then Johnson exclaimed:

"There's smoke coming out of her. Don't you see
it, like a blue line between her fore and main masts?"

"Maybe they're boiling the pitch-kettle abaft the

galley, as we used aboard the 'Mary Ann,'" said Winyard, wiping his forehead with his bare arm; "let's make for her, boys."

And he fell to his oar again.

The water rippled round the boat's sides once more, and the shawl at the mast-head fluttered.

Five minutes passed; and then Holdsworth, whose eyes never wandered from the vessel, saw something black pass up her sails, rise over her masts and there hang. Another followed; another yet; volumes now, and each volume denser, blacker than its predecessor.

"She's on fire!" he shouted; at which the men tilted up their oars and stood up.

Quicker and quicker the black volumes, like balls growing in size as they mounted, were vomited up, and resembled an endless series of balloons rising from the deck; they met when they reached a short height above the masts, mingled and formed into a livid line which gradually stretched north and south, but very slowly. The spectators in the boat were paralysed; but their emotions were too various and conflicting to permit the deeper, deadlier ones of disappointment and despair to make themselves felt as yet.

Holdsworth broke a long silence by exclaiming, "Can you see them putting off?"

"No—I see nothing. I reckon she's abandoned hours ago," answered Winyard.

The General sank upon his knees with a groan, clutching the gunwale and staring at the burning vessel over his knuckles. There was no sign of a boat anywhere—no sign of living creature being on board the doomed craft. The smoke, which appeared to have been pent up in the hold, had now escaped on a sudden;

and thick and thicker yet it mounted, marking an ugly
stain upon the pure morning sky, and hanging sombre
and menacing over the smouldering vessel like a thunder-
cloud.	Soon a short tongue of flame protruded; then
came another and a longer one, which seemed to whiz
with a yellow radiance up the rigging and bury itself
in the smoke.	Then the fire burst out in all directions;
in the time it would take you to count ten, the vessel
was a mass of flame, keen, brilliant, coiling, with streams
of thin blue smoke sailing out of each yellow ray, mingled
with particles of burning matter that winked among the
heavy cloud like fireflies in a dark evening.	She was
four or five miles off; a mere toy on the surface of the
sea; and yet those who watched her from the boat could
distinctly hear the crackling of the fire, and the seething
of her flaming spars as they fell into the water.	Anon
the fires flickered, and up drove new volumes of smoke,
which paled and thinned as the rekindled flames burst
forth again and darted their spear-shaped fangs into the
smoke-hidden sky.

For above an hour this terrible and magnificent
spectacle lasted, during which not a word escaped the
lips of the inmates of the boat.	Their minds seemed
incapable of understanding the extinction of the hope
that had sustained them since sunrise, by a catastrophe
so unexpected, by a horror which united the extreme of
sublimity with the extreme of misfortune, and which
appeared scarcely more than a vision—so unforeseen, so
incredible, so illusive, so ghastly, so terrific was it.

By this time the whole of the upper masts were gone,
adding fuel to the interior furnace of the hull, and the
three lower masts were burning stumps.	Suddenly the
blazing mass appeared to rise in the air; the fires went

out as if by magic, and an opaque cloud, burnished a livid blue by the sunshine, floated on the water. Not for many moments after the flames had vanished came a concussion that rent the air, loud and violent as a thunder-clap among mountains. The cloud lifted, and where the vessel had been the sea was a smooth outline, reflecting only the dark shadow of the slowly-mounting smoke, and dotted here and there with black remnants of the wreck.

"Mr. Holdsworth," said the General in a faint voice, sinking backwards against a thwart, "I am dying."

His hands were pressed to his heart; he was breathing quickly and convulsively, and his face was bloodless. His exclamation broke the spell that held the others gazing in the direction of the smoke. They turned quickly, and Holdsworth jumped over to the old man and supported his head on his knee.

"No, no, General; don't say that. This is a bitter disappointment; but we believe in God's goodness. He cannot mean that we should perish. Johnson, pour some rum into the pannikin. Mrs. Tennent, dip your handkerchief into the sea and kindly pass it here."

They put the spirit to the old man's lip, and he drank a little, but gasped for breath when he had swallowed it and clenched his hands. They spread the wet handkerchief over his forehead and loosened his cravat.

"I——I know not what this giddiness may mean," the General stammered, while the lustre faded out of his eyes. "If it is death . . . I am ready to meet it. God is merciful and good. His Son is my Redeemer . . . He will take me to Himself . . . how faint! how faint! But I have eaten nothing" . . .

He ceased with a sudden gasp.

"You will feel better presently," said Holdsworth, while Mrs. Tennent took the old man's hand and fanned his face. "The shock of the burning ship has been too great for you. But you will live to recall this time. You have as manly a heart as ever God blessed His creatures with. Don't let it fail you now."

"I have . . . I have striven to do my duty," murmured the old man, so faintly that his words were scarcely audible. "I have served my country . . . she is a great empire . . . a great empire . . . and my heart is with old England, too;" forcing a smile, "we should know each other better, sir, and our prejudices would leave us, for . . . . for . . . . See! yonder is Charleston!" he suddenly exclaimed, his eyes kindling, and drawing his hand from Mrs. Tennent's, to point with it into the infinite horizon. "Do you see that house on the left, there, with the green facing it? I was born there, sir. Observe the barberry-bushes with the red fruit on them—just there I fought my cousin, when we were boys . . . he's a senator now, and they tell me a good speaker. Oh, how the time goes!" he sighed wearily. "But there's my wife . . . she is holding the little one by the hand, and nodding to me to attend her. . . . A moment, Sarah, a moment! Gentlemen, farewell. I beg your kind word in my favour among your countrymen, whom I honour. I am a plain American gentleman—a general, gentlemen . . . but tell them that my sword was never drawn from its scabbard for any cause but a good one, and . . . Ah, farewell! You see, gentlemen, my wife awaits me, and the little one beckons."

He made a gesture as though he would bow; his venerable and honoured head sank upon his bosom;

then he started, looked about him with a glazing eye, and smiling sweetly, whispered, "Sarah, I am coming," lay back and spoke no more.

When, after long watching him, they knew that he was dead, they covered him over with the sail, meaning to commit him to the sea when the widow should be asleep.

Holdsworth was so greatly overcome that for many minutes he could not raise his head nor speak. The widow, with her eyes fixed on the water, sat motionless, a fixed image of despair. Her boy crept about the bottom of the boat at her feet, with somewhat weakly movements, though his body had not yet suffered enough to kill the infancy in his mind. The sailors, made selfish by the bitter disappointment of the morning, talked of their chances of rescue, and discussed the subject of the burning ship. Johnson probably solved the mystery of the deserted vessel when he suggested that during the night the hands had found the cargo on fire—and he judged by the blaze she made, and the smoke, and the long time she was smouldering, that she was freighted with cotton or coal—and had battened down the hatches; but not having the means of getting the fire under, they struck and took to the boats, obliging the skipper to go along with them, and left the vessel to her fate. Just such another case happened to a messmate of his in the Bay of Biscay. The crew left their ship smouldering under battened hatches. But *she* was boarded by a Frenchman, who smothered the fire and towed her into Bordeaux.

"Where was the brigantine's crew, now?" Winyard wondered.

"I wish we could fall in with them, if only for company's sake," replied Johnson.

But of that there was very little chance.

All the afternoon the calm lasted, with light mists hanging in wreaths upon the horizon. But about the hour of sunset the smoke that had risen from the burning ship, and which had not drifted more than a couple of miles to the southward throughout the day, came sailing slowly towards the boat and passed high overhead, thinning its bulk as it travelled in an easterly direction. A light breeze heralded it; they hoisted the sail, put the boat's head round, and stood east-south-east.

The night fell, but the light breeze held steady. When they thought Mrs. Tennent was asleep, they raised the body of the General in their arms from the bottom of the boat. The night was lustrous with yellow stars, which diffused sufficient light to enable them to see the old man's face. The eyes were closed, and, though the under-jaw was fallen, there yet lingered an expression both of firmness and sweetness about the mouth. The draught under the sail moved his white hairs.

"Mates," said Holdsworth in a whisper, "we pray that God has taken this noble gentleman's soul to Himself, and that, though his body be dispersed in the sea, it will rise again at the Day of Judgment, in the shape we now behold it, to become a partaker of life everlasting, through Jesus Christ our Lord."

The two sailors answered Amen!

All three of them then tenderly handed the body over the boat's side, and let it gently slip into the water. The white hair glimmered for a brief moment on the dark surface, and then the body sank or was swallowed up in the gloom; and the boat rippled onwards, cutting the star flakes in the sea with her stem, and leaving them glittering in silver fragments in her wake.

CHAPTER X.

THE FOURTH DAY.

A FOURTH day broke, and found the boat almost becalmed again. The intense tedium of their captivity
cannot be expressed by words. The eternal iteration
of the water-line became a torment and a pang, and
forced them to look into the boat or upon one another
for relief of the strained and weary eye. Their limbs
were cramped for want of space to stretch themselves.
Holdsworth's cheeks were sunk, and the hollows of his
eyes dark; and a black beard and moustache, sprouting
upon his chin and lip, gave him a gaunt and grizly look.
The men sat with rounded backs and hopeless eyes,
fixed downwards, and sinewy hands clasped upon their
knees.

But the effect of the sufferings, bodily and mental,
they were enduring, was most visible in the widow,
whose face was scarcely recognisable for the wasted,
aged, pallid, and heart-broken aspect that it presented.

When the little boy awoke he began to cry and complain of pains in his limbs and back. His mother
seemed too weak to support or even soothe him with
speech. Holdsworth took him upon his knee and talked
to him cheerfully, that he might inspirit the others as
well as himself.

I

"Louis, you are a little man; you must not cry, because it grieves your poor mamma, who cannot bear to see your tears. Your back aches because your bed has been a hard one; but you won't have that uncomfortable bed long. Don't you remember what the poor old General said: that God, whose eye is everywhere, sees us, and will pity us, and send a ship to our rescue if we will but have patience, and not murmur against Him. Many vessels have been wrecked as well as the ' Meteor,' and their crews taken to the boats, and rescued by passing ships, after they had suffered more anguish and misery than we can dream of. The fortune that befell them may befall us. We must put our whole trust in God, and watch the horizon narrowly. This is but our fourth day, and the very breeze that is now blowing may be gradually bearing us towards a ship. So no more tears, my man. Here is a biscuit for you. Give this one to your mamma. Here, Johnson —Winyard."

He handed the men a biscuit apiece, and bade Johnson serve out the water.

There were three kegs in the boat, as stated elsewhere. They had calculated that by allowing each person half a pannikin of water a day, their stock would last them ten days. But now there were two mouths less, and they might hope to make the water serve them for as long as thirteen days. It would seem, however, that, in spite of the injunctions of Captain Steel, the boats had been provisioned hurriedly. Of biscuit, Holdsworth had an abundance; but nothing but negligence or haste could account for the absence of other provisions, such as rice, flour, beef and pork, dried peas, and such fare; unless, indeed, it was considered that none of these things would be eatable unless cooked. Though Holdsworth's boat might not have fared the worst, it was manifest that the quantity of water that had been put into her was out of proportion with the biscuit that filled the locker. They had used the water in one of the larger kegs first, and Johnson, in measuring out the allowance, found that scarcely enough remained to fill the pannikin by a quarter. Holdsworth told him to pull the bung out of one of the other kegs, and when the little boy, who was first served, had emptied the pannikin, the next draught was handed to the widow. She raised it to her lips eagerly, her mouth being feverish ; but had scarcely sipped it, when she put it down, exclaiming that the water was salt.

"Impossible !" cried Holdsworth quickly, and tasted the water.

The widow was right. The water was not indeed salt, but so brackish as to be quite unfit to drink.

He spat it out at once, his instincts cautioning him that he would increase his thirst by swallowing it, and looked blankly at the men.

"What ! *is* it salt ?" exclaimed Winyard furiously.

"Try the other keg," said Holdsworth, throwing the contents of the pannikin away.

Johnson drew some of the water and tasted it, but also spat it out, as Holdsworth had done.

"Is that salt too ?" shrieked Holdsworth.

"Try it ! " answered Johnson grimly, coming aft with the pannikin.

That, too, like the other, was brackish and unfit to be drunk.

"Great God ! " exclaimed Holdsworth, clasping his hands convulsively ; " how could this have happened ?"

"It was the steward as filled these kegs," said Winyard. "I saw him myself pumping out o' the starboard water cask, which the sea was washing over when the masts went, and draining the salt water in." He added fiercely, "I'll lay he took care to fill the kegs of the boat he belonged to with the right kind!"

"Hand that pannikin here," said Holdsworth; and mixed some rum with the water and tasted it, but the dose was indescribably nauseous.

This discovery was a frightful blow; so overwhelming that it took their minds some minutes to realise it in its full extent.

They were now absolutely without a drop of fresh water in the boat; which fact was made the more terrible by the consideration that, up to the moment of discovery, they had believed themselves stocked with sufficient water to last them for another week at the very least.

They were appalled and subdued to images of stone by this last and worst addition to the series of heavy misfortunes that had befallen them.

Then Winyard, who was already tormented with thirst, for they had permitted themselves to drink no water during the night, began to blaspheme, rolling his eyes wildly and calling curses on the head of the steward for his murderous negligence. He terrified the boy into a passion of tears, which increased his fury, and he stood up and menaced the child with his outstretched fist.

"Sit down!" exclaimed Holdsworth, in a voice that fell like a blow upon the ear. "You are going mad some days too soon, you lubber! Do you hear me? Sit down!"

The man scowled at him, and then threw himself backwards into the bows of the boat.

"Will your shrieks and oaths give us water?" Holdsworth continued bitterly. "You are not more thirsty than I, nor this poor lady, from whom you have not heard one syllable of complaint since she was handed into the boat!"

He turned to her with a look of deep compassion.

"Try to sustain your courage under this awful trial," he exclaimed. "Our position is not yet hopeless. There is no sea more largely navigated than the Atlantic, by vessels bound to all parts of the world, and I say it is almost inevitable that we should fall in with a ship soon."

She forced a wan smile for answer, but did not speak; merely put her hand on her child's shoulder and drew him to her.

As the morning advanced the heat of the sun increased, and the rays seemed to absorb the light breeze out of the atmosphere; the sea turned glassy, and by noon the boat was becalmed. Meanwhile, Winyard remained doggedly buried in the bows of the boat, sucking his dry lips, with despair legibly written upon his countenance. Johnson appeared to find relief by plunging his arm in the water and moistening his head and face. The very boat took a white, baked, thirsty aspect; and the heat made the paint upon her exhale in a faint and sickly smell.

When the afternoon was waning, Winyard got up and crept stealthily to the after-part of the boat. Holdsworth kept his eyes steadily upon him. His intention, however, was no more than to take up the pannikin, which he snatched at hastily, as though fearing that his purpose would be frustrated.   He then hastened forward and filled the vessel from one of the kegs.

"Don't drink it!" exclaimed Holdsworth; "it will increase your thirst."

But the man, pointing to his throat, swallowed the briny draught hastily, then put the pannikin down with a sigh of relief and with a face cleared of something of its peculiar expression of pain.

Johnson seized the pannikin, meaning to follow Winyard's example.   Holdsworth entreated him to desist.   "The salt will madden you!" he exclaimed. He had scarcely said this, when Winyard began to roll his body about, uttering short, sharp cries.

Immediately afterwards he vomited, his face turned slate colour, and they thought he would expire.   Holdsworth drained some rum into his mouth, and poured sea-water from the pannikin in long streams over his head.   This somewhat revived him ; but he lay groaning and cursing, and clutching at the sides of the boat with his finger-nails for many minutes.

His sufferings frightened Johnson, who called out:

"Master, if the water in the kegs is poison, we should let it run away."

"It is worse than poison," replied Holdsworth.   "Pull out the bungs—the sea-water around us is as wholesome to drink as that stuff."

Johnson then turned the kegs over and let them drain themselves empty.

After this a silence fell upon the boat which lasted a full hour, when the boy said:

"Mamma, I am thirsty.   Give me something to drink."

It was shocking to hear the child's complaint, and

feel the *impossibility* of satisfying him. The mother started up with a wild gesture, and cried in a fierce whisper, that was thickened in its passage through her swollen throat:

"O my God! let us both die! End our misery now."

Holdsworth watched her mutely.

Her appeal died away, and she sank back, exhausted by the sudden outbreak.

The sun went down and some clouds came up behind the horizon to receive the glowing disc. These spread themselves slowly over the heavens, albeit the sea remained breathlessly calm; and thinking that the wind was coming up that way, the poor sufferers turned their eyes wildly and eagerly towards the west, hoping with a desolate hope for the vessel that was to rescue them, but which no day brought.

When the night fell, Winyard began to sing in a strange husky voice; but his tones soon died out, and then came the small weak cry of, "Mamma, I am thirsty! give me some water!" from the little boy, wounding the ear with an edge of agony in the stillness and the gloom.

Presently a soft sigh of wind came from the west, which backed the sail. Holdsworth put the boat's head round until the sail filled, and then hauled the sheet aft, meaning to lay close to the wind, that they might sooner encounter the ship that the wind was to bring. The air sank into a calm again; but another puff followed which made the water gurgle, and it was plain that a breeze was coming, by the clouds which were drifting eastwards. The wind freshened and then became steady, and the boat, bending to the weight of the full sail, stirred the water into fire, which flashed and vanished in her wake.

It mattered little which way Holdsworth steered the boat; but let him head her as he would, there was always the haunting sense upon him that he was speeding away from the ship that would rescue them; that by pointing yonder, or yonder, or yonder, a vessel would be encountered. The breeze and the movement of the boat revived Winyard, who lolled over on the lee side, finding relief in letting his hands trail through the water. The boy had ceased his complaints, and lay sleeping along the thwart, with his head on his mother's knee. Johnson also slept.

The thirst that had tormented Holdsworth during the afternoon had now in some measure abated. There were four or five bottles of rum still left in the stern locker, and, hoping to hit upon some means to deal with the sufferings with which they were threatened by the absence of water, he soaked a piece of biscuit in the spirit and tasted it. But he at once perceived that no relief was to be obtained by this expedient, but that, on the contrary, the spirit would irritate the throat and increase the dryness. He threw the piece of biscuit away, and began to think over all the stories he had ever heard of men who had suffered from thirst in boats at sea, that he might recollect any one way they adopted for diminishing their torments. He had been shipmates with a man, in one of his earlier voyages, who, together with three other men, had been miraculously rescued by a vessel, after they had been at sea in an open boat exactly twenty-one days, during which they had drifted above seven hundred miles from the spot at which their ship had gone down. Holdsworth could only remember two of the expedients they resorted to when maddened with hunger and thirst: one was, tearing off pieces of their shirts and chewing them; the other, cutting wounds in their arms and sucking the blood. This last was a remedy from which he recoiled with horror; nor were his sufferings so great just then as to tempt him to try the other.

"Master!" called out Winyard, in a husky voice, "what longitude do you reckon we're in?"

"We were in twenty-eight west when the ship went down, and I doubt if we are many miles distant from the same place."

"Ain't there no chance of our sighting a ship, master?"

"Yes, every chance."

"I reckon the skipper has run the long-boat into the regular tracks by this time," grumbled the man; "it's cursed hard upon us that we should be left to die here like dogs."

To this Holdsworth made no answer, and Winyard, after muttering awhile to himself, began to splash the water in his face by scooping it out with his hand. Then Johnson, in his sleep, called out for something to drink, on which Winyard, with an oath, answered, "Ay, you may call out! If calling 'ud bring it, I'd make noise enough, I'll lay!"

The clouds overhead, though widely sundered one from another, were heavy, and Holdsworth constantly directed his weary eyes at them, praying for a shower of rain. At midnight, or thereabouts, Johnson was awakened, and came aft to relieve Holdsworth at the helm. The two men whispered together about Winyard, saying that he was not to be trusted with the management of the boat whilst the breeze held; and it was agreed that Holdsworth should replace Johnson at the expiration of two hours, by the watch, which Johnson took and put in his pocket. But before lying down, Holdsworth dipped the sail and put the boat around. Her head on the port tack was north-west and by north.

"Keep a sharp look-out to windward, Johnson, and call me at once if you sight anything," said Holdsworth; then packed himself against the mast and fell into a doze.

When he was asleep, Winyard came out of the bows, and stepped to the stern-sheets and began to talk to Johnson. After awhile, he said he should like to see what quantity of biscuit they still had, and lifted the seat over the locker. Johnson, who suspected nothing, had his eyes fixed on the weather horizon; and Winyard, snatching at a bottle of rum, thrust it cunningly into his bosom, and hurried forward.

All this time the boy was sleeping; but it was impossible to tell whether his mother slumbered or not. She never once stirred. She sat on the weather side, close against Johnson. Her child's head was upon her knee, and her hands were clasped upon his shoulder. She kept her face bowed, her chin upon her breast.

At two o'clock by the watch, Johnson called Holdsworth, who instantly sat upright, and before rising, bent his head under the foot of the sail to take a look to leeward. He had scarcely done this when he uttered a cry, and then fell dumb, pointing like a madman. Johnson leaned sideways, and saw the outline of a large ship, about a mile distant, running with the wind free on her starboard quarter.

"Put your helm up! Head for her!" gasped Holdsworth, springing aft; and then as the boat swept round, he jumped on to a thwart, and hollowing his hands, shouted, but his shout was feeble and hoarse; the constricted throat dulled and choked his voice. Johnson also shouted, but his voice was even weaker than Holdsworth's.

"They will not leave us! they will not leave us!" shrieked Mrs. Tennent, rising suddenly and extending her hands towards the ship, which the movement of the boat's rudder had brought on the starboard beam.

As she cried, Winyard stood up in the boat's bows, reeling wildly, and mad with the drink he had abstracted. His gestures and fury were horrible to witness. His husky screeches sounded as the voice of one suffering indescribable torment. He brandished his arms towards the ship, which was drawing ahead rapidly, and in his drunken excitement leaped upon the gunwale of the boat, where he stood balancing himself, and tossing his clenched fists above his head. Just then the boat dipped and sank into the hollow of a swell; the drunken madman made a grab at the leach of the sail to steady himself—missed it—and went head backwards overboard.

Holdsworth bounded aft to catch him as he floated past; but he remained under water until the boat was some yards ahead; and then they could hear his bubbling cries and the splashing of his arms.

Holdsworth's first instinct was to bring the boat round; but Johnson divined his intention, and twirling the yoke-lines furiously around his hands, cried:

"No! no! we can't save him! he'll have sunk before we can reach him! Let's follow the ship—she may see us!" And he bawled "Ahoy! ahoy!" but his hoarse voice fainted in his throat.

Holdsworth grasped one of the yoke-lines, and there

was a short struggle. The boat's head yawed wildly. But by this time nothing was to be heard astern but the wash of the water as the boat sucked it into eddies.

Holdsworth let go the yoke-line, sprang forward and dipped the sail clear of the mast; crying that there were four lives to be saved, and it would be as bad as murder to stop the boat now.

The ship was distinctly visible on the port bow, every sail on her standing in a clean black outline against the sky. She showed no lights, and further than that she was a full-rigged ship, it was impossible to tell what she resembled. They watched her with wild despair, utterly powerless to attract her attention, and dependent upon the faint possibility of their glimmering sail being distinguishable on the black surface of the water. If the wind would only lull now, if such a calm as that which had held them motionless the day before would fall, their rescue was inevitable. But the light breeze remained steady, and the ship ahead slipped forward nimbly, and became soon a square shadow against the winking stars over the horizon.

How horrible to be abandoned for lack of means to make their presence known! Any kind of light would have served them.

The widow moaned and beat her breast as the vessel faded into the darkness; Johnson flung himself doggedly down, and sat resting his elbow on his knee, gnawing his finger-nails; whilst Holdsworth stood upright forward, gazing with wild, passionate, intense despair, in the direction of the ship long after she had vanished.

There could be little doubt that, had Johnson kept a proper look-out, he would have seen the ship in time to put his helm up, and run within easy hail of her. Holdsworth knew this, but would not increase the misery of their situation by useless reproaches.

The child, who had been awakened by their cries, now that silence had fallen began to ask eagerly and importunately for water, and even reproached his mother for not attending to him.

"I am hot—hot!" he petitioned. "Mamma, give me water."

Once during his appeals she started up and glared about her, as if there *must* be some means of relieving his sufferings; and then crying, "I shall go mad!" fell back with a low, heart-broken sob, and spoke no more, though the child persisted in his entreaties for a long while. Finally he burst into tears, and after plucking at his throat for a time, sank into an uneasy slumber, in which he uttered low moaning cries repeatedly.

A stupor now fell upon Holdsworth—a species of drowsy indifference to his fate and to the fate of his companions. He had fallen wearily upon a thwart and sat with his back against the mast, and visions began to float before him, and his whole physical being seemed lapped into a dreamy insensibility, that subdued, whilst it lasted, that subtle agonising craving for water which, since he was awakened from his sleep, had tormented him with a pang more exquisite than any other form of human suffering. He fought with the dangerous listlessness for some time, terrified at without understanding its import; but in spite of him, his mind wandered, and he presently thought that Dolly was at his side; whereupon he addressed her, and seemed to receive her answers, and asked her questions in a low, strange voice, often smiling as though the light of her eyes were upon his face and his arm around her.

His language was audible and intelligible; but Johnson, with one of the yoke-lines over his knees, his head supported in his hands, paid no more heed to him than to the flapping of the sail as the boat sometimes broached to; which insensibility was as shocking as the other's delirious chattering.

CHAPTER XI.

In this way the boat drifted on until the dawn broke, when the wind fell.

Johnson lifted his head and looked about him; and first for the ship that had passed them in the night—but she was nowhere visible; then at Holdsworth, whose delirium had yielded to sleep, and who slumbered with his feet on the thwart, his back arched like a bow, and his head between his knees; then at the widow, who drooped against the boat's side, her arm over the gunwale, and her hand in the water.

The boy was wide awake, reclining in the bottom of the boat, with his head against his mother's dress. His eyes looked large and glassy, his lips white, and his skin dusky-hued. When he met Johnson's gaze, he smiled as though he would coax him to give him what he wanted, and tried to speak, but his lips rather formed than delivered the word "water." The man stared at him with the insensibility of despair in his eyes: and the boy, thinking that he had not heard him, and that he would get what he desired, if he could but articulate his wish, tried to stand up, meaning to draw close to the man's ear; but his legs sank under him, and so he remained at the bottom of the boat smiling wanly and pointing to his throat, as though such dumb-show must needs soften Johnson's heart, and obtain some water for him.

Holdsworth awoke with a start and tried to speak; but the roof of his mouth was dry, and his tongue felt rusty like a cat's; moreover, his throat burned, and the sounds he uttered scathed and lacerated him.

The boy, seeing him awake, turned to him as a friend who would relieve him: and moaned his distress. The spectacle of his agony, and his own sufferings, maddened Holdsworth. All along he had dreaded the temptation of the rum, the fiery quality of which, whilst it momentarily allayed, would, he was sure, aggravate tenfold the craving for water. But suffering mastered him now. He seized the pannikin and pouring out some of the liquor, put it to the boy's dry lips. He drank greedily, but the ardent spirit checked his breath, and he struggled wildly, beating the air with his little hands.

But meanwhile Holdsworth had also drunk, and handed the remainder of the draught to Johnson, his throat softened, and his tongue capable now of articulation. Johnson drew a deep breath, and exclaimed:

"Thank God for that, master. I should have taken it before had I thought it good for me."

Holdsworth gave the boy a biscuit, which he grabbed at, and thrust large pieces into his mouth, as though seeking to extinguish the fire that the rum had kindled.

When the pain of the burning spirit had passed, he said, "Give mamma some. When you were asleep, Mr. Holdsworth, I heard her calling for water."

Holdsworth, thinking that she slept, would not arouse her; but noticing that her arm hung awkwardly over the boat's side, and left the half-closed fingers trailing in the water, he raised it gently to place her hand on her lap. In doing this, he observed a lifeless-ness in her arm such as sleep could not induce. He peered into her face, and cried out quickly :

"O my God !"

Then bade Johnson move, that he might get beside her, and reverently lifted her head.

There was no need to glance twice at her face to know what had happened, although the heart-broken expression in it would almost suggest that she slept, and was dreaming a painful dream. Her eyes were half-closed, her under-jaw had dropped, yet she looked even in her death a sweet, long-suffering woman.

"Give her something to drink," pleaded the little boy, passionately, imagining from her silence, and the expression on her face, that she was suffering as he had and could not speak.

"She don't want it—she's dead!" answered Johnson.

Holdsworth half turned, but checked the exclamation that rose to his lips, feeling that the bitter truth must be made known to the child sooner or later.

The boy did not understand the answer ; he crawled upon his mother's knee, with the pannikin in his hand, which he held out whilst he said : "Wake up, mamma ! Open your eyes ! Mr. Holdsworth will give you some-thing to drink."

Holdsworth removed the child, and seated him near the mast, and bade him stop there. He then returned, and lifting the poor woman from her seat, placed her gently in the bottom of the boat, throwing her dress over her face to hide the anguish in it, and blot out the mockery of the daylight.

The boy began to cry, and asked Mr. Holdsworth to wake his mamma up.

Neither of the men could answer him.

Shortly after this, the wind veered round to the north, and came on to blow in quick, fretful puffs. The sky grew cloudy, and indications were not wanting of the approach of a gale. Holdsworth took the helm, whilst Johnson lowered the sail and close-reefed it, and the quick jump of the sea, coupled with the small space of sail shown, making it impossible for them to head for the east, without driving bodily to leeward, they slackened out the sheet and let the boat run, keeping the wind about two points on her port quarter.

A squall of rain came up and wetted them. They turned their mouths in the direction whence it came, and gaped to receive the delicious drops; but it blew against their faces and slantwise along the sea, and was soon over. It left a little pool on one of the thwarts, and Holdsworth told the boy to put his lips to it. He did so, and lapped the moisture like a dog; whilst Holdsworth and Johnson removed the handkerchiefs from their necks which the rain had damped, and sucked them.

The wind increased, the sea became heavy, and the heavens overcast with a vast extent of lead-coloured cloud that stretched from horizon to horizon. At noon, when the boat was on the summit of a wave, Johnson caught sight of a vessel on their lee quarter. The boat plunged downwards, and the vessel was lost to view; but, on mounting again, they beheld the vessel, under double-reefed top-sails, standing westwards right across their stern. She was not above a mile and a half away, but she might as well have been a thousand, for the boat could no more have made for her in that sea than she could have sailed in the wind's eye. There was a faint chance that the people on board of her might catch sight of the shawl that streamed like a black flag from the mast-head; and, each time the boat sank into a hollow, the poor men waited with wild and dreadful eagerness for her to rise, that they might observe whether the vessel had seen and was following them. But she did not alter her course, and in ten minutes' time vanished in the haze.

Neither of the men spoke: Johnson, by the expression on his face, appeared to have resigned himself to despair, and all Holdsworth's thoughts were concentrated in keeping the boat clear of the seas which boiled around her. He was very weak; so much so that there were moments when, a sea catching the boat under the stern, he had scarcely the power to keep the yoke square and prevent the rudder from being jammed athwart-ships upon its pintles by the pressure of the water; which, had it happened, would have swept the boat broadside on and filled her.

Added to this, the torment of thirst was again upon him. He kept the end of his handkerchief in his mouth, literally chewing it to pulp, and constantly directing thirsty glances at the clouds, and praying for another shower of rain.

His own suffering made him perceive that the rum would be a curse to them whilst it lasted, inducing them to drink it, and presently maddening them with fresh accesses of thirst. The boy was suffering again, and was crawling upon his hands and knees over the thwarts in search of some rain moisture; and presently Holdsworth saw him put his tongue against the mast and lick it. Johnson hung, with an air of despairful recklessness, over the boat's side, dashing the water in his face, and letting the foam fly up his arm and soak his breast.

The boat presently made a plunge downwards—a long, wild, sweeping fall; the roaring of the waves sounded overhead; the sail flapped, ánd there was a pause of breathless calm that lasted some moments.

Holdsworth looked behind him and shrieked out: "Seize the boy, and throw yourself down!"

The man extended his hands, and, grappling the child, rolled backwards, under a thwart.

It came—a huge, green, unbroken sea, arching its emerald top on a level with the yard of the sail, and following the boat with a spring like a tiger's. Holdsworth stretched himself out, his feet hard against the aftermost thwart, his back squared, his elbows out, his hands grasping the yoke-lines with a death grip.

Up went the boat—stem up—yet up! as though she must be flung clean over on end; then came the rush and roar of water—it fell with a weight of lead on Holdsworth's back, and beat, with a ponderous single blow, the breath out of him, but could not root him from his seat; it broke into a vast surface of foam, divided, and swept forward, hissing spluttering, bubbling, raging; met at an angle at the boat's bows and half filled her! Down she swooped into another hollow, and half the water ran out over her bows, the remainder, as she rose, came rushing aft and filled the stern-sheets; and up and down, up and down, it washed.

But the boat still lived, and Holdsworth was her master.

"Bear a hand aft here and bale her out!" he shouted.

Johnson let go the half-drowned child, and struggled over the thwarts, blowing and shaking his soaked hair like rope-yarns off his face, his clothes streaming with water; flopped down, found the cocoa-nut shell, and baled with fury.

The child crouched in the bows, too terrified to cry.

The boat flashed along, skimming the frothing heads of the waves; she had outlived an exceptionally heavy sea, and seemed to feel her triumph as she flew.

But, oh! the ghastly burden that she bore! the dead and dripping woman, off whose face the water had washed the covering, and left it naked to the daylight; the gaunt bearded spectre baling out the boat on his knees, his wet clothes clinging to his frame like a skin of silk, and disclosing the piteous attenuation of the body; the steersman with wild and lustrous eyes sunk deep in livid sockets, the yoke-lines writhed around his lean brown hands, his lips pale and cracked, and his long neglected hair hanging like a wet mat over his forehead and down his back; and the shivering little figure in the bows, his hands squeezed together in an attitude of prayer, and his small face glimmering with unearthly ghastliness upon the gray background of the boat's interior.

Some flying-fish leaped out of the sea close to the boat, and buried their silver arrow-like shapes in a wave some distance ahead. Then the sun broke through a rent in the broad sombre cloud, and made the pelting ocean joyous with a snatch of cheerful light. But the strong wind lasted all the afternoon, and when it lulled just before sunset, Holdsworth was so exhausted, that in rising to give his seat to Johnson, he reeled and sank in a heap close beside the corpse at the bottom of the boat, and lay motionless and insensible. Johnson made no effort to restore him. Indeed, he thought he was dead. His own brain whirled; his tongue seemed to fill his mouth; there crept over him such a stupor as had visited Holdsworth; he let the yoke-lines go, and fixing his eyes on the sea, prepared to meet the death which his sensations led him to believe was at hand.

The boat, tossed like a cork on the troubled water, broached to; but happily the wind was momentarily dying away; her head came round to the seas and she rode with as much safety as if Holdsworth were at the helm.

For a whole hour the interior of the boat presented the same scene; the men motionless as the dead body, the boy squatting in the bows with nothing seemingly alive about him but his eyes, which winked as he rolled them seawards, where the sun shone on the water. Then Holdsworth began to groan and stir; whereupon Johnson fixed his dull eyes upon him, and watched him without any curiosity, without any sympathy, without any interest—indeed, scarcely, I might say, with human intelligence.

The boy, seeing Holdsworth move, came creeping aft and remained on his knees, first looking at the man awaking to consciousness, and then at his mother, whose motionlessness and drowned aspect, and face made unfamiliar to him by its total want of expression, terrified him.

Holdsworth raised his head and looked about him in bewilderment.

"Where have I been? What has happened?" he cried.

He fixed his eyes on the dead woman, his glance reverted to the boy, and then consciousness fully awoke.

He rose wearily to his feet, and sank with a heavy sigh near Johnson, at whom he looked, scarcely knowing whether the man slept or was dead.

The boy begged for water.

"Water!" exclaimed Holdsworth in a choking voice; "there is none."

But there was biscuit, and he turned to the locker to give him one, thinking that the food might relieve the child's thirst. He stretched out his arm to lift the seat of the locker and found the locker filled with salt water. With a cry of despair he dragged out a bag streaming with wet, and thrusting his hand into it found its contents soaked into pulp. The other bag was in the same condition; and to make matters worse, of the three bottles of rum that had been in the locker, one only was left; the other two were cracked and empty.

It was easy to understand how this had happened. A sea breaking over the boat's stern could not have filled the locker; the water which the boat had shipped over her bows had come rushing aft when the boat mounted the next wave, and filling the stern-sheets, raised the seat that formed the lid of the locker, and poured over the biscuit, at the same time forcing the bottles against each other and breaking them.

"Do you see what has happened?" exclaimed Holdsworth, grasping Johnson's arm. The man looked over his shoulder, shook his head, and muttered, "We're doomed to die. There's no hope, master."

What was to be done? Holdsworth thought that if the biscuits could be dried in the sun they might be fit to eat, and endeavoured to spread some of them along the thwart; but the stuff squeezed up in his hand

like thick paste. He tasted a little and found it no
better than salt, and he flung the bag down with a
groan that seemed to express the extinction of his last
faint hope.

But there was a bottle of rum left. He prised out
the cork with the blade of his knife, and gave a spoonful
to the boy diluted with two or three drops of sea water.
He then set the pannikin to Johnson's lips, who sucked
the hard metal rim as a baby might. Finally moistening his own throat with a small quantity of the liquor,
he carefully corked the bottle and stowed it away.

No! To say that hope had entirely abandoned him
would not be true. Whilst the heart continues to
pulsate hope will still be found to live, however faintly,
in its throbs, though each moment be heavy with pain,
and nothing seem sure but anguish and death.

The wind had died away, but the boat rose and sank
to the long and heavy swell that billowed the gleaming
surface of the sea to the horizon. Far away in the
south was an expanse of gray cloud with slanting lines
radiating to the sea from it, and a bright square of rainbow embedded in its shadow. It was travelling eastwards, and the rain would not touch the boat. Elsewhere the sky was a bright blue, with here and there
clouds of glorious whiteness and majestic bulk—mountains with shining defiles and a splendour of sunshine
in their skirts—hanging their swelling forms over the
sea. The sun was hot, but then, ever since they had
been in the boat, they had been steering more or less
south, and, taking the parallels in which the ship had
foundered as a starting-point, every degree the boat
made southwards would furnish an appreciable change
of temperature.

The rum had worked beneficially in Johnson, who now began to stretch his body and look about him.

"Another calm, master," he said, in a voice to which the dryness of his throat imparted a harsh unnatural tone. "I thought I was dead and gone just now. God help us! I don't think none of us three'll live to talk of this here time!"

"We must put that poor body overboard," said Holdsworth. "It isn't fit that her child should see her like that. Will you take him for'ard and stand between him and me, so that he can't see what I'm doing, and talk to him a bit? I almost wish they had both died together. The sight of his sufferings makes mine more than I can bear."

He stifled a sob, and Johnson getting up languidly and holding on to the gunwale of the boat with one hand, took the boy by the arm and led him into the bows.

Holdsworth slackened off the halliards to lower the sail and screen the after part of the boat from the boy's sight. He then, with what strength he had, and as quickly as he could, raised the dead body and let it slip over the stern, muttering a simple prayer as he did so, that God would let her meet her child in heaven, where they would never more be parted; and then turned his back upon the water and hid his face in his hands.

At the end of five minutes he stole a glance astern—the body had disappeared.

"Four," he muttered, "and three more to go! O God, what work—what work this has been!"

His thoughts went to Dolly. If he died, what would become of her? Not for many days yet, even supposing the other boats should make their way to land or

be rescued by a passing ship, would the news of the
" Meteor's " loss reach her ; and he thought of her
praying night and morning for him, straining her fond
eyes into the dim future, where the coming summer was,
with all its flowers and its sunshine ; where the happy
day was that should bring him to her.   If the news of
the shipwreck ever reached her, how would her gentle
spirit support the blow !   But worse would it be if she
remained ignorant of her loss ; because in that case she
would live on in hope for months and months, waken-
ing every morning with the idea that—To-day he may
come ! to-day he may come ! until hope sickened and
despair should bring cruel assurance of eternal separation—the more unendurable because she should not
know *why* he did not come—whether he were living or
dead—whether he were true or false to her !

Oh for the power of giving peace to that manly un-
offending heart !

We shed tears, and well we may, God knows, over
the privations of shipwrecked men, over the hunger and
thirst and the mortal bodily agonies of poor souls
doomed to die a lingering and shocking death in open
boats, storm-tossed, or baking in breathless calms under
the burning eye of the sun ; but do we think of that
deeper misery of theirs—that poignant mental torture
compared to which the sufferings of the flesh are as
naught—the thoughts of those they shall see no more—
of wives, and sisters, and mothers, and little children,
many of whom may perchance never hear the story of
their fate, and can have no tear for the famine and the
thirst that wasted the flesh off their skins and submitted
them to greater torture than the heart can bear to
think of ?

Holdsworth had believed that the sufferings of the boy would engross all his thoughts in himself, and that though he might miss he would not cry for his mother. But he was deceived; for, no sooner had the little fellow discovered that she was gone from her place in the bottom of the boat, than he uttered a sharp cry, and asked Holdsworth where his mamma was.

Holdsworth took him upon his knee, but could not answer. The child persisted in his inquiries, looking the while suspiciously and eagerly about him, particularly over the stern, where he had remembered seeing the actor disappear

" She is gone to God," Holdsworth said at last. " My little man, you will meet her again."

" To God !" cried the child. " That's where papa is !"

He looked up with startled eyes at the sky, and then sobbed passionately, " Has she left me alone ? has she left me alone ?"

" No, she has left you to me. Be a good boy now, and don't cry, and I will take care of you, and love you dearly."

His words smote him as the idlest mockery ; but apart from his mental sufferings, the mere effort of raising his voice pained him intensely. He put the child down, forcing a smile which seemed no better than a grin of pain upon his emaciated face, and then stood up to sweep the horizon, but soon sank down again with a sound as of a clanging of bells in his ears, and his throat constricted and burning with a dry, feverish heat, the pain of which was exquisite.

He was now sensible that his memory was going, for in trying to think of the child's name he found that he could not recall it. But this, somehow, gave him no

concern, for his whole physical being was in perfect
accord with such lapses of the intellectual faculties, and
the discovery bred not the lightest movement of surprise
or apprehension in his mind.

At noon, Johnson asked for more rum, and Holdsworth measured out a small quantity for the three of
them, diluting the draught, as he had before done, with
a few drops of salt water.

The boy never moved from the seat where he had
been placed by Holdsworth ; he knew not, in reality,
where his mother had gone, but there was plainly a
suspicion in him that she was in the sea, and he kept
his eyes fixed on the water, as though in expectation of
her rising at the side of the boat.   He shed no more
tears ; indeed, physical weakness had so far conquered
him, that it had rendered him incapable of tears.   The
sight of his white, young, piteous face, his head moving
on his shoulders in convulsive jerks, and his helpless
down-hanging arms, was enough to make one pray to
God that death might remove him speedily, if the term
of horrible misery were not to be ended at once.

The afternoon passed, and the sun went down behind
a calm sea.   While the crimson flush still lived in the
sky, a flock of sea birds came from the south, and
hovered awhile over the boat, as though irresolute to
quit it for their further destination.   They were at too
great an elevation to enable the men to judge what birds
they were ; but they emitted harsh sounds, resembling
in some measure the cry of gulls, mixed with the rough
intonation of rooks.   After this pause, they pursued
their flight, and soon winged themselves out of view,
but not without leaving behind them a species of desolate hope, such as would be excited in the minds of men

who had been long banished from the sight of living things, and by whom the most trivial incident would be interpreted as an auspicious omen.

Holdsworth and Johnson drew together and spoke of what these birds portended. The wildest phantasies were begotten, and they sought to encourage themselves with dreams which a listener would have shuddered over as the babbling of delirium. Their thoughts being loosened, they presently began to complain of hunger; and Johnson took up a piece of the pulpy biscuit which lay on a thwart and which the sun had hardened, and bit it, but instantly ejected it, saying that it was bitterer than gall. Indeed, had there been more light they would have seen the frost-like crystals of salt which had been dried into the biscuit by the sun's action. However, their hunger was not so fierce but that they could endure it yet awhile.

The night came down, quite radiant with stars, with not a cloud in all the great dome of glittering sky. The two men were now so regardless of their fate that they entered into no arrangement as to keeping watch, but folded their arms upon their breasts and slept or fell into a semi-unconscious state—lethargies so sinister that it was hard to tell whether they were not the sloping ways to death. Fitful cries sometimes broke from them, resembling the echoes which are awakened in the caverns of a bird-frequented cliff; but with notes of human anguish in them that made the glory of the stars a hellish mockery.

The boy slipped from his seat and lay prone at the bottom of the boat, unheeded by either Holdsworth or Johnson.

So passed the night.

CHAPTER XII.

THE SIXTH AND SEVENTH DAYS.

THE dawn awoke Johnson, who remained seated for some time motionless, with his open eyes fixed upon the sea half-way to the horizon. As he continued gazing, a wild smile of joy kindled up his face and parted his cracked lips into a grin so extravagant, so indescribable, that it converted his face into a likeness of humanity as repulsive and unreal as an ugly paper mask.

He thrust his bony fingers into Holdsworth's collar and shook him violently, whilst he pointed to the sea with his right hand.

"Look! look!" he cried. "Wake up! wake up! there is the land! See the houses, master! and the trees! . . . O Jesus! how green they are! Wake up, I say!"

Holdsworth started up violently and shook himself, with a mighty effort, clear of the benumbing torpor that had weighed him down throughout the night. He stared in the direction indicated by Johnson, then rubbed his eyes furiously with his knuckles, and stared again, but could see nothing but the ocean growing blue under the gathering light in the east, and stretching its illimitable surface to the horizon.

"Come, master, let's get the oars out. Why, where

have we drifted? O Lord, see the trees! how green and beautiful! I reckon there's water there—and I'll strip and souse in it! Will they see us? Wave your hat!"

He took off his own and brandished it furiously. But all on a sudden he let fall his arm—he stretched his head forward, and his glassy eyes seemed to protrude from their sockets; his breath went and came shrilly through his open mouth; and then, giving a scream, he shrieked, "It's gone! it's gone!" and as if the disappointment were a blow dealt him by some heavy instrument, he gave a great gasp, collapsed, and fell like a bundle of rags from his seat.

The fit of convulsive trembling that had seized Holdsworth passed; he caught sight of the boy lying on his side, with his eyes, wide open, fixed upon his face. The child was pointing to his throat. Holdsworth raised him and laid him along the seat, not conceiving that the little creature had fallen from his resting-place during the night, but that he had placed himself in that position the better to rest his limbs.

He moistened his lips with rum, but on looking attentively at his face, perceived indications denoting approaching death as clearly as though the piteous message was written upon his brow. This perception gave him exquisite misery. The bright eyes of the child, suggesting sweet memories of the little wife he had left at Southbourne, had endeared the boy to him; he had been his playmate and companion on the "Meteor;" he had watched the deep and beautiful love of the mother; and her death, recent as it was, had imparted the deepest pathos to the little orphan, and made his claims upon Holdsworth's protection and love infinitely eloquent and appealing. That he should be dying now—now that the bright sun was climbing the brilliant morning sky—dying for want of a cup of water, a morsel of bread—dying without a mother's love to enfold him in his last struggle and waft his young and innocent soul to God on the wings of a prayer, such as *her* agony, *her* devotion only could dictate—oh, it was too pitiful !

"My little boy—look up !—tell me—do you suffer ? Where is the pain ? Is it in your throat ? Oh my poor innocent ! "

His tears blinded him. He took his handkerchief and dipped it into the sea and laid it upon the child's throat.

The little creature seemed to feel his love, for he made a movement as if he would nestle against him, and smiled wanly, but could not speak. His young dying face was an unbearable sight, and Holdsworth, groaning, gazed wildly around the horizon as if there— or there—or there—must be the ship sent by God to save the boy's life !

A long hour passed ; the child still lived, and Holdsworth hung over him, heedless of the other poor creature who had awakened to consciousness, but yet lay in a heap, supporting his head against the stanchion of a thwart, and watching his companions with glazed eyes. Then a craving for food mastered Holdsworth, and he looked at the biscuit, but had yet sufficient control over himself not to touch it, knowing the penalty of increased thirst that must follow the absorption of the brine into his stomach. He went to the locker and plunged his arm into the water that half filled it, and groped about in search of he knew not what ; something to appease his craving might be there ; but he found nothing but slimy pieces of biscuit and the broken bottles.

In a sudden fury of hunger he tore off his boot and cut a piece of the leather from the top of it, and began to chew it.

The mere act of mastication somewhat diminished his suffering, and he returned to the boy. No marked change had occurred within the hour, but, imperceptible as the departure might be, it was only too evident that the child was dying. Thirst, exposure, and grief—for there had been something so akin to a heart-broken expression in the little fellow's eyes when he stared at the sea, expecting his mother to rise from it, that it would be impossible to doubt the keenness of his sorrow —these things had done their work.

Holdsworth bathed his face and throat with salt water, and again offered to moisten his lips with rum ; but the boy made a gesture of dissent. Indeed the rum served no other end than to irritate his lips and his tongue, which was swollen and discoloured.

As the day wore on, the torment of thirst abated in Holdsworth, and Johnson also seemed to suffer less. The first agony which thirst brings with it, and which endures for two or three days, was passing ; the next stage would be a kind of insensibility to the craving for water ; but this would presently be followed by a renewal of the suffering in its sharpest form, which would continue until death ended it.

Throughout the afternoon, Holdsworth remained at the side of the boy, who lay with half-closed eyes and no movement of the body, save the faint rise and fall of his chest as he breathed. They were neither of them much more than skeletons, and so ashen was the complexion of Holdsworth, so lustreless his eyes, so wild and gaunt and ragged his whole face with the grisly beard, the white lips, the livid hollows beneath the eyes, and the twisted knotted hair upon his forehead and down his back, that he seemed much nearer to death than the child, whose infancy saved his face from being made actually repulsive by suffering.

Before sunset the boy became delirious, and mouthed shocking gibberish, being unable to articulate. For a whole half-hour this babbling lasted, and then died out, and the boy grew conscious. Holdsworth supported his head on his knee, but he slightly twisted it round to look at the sun, which was just then resting, a great orb of burning gold, upon the line of the horizon. He watched the sun intently, undazzled by the splendour, until it vanished, when he uttered a low wailing cry and stretched his arms out to it. Holdsworth felt his little body trembling, and some convulsive movements passed through him. Holdsworth kissed his forehead, and the boy smiled, and with that smile his spirit passed away.

When he could not doubt that he was dead, Holdsworth removed the little jacket from the child's back, covered his face with it, and laid him in the bottom of the boat.

The mere exertion of doing this made him fall half-swooning upon a seat, on which Johnson came staggering over the thwarts and gave him some rum. There was now no more than a quarter of a pint left in the bottle.

"Master," said the man, bringing his lips close to Holdsworth's ear, "if I die first, please throw my body overboard. I don't like the notion of drifting about in this boat maybe for weeks, and becoming a sight not fit to be looked at, if e'er a ship should come by."

"I shan't live to do you that service," muttered Holdsworth. "I don't feel as if I could last out much longer."

"The curse of God is on us!" said Johnson. "There's nothing but calms, and to think of two being left out o' seven!"

The night fell quickly. At about ten o'clock a breeze came up from the north, and blew coolly and gratefully over the burning heads of the two men. It took the boat aback, and Holdsworth, acting from sheer instinct, put her before it, and hauling the sheet aft, steered east. No clouds came up with the wind; it was a summer breeze which might lull at any moment, or veer round, perhaps, to the south-west, and bring up a change of weather.

Lying pretty close to the wind the boat required no steering, which was fortunate, for the yoke-lines soon slipped out of Holdsworth's hands, and a torpor stole over him, which, without actually suspending his consciousness, rendered his perceptions dreamy and useless. He rested with his back against the side of the boat, his head upon his breast, and his eyes half closed. Johnson crouched near the mast.

The breeze proved steady during the night, but died away towards the small hours; then, at daybreak, sprang up afresh from the west. The heeling over of the boat aroused the two men, who languidly, and with gestures terribly significant of their growing indifference to their fate, dipped the sail, and again let the boat lie close to save the trouble of steering her.

When the morning was a little advanced, Johnson

crept to the side of the dead boy and groped about him.

"What are you doing?" cried Holdsworth fiercely.

"Feeling if there isn't a piece of ship's bread in his pockets," answered the man doggedly, and looking up with a wolfish light in his sunken eyes.

"Let him alone!" said Holdsworth.

The man dragged himself away reluctantly, grumbling to himself, and resumed his place near the mast, keeping his eye steadfastly fixed on the dead body.

A sick shudder passed through Holdsworth as he observed the man's peculiar stare, and sinking on his knees, he uncovered the child's face and inspected it attentively, to satisfy himself that he was actually dead. He then raised him in his arms with the intention of casting him overboard. But Johnson came scrambling over to him and gripped him by the wrist.

The expression of his face, made devilish by suffering, was heightened to the horribly grotesque by the action of his mouth, which gaped and contorted ere he could articulate.

"What are you going to do? Keep him!" he exclaimed.

"Why?" answered Holdsworth, looking him full in the face.

But the man could not deliver the idea that was in his mind; he could only *look* it.

Holdsworth turned his back upon him and raised his burden on a level with the boat's gunwale, but Johnson grasped the body with both hands.

"Let go!" said Holdsworth.

The man with an oath retained his hold. Weak as Holdsworth was, the passion that boiled in him at the desecration the half-maddened wretch was doing his poor little favourite, gave him temporarily back his old strength. He raised his foot, and, planting it in Johnson's chest hurled him back; the man fell with a crash over the thwart, and lay stunned.

Holdsworth leaned over the boat's side and let the body gently sink in the water; which done, he felt that his own turn was come, and dropped in the stern-sheets groaning, with drops in his eyes that scalded them.

But he still lived, and whilst his heart beat nature would assert herself. Towards the afternoon a torturing craving for food beset him, started him into life, and made him sit upright. He wiped the foam from his lips and beheld it discoloured with blood. He looked savagely around him like a wild beast, and, beholding nothing but the dry, bare seats, the boat's hot interior with the gratings whitened by the heat of the sun, and underneath them the glistening water that bubbled coolly and with a maddening suggestion of sparkling, refreshing springs, he dragged his knife from his pocket, pierced his arm, and put his lips to the wound.

*　　　*　　　*　　　*　　　*

CHAPTER XIII.

THE TENTH DAY.

IT was morning on the tenth day, dating from the foundering of the "Meteor."

A barque of about six hundred tons, named the "Jessie Maxwell," three weeks out from the port of Glasgow, having been becalmed all night, was standing south, with all sail set, and a gentle breeze on the beam.

It was the second officer's watch on deck; he was sitting trimming his nails on the grating abaft the wheel, when the man who was steering, pointing to the horizon a few points before the port beam, asked him if he could see anything black there. The second officer not having very good sight, stared awhile and declared that he saw nothing; then, going forward, called to a man in the main-top to tell him if there was anything to be seen on the port beam. The man, shading his eyes, sang out that he could see a black object, but whether it was a boat or a piece of wreck he couldn't say. Whereupon Mr. Anderson stepped to the companion-hatchway, took down the glass, and, having adjusted it to his sight, levelled it.

"By thunder!" he cried, keeping the glass to his eye, "it's a boat—and there's a mast, and a lug-sail—

and something black at the mast head. But the de'il a soul can I make out aboard of her."

He had another good look, and then, tucking the glass under his arm, went below.

In about three minutes' time he returned, followed by a small stout man with a good-humoured face, and a grave, middle-aged gentleman with a long black beard.

"There, sir; there she is yonder!" said Mr. Anderson, incapable of seeing her with his naked eye, but concluding that she must still be where he had at first sighted her, and willing to obtain the credit of a good sight by a simple device.

"I see something black," said the grave gentleman.

"Give us the glass!" exclaimed the short man, who was the skipper, and applied the telescope to his eye. "It is certainly a boat," he observed, after a bit; "but I don't see anybody moving in her. What's that black thing at the mast-head? Is it a signal?"

He turned to the man at the wheel: "Starboard your helm. Mr. Anderson, trim the yards. Yonder may be some perishing human beings."

The whisper soon went through the vessel that there was a boat in sight; the watch below turned out of their hammocks and came on deck; and soon the forecastle was lively with a crowd of hands gazing earnestly at the boat, which the alteration in the barque's course now made distinguishable, and speculating as to the people who were on board of her.

"She looks to me like a ship's quarter-boat," said the skipper, with his eye to the glass. "The sheet of the sail is to windward, and she's driving bodily to leeward. What in the name of conscience is the meaning of that black flag at the mast-head?"

They neared her rapidly, but were puzzled to discover no living thing stirring in her, for though it was
perfectly true that the sail had not been dipped, she
had all the appearance of being manned. The water
was so calm that the barque was able to run almost
alongside the boat. There was a rush to the vessel's
side, and then, as the boat was passed at a distance of
forty or fifty feet, cries rose from the forecastle: "There's
a man in the stern-sheets!"

"Do you see him, sir, lying with his head under the
aftermost thwart?"

"There's two of them! See there—hard agin' the
mast!"

The boat dropped astern and revealed her interior
to the people aft.

"My God! Two corpses in her!" cried the second
mate.

"Man the starboard fore braces!" shouted the
skipper.

The wheel flew round; the port fore-braces were
let go, and the yards backed. The vessel's way was
stopped and a dozen hands came aft to lower away the
port quarter boat. In jumped four men, the second
mate at the tiller. "Lower away!" Down sank the
boat, soused upon the water, the blocks were unhooked,
out flew the oars.

In a few minutes the boat was alongside the coffin
with the black flag at her mast-head. The men grabbed
her gunwale, and stood up to look in.

God in Heaven! what a scene!

Holdsworth lay on his back, his legs bent double
under him, his arms stretched out, and his ghastly face
upturned directly under a thwart. Johnson lay in a

heap near the mast, and they thought him at first a
bundle of clothes, until they caught sight of his hair
and the fingers of one hand. *His* face was hidden; but
Holdsworth looked a gray and famished skeleton, with
God's signal of humanity eaten by suffering out of his
face; his wrists, like white sticks, covered with sores,
one foot naked, and the skin of that and of his face of
the complexion and aspect of old parchment.

Crumbling fragments of salted biscuit were scattered
on one of the seats. Aft was the open locker half-filled
with water, coloured like pea-soup by the ship's bread
that was soaked and partially dissolved in it. In the
bows were the empty kegs with the bungs out, and as the
boat swayed to and fro to the movements of the small
waves with which the wind had crisped the sea, these
kegs rolled against each other with hollow sounds.

The dry, baked appearance of the boat, the fragments
of biscuit, the empty kegs, and the skeleton men, formed
a spectacle of horror and extreme misery, such as the
wildest imagination could not realise without memory
and experience to help it. Nor in this picture of pure
ghastliness was the least ghastly item the black shawl,
which fluttered its sable folds at the mast-head, and to
the sailors typified, as no other image could, the character and quality of the horror they contemplated.

" Can they be dead ?" gasped one of the sailors, whose
white face showed him almost overcome.

"Mr. Anderson!" came a voice from the barque's
quarter-deck, "take the boat in tow and bring her alongside."

They made the painter fast to their stern, lowered
her sail, and started with their grim burden gliding after
them. The voices of the men overhanging the vessel's

bulwarks rose in a low, deep hum, when the boat was near enough to enable them to see its contents again. The port gangway was unshipped, and some hands stood by with lines to hoist the bodies inboard.

Do they live ?" called out the skipper.

"They both seem dead, sir," answered Anderson.

The boat was now brought right under the gangway, and the top of her mast being level with the bulwarks, submitted the shawl to the close scrutiny of the sailors. They examined it with awe and curiosity.

" It isn't bunting," said one.

" It looks like bunting too !" exclaimed another.

" See how it's rigged up !" observed a third ; " hitched on anyways."

" If it ain't a woman's dress tore in two, I give it up," said a fourth, " though there ain't no woman in the boat as I can make out."

By this time they were slinging Johnson under the arms and around the middle, ready to be hoisted over the gangway. Now that he was exposed, he made a more gaunt and sickening object than Holdsworth. He was an image of famine—of manhood killed by suffering —a picture such as the memory would retain when years had impaired its powers, and driven all other vivid impressions from it. The men fell back as the piteous object was reverently raised over the vessel's side, and placed upon a sail near the main-hatchway. Then followed the form of Holdsworth.

The captain and the gentleman with the long beard approached the two bodies.

" Can you tell me if there's any life in them, Mr. Sherman ?" said the captain.

Mr. Sherman knelt and examined the two faces. The

seamen pressed eagerly around to listen. The elements of the picturesque and the tragical entered so deeply into the scene as to make it extraordinarily impressive— the brown and rugged features of the sailors ; the grave figure kneeling ; the two bodies on their backs resembling skeletons poorly disguised by a rude imitation of human skin ; the black shawl streaming alongside, symbolising a story of cruel, lingering, horrible death ; above, the white sails of the vessel, and over all a beaming sky and a joyous sun ! And add the mysteriousness of these famished and motionless visitants—their name, their country, their story unknown—their white lips sealed !

"What do you think ?" asked the captain.

"This man," answered Mr. Sherman, indicating Johnson, "is certainly dead ; and in my opinion——"

But at that moment the feeblest of feeble tremors passed through Holdsworth.

"Quick !" cried Mr. Sherman, springing to his feet. "This man lives ; they may both be alive ! Have them taken below, Captain Duff ! Quick, sir ! every moment is precious !"

His excitement was contagious. The captain bellowed for the steward. Others seized upon the bodies and hurried aft with them. The murmur of many voices rose and swelled into a hubbub.

"Aft here to the davits, and hoist the boat up !" sang out the second mate ; who, while this was doing, went below to take instructions as to the other boat, and returned with orders to get it inboard.

The curiosity of the men to handle and examine this boat was so great, that when the order was given for some hands to get into her, the whole ship's company made a rush to the gangway. But this tumult was soon

quelled by the help of a few Scotch curses. The boat
was hauled round to the starboard side, and tackles
rigged on to the fore and main yard-arms. Up came
the boat cheerily, with her mast unshipped, and was
lashed athwart-ships just before the main-hatchway.
The vessel's yards were then trimmed, and away she
slipped through the water.

The hands could not be got away from the boat.
Had she been the fossilised remnant of some antedilu-
vian Armada, she could not have been examined by the
men with more intense and breathless curiosity. There
was no name on her, no clue of any kind to tell the ship
she had belonged to, where she was built, what port she
hailed from. There was, indeed, the word "London,"
together with some figures branded upon the kegs; but
this indicated nothing. They dragged the soaking bags
of biscuit out of the locker, where they also found the
fragments of the rum-bottles; and deep and numerous
were the ejaculations these simple things called forth
from the sailors, who gathered a story from them of
which my hand is powerless to impart the thrilling
pathos to my unvarnished version.

"See here!" said a man, shaking the kegs; "not a
drain of water in them!"

"Here's a boot with a piece cut clean out from the
top of it," said another.

"Some one has tried to make food out o' that!"
said an old salt, shaking a quantity of ringlets. "I've
heerd tell of worse stuff nor boots being eat by castaway
men!"

The fragments of dried biscuit were passed around
and examined with wondering attention. The sail, the
oars, the gratings—all came in for their share of closest

and absorbed scrutiny. But the object that most excited speculation was the poor widow's shawl, which, having been drenched and dried, and drenched and dried again, had become rotten, was full of holes, and as much resembled a shawl as a waistcoat.

"If this ain't a curio, I should like to know what is!" said a seaman.

"It's a bit of a gownd, that's what *I* say it is!" exclaimed another authoritatively. "Think I can't tell what a woman's dress is like?"

"My notion is," said an old man, standing aloof, "that there ain't nothing mortal about it at all, but that it's just a bit of bunting hoisted by death, to let the people as was in the boat know who their proper skipper was. I hope nobody means to bring it into the forecastle. I'll not go a-nigh it for one."

"Bring that thing aft here!" called Anderson; "and turn to there and get about your work."

The men dispersed, and the watch below rolled into the forecastle, talking under their breaths, and making each other miserable with horrid legends of fire, disease, drowning, and starvation.

The night came. The "Jessie Maxwell" was heeling over to a spanking breeze, and in her cabin the lamp was lighted, and Captain Duff and his chief officer, an Orkney Islander named Banks, a huge, rough, shaggy, honest-looking being, as like a Newfoundland dog as it is possible for a man to be, sat, each with a big glass of whisky and water at his elbow, smoking pipes.

Here was a very different interior from what the "Meteor" had presented. The cabin was about twenty feet long and six feet high, with a broad skylight overhead, and half a dozen sleeping berths around. No gilt and cream colour, nor polished panels, nor Brussels carpets, nor the hundred elegancies of decoration and furniture, that made the "Meteor's" cuddy as pretty as a drawing-room, were to be found; but solid snuff-coloured doors, with stout hair-cushioned sofas on either side the table that travelled up and down a couple of portly stanchions, so that, when it was not wanted, it could be stowed out of the road. But how suggestive, every plank and beam that met the eye, of strength and durability! Here was a vessel fit to trade in any seas, well manned, with a snugly-stowed cargo, not a quarter of a ton in excess of what she ought to carry, commanded by a shrewd and able seaman out of Glasgow, and by two mates as competent as himself.

The steam from the toddy mingled the fragrance of lemon and honest Glenlivet with the more defined aroma of cavendish tobacco. The captain sat on one sofa and Banks on the other; and they smoked and sipped, and looked steadfastly on one another, as if time were altogether too precious to be wasted in conversation, which must oblige them to devote their lips to other purposes than the pipe-stem and the tumbler.

"I think I did well to get that boat inboard," said the skipper presently; "a boat's a boat."

There was no controverting this position; so Mr. Banks acquiesced with a nod, which he executed like Jove, in a cloud.

"Do you remember the time, Banks," observed the skipper after a long pause, "when little Angus McKay spun us that yarn in the "Bannockburn," about his falling in with a ship's long-boat off the Cape of Good Hope, with a nigger boy and three sheep aboard of her ?"

Mr. Banks, after deep deliberation, replied that he minded the story weel.

" A verra curious circumstance," continued the skipper, " if it wasn't a lee !"

Another pause, during which the two men sucked their pipes, never remitting their steadfast gaze at each other, unless to turn their eyes upon the tumblers before raising them to their lips.

" Mr. Sherman seems to know what he is about," said Captain Duff. " He has a fund of humanity in his bosom, and I like to reflect, sir, on his sitting by the poor de'il's bed watching by him as though he were his ain son."

Nothing could have been more *à propos* than this remark, if it were designed to reach the ear of the gentleman referred to ; for, as the captain spoke, one of the snuff-coloured doors was opened, and Mr. Sherman came out.

" Hoo's the patient ?" asked the captain.

" He has his senses, though there is such a bewildered look on his face as I don't think I ever saw on the human countenance," replied Mr. Sherman, seating himself near the skipper, and looking about for a tumbler ; whereat Mr. Banks called in a hurricane-note for " Atam," meaning Adam. A small red-headed man emerged from somewhere and placed the materials for a glass of whisky toddy before Mr. Sherman.

" Ech !" ejaculated the skipper, " I daresay he *is* puzzled. So would I be if my last memory left me starving in an open boat and my next one found me warm in bed with the flavour of old Nantz brandy in my inside."

" I have asked him no questions," continued Mr.

Sherman. "I know enough of doctoring to understand that his life may depend upon rest and silence."

"My word, sir, you are a very gude-hearted man!" exclaimed the skipper; "and if ever I am shipwrecked, may it be my luck to fall into just such hands as yours. Your health, sir."

Saying which, he half-emptied his tumbler, a performance that made his merry eyes glisten with delight.

"And the other man is ted?" said Mr. Banks.

"Quite dead, poor soul! Did you ever see anything more heart-rending than his body, captain? Mere skin and bone—and, oh! sir, the expression of his face!" exclaimed Mr. Sherman, holding his hands over his eyes a moment.

"Thirst is an awfu' thing," said the skipper, glancing at his tumbler.

"And so is hunger," observed Mr. Banks, who looked as though a whole ox might hardly serve him for a meal.

"I expect, when the other poor fellow is capable of speaking, that we shall hear a terrible tale," said Mr. Sherman. "It is very providential that my slight knowledge of medicine should qualify me to deal with him. The greatest care is required in treating persons nearly dead of starvation. I have fed him so far in spoonfuls only. It is my intention to remain with him through the night. I'll borrow one of your easy-chairs, captain, which will serve me very well for a bed."

"Certainly. I am sleeping close at hand, and if you want me, just give my cot a shove, and I'll be out of it before you can tell which side I drop from."

This settled, the captain mixed himself another tumbler of spirits, refilled his pipe, and entered into speculations as to Holdsworth's nationality, the length of time he had been in the boat; the probable longitude and latitude in which the ship had taken fire or foundered, with many other matters, all of which he relieved with long pauses, and a variety of thoughtful puffs and attentive glances at the light through the medium of his tumbler. Presently four bells—ten o'clock—struck, which made Mr. Banks rise from his seat, wish his companions "Coot night," and withdraw to his cabin to get a couple of hours' sleep before his watch came on. The others remained chatting for half an hour, and then the skipper went on deck to have a look around before turning in for the night.

CHAPTER XIV.

HOLDSWORTH'S RECOVERY.

THE cabin in which Holdsworth lay was a spare one, next the captain's. It was lighted by an oblong piece of frosted glass let into the deck overhead, and by a porthole which was a standing and comfortable illustration of the immense thickness of the timbers that separated the inmate from the sea. There was a square of cocoanut matting on the deck to tread on; up in a corner an immovable washstand, containing a pewter basin; a row of pegs against the door; and a mahogany bunk.

In this bunk lay Holdsworth, and at the hour of which I am now writing, Mr. Sherman sat beside him in an easy-chair, his legs up and his head back, in a deep sleep. From the centre of a beam hung a small oil-lamp, the frame carefully protected by wire network; and the light diffused by this lamp was clear enough to exhibit Holdsworth's face distinctly.

He, too, was asleep, if sleep that can be called which, plunging the senses into unconsciousness, yet leaves pain and misery to play their active part upon the darkened stage of the mind. Of his youth, of his beauty, I might almost say of his very manhood—such as was wont to be suggested by the open, brave, and winning expression of his face—not a trace was left.

The spoliation of suffering had been so complete, that
the bare wreck of the noble temple it had ruined was
all that remained. Now, even more completely than in
his waking hours, might we master the full extent of
the cruel transformation that had been wrought, since
the candour of sleep was on the slumberer, and the self-
consciousness that masks the subtle facial truths, in-
active. His hair, formerly dark and luxuriant, was
thinned about the forehead, was tangled and coarse,
and mixed with gray and white. The protrusion of the
cheek-bones formed a conspicuous feature; under them
the flesh fell into a hollow, and, as much of it as the
bristly moustache and whiskers suffered to be seen, was
puckered and dried up like the rind of an old winter
apple. The under lip was enlarged, and entirely altered
the remembered aspect of the mouth. The eyebrows
drooped where they had formerly arched, and the hair
of them near the temples had fallen off. Time might,
perhaps, efface some of these disfigurements deep graven
by the stylet of pain; but no man could have looked
upon that sleeping face without a conviction of the per-
manency of much that he beheld.

He slept; but though his slumber was deep, his
movements were so restless, convulsive, and feverish,
that it seemed every moment as if he must start up.

Once during the night the ship's bell sounding seven
awakened him, and he opened his eyes and raised his
head, but soon let it fall again. Then it was during
this short interval of wakefulness that the bewildered
look of which Mr. Sherman had spoken might have
been perceived; and it lingered for some minutes on
his face after he had dropped asleep once more.

Several times during the night the kind-hearted man

who watched by the poor fellow's side rose from his
chair, and scrutinised him anxiously; and once Mr.
Banks popped his shaggy head in to ask how the sufferer
did, but found both patient and doctor asleep.

The morning crept over the sky, and turned the
port-hole and the piece of deck-glass white; and at six
o'clock Mr. Sherman woke, and crept quietly to his
cabin to refresh himself with a plunge in cold water;
then went on deck, where he found the captain smoking a cigar, his feet in galoshes, and the hands washing
down.   A sparkling, genial morning, with a warm
breeze from the west, the barque in full sail, and the
green seas caressing her bows, and leaping back from
their keen salute in avalanches of foam.

"Good morning, Mr. Sherman," said the skipper.
"This is the weather, eh, sir?   Out of the Doldrums
by Tuesday week, I hope.   How's your patient?"

"Sleeping soundly.   He has passed a good night.
If he can only get over the next few days, the tropical
sun will set him to rights."

"Is he awake now?"

"I think not.   But we'll go and see if you like."

The captain threw away his cigar and followed Mr.
Sherman below, not, however, before casting a look
above and around, and singing out to the man at the
wheel to "keep her at that."

Opening the cabin door they crept to the bunk and
stood looking at the sleeping man, who, aroused perhaps
by the magnetic influence of four eyes upon him, started
and stared up at them from his pillow.

Captain Duff drew back a step, scared a little by the
wild gaze that Holdsworth fixed upon him, and which
was made in some measure repellent by his gaunt and

wasted face, and by the pitiable expression of bewilderment that passed slowly into it, and made it almost as meaningless as an idiot's.

"How do you feel, my poor fellow?" asked Mr. Sherman; "stronger, I hope?"

Holdsworth made no answer, but knitted his brow with an air of profound perplexity, gazed slowly round him, then attentively at Mr. Sherman, then at the skipper, then at himself, finally pressing his hand to his head.

"How do you know he is English? Perhaps he don't understand you," said Captain Duff.

"I heard him mutter in English before I joined you last night," answered Mr. Sherman.

"Pray tell me where I am?" said Holdsworth, in a faint voice.

"That's English!" exclaimed the captain, though he looked as if he must take a thought of it yet, before he should allow himself to feel sure.

"You are among friends," replied Mr. Sherman softly, and in a voice full of sympathy; "on board a vessel called the 'Jessie Maxwell,' bound to Australia. We sighted your boat yesterday morning."

"My boat!" whispered Holdsworth, with an expression on his face of such deep bewilderment that it was painful to behold it.

"Do you not remember?"

"My boat! my boat!" repeated Holdsworth; but no light came into his eyes to show that he apprehended the other's meaning.

"He has lost his memory," said Mr. Sherman aside to the captain. And then to Holdsworth: "Do you feel as if you could eat anything?"

"Yes, I am hungry," answered Holdsworth.

"That is a good sign!" exclaimed Mr. Sherman, cheerfully. "Captain, will you stop here a few minutes, while I ask the steward to get the soup heated?"

The skipper, being left alone, stationed himself near the door, and watched Holdsworth with mixed emotions. Brave to foolhardiness in a gale of wind, on a lee-shore, in confronting a mutinous crew, in dealing with the severest of marine exigencies, this little gentleman, in some trivial matters, was as timorous as a mouse, and would have made his escape overboard, rather than be grasped by Holdsworth, who, if he were not the dissembled madman his ragged, withered face suggested him to be, was still hedged about with enough of mysterious and secret horror to make him awful in the practical little Scotchman's eyes.

Meanwhile, Holdsworth rested upon his pillow, casting eager and restless glances about the cabin, and at the skipper, and battling with an oblivion of the past as thick and as impenetrable as that mystery of being which the infant emerges from at its birth.

"Tell me, sir, who I am—where I have been taken from!" he exclaimed, presently, looking with imploring eyes at the skipper.

"Indeed, my man, I can't tell you who you are," replied the captain, wishing that Mr. Sherman would return, or that a squall would give him an excuse to withdraw. "All that I know is, we found you in a boat, and picked you up, and that the gentleman who has just gone out, saved your life."

"Strange!" muttered Holdsworth; "I remember nothing."

"Oh, it will all come if you give it time. Memory

often leaves people after a bad illness, but returns again with the strength. Ech!" he cried, struck, as though for the first time, by the poor creature's lean and hollow face. "But you have kenn'd some awfu' times, man, since ye last stood upon honest shipboard. Sailoring, if you are a sailor, is a poor look-out when it comes to wanting bread and water."

The door opened and Mr. Sherman came in, followed by the steward bearing a dish of soup and some mild brandy and water, with which Mr. Sherman proceeded to feed Holdsworth. When as much of the soup as was thought good had been administered, Mr. Sherman bade his patient turn his back to the light and get some sleep.

"I will, sir; thank you for your kindness," returned Holdsworth, with affecting docility. "But, first, will you help me—will you help me to recall something—anything—to give my mind rest? I can see nothing for the darkness that is over me."

"I have told him that his memory will come back with his strength," said Captain Duff.

"Yes, have a little patience!" exclaimed Mr. Sherman. "We will get you on deck in a day or two, and when you see the boat we took you from your memory will return to you."

"Can you not tell me my name?" asked Holdsworth, with that striking expression of painful anxiety you may see on the face of a blind man deserted by his guide and totally at fault.

"We will endeavour to find it out," replied Mr. Sherman. "Come, captain, our friend must talk no more, or all our trouble to get him well will be of no use."

Holdsworth put out his hand with a smile of grati·
tude that softened and almost sweetened his miserable
and skeleton-like face ; then turned in his bunk and
closed his eyes.

"A strange thing to happen to a man," said the captain to Mr. Sherman, as they went on deck.   " I never
could have believed that the memory of a creature could
go out of his brain like that !"

" We may guess the nature and magnitude of his sufferings by this effect," answered Mr. Sherman.   " God alone
knows how many days he may have passed in that boat,
and what scenes of horror he has witnessed and what
torments he has endured.   But we must help his memory
as far as he can.   Will you allow me to go forward and
examine the boat ?"

They walked to the main-deck, where the boat was
stowed.   A little knot of men gathered around and
watched their movements with interest.   But, in truth,
the boat was as unsuggestive as a sheet of blank paper.
There was no name in her ; nor by her build, sail, oars,
shape, or anything else, was it possible to tell her pater·
nity.   The broken bottles and bags of bread that had
been fished out of her locker were in her bottom, but
no clue was to be got from them ; nothing but a story
of deepest tragical misery.   The captain sent for the
shawl that had been unhitched from the mast-head, and
he and Mr. Sherman held it open between them and
inspected it.   Browned by the wet and the heat—in its
frayed and tattered shape, its very texture modified by
exposure—it was positively no more than a black rag.

They returned to the after-deck, and sent the steward
for the clothes which had been removed from the two
men.   Holdsworth's pilot coat was of good quality, and

his linen also seemed to suggest that he had held a very superior position to that of Johnson, whose dress was a sailor's, a brown woollen shirt, serge trousers, boots with high tops, and the invariable belt and knife. Holdsworth's linen was marked with H ; nothing more. They found in his pockets a watch, a clasp-knife, some money, and one or two other articles, which Mr. Sherman made into a parcel, hoping that the sight of things which would be familiar might help the poor fellow's memory.

"It is evident," says the skipper, "that whatever we are to learn must come from the man himself. His clothes tell us nothing."

"They are a sailor's, don't you think ?"

"Why, they are such clothes as I or Banks might wear ; but that don't prove that the man was a sailor. He certainly hasn't a nautical cut."

"His language is that of an educated man, and his linen is that of a gentleman. Pray God that the poor soul's memory will return. Without it he will be scarcely better off with us than he was in the boat."

"Eh ?" cried the literal skipper, "not better off with good meat and drink and a good bunk to lie in, than when he was perishing of thirst, with no better blanket than the sky to cover him ?"

"I mean that he may have friends at home who, while his memory remains torpid, must be as dead to him and he to them, as if he had remained in his open boat."

"Yes, I see your idea, sir," replied the skipper. "And now about the other puir creature. We must bury him this morning. He is dead you say ?"

"We will go and look at him."

"Why," returned Captain Duff, shrinking, "to tell you the plain truth, I am not over fond of these girning

bodies. By your leave, sir, I'll hae the puir creature
sewn up in canvas, and if you'll tak' the reading of the
Burial office I shall feel obliged, Mr. Sherman, as I
have but a varra moderate capacity for the delivery o'
written words."

At this juncture, Adam, the steward, rang the
breakfast-bell, and the captain and Mr. Sherman went
below.

*   *   *   *   *

There is scarcely any ceremony more impressive than
a burial at sea ; perhaps because nowhere does man feel
his littleness more than when the mighty ocean surrounds
him. The graves of the dead on shore in a measure
localise their inmates, and our associations are fortified
by the power of referring to the departed as beings who
slumber in green places, and are at all seasons visitable.

But a burial at sea is the launching of the dead into
infinity. The sense of his extinction is absolute. He is
swallowed up and annihilated by the universe of water,
which also seems to overwhelm his very memory.

At twelve o'clock the body of Johnson, sewn up in
canvas, with a weight of lead attached to his feet, lay
extended upon one of the gratings of the main-hatchway,
one end resting on the bulwarks of the ship, the other
upon the shoulders of two sailors. The crew stood round,
holding their caps in their hands ; and near the body
stood Mr. Sherman reading the Burial Service. The
mournful and impressive spectacle was greatly heightened
by the tolling of the bell on the quarter-deck, which
mingled its clear chimes with the words delivered by
Mr. Sherman. The vessel was sailing on an even keel,
her white sails swelling and soaring one above another,
and forming a lovely picture against the bright blue sky.

The water leaped and sparkled and frothed against her clean sides, and those swallows of the deep, the stormy petrels, chased her flashing wake, and gave by their presence a finishing detail to the whole of the sun-lighted scene.

How unutterable the mystery hedging the motionless figure in the canvas shroud—his name unknown, a waif of dead humanity snatched for a brief moment from the imperious deep, whose will it was to keep him! The seamen sent shrinking glances at the bundle on the grating. That he had suffered; that famine had made a skeleton of him; that thirst had twisted his lean face into an expression of agony which death was powerless to smooth out, was all they knew.

"*We therefore commit his body to the deep, to be turned into corruption——*"

The captain motioned with his hand; the grating was tilted, and its burden went like a flash from the bulwarks; the steersman turned his face upon his shoulder, hearing the hollow plunge; but those on the main-deck stood without a move among them, listening to the final, comfortable, glorious words :—

"*Looking for the resurrection of the body (when the sea shall give up her dead), and the life of the world to come, through our Lord Jesus Christ, who at His coming shall change our vile body, that it may be like His glorious body, according to the mighty working whereby He is able to subdue all things to Himself.*"

The reader closed the book; the grating was restored to its place; and the men in twos and threes moved slowly forward, talking in subdued tones; and for the remainder of that day at least no sound of loose laughter or reckless words was to be heard in the forecastle.

CHAPTER XV.

HOLDSWORTH regained his strength slowly, and on the fourth day Mr. Sherman, who attended him with the gentle and unobtrusive solicitude of a perfectly bene-volent mind, suggested that a visit on deck might freshen him up and contribute to his recovery.

To this Holdsworth had been looking forward with indescribable eagerness, believing that the sight of the boat of which Mr. Sherman had spoken would recall his memory. His mind, indeed, presented a phenomenon. He remembered nothing—literally *nothing*. His actual life, as he was then living it, practically dated from the moment of the return of his consciousness. All that had gone before was pitch darkness. That the faculty of memory was not *dead*, was proved by his capacity to remember his thoughts and feelings, the offices and faces of those who waited on him, the food he had eaten, the names of those he conversed with, during the time he had been in the cabin of the barque. But behind this was impenetrable gloom, every glance at which tortured him, so inexplicable was his helplessness to penetrate it.

The mind of an infant has been likened to a sheet of blank paper; we may extend the image in Holds-worth's case by conceiving that all the characters which experience had written upon his mind had been effaced, and that, what new characters there were upon it, were the impressions only which he had received since he had been awakened from the deadly stupor that had conquered him a few hours before his rescue.

Mr. Sherman was fully persuaded that Holdsworth's memory would return with his strength; and had therefore foreborne from making any experiments by questions or allusions until the time should come when the renewal of health would enable the sufferer to sustain the fatigue of thought. He was impressed and touched by the poor fellow's docility, his sweetness of temper, and his gratitude, which moved him to tears as often as he attempted to express it. But no clue was to be obtained from his conversation as to the profession he had followed. There was not a shoppish expletive in his language. He named things after the established prescription of Johnson's Dictionary, and might as well have been a clerk, a dentist, a builder, a Member of Parliament, or even an attorney, as a sailor.

The "Jessie Maxwell" was now in the hot latitudes. The fourth day was lovely, with a north-east breeze on the port quarter, and a burning sun, from which an awning protected the deck. An easy chair was placed near the skylight for Holdsworth, who gained the deck, leaning on Mr. Sherman's arm. He halted on the last step of the companion-ladder, and clung to his friend with a look of mingled surprise and fear in his face.

Had there been any one, among those who watched him with curiosity, who had known him as the chief mate of the "Meteor," he could scarcely have contemplated this wreck of a man without deep emotion. Conceive, if you can, a face with every characteristic

that had once contributed to give it manly beauty,
wrung out of it by sufferings which had left ineffaceable
marks on every inch of the whole surface of the countenance. Conceive a stooped and trembling figure, the
shoulders forward so as to hollow the chest, and the
back bowed like an old man's, the arms lengthened by
the abnormal attitude and defeating every faint suggestion of symmetry which the eye might still hope to find.
But this expresses nothing of the real transformation
that had been wrought; of that subtle modification of
expression, of the spiritual conditions of the face, of
changes achieved by the most delicate strokes, but
which were as effectual as a recasting of the whole figure
and countenance could have been. He was dressed
partly in his own clothes, partly in some of the clothes
belonging to the second mate, who was a slight man,
but whose garments hung loosely on Holdsworth. He
wore his own coat, which formerly had buttoned tight
across his chest, and which his muscular arms had filled
out, as the fingers a glove; and he could now have
buttoned it nearly twice around him. The ring that
he had worn on his left hand had slipped from his
skeleton finger long ago, when he had been splashing
the sea-water over his face in vain endeavour to quench
the burning agony in his head and throat. He might
have worn Dolly's wedding-ring on his middle finger
now, for his hands were indeed scarcely more than bone.

Mr. Sherman eyed him anxiously as he stood tottering at the companion-hatchway. It seemed as if the
long-desired revelation had come to the suffering man,
and that he could now remember.

"Look about you," he said, "and tell me if there is
anything you see that recalls old impressions."

"I see nothing that does this," replied Holdsworth in a low voice. "Where is the boat I was taken from?"

"On the main-deck yonder."

"I should like to see her," said Holdsworth eagerly. "*One* idea may light up all."

They walked slowly forward. Here and there a seaman repairing a sail, or working in the lower shrouds, or doing one of the endless jobs of splicing, whipping, tarring, cleaning, which are so many conditions of the maritime life, looked at Holdsworth earnestly, but never intrusively; and when he was at the boat some of the hands came up to him with a spokesman, a middle-aged sailor in ear-rings, who said :

"Beg pardon, sir, but all hands wishes to say as they're werry glad to see you up and doing; and if there's e'er a thing any man among us can do in helping to make you comfortable while you're with us, they'll do it and welcome; and no liberty is intended."

"Thank you, and God bless you !" answered Holdsworth, greatly moved by this speech, and with an expression on his face that could hardly fail to let the honest seamen know that their goodwill was not the less appreciated because it provoked no lengthened reply. The men retired, saying among themselves that, "though the gentleman warn't a sailor, he ought to be one; and though he was nothing but a skeleting, he had as honest a face on him as ever they seed."

"This is the boat," said Mr. Sherman.

Holdsworth steadied himself by holding on to the gunwale and looked into it. The bags of bread lay under the aftermost thwart; there was the open locker which the sea had filled with water; there were the empty kegs, whose hollow rollings, as the boat had swayed to and fro, had formed such suggestive notes of torture, as one might think would nevermore depart from the ear that had received the echo. If there were impressions like red-hot brands to sear the mind with burning transcripts of the ugly agonising facts they counterfeited, one, if any of them, would surely be the impression conveyed by the scenes of which the interior of the boat had been the theatre. Here the widow had died, with her arm hanging over the side; yonder the General had expired, pointing to the phantom of his native town, which dying memory had evoked from the air; from that spot the actor had leaped; and on that seat the boy had died, holding out his hands to the sinking sun. The little arena should have been vital with memory, so small was the space in which infinite human misery had been packed. But to Holdsworth it conveyed no ideas. Not the faintest illumination entered his face in surveying it. To Mr. Sherman it was a thousandfold more significant than to Holdsworth, who was the chief actor in the heart-breaking tragedy that had been enacted in it. Yet he knew that it *ought* to have an interest for him; and he stood clutching and staring at it, with a frowning forehead, wrestling wildly with his mind, in which the corpse of memory lay deep and hidden.

After a long interval he passed his hand across his eyes, and turned to Mr. Sherman.

" It will not come," he said.

Mr. Sherman was both disappointed and astonished; disappointed by the fruitless result of an inspection, the good effect of which he had counted upon, and astonished by this phenomenon of the utter extinction of the most life-giving faculty of the mind.

He drew him to the boat again, and said:

"See now; you were found there, lying under that seat, and beside the mast lay another man, a dark-faced man, dressed in sailor's clothes. Do you remember?"

"No."

"Look at those bags of biscuit. They were found soaking in the locker. Those bags contained all the food you had on board. You must have suffered horribly from the dread of starvation when you found the biscuit spoilt by the salt water. Recall your thoughts on making the discovery. Can you?"

"No," replied Holdsworth, pressing his hand to his head.

"There was a black flag—a piece of stuff, a portion of a woman's dress it seemed—fastened to the masthead. Do you remember?"

Holdsworth said "No."

"Had you a woman with you?"

"I cannot tell."

"See if you can go farther back. Try to recollect where your ship sailed from. Was it England?"

"England? Yes—I know England—but I do not remember if I came from England," Holdsworth replied, with profound anxiety in his eyes.

"Come! you remember England! Did you sail from Liverpool?"

"I know Liverpool!" he exclaimed quickly.

"And London?"

"Yes! yes!"

"And what was the name of your ship?"

Holdsworth thought and thought without avail.

Herein was the deception that misled Mr. Sherman Holdsworth could perfectly remember familiar names, but they had to be pronounced in his hearing before he could recall them. In like manner he could tell the names and discourse of the things he beheld, *because he saw them.* Had Johnson lived, he would have known and called him Johnson. Had Mr. Sherman spoken of Dolly, of Southbourne, of the London Docks, of the "Meteor," of any of the incidents connected with the "Meteor's" loss, Holdsworth would have remembered exactly as much as he heard. But, in the absence of suggestion, his memory was powerless—absolutely helpless—to generate independent conclusions as to the impressions his mind had received previous to his rescue.

The real miracle lay in *this* contradiction—in the death of memory, dating *up to* the moment of the swoon in the boat; in its resurrection to health and vigour, dating *from* the moment of his recovery.

He returned to the chair that had been placed for him near the skylight, and Mr. Sherman, still not despairing of arousing this dormant faculty, went below and returned with the parcel of things that had been taken from Holdsworth's pockets. These were given him one by one, but he handled them without recognition.

"But you know their names?" said Mr. Sherman.

"Yes. This is a knife. This is a watch."

"They are yours; found in your pockets."

His hand trembled, and he gazed at them with devouring eyes; but no other idea was conveyed to him by Mr. Sherman's assurance than the bare fact that they were his property. He could not remember having purchased or owned them.

"It's only a question of time, my man," said Captain Duff, who stood by looking on at these strange ineffectual experiments.

No mere effort of imagination can do justice to Holdsworth's suffering. The feeling that he *ought* to remember, coupled with his incapacity and the sense of the past holding, perhaps, memories of vital consequence to him to recall, created a mental torture more afflicting than it is in the power of any man, who has not suffered in this way, to conceive. Loss of memory, even in trifling matters, always partakes of the nature of pain. The fruitless effort to recall a name, a date, begets uneasiness, and is soon converted into a positive torment. But figure your mind haunted with a sense of the significance of the past, not one faintest glimpse of which it is permitted to you to obtain. Figure yourself groping in a dense gloom, saying : "There are things here which I *feel* are precious to me, which are of deep consequence to my happiness and to the happiness of others, but I cannot recall their names or their aspect !" and meanwhile the subtlest of your instincts is driving you mad with importunities to prosecute your search and lay the store of memory open to the light ! This is worse than · blindness ; it is death in life. The years that you have lived are cut away from your existence, and with them all the precious accumulations of experience—love, sorrow, and thought itself. God preserve us all from such an affliction !

CHAPTER XVI

SAILORS' SYMPATHY.

THE "Jessie Maxwell" was bound for Sydney, New South Wales, freighted with what is called a general cargo — pianos, nails, scents, and such matters. She carried only one passenger, Mr. Sherman, whose cabin was given him as a favour by Captain Duff, who partly owned the barque, and who had a great friendship for the gentleman, whose house he visited in Sydney. Mr. Sherman was a merchant, doing business in wool, tallow, and other Australian exports, and had been visiting London and Glasgow for agents and consignees, and also to benefit his health by a sea voyage. He was one of the most humane men in the colony, very well to do, but prosperous by his own efforts. He had a commanding figure, a large, mild, intellectual eye, and the kindliest smile that ever graced the human face. The strong benevolence of his character made his manner singularly fascinating ; and before Holdsworth had known him a fortnight, he was bound to him by a feeling of affection, which, though it might have owed something of its depth to gratitude, must have existed in a complete form, without reference to the great kindness that had been shown him.

The days passed quickly. In the equatorial latitudes

the barque was becalmed for two days; and then a gale rose, and drove her into the south-east trade-winds.

If Mr. Sherman and Captain Duff had ever felt disposed to believe that Holdsworth might have been a sailor, they considered that probability entirely disposed of by his behaviour on the first day of the gale.

He was on deck when the wind was freshening, walking to and fro with Mr. Sherman, whose arm he could now do without, having recovered as much of his strength as it seemed likely he would ever get back. The wind came up in a sudden squall, and took the barque on the starboard beam. Her royals were set, but the yards fortunately were trimmed to receive the breeze. The vessel heeled over under the great weight of canvas, and there was some hurry amongst the men as they let go the royal and topgallant halliards, though there was nothing in the confusion to occasion the least alarm, even in a passenger who had been a month at sea. But the effect of the squall upon Holdsworth was extraordinary. As the vessel lay over, he grasped Mr. Sherman's arm with looks of terror in his face, and ran to windward, flinging fearful glances at the sea on the lee side. Mr. Sherman offered to help him to go below, but he declined to leave the deck, and clung to the weather mizzen rigging, apparently speechless with alarm.

As it came on to blow heavily, the men reefed the topsails; and Holdsworth literally trembled as the yards rushed down upon the caps, and the canvas thundered as the helmsman luffed to enable the hands to pick up the sails more easily.

"My dear friend," exclaimed Mr. Sherman soothingly, "you must endeavour to control yourself. There is no danger, indeed. This uproar will cease presently. We encountered much worse weather than this in the North Atlantic, shortly after leaving Glasgow."

"Yes, I am ashamed of my weakness; my nerves are gone," answered the poor fellow. And then, seeing the men tumbling up aloft and laying out upon the yards, he covered his face with his hands, saying he dared not look, lest he should see them fall.

The ship was made snug presently; but the sea rose, and now and again a shower of spray came flying over the forecastle and the main-deck, which so violently agitated Holdsworth that he let go the rigging and made for the companion. He walked like a paralysed man: his hands outstretched, and his head turning about on his shoulders. He gained his cabin and laid himself down in his bunk, exquisitely alive to his pusillanimity, and weeping over his incapacity to control himself.

The skipper went up to Mr. Sherman.

"Our friend is no sailor. I think you can tell *that*, Mr. Sherman?"

"No; that is proved. The instincts of his old life, had he been a sailor, would have kept up his courage without respect of his memory. But let us bear in mind that his nervousness is the result of the terrible experience he has gone through. If illness—if fever, for instance—will rob us of our nerves, how much more the unspeakable agony of hunger and thirst, and the deadly, hopeless captivity and exposure in an open boat for days, and maybe for weeks! It would drive me mad!"

"Ay, that is verra true. Understand me, I am not speaking disrespectfully of the puir soul. I would only

bid you obsairve by his fear that he canna hae been a
tarry-breeks. The auld speerit would live in spite o'
his nerves, and would have risen to the cries of the men
and the bocking o' the water. That's my opeenion."

Thus we may learn how some opinions, delivered in
sound earnest, are manufactured.

Not a tarry-breeks!

There had never sailed out of any port in Christen-
dom a finer, a more courageous sailor than Holdsworth.
What would Captain Duff have thought of his "opeenion," had he been told that that same halting, crippled
figure, who had hastened to his cabin with movements full of fear, had been, only a month before, an
upright, handsome man, with an eye full of light and
spirit, with nerves and skill equal to occasions which
would have overwhelmed the honest Scotch skipper and
left him nowhere, with a heart as gentle as a maiden's
and manly as Nelson's; always foremost in the moment
of danger, with the voice of a trumpet to deliver unerring commands; a leader in measures of which the peril
made the stoutest-hearted tremble and stand still;
scaling the dizzy heights of whirling masts and spars,
to whose summits he might have beckoned in vain to
those very seamen of the "Jessie Maxwell," whose
movements, now in the weakness of his crushed and
broken life, he dared not even watch?

Of all sights, that of the strong and lion-hearted
man, smitten down by sickness, by misery, by misfortune to the feebleness of an infant, to the timidity of a
girl, is surely the most affecting. Such a man I have
seen—a sailor—entering the forecastle full of the courage
that makes heroes of men, and leaving it, after two
months of confinement, with nerves and health so

shattered, that he has not dared to approach the bulwarks of the ship for fear of falling overboard!

Give the full measure of your pity, kind reader, to
such as these. There is no form of human suffering
whose pathos is more unqualified.

So Mr. Sherman, agreeing with Captain Duff, was
confident that, whatever else Holdsworth might have
been, he was not a sailor. This was, at all events, a
negative discovery, which lopped off one of the numerous
conjectures with which the mystery of Holdsworth's
past was considered. Strange it was to talk to the
poor fellow, to hear his rational language, his discus-
sions, his sensible remarks, and to feel that he was
speaking, so to say, on this side of a curtain, behind
which were hidden all the true interests of his life.
Once or twice he staggered Captain Duff by a nautical
question, the very nature of which implied an intimate
acquaintance with the sea; but his unaffected timidity
when the vessel rolled, or when the weather was squally,
always drove the skipper back upon his first conclusion,
and made him think that the knowledge of sails, ropes,
yards, etc., which Holdsworth displayed, had been picked
up by him as a passenger, or even out of books.

However, his marine allusions were few and far
between. His horror of the sea was remarkable, and
he repeatedly inquired how long it would be before
they reached Sydney. Moreover, he was rendered
taciturn by his ceaseless struggles with memory; and
would pass whole hours lost in thought, during which,
it was observed, no gleam ever entered his face to indicate his recurrence to any action, phase, or condition
of his past.

Often, when the main-deck was clear, he would steal

to the boat and stand contemplating her with his hands locked, and his brow corrugated with anxious thought. It was strange to see him running his eyes over her, handling the yoke-lines, peering into the locker, and literally groping for an inspiration.

Once, the boatswain of the vessel, a shrewd English seaman, who, as well as every other soul on board the barque, knew of Holdsworth's total loss of memory, seeing him alone staring at the boat, came out of his berth, and addressed him :

"They say, sir, that you don't remember this boat?"

"I am trying to recollect," answered Holdsworth, looking at him with the expression of painful eagerness that was now almost a characteristic of his face.

"See here, sir, when that there boat was sighted, there was only two persons found aboard of her. You was one, and the other was the poor fellow we buried. Now, what I'm always saying to my mates is this : this here's a ship's quarter-boat, and more hands went in her than two when she put off. Now, sir, try and think how many there was."

"I remember nothing. I would to God I could !"

"But don't you reck'let what your thoughts was when the bread got soaked with the salt water?"

Holdsworth shook his head.

"Here," continued the good-natured boatswain, "might be the bread," pointing to the locker. "Here," he went on, pointing to the stern-sheets, "might you be sitting, steering of her; when up comes a sea and washes over you or the chap that has the yokes. Now, may be, you notices this, but can only groan, having to keep her head well before it—putting you for the man as steers. But you can think, for all that ; and it must ha' scared the blood out of you to guess that the little food that remained was all spoilt. Can't you remember?"

Holdsworth, who had followed every syllable with trembling anxiety, shook his head again.

"Many things have happened; something tells me that," he answered; "but I can remember nothing."

"Would you like to step into the foks'le, sir? Perhaps you might see something there as will help you," said the boatswain, who was moved by Holdsworth's hopeless reply.

They descended through the fore-scuttle into the dim semicircular abode, with huge beams across the upper deck, from which depended a number of hammocks, and bunks all around, with their edges chipped and hacked by the men, who used them for cutting tobacco upon; and on the deck, sea-chests and bundles, and pannikins and tin dishes scattered everywhere. The gloom was scarcely irradiated by a couple of lamps resembling tea-pots with wicks in their spouts; and the faces of the men glimmered over the sides of the hammocks or in the darkness of the bunks. Up in a corner was a group of men, consisting of a portion of the watch on deck, assembled around two sea-chests, on which were seated a couple of ordinary seamen, fastened down by nails driven through the seat of their breeches into the lids of the chests. Their sleeves were tucked above the muscles of their arms, and they were deciding, by means of their fists, an argument which had been commenced half an hour before in the main-top. Being nailed very nearly at arm's length from each other, their efforts to deal each other blows threw them into contortions irresistibly ridiculous; but the lookers-on, having probably no very lively sense of the absurd, stood around with grave faces, thoughtfully chewing tobacco, and now and then offering the combatants a friendly suggestion where best to hit each other. Some men lay in hammocks directly over the heads of the pugilists, but took no further interest in the proceedings going on under their beds, than now and again to pop a burnt and hairy face over the edge of the tight canvas, and in polite and genteel terms recommend the youngsters not to make too much noise if they didn't want to be nailed fore and aft upon the lids of the chests like bats.

"Now, sir," said the boatswain, advancing a few steps into the forecastle, but not even deigning to notice, much less offering to interfere, between the combatants, "see if there ain't nothing here to give you an idea."

There should have been many things ; for the forecastle of a ship was as familiar to Holdsworth as any part of her ; and though, when he had first gone to sea, he had slept in a cabin near his father's, he had spent the greater part of his time forward among the men, taking instructions from them in all kinds of seafaring work, and never more happy than when squatting on a chest, plying a marlin spike, and listening to the yarns of the sailors around him.

The boatswain watched him with looks of interest, which faded into disappointment.

"Is there nothing ?" he asked.

"Nothing," said Holdsworth gazing blankly around him.

"But you know those things are called hammocks ?"

"Yes, I can tell you the names of everything that I see, but that don't help me."

"Well I *am* blowed !" muttered the boatswain, under his breath ; whereupon Holdsworth, thanking

him for the trouble he had taken, withdrew, pained by
the glances and whispers of the men, and rendered
nervous and dispirited by the smells, the fight in the
corner, and the strong movement of the ship, felt here
more than anywhere else.

CHAPTER XVII.

NOT knowing how to address or speak to Holdsworth, the skipper and Mr. Sherman and the others called him Mr. H., that letter being all they knew of his name.

He was treated by captain and officers with great kindness, shared their table, and was even furnished by them with clothes, of which, you may conceive, he stood very much in need.

None of them could doubt that he had friends, that he held a position, that he might have money; and they waited day after day for the return of his memory, which was to solve the mystery his silence wrought, and set him square with the world again. Indeed, his utter incapacity to recall the smallest incident connected with his past, was almost provoking, despite its pathos. Captain Duff wanted to know the name of the vessel that had been wrecked, the port she hailed from, the port she had been bound to, her cargo, who her captain was. How astounding to this healthy little man that such plain and easy questions should provoke no replies. Perhaps, had he been kept without food and water for six or seven days, subjected to a long series of appalling mental tortures, exposed on the sea in an open boat that was scarcely visible a mile off, with Death the skeleton for a helmsman, he might have moderated his wonderment—nay, even admitted that such experiences were not only highly calculated to deprive a man of his memory, but to drive him raving mad for the remainder of his life.

But the barque was drawing near her journey's end, in long. 120°. The pale outline of Van Diemen's land must heave in sight shortly away on the port bow.

They were now in the beginning of November, and had been seventy-two days from Glasgow. One bright morning Holdsworth was seated on the skylight, with his eyes on a book that had been lent him, but with his mind groping, as it more or less always was, in the darkness that hid the past from his sight. There was a blind man's look on his face when he was thus thinking, that was more conclusive of the ghastly sincerity of his intellectual bereavement than anything that could be said or done. You saw by the blank expression in his eyes that his gaze was turned inwards, and by his general air that the search he was making was a fruitless one.

He had been taken out of the boat a ghost—a gray skeleton; he had picked up a little since that time, but his present aspect was merely a slight improvement on the forlorn image he had presented when rescued. The familiar picture of a broad-shouldered, hearty, vigorous, handsome young man, smooth-cheeked, clear-eyed, was gone : in its place was a wasted shadow, a drooping, hesitating figure, with a characterisation of deformity in its movements, though there was no positive deformity ; thin, feeble hands whitened by sickness, and a pale face hollowed in the eyes, and made ragged with a growth of black beard and moustache.[1]

The change was altogether too remarkable to have been effected by physical suffering only; the heart had worked the deeper transformation—the soft, tender, womanly heart brought face to face with sufferings it was constrained to contemplate, to hearken to murmurs of agony it could not soothe nor silence. Consider, I pray you consider, that he had beheld five shocking deaths, each one accompanied by circumstances of unspeakable horror or misery. Stretched over a longer space of time, they might, by giving his heart breathing-spaces between, have inured it to the inevitable scenes; but crowding upon him one after the other in quick succession, they ground his sensibility to dust, and though he had now no memory whereby to renew the sufferings of those ten days, its blighting effect was not the less clearly visible in him, its operation had not been the less complete.

Whilst he thus sate, as lonely now in a ship full of men as ever he had been in the boat with Johnson dying under the thwart, Mr. Sherman came on deck and took a seat at his side. Holdsworth was so engrossed that he did not perceive his companion, and Mr. Sherman, unwilling to break in upon his thoughts, remained silent, watching him.

Suddenly Holdsworth turned; the blank dead look went out of his eyes, and he smiled.

[1] " Famine, despair, cold, thirst, and heat had done
    Their work on them by turns, and thinn'd them to
    Such things a mother had not known her son
    Amidst the skeletons of that gaunt crew."
                                    Don Juan, Canto ii. 102.

"So memory still defies you?" said Mr. Sherman kindly, and with just as much anxiety as would let his companion understand the sincerity of the interest taken in him.

"Yes," answered Holdsworth, the smile fading off his face. "Once—once only, just now, a fancy came into my mind—I cannot explain its nature, or what it betokened, but it vanished the instant I attempted to grapple with it."

"Did it leave no impression—no idea whatever?"

"None. I can compare it to nothing better than a dim light stealing across the wall of a dark room and disappearing."

Mr. Sherman was silent; and presently said:

"What do you propose to do when you reach Sydney?"

"I have often thought of that. I must seek work and wait."

"Wait until your memory returns?"

"Yes."

"The captain and I were talking about you just now, and I suggested that, were you to return to England, which I am persuaded is your native country, you might come across a friend who would give you your memory back at once; or failing such a friend, you might encounter some scene which would achieve the same end."

"I don't think I could bear another long voyage just yet," answered Holdsworth, glancing at the sea. "What should make the water so hateful to me?" Sometimes I fancy I must have passed many years upon it, and that it has served me badly."

"Oh, your dislike is easily understood. But now

with regard to your prospects.   Will it be wise for you
to remain in Australia?   You must have friends at
home—supposing England to be your home."

"But how shall I find them?"

"Ay, that's it.   Much might be done if I could only
discover your name.   I must make a list of all the
names beginning with H.   The only question is, would
you know your name if you were to see it?"

"I would try," answered the poor fellow humbly.

"Well, now, I'll tell you what I have in my mind,"
said Mr. Sherman, laying his hand kindly on Holdsworth's.   "I look upon you as a man whom, having
brought to life—for I take the credit of your recovery
to myself—it is my proper privilege to support.   But
I shall not allow you to be dependent on charity.   I
have an office in Sydney, and you shall have a desk in
that office, and so earn a salary that will maintain you
in comfort.   By-and-by your memory will come back.
You will then return to England, and I shall heartily
wish you God's blessing, for you have suffered—yes,
you have suffered very much—more than I, more than
any of us, can conceive."

He broke off suddenly, his voice faltering.

Holdsworth seized his hand.

"Mr. Sherman . . . good, kind friend . . . God
will reward you . . . I have suffered . . . I . . . I
feel it here," pressing his hand to his head.   "Sir, dear
sir, believe me grateful!"

"I do believe you grateful, and it pleases me to
believe it, for it is a pleasure to serve the grateful.
Well, we have settled that.   But understand, though
you will remain with me as long as you like, yet, at the
first prompting of your memory, I shall exhort you to

O

return to England, for I cannot persuade myself that you are not leaving relatives and friends who will mourn you as dead, and suffer unnecessary sorrow on your account."

"Yes—yes! I think this sometimes!" cried Holdsworth passionately. "*That* is the haunting thought—but it may not be! Oh, sir, it *cannot* be! Were there dear ones belonging to me, *could* my memory forget them? Could they be *very* dear to me, and be forgotten?"

Mr. Sherman drew a deep breath, and said, "No, I believe that would be impossible. If love united you to any person at your home, that love would be an instinct to prompt you with an influence that should have no reference to memory. But the mind of man is a great mystery."

There was a short silence, and then Mr. Sherman asked: "Do you ever dream?"

"No."

"But you may dream, though your mind cannot retain the impression of its dreams. Could you awaken from a dream of home, your darkness might be made light."

"I have thought of that," answered Holdsworth, with the air of a man who, having exhausted speculation, can find no inspiration in any kind of suggestion.

"And you have no inclination to return to England?"

"It cannot matter where I am whilst my memory remains dead. England! You speak a familiar word, and I know it is a country, but I cannot bend my mind back to it. It gives me no ideas. I stretch my thoughts over the great waste of waters we have traversed in this ship, and find nothing more than sea and sky—sea and sky! I can find no country lying beyond—nothing to give me thoughts of home. Oh, sir!" he cried, "you cannot understand this! How should you? It is horrible for me to look back and see the whole of my life eclipsed—to see a wall of darkness reared close behind me through which I *cannot* see! What things precious, infinitely precious to me, may be hidden! It would ease me, sir, greatly ease me, if God would but illuminate my mind only for a moment, that I might know what is lost to me. And the loneliness of it all! —the feeling of desolation that comes over me in my solitude! Mr. Sherman, consider how lonely I am! Not a voice, not an echo of anything that may be dear to me, comes out of that darkness behind me. Who would believe that memory is life, and the loss of it worse than death?"

He bowed his head and covered his face with his thin hands, and some tears trickled through his fingers.

God help him! Suffering had subdued that manly nature to the feebleness and weakness of a child, and tears, though there had been a time when no anguish of his own could have wrung such things from his eyes, now easily rose with the expression of his feelings.

Here Captain Duff, coming up to Mr. Sherman, interrupted the conversation, and Holdsworth, ashamed of the weakness he had no power to control, went with his slow step and shaky movements below.

* * * *

When they were within two days' sail of Sydney, the boatswain and two hands came aft to the skipper, and the boatswain, touching his cap, spoke as follows:

"Sir, the ship's crew have asked me to turn-to and say this here for them: that they werry well know

that the gentleman who has lost his memory hasn't any
clothes, and, maybe, no money ; and as shipwreck's a
thing that may happen to any of us, and as the poor
gentleman's suffered more nor he's allowed to remember,
though, as my mate Bill here says, it ain't werry hard
to guess what he's gone through, as there are some of
the men for'ard who have bin short of water in their
time, and spin 'arrowing yarns such as I never heerd
the like on ; why, what I was a sayin' was this : that
the ship's company, barrin' one, which is an Isle o'
Dorg's man—but *he'll* come over—want's to make up a
purse o' money for the poor gentleman, and though
some o' them ain't got much to give, leastways to spare,
they'll all lend a hand, and only wait to hear if you and
the mates 'll start the list, which 'ud be more ship-
shape."

The boatswain delivered this speech with great
hesitation—not from nervousness, but from a perception
of the puzzling nature of words, which had a trick of
falling athwartships along the course of his meaning,
and bringing him up with a round turn. Having concluded, he glanced at his mates to see if they approved,
on which they nodded a good deal of hair over their
eyes, and then wiped their mouths with their wrists.

"Right you are," said the skipper, addressing them
with his eyes fixed on the main-topsail, and his hand
out to motion the man at the wheel to keep her steady.
"You can put me down for five pounds, and Mr. Banks
and Mr. Anderson for a sovereign apiece. If they don't
fork out, I'll pay for them. Steady, I say, steady !
Dom it, man, you're a point off your course !"

That evening, the weather being mild and balmy,
and a glorious breeze right astern of the barque, Holds-

worth was seated aft when the skipper came up to him
and said :

"The ship's company have been making you up a
purse, sir, as a token of their sympathy with the
temporal losses you must have sustained by the wreck
of the vessel, which there canna be a doubt you were
on board of, and with the suffering you endured in the
boat. The bo'sun waits to know when it'll be agreeable
to you to receive the gift."

"No—no—really—the poor fellows must keep their
money—I cannot accept it," replied Holdsworth, greatly
agitated and moved.

"Oh, you must tak' it, sir, or they'll think you
paughty, as we say in Scotland. The bo'sun is waiting
at the capstan yonder, and the men are on tiptoe for'ard
—look at the heads louping in the fore-scuttle!"

Holdsworth left his chair and went slowly to the
boatswain. When the hands saw him draw near the
capstan, they wriggled out of the forecastle, out of the
galley, out from behind the long boat, and came slipping
aft, advancing and drawing back fitfully, and some on
tiptoe, to catch the speeches. A seaman somewhere
aloft came hand over fist down a backstay, finally landing himself on the bulwarks, where he stood looking on.

The skipper, and Mr. Sherman, and the second mate
approached ; and when the boatswain was going to
speak, the captain called :

"Draw closer, my lads. The gentleman can't talk
to you out of earshot."

The men, like shy schoolboys, elbowed each other
into a smaller semicircle, and stood staring and grinning
over one another's shoulders.

"All ready, sir?" asked the boatswain.

"Fire away!" answered the skipper.

The boatswain took off his hat and placed it on the capstan; then drew from it a handkerchief of the size of a union-jack, with which he dried his face and mouth; he next fished in his coat pocket and produced a small canvas bag, very neatly sewn. This he held in his hand, and turned to Holdsworth.

"We don't know your name, sir, and we're werry sorry that we don't, 'cause there's a great deal in a name when you give a thing, 'specially to them as has to speechify, and it helps 'em along like. ('So it dew, mate!' from the crowd, and several heads nodded emphatically.) I'm a seafarin' man myself, and come from Greenwich, and had no larnin' taught me when I was a boy, and so the present company will please hexcuse bad grammar and the likes of that, seein' that a seafarin' man don't want to know many words besides those as consarn a ship. We're all sailors here, if the skipper will let me call him a sailor——"

"Ma conscience! and what else am I?" cried the skipper.

"Well, as I was a sayin'," continued the boatswain, looking discomfited for a moment, "we're all sailors here, barrin' you, sir, and Mr. Sherman, and it's only men as go to sea as can know what an awful thing a shipwreck is, and what a bad look-out thirst and hunger is, and the feelings that overcome a man when he is in a open boat miles away from the shore. We reckon that you've passed through a deal o' sufferin', and being sailors, it's only right and proper that we should all of us, from the skipper down, let you know by a better sign than mere talk, which don't go far, though it may be werry comfortin' sometimes, when you can understand what's said to you—I say that we want to let you know how sorry we are for you, and how werry grateful we are that we belong to the wessel that picked you up; and so, sir"—here he handed the bag to Holdsworth—"all hands clubbed together to make up this trifle o' money jist to buy you a few things when you get ashore; and I'm proud to say there ain't a man among us, though I *did* think one was goin' to back out, that hasn't given something——Beggin' your parding a moment; them scraps o' paper in the purse are horders wrote by me, and signed by the men as hasn't got ready money about 'em, for the captain to pay you the valley in silver which they bear in figures; and that money to be deducted from their wages. That's all, I think, sir," he concluded, looking at the skipper.

A voice called out, "Three cheers for the gentleman!" and forth burst a roar from the iron throats of the men that made the decks ring again.

Holdsworth was unmanned, and looked downwards, struggling with his emotion. But glancing up and catching sight of the swarm of rough kindly faces around him, he broke away, so to speak, from his agitation, and answered as follows:

"If it had pleased God to leave me my memory, I believe I could have done my gratitude more justice, though I couldn't have felt more grateful. For, sometimes, when I have watched you at work, it has come over me—not as a conviction—no! I wish it had; but as a mere fancy only—that I too have been a sailor; and if that be so, then I can understand why your kindness does not overcome me with surprise, because I ought to know that sailors' hearts are the largest, the truest, the most manly in the world, that there's not a sorrow their purses will not fly open to relieve, and that a man, let him be what he will, is never so well recommended to them as when he is poor and broken down and friendless. I don't know how properly to thank you for your generous gift. ('We don't want no thanks,' said a voice; 'if there's enough to rig you out and put some 'baccy in your pocket, that's all we want.') Miserable, indeed, I shall be if my memory plays me false in this—if it does not suffer me to carry the recollection of your kindness to my death-bed. May God bless you and guard you all back in safety to your homes."

He ceased, unable to say more.

"Sir," said Captain Duff, "we have done no more than our duty in all this business from beginning to end. In the name of all hands I return your good wishes by praying that God may speedily give you back your memory, and make you happy for the rest of your days, as a proper compensation for what you have gone through."

He shook him by the hand, and then Mr. Anderson stepped forward; then came the boatswain; and then an able seaman; and then another able seaman; until presently Holdsworth was engaged in shaking hands all round, scarcely a man quitting the quarter-deck until a grasp had been exchanged.

When all this hand-shaking was over, Captain Duff ordered rum to be served out to the men, who then returned to the forecastle with a sense of festivity upon them, and passed the rest of the second dog-watch in singing songs and dancing.

CHAPTER XVIII.

SYDNEY.

At nine o'clock on the morning of the third day from the time occupied in the last chapter, a hand stationed on the look-out in the fore-top sent a roar from the sky:

"Land right ahead!"

In half an hour's time it was to be seen from the deck, a mere blue vision stretching eel-shaped, upon the horizon.

Australia! the great and wealthy continent of which there were men then living whose fathers could recall the time when this vast tract of land had no place in the world's knowledge of the Pacific.

Of all sensations, the first glimpse of the land towards which a ship has been steering for weeks and weeks, with seldom even so much as a passing sail to relieve the monotony of the ocean, is the most thrilling. The oldest seaman will desert his bunk or hammock to make for the forecastle and have a look at the dim cloud. The pale-faced steward, seldom seen on deck, sneaks from his berth in the steerage redolent of luke-warm soup and resonant with the ceaseless clattering of crockery, to peer over the bulwarks at the far-off coast.

If there be passengers on board, you are sensible of an uneasy movement among them, strangely suggestive of mingled excitement and reluctance, as though they were at once eager and loath to quit their floating home, the familiar cabin in which so many hours have been passed, the white decks which have become to them what the pavement in front of your house is to you. The ship is endeared to them, and the hold she has upon them is felt now that they shall shortly leave her. How nobly she has struggled with the waves and the wind! What grandeur she assumes when thought of with respect to the immense universe of water she has traversed in safety! But a few weeks ago, one might say, she was in English waters, and now she is breasting the waves of the antipodes, raising her graceful canvas to the heavens with almost conscious elegance, as though exulting in the knowledge of the feat she has performed—a feat of which no repetition can ever diminish the wonder, the courage, and the triumph.

And now the land loomed large and bold upon the horizon, a gray and iron coast, inhospitable enough to scare away all rash adventurers, one might think, in search of new homes and brighter fortunes.

What was Captain Duff about! Did he mean to run his ship bow on to those granite-coloured cliffs stretching to right and left, with their swart base marginated with a line of crawling foam? Screw your eyes up attentively, and you will see two breaks in the shore. The bowsprit of the "Jessie Maxwell" heads for the break on the right. Slowly the coast grows clearer. That break on the left is but a deceptive hollow, with a vast block of rock lying in the blue, shark-studded water, upon which, many years later, a noble ship called the "Dunbar" shall be wrecked, and, of a great crowd of human beings, but one man saved.

And now behold the miracle of the seaman's art!

For weeks and weeks, counting from the English summer, the "Jessie Maxwell" has been surrounded by the ocean, directed through light and darkness, through bright sunshine and howling tempests charged with sleet and spray, by no more than a little needle, but gifted with a steadfastness of intelligence more unerring than the loftiest that humanity is endowed with. For weeks and weeks this little needle points and the helmsman obeys, and onwards the ship sails through hundreds of miles of water, until one morning those on board awake and look ahead, and lo! there is the land, with the ship's head pointing accurately towards the little cleft in the coast through which the great Bay of Sydney is to be entered.

This bay is a vision of beauty. No hint of its existence is given until you have sailed into it. The effect produced by the contrast between the rugged, iron, sterile coast beheld from the sea, and the loveliness of deep blue water and summer islands richly wooded, and green hills sloping to the water's edge, and sandy creeks, with the heavy bush to the right, and the tropical splendour of vegetation that meets the eye upon the outlying land—all which form the noble bay into which you pass through the narrowest and most repellent of headlands—is not to be described. One might think that Nature had stooped to the human device of a pantomimic surprise, and reared the bleak Australian coast in this latitude for no other reason than to give effect to the grand transformation scene she exhibits behind it.

To the eyes of Holdsworth, wearied by the eternal glancing or leaping of the sea, how sweet and refreshing were the green shores, the houses peeping out here and there upon the outskirts of the bush, the trees overhanging the margin of the islands like living things never weary of admiring their own shapes! Here and there a boat rowed from shore to shore. Small coasters lay at anchor, their sails clewed up but not furled, and the men lounging drowsily aboard of them. Hark to the humming of the locusts!—comparable to nothing so much as the murmurs of a sleepy congregation reciting the responses in church.

Anon the city of Sydney opened; at its foot a great semicircular basin of water, with the masts of many vessels standing out against the farther houses, and the green hills backing all. How picturesque from a distance the combined colours of the streaming flags, the white-fronted houses, the green of the hills, and the heavenly azure of the sky! All the way on the left ran the houses into the country beyond, and close at hand were shaggy abutments of wooded land, with deep shady recesses through which the sunlight sparkled on the emerald ground, with many boats upon the water to give variety and life to the picture. Far, far away, almost like an echo from the old world, the strains of a band playing a hearty English melody could be heard.

No thoughtful man can behold such a colony as this without finding something at once pathetic and inspiring in the spectacle. A great rugged continent, lying hidden in the distant Pacific main, is encountered by

human enterprise; and in a few years we witness towns
and cities thronging its seaboard, and all along the surf-
beaten shores is heard the hum of industry. We mark
the inalienable love of home, of the mother-country, in
a thousand tokens, and find the measureless ocean
bridged by sympathy and memory, and Old England
renewed in such forms as make us scarcely conscious
of our distance from it; though sometimes thought itself, when the thousand leagues of waters that flow
between are remembered, seems almost powerless to
present our beloved home to us as something real, so
vague, so dim, so inaccessibly remote has it become
since we left its shores. Signs of remembered things
are about us. We think of the home love which gave
that name to that street; which reared yonder house
in the likeness of one in the far-off land, that enshrines
the emigrant's most precious memories of childhood;
which parcelled out yonder garden in the fashion of the
little tract of land in the distant country, whose soil is
sacred to the mind as the favoured retreat of a beloved
parent. The very nomenclature by which the colonist
dignifies some mean spot or small building by the name
of a noble city or a spacious edifice in the old home, is
full of pathos, since it can signify no more than a deep-
rooted affection (not to be weakened nor divorced by
the harshest recollection of the impracticable struggle for
bread which drove whole families across the sea) for
England, and a tender impulse to give permanent form
to memories which survive through many generations,
and create loyalty and patriotism among a people who
owe nothing to the country and the sovereign whom
they reverence, and would at any moment serve.
British faces are around us; British accents sound in

our ears; and on all sides we behold signs of that British courage, audacity, and genius, which grow sublime under our gathering appreciation of the difficulties which have been conquered and the triumphs which have been achieved.

CHAPTER XIX.

In the year 1832, within a week or two of the date that would make the time exactly five years since the "Meteor" lay off Gravesend, waiting to embark her captain and start for the port it was her doom never to reach, a large ship was sailing slowly up the river, her poop crowded with passengers, and many heads ranged along her bulwarks.

Far away aft, hard by the wheel, stood a man thickly bearded, dressed in dark clothes, his arms folded, and his eyes bent steadfastly upon the passing shore. He was alone; for the rest of the passengers, of whom there were many, were grouped about the break of the poop talking to one another excitedly, or pointing to the houses ashore, or watching the steerage passengers on the main-deck cording their boxes, cramming their clothes into bundles, and making preparations for landing that afternoon.

There was something in the expression of this man's face which would have attracted and detained your attention; a mixture of profound melancholy and struggling surprise, clouded with what might have passed very well for a mood of deep abstraction. His features were thin and haggard, the nose pinched and white, his eyes dark and gleaming, and sunk in hollows, shagged by eyebrows of black hair mingled with white, which met in a perpendicular seam in his forehead.   He presented the appearance of one suffering from some incurable constitutional malady which had wasted the flesh off his bones, arched his back, hollowed his chest, and brought into his face a permanent expression of mingled pensiveness and sorrow.

A round-faced, brisk, and busy-looking little man happening just then to pop his person out through the companion, stood looking awhile at the shore with eager twinkling eyes, and then, directing his gaze aft, caught sight of our lonely individual and approached him.

"Ah, Mr. Hampden! there you are! still puzzling, puzzling, eh?" he exclaimed in a hearty manner. "Come now, you have seen Folkestone, Margate, the Reculvers, eh, now? Confess that those places have helped you to remember all you want to know."

The person addressed as Mr. Hampden, but whom we will continue to call by his proper name of Holdsworth, turned his eyes from the shore and answered with an effort, as though he could not at once break away from his thoughts.

"I know all those places well; and there's not a house yonder, I may say, that doesn't assure me I am on familiar ground. But they tell me nothing. My past is still a puzzle, doctor, of which these scenes are only fragments. There are many more things to come before I can piece it into a whole."

"What *is* a cure for a decayed memory? what *ought* to revive old impressions?" exclaimed the little doctor, hammering a snuff-box with his knuckles. "You'll never know, Mr. Hampden, how you have weighed upon my mind. I feel, sir, that I have no business to let you quit this ship uncured. And yet, what more than I have done *can* I do? I have exhausted my imagination in questions."

"Yes, doctor, you have been very kind, and I thank you heartily for the interest you have taken in me."

"Ay, but interest is of no professional use," returned the doctor, sniffing up a huge pinch of snuff. "We look to results in our calling. I must say I should like to have been able to tell Mr. Sherman when I get back that I left you remembering everything. Eh, now? But I don't believe there's a medical man living who ever encountered such a case as yours. So much density of mental gloom, sir, seems psychologically impossible. If you could only have given me one end of the thread, so to speak, I might have drawn the whole skein out smooth. Look about you now. Here is genuine Thames scenery, which, if you are an Englishman, ought to go home straight to your heart and recall a thousand matters."

Holdsworth stared around him, puzzling and biting his lip.

"I have often felt, and I feel now," he exclaimed, "that if I could see something which was prominently identified with my past my memory would return. When we were off Margate, I grew breathless—breathless, doctor, believe me, under the shock of an indefinable sensation. I made sure that my memory was about to rush upon me—oh! it is impossible to explain what is inexplicable to myself. But there have been moments, since we first entered the river, when I have felt that a revelation was close at hand—and I have trembled whilst awaiting the flooding in of memory, which will not come—which *will* not come !"

"It *will* come. The power that you possess to remember the names and qualities of things which you see, has long ago persuaded me that your memory is not dead, but torpid. Keep your body up, when you get ashore, with nourishing food. Walk the streets constantly and use your eyes, and, when a recollection rises to the surface, don't rush upon it voraciously, but leave it to its own will. Consider, memories are nothing but shadows; you can't dodge and drive them into corners . . . "

Here somebody called to him, on which the little man shook Holdsworth's hand, and darted towards the group of passengers.

The ship was rapidly nearing Gravesend, where she would disembark her passengers. The Thames looked noble, with many vessels of all shapes and sizes breaking its shining waters, with the houses and wharves ashore, with here and there a short wooden pier running into the stream, and the green summer country smiling beyond.

It was a bright July morning, and the air had an exquisite transparency that so clarified and sharpened the outlines of objects, that it was like looking at them through highly-polished glass. Just such a day should greet all homeward-sailing ships, and make their inmates merry with a foretaste of the shore-life they are to enjoy after their long strife with the distant treacherous ocean.

Anon Gravesend opened, and then the pilot volleyed some quick orders along the ship. Down rattled staysails, and jibs, and yards with their spacious breadths of canvas ; and the stately vessel, denuded of her towering costume, swam lazily into position off the town. Then rose a cry, "Stand clear of the chain-cable !" and the second mate, on the port side of the topgallant forecastle, brandished his arms as a warning to the people on the main-deck to crowd out of the road.

"Let go the anchor !"

Clank ! clank ! went the carpenter's hammer. And then, with a deafening roar, down plunged the mighty weight of iron, and tore the huge cable with shrieks through the hawse-pipe. The ship swung slowly around and became stationary, with many hands aloft furling the sails, and the quarter-deck throbbing with the movements and struggles of excited passengers.

And now a dozen boats, some large some small, came tearing through the water to the ship. How the watermen pulled ! Their faces all veins, and their arms all knots, and their hats anywhere ! The canoes of cannibals, sneaking from the secret creeks and hidden points of an unexplored island, advance not more swiftly, nor, maybe, with feller or more rapacious designs, upon the intruder in their waters, than did our Gravesend wherries upon this ship fresh from Australia.

Many of the watermen were soon upon the quarter-deck, demanding monstrous sums to row three-quarters of a mile. You saw boxes and bundles seized and disappear, and excited 'tween-deck passengers elbowing a lane to the gangway, fired with a resolution to disembark or perish, while children screamed, and women implored, and men gesticulated, and even menaced one another. One by one the wherries put off, loaded to the gunwale with people and baggage. These wherries returned and returned again, until the ship was cleared of the majority of her passengers.

" Good-bye, captain," said Holdsworth.

A sunburnt man in a blue cloth coat with gilt-buttons took Holdsworth's hand, and grasped it cordially.

" Good-bye, Mr. Hampden, good-bye to you, sir. Any time these three months, if you have a mind to let me see your face, you will be able to find me out by calling at the Jerusalem Coffee House. I shall be glad, sir, as we all of us shall be, to hear that London has stirred up your recollection and restored your memory."

Then the chief mate and second officers and some midshipmen pressed forward and shook his hand, and Holdsworth, pointing out his luggage to a waterman, descended the gangway ladder, and was rowed to Gravesend.

And now, whilst our hero, having been put ashore and eaten a hurried dinner, climbs on top of the coach that is to land him at Southwark, let us beguile an uninteresting interval by casting a brief glance backwards.

On the arrival of the " Jessie Maxwell " at Sydney, Holdsworth had accompanied Mr. Sherman to his house, and been then and there established as an inmate as long as he chose to remain. He was also given a clerkship in Mr. Sherman's office, worth £250 a year, which was by no means an out-of-the-way price for a man's labour in Australia in those days, though in Holdsworth's case the salary was rendered nearly worth as much again by his friend providing him with board and lodging free. The truth was (1) Mr. Sherman wanted an honest man in his office; (2) Holdsworth's sufferings, friendlessness, and perfect amiability, coupled with his deprivation of memory, which affected all whom he conversed with as something worse even than blindness, had obtained a permanent hold for him on his generous patron's sympathy long before the "Jessie Maxwell" had sighted the Australian shore.

Mr. Sherman was a widower and childless. A maiden sister of his lived with him, a woman whose character and face were as like his as an egg is to an egg. Not knowing Holdsworth's name, they agreed to call him Mr. Hampden, which would serve as well as any other, and which had at least the merit of beginning with the letter of his real name.

As Mr. Hampden he was introduced to Mr. Sherman's friends, who took a very great interest in him. Indeed, some of these people went to the extent of giving dinner-parties in his honour, and for a time he was a lion. All this attention, meant in perfect kindness, greatly disturbed him, for his loss of memory made him singularly sensitive, and his nervous system had entirely given way under the extraordinary sufferings he had endured. Mr. Sherman would have kept his secret, but Captain Duff and the officers and men of the "Jessie Maxwell" went and talked of him all over the city, and then the tale of his discovery and rescue was published in a newspaper and made the property of the public.

But the public soon forgot him. The colony was young, and the New Hollander had too many mines to sink, and houses to build, and acres to clear, and convicts to protest against, and home oppressions of every species to deal with, to keep his mind long fixed on one object. Holdsworth settled into a regular clerkly routine, and every day improved himself in Mr. Sherman's opinion, by the peculiar sweetness of his amiability, and by his gratitude expressed in every delicate form that could vehicle the emotion of his full heart.

There was an able doctor at that time practising in Sydney, and Mr. Sherman invited him to his house, and introduced him to Holdsworth, believing that, by skilful handling, it was possible to restore the poor fellow's memory. But the doctor after a few weeks shook his head, and pronounced the case hopeless, or at least beyond the reach of human skill.

Indeed, rarely had a more curious and baffling problem been submitted, than Holdsworth's mind in those days.

Here was a man capable of recollecting with precision every incident that had befallen him since his rescue, exhibiting shrewdness in conversation, and accuracy in matters of current fact. His intellect was as healthy as that of the healthiest-headed man who conversed with him, but up to the period of his rescue everything was in darkness. The conjectures which were offered him—so close to the mark some of them, that they brushed the very skirts of real facts, and told the truth by implication — conveyed no ideas. His eternal rejoinder was no more than a shake of the head. Had he been a sailor? Did he remember the port from which he sailed? the rig or name of the vessel? his native town? Such questions, and hundreds of them, were asked, but though he grasped familiar names with almost passionate eagerness, they established no faintest clue as to his real past. And then inquiries becoming at last no better than fruitless importunities, were dropped, and Holdsworth was considered incurable.

Yet this could hardly have been thought, had those who gave in this opinion been conscious of the undercurrent of secret, but not the less powerful, yearnings, absolutely objectless, scarce owning definite forms, which yet the restless instincts of the man urged with greedy emphasis. .These movements were, indeed, purely spiritual—the action of the soul groping in her cell and searching for that window of the mind which had been blackened, and through which no light could break. Of the mental torments this intellectual blindness occasioned, no words that I possess can describe the anguish. Month after month went by and still found him searching heart-brokenly in the gloom for some image, some substance, some sign, that should appease the piteous cravings of his instincts, *which knew all, but could not speak.*

Whatever feminine tact could suggest to give light to his mind, Mr. Sherman's sister did. She made out a long list of names beginning with H, trusting that one among them might be his, and that the sight of it would recall many things or all.

But, long and patiently compiled as the list was, many names there must be which she would omit; and amongst them his own. Then she made out a list of the names of the ships; but here was an endless job, prosecuted for a long while with benevolent industry, and then abandoned in despair. She read the European papers carefully, hoping to find some account of the loss of the vessel in which, it was surmised, Holdsworth had been a passenger; but no such account ever rewarded her search. Numerous were the other remedies she resorted to, but none of them produced any result.

A few months of such unavailing work would soon extinguish hope. Both she and her brother desisted at last from their merciful endeavours in the full and final conviction that nothing but the hand of God could ever draw aside the black curtain that hung over Holdsworth's past.

But not to dwell at needless length upon this part of the story:

More than four years had passed since Holdsworth had arrived in Sydney. Mr. Sherman had long learned to think of him as settled in the colony, had increased his salary, and congratulated himself not only on the possession of a valuable and trustworthy assistant, but upon a pleasant, amiable, and thoroughly gentlemanly companion. No expression of a wish to leave had ever escaped Holdsworth's lips. He appeared not only contented, but resigned to the affliction that had practically deprived him of all knowledge of his past existence.

He came down to breakfast one morning with a face betokening great agitation. Mr. Sherman was in the breakfast-room, and instantly noticed Holdsworth's air of bewilderment and distress.

"Mr. Sherman," exclaimed Holdsworth at once to him, "do you remember telling me that it was possible for my memory to be revived by a dream?"

"Yes—has it happened?"

"I cannot tell; but this much I know, that a voice sounded last night in my ears, and bade me return at once to England. It was a woman's voice—it had a clearly-remembered tone—and I knew it in my sleep; but when I awoke and tried to recall it I could not."

"But your dream?"

"That was all."

"Was your dream merely confined to the utterance of this voice?"

"I can remember nothing more than the voice."

" And you cannot recall whose voice it resembled ?"
" No."

Mr. Sherman was silent, and Holdsworth watched
him with anxiety, that was almost pathetic, so eager
was his hope that his friend would find some light in
this dim and curious night-fancy to help him with.

" I can see nothing serviceable in this," said Mr.
Sherman presently, " but it is hopeful. Wait a while.
This voice may return, or you may dream something
more tangible. Remember," he added with a smile, " that
the morning light does not flood the world suddenly.
The pale, faint gray comes first, and there are many
gradations of brightness between the first peep of dawn
and the rising of the sun."

But though Holdsworth waited, the voice did not
return. Nevertheless it had sounded in his ears to some
purpose. Day by day a longing grew in him to return
to England, which became in time deep and fervent and
irresistible. Superstition was the root of this yearning ;
but the poor fellow, urged by his instincts into an eternal
searching amid the darkness, would scarcely pause to
consider the nature of his keen desire, but submit to it
as an ordinance from God commissioned to impel him
into the Divine light of memory.

Mr. Sherman watched his increasing restlessness in
silence, waiting for him to declare his intention. He
announced it one day.

" Mr. Sherman, I feel guilty of deep ingratitude in
harbouring a wish to leave you. But my longing to
return to England has become so strong that I can no
longer resist it. God knows if I am not taking a foolish
step in voluntarily quitting so good and beloved a friend.
But what are these instincts which govern me ? Ought

I to blind myself to them?   Are they not given me for
some end which can only be accomplished by my obeying them?   I do not know what I am leaving you to
seek ; but I *feel* that whatever my past may hold which
is precious to me is to be found in England."

"If you have this confidence in your impulse,"
answered Mr. Sherman, "you are right in obeying it.
I am at least sure that your memory stands but a poor
chance of recovery in a strange land, surrounded by
objects which have no possible reference to your past,
and can, therefore, have no value as an appeal.   I shall
be sorry, very sorry, to lose you, Mr. Hampden, but I
think I can trace the hand of Providence in this longing
of yours, and in all humbleness and sincerity I ask God
to bless your endeavours and restore you the illumination
of your memory."

This resolution, now taken, was final.   Mr. Sherman's encouragement gave new strength to Holdsworth's
wishes, and the restlessness that beset him became almost
unbearable to him.   In ten days from that date a ship
named the "Wellington" sailed for London ; she was
to carry many passengers, but one saloon berth was still
vacant, and that Mr. Sherman himself procured and
paid for, for Holdsworth.   Nor did his kindness stop
with this.   A few days before the ship left Sydney he
asked Holdsworth if he had saved any money.

"Yes, four hundred pounds."

"Come ! that will help you along for a time.   Dr.
Marlow, a friend of mine, is attending an old lady to
England.   I have explained your case to him, and
begged him to give you his closest attention.   He is
clever, and the long term of intimacy you will enjoy
before you reach London may be productive of some

good to you. And now do me the favour to put this in your pocket," he continued, handing Holdsworth a little parcel. " No need to examine its contents now. It is a small gift from my sister and myself. You will find my address inside it, which will remind you to write to us ; for be sure that nobody can take more interest in you than we do. Above all, remember that if ever you should want a friend, you will find two very steadfast ones in Sydney, who will rejoice to welcome you back."

The parcel contained bank-notes to the value of three hundred pounds.

CHAPTER XX.

In the fine old times—the good old times—a short journey took a long time ; and it was evening when the Gravesend coach put Holdsworth down at the door of an old inn in Southwark named the "Green Dragon."

He was now in London, but in an unfamiliar part of it, and he stood for some minutes gazing up and down the wide long street, with its hurrying crowds, and thronging vehicles, and endless shops, without getting one idea more from it than ever he had got out of Pitt Street or George Street, or any other street in Sydney.

It mattered little to him where he should sleep that night. He had as yet formed no plans as to how he should act with respect to beginning the inquiries which were to give him back his life's history. So he entered the bar of the "Green Dragon" and asked for a bedroom, with which he was at once accommodated.

On descending the stairs he was encountered by a very polite waiter, who begged to receive his orders for refreshments. The house was a very old-established one, and the waiter, with a smile of concern, as though the necessity were a melancholy one that obliged him to suggest such obvious truths at that time of day, ventured to observe that the gentleman might travel the whole breadth and length of the United Kingdom without meeting with better wines and choicer cooking than were to be found at that inn. On the strength of this and a small appetite Holdsworth ordered supper, and was conducted to the coffee-room, where he seated himself, the only occupant of the dark bare apartment, at a table furnished with a mustard-pot large enough to have supplied a hospital with poultices, and amused himself as best he could with staring at some grisly, faded prints after Hogarth, and a map of London, to which several generations of flies had contributed squares, streets, and blind alleys nowhere to be found in the metropolis proper.

Having eaten his supper, he was leaning back in his chair, with a half resolution in his mind to stroll forth into the streets for an hour, and see what suggestions his wanderings might obtain for him, when the waiter came up, and leaning confidentially upon the table, informed him that there was an " 'Armonious Meeting going on in the public room at the bottom of the passage, and if the gentleman liked, the sperits he was pleased to horder could be served him there."

" Who are they ?" asked Holdsworth.

" All sorts, sir. The 'armony is done by some gents as lives in the neighbourhood, who look in every Wednesday night to drink and converse. The governor takes the chair, and every gent as is stoppin' in the house is made welcome. I think you'll be pleased, sir."

" This is dull enough, at all events," said Holdsworth, looking around him. It was too early to go to bed, and he felt too tired to take his half-projected stroll. So, conceiving that a quarter of an hour's inspection of the convivialists in the public room might cheer him up, he rose and followed the waiter down the passage.

The scene into which he was admitted certainly
wanted no feature of liveliness.   The room was long and
low pitched, with two immense grates in it, and wooden
mantelpieces carved into all kinds of quaint embodi-
ments of Greek and Roman mythology.   Common brass
sconces were affixed to the walls with a couple of candles
in each.   Around were pictures of fighting and theatrical
celebrities of that and an earlier day ; Humphreys and
Mendoza, stripped to the waist, and working into each
other's eyes in wonderful style, watched by a distant
and pensive crowd in hats of the Tom and Jerry school,
uncomfortably tight breeches, and coat collars above
their ears ; Kemble in furs ; Incledon dressed as a
sailor ; Braham, as little Isaac, in the "Duenna ;" and
Dicky Suett, with a thing like a balloon coming out of
his mouth, and "Oh la !" written upon it.   At the head
of a long table sat a stout man in a striped yellow
waistcoat, a bottle green coat, and a white neckcloth ;
several black bottles, steaming jugs, and a plate of
lemons were in front of him.   And down the table on
either side were seated a number of individuals, some
of them dressed in extravagant style, a few clad soberly,
and most of them smoking cigars, or rapping snuff-boxes,
laughing, talking, and drinking from fat one-legged
tumblers.

As Holdsworth entered, either a speech, a song, or a
sentiment had just been delivered, for there was a great
hammering going on, mingled with cries of "Bravo !"
The "cheer," who was the promoter of, and the sole
gainer by these Wednesday festivities, bowed to Holdsworth, and getting on to his legs, came round and bade
him welcome in the name of all the good fellows there
and then assembled, and gave him the sign, which

Holdsworth, not having been made, did not take. He then led him to a vacant chair between two of the more soberly clad of the company, and having received and transmitted his commands to the waiter with a host-like and hospitable air, as though such a low arrangement as a reckoning had no existence, resumed his place at the head of the table, knocked loudly with his knuckles, and called upon Mr. Harris for a song.

On this, up started a thin young man with a yellow beard, and, leaning on his hands, gazed slowly around him with a leering and perfectly self-possessed bloodshot eye. Whereat there was a laugh.

"Gentleman!" he began.

"Order! silence!" cried the landlord. "Mr. 'Arris has your ear!"

"And I wish I could say ladies: I am asked to sing a song, and I'll do so with the greatest of pleasure. But before I begin, permit me to make an observation; as I don't want to wound any gentleman's feelings, though no fear of that kind will prevent me from expressing my sentiments, which are those of a Briton and a reformer, who has no opinion of the present, looks upon the past with contempt, and only lives for the future."

"Hear!" from several reformers.

"There's a good deal to be said against this age; and there's no abuse which the past don't deserve! The past! gentlemen, it did for our grandmothers. The present! it does for our fathers. But we, gentlemen— we who possess young and ardent minds——"

"Give us your song!" cried a voice.

"We, gentlemen—we, the young blood of this great nation—we," cried the orator, swinging his fist, and nearly knocking a cigar out of the mouth of a man at his side, with a face on him filled with idiotic admiration, "are for the future!"

An old man uttered a cheer; the speaker then coughed, swallowed a draught of brandy-and-water, expanded his chest, ran his fingers through his hair, and began as follows, throwing out his arms in approved comic style :—

THE DAYS WHEN I WAS YOUNG.

Of the days when I was young, sir,
  Sing the splendour and the fame,
When the fields and woods among, sir,
  Traps were set to guard our game ;
When our clergymen got drunk, sir,
  And our Prince was made of waistcoats,
When our soldiery had spunk, sir,
  And wore epaulets and faced coats.
      Chorus—Sing the days when I was young !
        Such a song was never sung !

When Madeira, port, and sherry
  Were such wines as made men wits :
When our songs were coarse and merry,
  And our pockets full of writs !
When we fought like hungry Spartans,
  And told tales like Jemmy Twitcher's ;
When cognac was drunk in quarterns,
  And October ale in pitchers !
          Sing the days, etc.

When the House was full of quarrels,
  And our hustings the arenas
For dead cats and bilious morals
  And the music of hyenas !
When our Avershaws were strangling,
  And our Mrs. Frys were preaching :
And our priests and bishops wrangling,
  And our patriots a-screeching !
          Sing the days, etc.

When a Tory *was* a Tory,
    Armour'd tight in old tradition,
Quoting nothing but the hoary,
    And a friend to superstition :
Hating Irishmen and priests, sir,
    All excisemen and dissenters,
Holy fasts and holy feasts, sir,
    Whigs and Jews and ten-pound renters !
               Sing the days, etc.

When our fiddlers were true artists,
    And our singers all had voices :
Ere our labourers were Chartists,
    And the land was full of noises.
When our "bloods" were breaking knockers,
    Smashing bells all free and hearty,
And when little else could shock us
    But reports of Bonaparte.
               Sing the days, etc.

When our coaches turn'd us over,
    And our watchmen snored in alleys :
When it took a day to Dover,
    And a week or two to Calais.
When Jack Ketch was hanging women
    Who stole bread for starving babies,
And our rogues were just as common
    As new honey in old May bees.
               Sing the days, etc.

Never more shall we survey, sir,
    Times so splendid and so stirring,
Social life and tastes more gay, sir,
    Laws and statesmen more unerring.
Fights and factions more unsparing,
    Tories truer to traditions,
Foreign policy more daring——

(Here the vocalist took a deep breath),

    And more brutal superstitions !

The sounds excited by this song were somewhat
discordant, owing to the bravos being mingled with

Q

hisses. Mr. Harris resumed his seat with a contempt-
uous expression, and the chairman, rapping the table,
called out:

"Gentlemen! 'issing isn't 'armony to any ear but a
goose's!"

"I don't like the sentiments of that song," exclaimed
a man at the bottom of the table.

"Why not, sir?" demanded Mr. Harris, warmly.

"First of all, I don't understand 'em," said the
other.

"Oh!" said Mr. Harris with a sneer.

"Much of what that song says is to be applied to
the present as well as to the past," observed an old
gentleman, looking staggered at his own boldness in
talking amid a silence. "For my part, I don't think a
man fights fair who uses a two-edged sword."

Several voices murmured acquiescence.

"I'm for the future," said Mr. Harris, "and told you
so at the beginning."

"See here, gentlemen," called out the landlord; "the
meaning of Mr. Harris's song, so far as I understand its
hallusions, is this: he supposes himself to be old——"

"No, I don't," growled Mr. Harris.

"Quite the contrary, *I* think," snarled a little grocer
near the chairman. "I reckon there's more swaddling-
clothes nor expirience in *them* sentiments, or I'm gone
deaf since I sat down."

"The meaning of my song is just what it says,"
retorted Mr. Harris. "I'm not ashamed of being a reformer. Better men than I or any other gentleman in
this room, begging *nobody's* pardon, have been reformers.
Thank God, my politics are not of a kind to call up my
blushes when I own them."

As the Tories in the company judged that something offensive was meant by Mr. Harris, several persons spoke at once, and a clamour ensued which threatened to establish the meeting on any other basis than that of harmony. Indeed, one man, who was nearly intoxicated, went so far as to get upon his chair and exclaim, while he brandished his fist, that if he had it in his power, he would hang every Whig in the country. And there is no telling what further extravagances of language and gesture he might have indulged in, but for the prompt interference of a neighbour, who, catching hold of his coat-tail, pulled him under the table.

However, by dint of shouting pacific language at the top of his voice, the chairman succeeded at last in restoring tranquillity. More grog was brought in, snuff-boxes were handed about, hands were shaken across the table, and loud cheers greeted the sentiment delivered by a gentleman who appeared to be vice-chairman: "That 'armony of feeling was the music of humanity." Mr. Harris apologised for having sung anything distasteful to the company, who he hoped were all his very good friends; and amid the clanking of spoons in glasses, and polite calls of "After you" for lighted spills, the conversation streamed into milder channels, and everybody did his best to look harmonious.

Though Holdsworth was a good deal amused by this scene, and by the manners and dress of the people around him, he hardly felt himself equal to enduring very much more of this social harmony, and sat twisting his glass on the table, watching the faces of the company, and waiting for another "row" to make his escape without attracting notice.

He was presently addressed by a man sitting on his

left—a middle-aged individual, with a thin, smooth-shaven face and a keen eye, and very high shirt-collars.

"A stranger, I make bold to think, sir?"

"Yes," answered Holdsworth.

"I judge so by an air of travel about you, if you'll pardon me. Forgive me, sir, if I inquire your secret—understand me—your secret opinion as to that song just sung by the gentleman opposite."

"To tell you the truth," replied Holdsworth, who imagined that his companion wanted to draw him into a political argument, "I only caught a few of the verses, and am therefore scarcely able to give an opinion."

"Humph!" exclaimed the other. "Now, sir, *I* call that song clever—damned clever, and I'll tell you why: it's ironical. Without irony, sir, I wouldn't give a pin's head for the best piece of humour in the world. You'll excuse what I am about to say, sir, I'm sure. You are a traveller—I flatter myself I can tell that with half an eye. Now, sir, as a man who has visited other countries, and observed human nature in a hundred different forms, you can't help being a Whig. Confess, sir, that you share my political views, which are those of a man who has only one cry—'Down with rubbish!'"

"I hate rubbish as much as any man," replied Holdsworth.

His companion looked struck and delighted.

"Your hand, sir. Permit me to shake it. I love a Whig, sir. Here's to your good health."

"Are you a native of this country, sir?" he continued, glancing at Holdsworth's dress, which had a decidedly colonial cut.

"I believe so."

" But not a resident ?" said the other, whose turn of mind was decidedly inquisitive.

" No."

" Now what part might you have come from, sir, if you'll excuse the liberty ?" asked the man confidently.

" From Australia."

" God bless my heart and soul ! You don't say so ! Dear me ! Australia ! Is it possible ? I consider myself a bit of a traveller ; but in your presence, sir, I feel my insignificance."

Holdsworth laughed, but made no answer.

" They say that Australia is a wonderful country, sir : that you grow cherries with the stones outside, and that your parrots are like sea-gulls. Fine climate though, I believe, sir, if you will pardon me ?"

" Very fine."

" And yet not equal to ours ?"

" Perhaps not."

" They talk of scenery, sir. Now I was never out of England in my life, though there's not a hole or corner in it that I don't know. But what can equal English scenery ? Take Devonshire. Take Cumberland. Were you ever in those counties ?"

" Never."

" Yorkshire ?"

" No."

" Talk of desolation—see the moors : great plains of the colour of tripe stretching for miles, with one dwarf tree for every league of ground, and that's all. Now, sir, my taste may be wrong, or perhaps it's right ; I wouldn't flaunt it in any man's face, though I'd hold on to it if I was on my death-bed. Of all the counties in England, which think you I'm the most partial to ?"

" I cannot imagine."

" Kent, sir !" exclaimed the man, drawing back triumphantly.

The name sent a thrill through Holdsworth. He pricked his ears and looked at his companion earnestly.

"The Devonshire people may crack up their county, but give *me* Kent. I am a native of Kent, sir !"

" Indeed !"

" I was born at Canterbury. Ever seen the cathedral ?"

" Canterbury Cathedral !" muttered Holdsworth, struggling to grasp an illusive, half-formed fancy that flitted across his mind.

" Take the country about Hanwitch, now . . ."

"Hanwitch!" echoed Holdsworth. The name pierced him as a sword might. He pressed his fingers tightly over his eyes, his face turned white, and his whole body trembled.

His companion stared at him.

"Do you know Hanwitch ?" he asked, wondering if this singular-looking person with the haggard face, Australian clothes, and thick beard was in possession of his right mind.

"The name struck me," answered Holdsworth, removing his hands and frowning in his effort to master tho meaning of tho extraordinary emotion excited by the name of that town.

"There's not a spot of land anywhere within thirty miles of Canterbury all round," continued the man, looking at Holdsworth watchfully, "that I don't know. I name Hanwitch because there's a bit of river scenery near it which is prettier than anything I've seen in any other part of England. If you've got the leisure, and would like to see what this country can show in the way of good views, take a run down to Hanwitch."

He pulled out a pocket-book, and extracting a card, handed it to Holdsworth, observing in a tone that at least showed he had regained his confidence in his neighbour:

"Show that, sir, at the bar of the 'Three Stars' at Hanwitch, and if you don't get every attention, be good enough to write to me, and see if they don't lose my patronage."

Holdsworth looked at the card, whereon he might have seen a very commonplace name, printed in capitals, with "Commercial Traveller" squeezed into the corner; but he saw nothing. A name had been pronounced which quickened the dormant memory in him into a vitality that threatened to make it burst through the shell that imprisoned it, and proclaim all that he passionately longed to know.

Powerless must his mind have been not to find in the name of the Hanwitch inn the magic to give him back his memory. Could not his heart recall the sweet day he had spent in Hanwitch with Dolly at his side? —the sweetest, happiest day of all the days he had passed in the brief three months during which they had been together? One might have thought that, saving her own dear face, there was nothing more potent to roll back the deep mantle of darkness, and lay bare the shining panorama of those far-off times, than the name of the inn in whose deep bay window they had sat linked in each other's arms, watching the soft sunshine shimmering through the summer leaves, and the clear river wandering gently along its emerald-banked channel

Further conversation was out of the question for a while, by the chairman hammering on the table and calling silence for a song. The disagreeable effects produced by the last song had completely passed away, and the landlord thought that another "ditty," as he called it, might safely be sung.

A very corpulent man stood up, with a face upon him of which the quantity of flesh had worked the expression into an aspect of fixed amazement. An immense blue-spotted cravat adorned his throat, and long streaks of hair fell slanting down his cheeks. His small clothes and arm-sleeves were distressingly tight, and suggested that any display of pathos or humour, of gesticulation or laughter, would be in the highest degree inconvenient. It was not hard to guess that this fat man sang comic songs, that he dropped *every* h, and that he was in the eating-line, in a commercial sense.

He was saluted with a round of laughter, which, being hammered down, he began in a soft, oily, tenor voice—

> " A dawg's-meat man he loved a voman,
> Sairey her name vos—not uncommon ;
> He had vun eye, and he hown'd a barrer.
> Coopid up's vith his bow and lets fly a arrer.
> ' O dear !' cries this dawg's-meat man,
> Fingerin' his buzzum and looking vith his eye ;
> ' Vot can this be a-sticking in my tan ?'
> Ven Sairey draws near a-lookin' very shy.
> ' Tell me,' sez he, ' the name o' this here thing ?'
> ' Vy,' sez Sairey vinkin', ' it's vun o' Coopid's darts.' "
>   etc.   etc.

This song gave such exquisite satisfaction to the company that, on his concluding it, he was entreated, amid cheers, to sing another; on which, squaring his breast, but preserving his wooden face of fat astonishment, he began as follows:

" There vos a 'ot pieman as vurked in the Strand,
        Singing hey, ho! 'ot pies, all 'ot!
Vun night he was kickin' his 'eels at his stand
Ven who should come up but a lady all grand,
Vith a dress all of satin, and rings on her 'and,
                And she asts for a pie
                Did this lady, oh my!
                Let us cry.
        Singing hey, ho! 'ot pies, all 'ot!

" Now, our friend was genteel, as all piemen should be,
        Singing hey, ho! 'ot pies, all 'ot!
And he sez to this lady, so grand for to see,
'My pies, mum, are meant for sitch people as me,
For poor cabbies and sitch; not for folks of degree,'
                And she jest sez, 'O fie!
                Hand me quickly a pie,
                Or I'll cry.'
        Singing hey, ho! 'ot pies, all 'ot!"

I spare the reader the remaining six verses of this delectable song. The company joined in the chorus with the full force of their lungs, and so exhilarated the fat vocalist, that at the end of the second verse he pushed away his chair, and folding his arms on his breast, actually danced an accompaniment to the words, amid shrieks of laughter and wild stretching forward of necks at the farther end of the table to see him. Holdsworth's companion laughed until he grew faint, and then, to recover his strength, drank brandy and water, and then laughed again. The song was encored, genuine vulgarity seldom failing to please; and then a brief breathing-space of silence falling, Holdsworth said to his companion:

" Will you tell me how I am to get to Hanwitch from here ?"

" Certainly. All you've got to do is, step across to the ' Canterbury Arms '—it's five minutes' walk from this house on the left—the coach starts for Canterbury at half-past seven in the morning, every day."

" Thank you," said Holdsworth, who found it impossible, amid the renewed hubbub of conversation that had burst out, to ask some questions about Hanwitch, which might help him to understand the longing that possessed him to visit it.

" You're not going—the night's very young, sir ?" said the man, seeing Holdsworth rise. But Holdsworth merely wished him " Good night," and slipped out of the room unnoticed by the company, who were at that moment busy in entreating the fat man to give them another song.

The cool air and silence of the passage were a great relief after the heat and noise of the public room. It was now drawing near to eleven o'clock. Holdsworth went to the bar and asked for a candle, and was lighted to his bed-room by a chambermaid with ringlets and black eyes, who probably felt surprised that her charms attracted no notice whatever from the gentleman, who seemed to find pleasure in no other object than the carpet on which he trod.

Holdsworth closed the door, and a whole hour passed before he rose to remove his clothes. There was something in the recollection of the thrill which the name of Hanwitch had sent through him, that impelled him to bend the whole energies of his mind to the word, and he strove with memory passionately and fiercely, but could not wrench a syllable from her. He repeated the name until it lost even its sense as the designation of a town. Nevertheless, every moment made his longing to visit it deeper. There must be *some* reason why this name had so stirred him. The names of other English counties and cities had been pronounced before him and by him over and over again, but they touched no chord, they awoke no echo in his mind, however dim and elusive.

If memory would only define the object he sought! This it would not do. He was a wanderer, obeying the dictation of blind instinct, which urged without guiding him. Of all his past, nothing was present to his mind. He knew not what he sought. His was an affliction crueller than blindness, for a blind man could say: "A beloved one has strayed from me. I seek her. I see not, indeed, those who surround me, but my mission has form and substance in my mind, and my inquiries cannot *always* prove fruitless." But Holdsworth was commanded by a mysterious emotion which controlled without enlightening him. *Something* had been lost— *something* was to be found. He felt his want, but could not explain it to himself. No man could help him, since no man could guess what was the thing he looked for.

When he left his chair he sank upon his knees and asked God in broken tones to help him—to direct him into the path that should lead him to the light—to aid him in his yearning to re-illuminate his memory.

CHAPTER XXI.

FOR HANWITCH.

IF a man has one good reason for being grateful for living in these times, it is because they are *not* coaching days.

The old stage-coach, the Wellerian coachman, the spruce guard with his horn and his jokes, the fat people inside, the gruff people outside, all contributed a picturesque detail to the age they belonged to; but I have generally found that the more picturesque an object is, the fitter it is to be surveyed at a distance only.

If in the days to which the old stage-coach belonged it never rained, it was never cold, one was never in a hurry, there were no missions of life and death to make one curse the delay of a moment—if one's companions were always good-tempered, and one's body was so constituted as to endure jerks and jolts and a sitting posture for hours at a stretch without inconvenience—then the old stage-coach may be conceived to have been a very agreeable means of locomotion. But as I have been informed by several elderly gentlemen that the weather forty years ago was pretty much the same sort of weather that it now is, that strokes of death and strokes of business requiring immense despatch happened then as they

happen every day; in a word, that in most atmospheri-
cal, moral, and civic respects the early years of this
century differed but very little from these its maturer
days, I can only repeat, in spite of the protests of several
venerable friends who seem to find most things (even
whilst enjoying them) objectionable which are not as
aged as themselves, that if we have one excuse better
than another for being on good terms with the times
we live in, it is because the picturesque old stage-coach
makes no condition of our daily existence.

Hanwitch was about fifty miles from London. To-
day a traveller would be carried the distance in about
an hour and three-quarters. Holdsworth, starting at
half-past seven in the morning, would, providing that
the coach did not break down or overturn, reach the
town at about four o'clock in the afternoon.

He awoke at half-past six, and at once rose. The
morning was a bright one, but all the efforts of the
sunshine to squeeze itself through the wire blinds and
dusty panes of the coffee-room windows could not avail
to communicate the faintest spark of cheerfulness to the
dingy apartment, with its bare tables and blue-coloured
looking-glass over the chimney, and the old-fashioned
prints around the walls, suggestive, one knew not why,
of London milk and discoloured blankets.

The waiter came in, looking dejected, limp, and fluey,
and perhaps to pay Holdsworth out for neglecting to
leave word at the bar before going to bed, that he should
want to breakfast at an unreasonable hour, declaimed a
bill of fare, nearly every item of which, as Holdsworth
named it, he declared could not possibly be got ready
before half-past eight. Cold ham and tea must suffice,
with which order the waiter sleepily withdrew, and after

a long absence returned—when Holdsworth was on the point of starting up and leaving the house in the full belief that he should miss the coach—bearing a teapot of which the contents looked like rain-water, a loaf of bread as hard and slippery as glass under the knife, a lump of butter of the colour and perfume of soaked cheese, and a ham of which what was not bone was brine.

Very lightly breaking his fast with these things, Holdsworth called for his bill, and obtaining the services of the Boots to carry his portmanteau, which was all the baggage he had brought with him from Australia, walked to the house from which the Canterbury coach started.

It wanted but ten minutes of the starting-time, but no coach was visible. However, it was up the yard, and would be brought round in a few minutes, the book-keeper said. As these few minutes threatened to expand into half an hour, Holdsworth entered the bar of the "Canterbury Arms" to obtain a biscuit and some brandy-and-water, partly to complete the wretched breakfast he had made, and partly to exterminate the vile flavour of the tea that lingered in his mouth.

When he returned, the coach was out, the horses were in, several passengers were getting into, or climbing on top of, the vehicle; the coachman, muffled about the throat as though the month were November, and the air full of snow, stood on the pavement, smoking a cigar and surveying the whole picture with a lordly and commanding, though a somewhat inflamed eye; and the busy scene was completed by a body of boys and men offering newspapers, walking-sticks, knives, combs, and broad sheets of songs to the passengers, and striving to drown each other's importunities with loud and ceaseless clamour.

Off went the coach at last, with Holdsworth by the coachman's side. The wheels rattled over the hard roads, the houses in long lines swept by, lost by degrees their frowsy exteriors and dingy metropolitan aspects, and attempted little revelations of bucolic life in small gardens, with glimpses of trees in the rear. Then came houses standing alone in grounds of their own, cottages purely pastoral in appearance, with the noise of farmyards about them, and their atmosphere sweetened by the smell of hay and flowers. These dropped away, the breeze grew pure and elastic, the country opened in wide spaces of waving cornfields spotted with bright poppies, and swelling meadow lands and green fields shaded by groups of trees, with here and there a lark whistling in the blue sky, and all London lying behind, marking its mighty presence by a haze that seemed to stretch for miles and miles, and paled the heavens to the hue of its own complexion.

. Holdsworth was such bad company that the coachman soon ceased his "observations" touching the different scenes through which they passed, and addressed himself to his companion on the right, a young gentleman who was going as far as Chatham, and who lighted several large cigars in less than half an hour, pulling at them with hollows in his cheeks, and looking at the ash of them, and preserving a very pale face. Holdsworth had something else to think about than the coachman's refined and classical remarks, delivered from the depth of three shawls. The quick rolling of the coach over the smooth turnpike-road was inducing an exhilaration that acted upon him as good wine acts upon the brain,

giving clearness and freedom to thought, and causing
life to be felt at her most secret sources. There was
the impression in his mind that he had once before
travelled on the top of a stage-coach along this very
road, though when, or under what circumstances, or
whether he had actually performed the journey or had
read of some one else having done it, he could not tell.
The scenery they were travelling through was altogether
delicious, and better than a cordial to a man who had
just landed from a three and a half months' voyage at
sea. The aspect of the country was full of that sober
sweetness of general effect which soothes the heart with
a deep sense of home; of broad yellow tracts burnished
by the sunshine, of the delicate shadowing of green, and
the neutral tint of fallow soil; houses made as dainty
by distance as pictures on ivory; great trees spreading
their broad abundant leaves over cool spaces of gleaming water; with the animation, now and again, of
human life, where men worked in the fields, or where
children sported before the houses, stopping their frolics
to cheer the coach, while women held babies high in
their hands and swayed to the delighted plunging of
the chubby limbs.

Holdsworth, however, was by no means a sample of
the " outsides " carried by the coach, whatever the de-
portment of the invisible " insides " might have been.
There were some half-a-dozen people on the roof, includ-
ing two girls, one of whom was decidedly pretty and the
other decidedly coquettish. These young ladies, at the
first going off, had been ceaseless in the expression of
their fears that, though it was true they were up all
right, they should never be able to get down again. A
gentleman with a turn-up nose, expressive of the utmost

self-complacency, had taken it upon himself to comfort the ladies, by remarking that getting down was in every case easier than getting up, because the natural tendency of the human body was to fall; at which the ladies had murmured "Impertinence!" and "Some people are better seen than heard," and such-like scathing phrases, thereby sanctioning the display of such wit as the turn-up-nosed gentleman possessed, which he exerted with such good effect that the ladies grew crimson under uncontrollable fits of laughter. Then the guard struck in, and provoked the other outsiders to talk; and presently a large flat bottle was handed around, which had the effect of making everybody who put it to his or her lips merrier still. Onwards rattled the coach with its noisy, laughing burden, flinging sounds of life broadcast over the green country, provoking many a pair of slow bucolic eyes to stare it gravely out of sight, raising clouds of dust as the wheels went softly over the floury highway, spinning under mile-lengths of trees darkening the road with twinkling shadows, and throbbing with the piercing shrilling of innumerable birds buried in the dense foliage, catching the hot sunshine again in the open, and gleaming like a gigantic looking-glass as it sped gaily forward under the broad eye of Heaven.

It was two o'clock when they changed horses for the second time at a smart little Kentish town, with a gray ruin right in its midst, and an old church hard by it, with one of the snuggest of rectories peeping at the world out of the silence and shadow of a rich orchard. Some of the "insides" got out here and went their ways, and were no more seen. The young ladies on the roof were entreated to alight by the small-nosed man, but this they noisily refused to do, the mere idea of such a

R

thing causing them to catch hold of each other. The
delay, however, was a short one. The jaded horses,
with streaks of white foam upon their polished hides,
were taken out and fresh ones put in ; the coachman,
smelling strongly of gin and peppermint, climbed into
his place, cracked his whip, and off started the coach,
followed by a crowd of excited boys, who chased it clear
of the town and then threw stones after it.

"Where might you be for, sir ?" inquired the coachman of Holdsworth, speaking out of his stomach like a
ventriloquist.

"Hanwitch."

"Several stoppages afore Hanwitch," said the coachman.

"How many ?"

"Vy, there's Saltwell, Halton, Gadstone, and Southbourne."

"Southbourne ?"

"Yes, Southbourne, of course. That's the willage
jist afore Hanwitch."

"Southbourne ! Southbourne !" repeated Holdsworth,
with the old look of bewilderment that invariably entered
his face when some familiar name was sounded in his ear

The coachman glanced at him over his shawls, and
said to himself, quite in the pit of his stomach. "You're
a rum 'un, you are !"

"P'raps you ar'n't acquainted with the road, sir ?"
said he.

"I think—I am sure I know Southbourne," replied
Holdsworth. "What sort of place is it ?"

"Vot sort o' place ? Vy, a willage."

"But what kind of village ?"

"All that I know is this, there's a hinn there vere

they serves you vith werry good liquor. Blow'd if I can tell you anything furder. But that's my veakness, sir. Vould you believe me, I've drove coaches through that willage for the last two-and-twenty year, and may I be bil'd if I can tell you anything about it."

Holdsworth sank into deep thought, while the coachman, twisting his eyes over his shawls, examined his face and clothes with side-long attention; then his curiosity being evidently aroused by something in Holdsworth's appearance which widely differed from the cut and style of the passengers he was in the habit of carrying, he said :

"Might you be a furriner, sir ?"

"No," answered Holdsworth.

"I've a brother in Californy. P'raps you might know them parts, sir ?"

"I have just returned from Australia."

"Oh !" exclaimed the coachman, looking staggered ; "that's a good vays off ain't it ?"

"The other side of the world."

"Gor bless me ! A queer place, I've heerd. Full of conwicks. One of our guards was sent out there t'other day for abstracting of money from a wallis."

This reference operating upon his sympathies, he entered into a story, as long as a newspaper account, of the trial ; "how beautiful the counsill as hadvocated the pore fellow spoke, vich the court vos crowded vith coachmen, who groaned venhever the hadvocate as vos opposed to the guard began to speak, vich behaviour, though it warn't p'raps quite correck, vasn't to be stopped nohows, although the judge looks werry fierce, and the counsill kep' on sayin', 'My lud, if this here noise ain't stopped, I'll throw the case up,' vich was just the thing the coachmen vanted" (here he made as though he would poke Holdsworth in the ribs with the butt-end of his whip); "but, lor' save yer, it was no go."

Holdsworth paid no attention to this story, his mind being engaged in a desperate struggle with memory. Indeed, the word "Southbourne" had affected him as no other allusion had. Pale, dim phantoms of memory, comparable to nothing so much as the phosphorescent outlines which the eye may mark fluctuating in the black sea-water, rose and sank in his mind; and though whispering nothing to his breathless anxiety, clearly proving that the faculty which he had long believed dead was beginning to stir and awaken.

One by one the towns and villages named by the coachman had been passed, and now Southbourne was to come.

An indescribable anxiety, at once breathless and thrilling, suspending, it seemed to him, the very pulsations of his heart, making his breath come and go in quick, fierce respirations, possessed Holdsworth.

He held his hands tightly clasped; all colour had fled from his face, and his deep-sunk eyes glowed with unnatural fire.

Repeatedly he muttered to himself, "What does this portend?"

Already his prophetic soul had caught the light, and seemed to know herself, and maddened him and wrung his frame with her wild and bitter struggles to proclaim her inspiration and pierce her reflected beam through the film that still blinded the eye of the mind.

The sun was still high, and flung its yellow brilliance over the fair and gilded prospect. The coach had turned the corner of the long road that led straight as an arrow into Southbourne; and far away at the extremity, in mingled shadow and shine, the few houses could be seen, with the spire of St. George's Church rearing high its flaming vane, and on the left the gleam of the river shadowed by many trees.

"There's Southbourne!" said the coachman, pointing with his whip.

The dust whirled in a cloud behind the wheels, the guard sounded his horn, and with a rush and a rattle the coach drew up opposite the "Hare and Hounds," a tavern as familiar to Holdsworth as the sight of his own hand.

"Hullo!" cried the coachman. "Hi, you there! Help! A glass o' brandy! Blowed if the gentleman hasn't fainted!"

"Fainted!" cried the young ladies on the top of the coach, leaning forward to catch a sight of his face.

No, not fainted; but struck down by a revelation such as, had the two young ladies and the small-nosed man and the coachman been told the story of it, would have supplied them with enough matter to keep them talking without intermission as long as the coach-wheels turned.

Memory, coming out of the little house at the bottom of the long familiar thoroughfare, out of the little house that turned its shoulder upon the highway and parted it into lanes, had rushed upon him like an armed man, and struck him a staggering blow. He had dropped under it, and, but for the support of the apron over his knees, would have fallen to the ground.

The guard ran into the tavern and returned with a glass of brandy, which the coachman put to Holdsworth's lips.

"Thank you, I am better now," he exclaimed.

"Glad to hear it," said the coachman.

"I will get down here."

"Aren't you booked for Hanwitch!" exclaimed the guard, who imagined that the gentleman's head wandered.

"No—this will do—I will go no further. Help me with your hand—thank you."

He reached the ground, watched by a group of persons who made a movement as though to support him, when they saw him swaying to and fro like a drunken man, and staring fixedly down the road. But in a moment or two, with a struggle, he stood firm. His portmanteau was handed out and carried into the bar. The guard took his place; the coachman, with a glance over his shawls to see that Holdsworth stood clear of the wheels, jerked the reins, and the coach rattled out of sight.

CHAPTER XXII.

RIGHT in the middle of the road stood Holdsworth, casting his eyes first to the right, then to the left, then letting them rest fixedly on the house at the extremity.

Here was the scene, the place at last, that was to roll back the curtains which hid the past from him, and to proclaim the resurrection of the life within him that for years had slept a sleep as deep as death.

There he stood, brought by God's hand from a far-off world into the little Kentish village, where his memories lay heaped, where association made a beacon of every humble house to lead him with unerring step backward and backward to the sweetest, the dearest of all his memories.

How remembered, how deeply remembered, the scene! The old tavern on the right, with its swinging signboard, its burnished latticed windows, the great elm tree spreading its branches, like soft fingers, over the red-tiled roof; the farmhouse facing it, with the clamour of hidden poultry all about it, softened by the cooing of doves; and the cherry and apple trees stretching forth their fruit over the wooden railing, and the strings of white linen drying in the open spaces among the trees; the vista of gable-peaked houses, the old shops, the grassy land between the houses, the blacksmith's shed, the hens in the roadway, the children on the doorsteps, the women working at the open windows, and the little house at the extremity, backed by soft masses of green trees and the delicate blue of the afternoon sky.

He knew his life's history as he surveyed this scene, as though a voice in his ear were whispering it all to him. The chain was too complete not to suggest the unseen links; the throng of associations was too manifold and pregnant not to reveal to his mind the things which his eyes beheld not. Swiftly and fiercely—a very whirlwind of logic—thought flew over each stepping-stone to the hidden past; and then he knew what he had left, what he was now to seek, and what had been the WANT which his instincts—that deeper life of his of which the movements were independent of the senses —had never lost sight of.

When his faintness had passed, a great joy took possession of him—an impulse so keenly exhilarating, that he could have cried aloud in his rapture. But then came a revulsion—a deadly fear—of what he knew not, save that its presence turned him into ice, and damped his forehead with sweat.

He was all unconscious of the eyes that were upon him; but some one approaching made him turn his head, and he saw several persons watching him curiously from the door of the inn, while others, plain country people in smocks and highlows, muttered to one another as they stared from the pavement.

" Won't you please to step in, sir ?" said the man who came forward, a short, square-faced individual, in a black calico apron and a white hat.

" Who lives in that house ?" returned Holdsworth, pointing down the road.

"That one yonder, with the chimbley looking this way? Why, I don't think anybody's living in it just now, although I did hear that it was taken by a party from Ashford.—Emily!" he called.

A stout, well-looking woman elbowed her way out of the tavern, and stood on the lower step.

"The gentleman wants to know who lives in that house at the bottom."

"It's to let. Mr. Markham has the letting of it," answered the woman.

"His is the shop yonder," said the man. "You'll see 'Undertaker and Joiner' wrote over the door."

"I'll send a boy to fetch him, if you like," said the woman.

"I'll goa, missus," remarked an old man in a long blouse, turning about on his stick in his eagerness to earn a glass of yale.

"No, I don't want him," said Holdsworth.

"Won't you step in and rest yourself, sir?" exclaimed the woman, exerting the seductive smile with which she was wont to greet every passenger who stopped at her door.

Holdsworth hesitated a moment, as though there were a magic in the little distant house that constrained him to keep his eyes upon it, and then entered the tavern, heralded by the landlady, and followed by the landlord.

The parlour into which he was conducted was as quiet and private as he could wish, screened by a red curtain across the glass of the door from the bar, with a window opening on to a square of ground well stocked with shrubs and vegetables. The sunshine streamed into the room, and lighted up the queer ornaments on the mantelpiece, the fine old china hanging upon rows

of hooks in a mahogany cabinet, the well-worn carpet,
the velvet sofa, the black bottles and glittering tankards
on the shelves of the sideboard.

The landlord went behind the bar to look after some
besmocked gentry who were drinking in front of it,
leaving his wife to attend to Holdsworth.

"What might you like to order, sir?" she inquired,
presenting herself at a side door.

He asked her to bring him some wine and biscuits,
saying that he had no appetite now, but would dine or
sup later on. He looked at her very attentively as he
spoke, with an idea in his mind that he had seen her
before.

She went away, and he left his seat and paced the
room with a wild look of distress on his face, and bitter
anxiety and fear in his heart. Once he snatched up
his hat and advanced to the door, but hesitated and resumed his agitated walk. His feelings were those of a
man just awakened to consciousness from the effects of a
blow that had stunned him. His body trembled, his lips
worked, and he held his hands squeezed tightly together.
His sufferings were indeed terrible. He looked back
upon the blank of five years and recoiled before the
conjectures his heart prompted as to the things which
had happened in that time. Sometimes his impulse
was to rush forth and cry aloud for Dolly, and then a
deadly chill came over him, and he shut his eyes and
beat aside his thoughts, as though they were something
tangible and apart from him, with his hand.

When the door opened, he bit his lip to control
himself, and kept his back turned upon the woman in
feigned inspection of a print upon the wall. As she
was about to withdraw, he looked at her and said :

" Have you lived long in Southbourne ?"

" Yes, sir, many years."

He seated himself and drank a glass of wine.

" How many years ?"

" Oh, twelve, thirteen. Ah, more like fifteen years, sir !"

" So long ! Then you know all the people here ?"

" Yes, sir, I daresay I do," answered the woman, putting her hands under her apron, and examining Holdsworth's face and clothes with great curiosity.

" Who last lived in that house at the bottom of the street ?"

" You mean the one you was askin' my husband about ?"

" Yes."

" Mr. Fairchild, the butcher, after he sold his business about two years ago."

" Who before Mr. Fairchild ?"

" It stood empty awhile after Mrs. Holdsworth left it."

" Where is she now ?"

" Livin' at Hanwitch, along with her husband, Mr. Conway, the dentist."

The woman's eyes, when she made this answer, were on the garden ; when she looked again at Holdsworth, his face was turned from her.

" Did you know any of the parties, sir, as you're asking about ?" she inquired.

He did not answer her, and she, thinking that he had not heard her, continued :

" I was servant along with poor Mr. Newcome before the old gentleman died, and saw a good deal of Mrs. Holdsworth, as I always call her ; for, somehow, I can

never bear to think of her as Mrs. Conway, for her
heart never went with her hand when she married that
gentleman, as I can bear witness to, for I was at the
wedding, and never saw a poor body cry as she did.
She and her grandmother, old Mrs. Flemming, was often
at the rectory . . . but I beg pardon, sir; you was
speaking of the house. I can't remember who had it
before Mrs. Holdsworth. It's a long time ago."

Holdsworth raised his head.

Up to the moment of her speaking of Dolly he had
not known his own name; all other memories had returned to him, save that. His face was very white, but
there was a strong expression in it. If the woman were
to talk for another twelve hours, she could add nothing
more to what she had already said. Dolly's death he
had expected as he had expected a hundred other nameless possibilities, when memory swooped upon him and
set him peering over the edge of the chasm that separated the Then from the Now; but not her marriage.
Not that. In all the hours he had passed in the open
boat at sea, beholding death striking down his companions about him, suffering the exquisite torture of
thirst, the yet more exquisite pang of hopelessness, there
was no moment of agony in all that time comparable to
the agony that now wrenched him. It might be one of
those terrible experiences which break the heart or
transform the nature, but it gave to or found in Holdsworth a quality of endurance that enabled him to front
the extremity with a face of marble.

When next he spoke his voice was low, but without
a tremor in it.

"I am interested in Mrs. Conway and her old
grandmother. Tell me what you know about them."

" Surely, sir, you don't bring news of Mr. Holdsworth
—of the fine young man that went to sea and was
shipwrecked ?" inquired the woman with a face of
excitement, and staring hard, as if she were about to
receive some astounding news.

" No, no !" he answered, almost under his breath ;
and then he added, " Tell me what you know of the
widow."

" I remember Mr. Holdsworth well," said the woman,
her speech answering to her mood. " A handsomer
young fellow I never saw. He used often to be at the
rectory with his wife, and the love between them was
something beautiful. How she ever had the heart to
let him leave her I never could guess. But he went
and was drowned, and left the young thing without
a friend or a shilling in the wide world, God help
her ; and though I said it was almost stupid her marry-
ing Mr. Conway, remembering what love there was
between her and Mr. Holdsworth, yet I have always
believed it was for her child's sake that she married the
dentist, for they were in desperate want when he
courted her, and must have starved for want of help."

" You are speaking of Holdsworth's child ?"

" Yes, sir. A bright little thing, and fair as a lily.
I saw her the other day when I was over at Hanwitch.
She was with her mamma, and I never see such a likeness as there is between her and her poor drowned
papa. But you're askin' about old Mrs. Flemming.
Why, she died four years ago. She was very old, and
went off quite peaceful, they said. What with Mrs.
Flemming's death, and her never getting any news of
her husband, and having a tiny little baby to find food
for, I do think the poor young lady's heart nearly

broke. I never heard exactly how the money matter was with her, but I believe that when Mrs. Flemming died she would have nothing to live on but her husband's pay, which was stopped when he was given up for lost. Mr. Newcome was very kind, and paid her rent, and helped her along while he lived; and then Mr. Conway saw her; but it was a long time before she would marry him, long after the poor old rector was dead and gone, and she found that taking in needle-work was worse than going on the parish. I often think of her—I do, indeed, sir—waiting day after day for her husband, who was never to come home. I'd rather, myself, have married anybody than a sailor. There's no telling, when once they go, whether they'll ever come back again. They're worse nor soldiers for that."

Here the woman, suddenly conceiving that she had talked quite enough, and perhaps a little too much, dropped a courtesy and left the room; but came back again to ask two questions—At what hour would the gentleman please to dine? and would he like to have a bed-room in her house? She could recommend her bed-rooms. Her linen was clean as snow.

"I will tell you presently," answered Holdsworth. "I have not yet decided upon my movements."

"There's a nice plump fowl——"

"Yes, cook me that by seven o'clock," said Holdsworth, who was feverishly impatient to be left alone.

She closed the door, and Holdsworth leaned his temples on his hands and fixed his heavy eyes on the bare table, taking the attitude of a student striving to master some difficult problem.

For many minutes he held this posture, presently

lifted his head, and looked about him; then took his hat and went out.

The landlord behind the bar made him a low bow, and offered his services to show him over the village. Holdsworth declined his offer with a "Thank you," and walked into the road. He glanced over his shoulder suspiciously as he advanced, disliking the inquisitive stare with which he had been followed through the bar of the inn by the people drinking there, but no one watched him. He held a stick, on which he leaned as he moved, like an infirm man; and often he paused and gazed around him. The people in the roadway, or in the houses, eyed him as he passed with the curiosity a stranger seldom fails to excite in small unfrequented places; but he took no notice of them; his mind was intent on vivifying the impressions it was receiving with old memories, and adjusting the ideas which had been restored to him out of the dark and secret hiding-places of the past.

Few changes had been made in the aspect of the little village to embarrass the picture which his recovered memory had submitted to him. Some alterations in the external form of one or two shops, and two freshly-built houses on the left-hand side facing the blacksmith's shed, were the only new features in the familiar scene of this quaint broad thoroughfare.

His steps grew more reluctant, his face took a sharper expression of pain, though never losing its characteristic of hardness and severity, as he drew near to his old home. He forced himself forwards, and, when abreast, halted and looked at it.

The windows were blindless, the garden showed signs of long neglect, and a board nailed to a post leaned towards the road, bearing the announcement, in painted letters, that the house was to let. A row of cobwebs garnished the woodwork of the gate, and glistened in the sunshine; the bare rooms, visible through the windows, looked cheerless and inhospitable; the window-glass was dirty, and some of the panes in the kitchen window were broken. The grass about the house was tall and vividly green. That window, looking towards the trees between the lanes, belonged to Dolly's room. There were white soft curtains to it in those days, and the glass was pure and transparent as spring-water. That room on the left was the sitting-room. There they had taken their meals; there they had played forfeits, had hunted the slipper, had made the walls ring with innocent laughter. He remembered the old grandmother's placid smile, the rector's kindly jokes, his Dolly's sweet face, throwing a light of purity and beauty about her. And under the sill· were the dead branches of the clematis, still held to the wall by the pieces of black leather Dolly's own hand had nailed. Such humble signs make grief sharper than large memorials.

He stood leaning upon his stick, losing all sense of the present in this vision of the past. His thoughts, taking their departure from the time when he first fitted out that house as a home for Dolly, flowed regularly downwards. He was a bridegroom again, and his wife was at his side, and her eyes upon his, and their hands clasped. Now the shadow of separation that was to darken them presently was felt; and then came the eve of his departure, thronged with the memory of kisses sweet and bitter, of tears and broken prayers, and brave hopes battling with sullen misgivings. He was now on board the "Meteor," and now in the open boat, surrounded by the dying, and himself suffering tortures it broke him down to recall; and now he was in Australia, striving with memory, which would yield no answer to his passionate prayers. But the finger of God pointed the way to his old home; and now he was returning to England, with his past still hidden in gloom, but with his heart not unhopeful of the morning that was to break after the long darkness of the night. And finally, with the old village of Southbourne before him, came the rush of memory—the brief exultation—the spasm of fear—the terror that held him mute—the disclosure that showed him his wife less his than had he traversed all the desolate miles of water only to kneel by her grave . . . .

Tears would have relieved him, but he could not weep. He turned and moved slowly away, stopping again and again to look back at the little empty house, while sobs convulsed him, and a sense of supreme desolation and friendlessness weighed him down.

CHAPTER XXIII.

REFLECTIONS.

THE fowl dished up by the landlady and served upon fine linen, was plump, and juicy and aromatic enough to re-excite the appetite of an alderman after Mansion House dinner; but Holdsworth hardly touched it. The woman looked vexed as she removed it, for the neglect of such a dainty was as good as a spoken disparagement of her skill as a cook. She set a fine cheese, fresh from the farmhouse over the way, upon the table, and butter from the same dairy, firm and sweet-smelling, as butter should be; but these were left untasted.

"I don't know who he may be," she whispered to her husband, outside, "but if he don't make a better dinner than this every day, it's no wonder his body's a shadder."

The setting sunshine streamed into the little parlour in which Holdsworth sat, and enriched the room with its vivid crimson light; the soft evening breeze wafted pleasant perfumes through the open window; and in the air was the tender and delightful peace which falls with an appreciable hush over little country villages, where the sinking of the sun is the signal for rest.

Holdsworth had made up his mind to sleep in South-

bourne that night. He needed the silence and the solitude the little inn promised him, that he might meditate
upon the steps he should now take.

The feverish misery that had been born in him by
the landlady's story was, in some measure, tranquillised,
and he had now the power, at least, to think with
tolerable clearness. And yet he was sorely perplexed,
as he sat with his head resting on his hand and his
weary eyes fixed on the little garden outside. Impulses
were governing him that made his mind incline from
side to side like a pendulum. Had Mr. Newcome been
alive—the kind and good old rector, whom he recalled
with love—he would have gone to him, avowed himself,
and entreated his counsel.

He felt that Dolly was dead to him. He felt this,
though no words that he had at his command would
have enabled him to explain his ideas. His own grand
sense of honour witnessed this truth, that she had
married another man in full belief that he—John Holdsworth—was dead; and he recognised and appreciated
the force of the overwhelming claims of the moral obligation imposed on him to leave her belief undisturbed.
Why? Because its disturbance would generate a heavy
burden of shame, would make her practically false to
both men, and stain her nature with a sin whose hue
would not be the less dark in the sight of the world
because her conscience had no share in it.

Such instinctive perception of the high needs of the
seldom-paralleled situation his fate had placed him in,
could only have possessed a man of deep honour, great
humanity, and rare unselfishness.

But his child!

The child of his own passionate love for Dolly.

There was the magnetic power that drew all his inclinations away from the silent command of honour.

To see her—to behold himself renewed in a sweet child's face—to press his lips *once* to her cheek—once only, if nevermore!

Oh! not once—not once only! To dwell near her, to have her in his sight, to watch them both, and live out the years that should be allotted him in secret contemplation of the joy, the sacred pleasures, the divine emotions embodied in this woman and her babe; happinesses which had been broken away from his life—could not this be?

He started up and looked at himself in the glass over the mantel-shelf. Had suffering wrought in his face to such poor purpose, that even the eye of love could pierce through the sunken mask? His child knew him not— and Dolly, deeming him dead, and holding him a thing of the irreclaimable past, could not behold—could never imagine that she beheld—in that bowed figure, that bearded face, those hollow eyes, that hair with patches of gray all over it, the handsome, vigorous, upright, clear-eyed man whom she had called husband.

Husband! . . . and she had left him.

Stop! Passages of the landlady's story echoed in his ears; how the poor young lady was starving; how she had a tiny baby to support; how the workhouse seemed better to her than the hopeless, scanty produce of the needle; how she held back, reluctant to give her hand to the man who wished to marry her; how she had wept when her hand was given!

Oh, husband! oh, lover! though to the past only those titles now belong; by your own sufferings, remember hers! By your own misery, when, feeling yourself dying alone on the great deep, your physical torments yielded to the fiercer tortures of your heart when you thought of your wife praying for him, whom, you said to yourself, she shall never see again, remember her! pity her! Was his imagination so poor that he could not find it in him to make, out of the landlady's brief tale, a pregnant, bitter picture of his wife's trials? Not so! To such a heart as his, one hint of misery would bring with it many piteous details. There was infinite anguish in the picture his fancy drew; but he forced himself to contemplate it, that the jealousy, the disappointment, the despair of unfulfilled hope, might melt out of his heart, and leave it a fit shrine for the consecration of the two images which the uncontrollable will of his humanity as a father and a husband declared should be placed there.

His fingers had stolen over his face as he stood before the looking-glass. A long time he thus remained, while the sun went down behind the trees in the far-off fields, and the twilight stole softly into the room and made his figure visionary. When he withdrew his hands from his eyes, they were wet; but the one star shining clearly in the dark blue overhead had dawned out of the light to witness a fairer sight than the sun had shone upon—a face from which all vestige of hardness and severity had passed, eyes heavy with tears upturned to God's kingdom, and lips whispering a prayer for help, for courage, for counsel, to aid the resolution of his heart, intent upon a noble self-sacrifice that should yet not remove it from the sphere of all that it held dearest on earth.

CHAPTER XXIV.

HANWITCH is nowhere seen to greater advantage than from the summit of the little hill that flanks it on the west. Here, if you are an epicure in your enjoyment of what is picturesque in scenery, you will take your stand at sunset, while the splendour still flushes the heavens, and the country all around is tinted with a delicate crimson haze. In this fairy light, Hanwitch, from where you stand, will resemble some architectural dream; for the serene sky gives an ideality to the proportions which are magnified by the soft combining shadows, and peace broods in the streets. The noble church dedicated to St. James towers in the midst of the houses; its spire glows with the red fire, which a little while before had bathed the whole pile and kindled brilliant stars in its long and narrow windows; and all about the church rise and fall the roofs of closely-grouped houses, manifold in colour, with lines of thin blue smoke mounting straight into the sky. The town lies backed with wooded scenery, and the picturesque outlines of the houses take a new detail of beauty from the relief they give to the soft dark masses of trees and lightlier-coloured fields which make up the farther landscape.

And as you watch, a human interest will be communicated to the town by the breaking out here and there of little yellow lights. Darkness soon falls when the crimson flush pales upon the sky; but where you stand daylight is still around, mellowed into deepest, richest, beauty of colour, and so lingering ere it fades into the gray and gloom of twilight.

The town has been enlarged since the days to which this story belongs; but elderly people are living whose love for the old High Street scarcely reconciles them to the "improvements" which have been made in its aspect. Surveyors and local boards press sorely upon gentle prejudices. These elderly people remember the row of antique houses where the big bank building now stands. They remember certain primitive shops, the windows of which were furnished with diamond-shaped panes of glass that discoloured to the eye the wares exposed for sale within. They remember the picturesque alley out of the High Street, with a cottage at the end of it that had a green porch; it looked from its cool retreat upon the narrow slice of the main thoroughfare with its passengers flitting like shadows past the brief opening. And I myself can recall the wonderful effect of light and shadow in that tranquil embrasure when the evenings lengthened, and as I beheld it once—a maid-servant, picturesquely attired in a red petticoat, lolling within the porch, her hand upon her hips, laughing at a dog that stood on its hind legs begging; the figures shadowed, the windows above burning with the light of the setting sun, the pavement a deep gray.

In Holdsworth's time, the vehicles and passengers were in perfect keeping with the venerable and faded but dignified aspect of the old street. The townspeople still lingered behind the transition-epoch of that bygone day, and held for the most part tenaciously to the costumes and the indolence of their fathers.

The town was about an hour's walk from Southbourne. After quitting the handful of houses which formed the village, Hanwitch came upon you as a metropolis. To describe it in homely guide-book fashion :— It had two good churches, and a public square full of evergreens, rock-work, and stone images; several snug inns, one wide street and a quantity of narrow ones; a town-hall, a market-place, a prison, and a town-crier; a large number of old ladies and fat poodles, invalids, sedan-chairs, and camp-stools. In olden times—and now I am talking of the eighteenth century—it had held some sort of position as a third-rate inland watering-place; but what had become of the springs which had brought the gout, the vapours, and the spleen from places as distant as London to drink, the oldest inhabitant never could remember. But one thing was certain : there was no lack of water in the place. A river ran close to it, and from this river meandered some crystal streamlets which ran right into the town. And where the river was, the scenery was exquisite in summer—cool, deep, and leafy, with a bridge at each end of the town, a little landing-stage, a punt or two, and midway between the bridges, a cluster of trees on either bank, with huge gnarled trunks and roots which ran naked for many feet along the ground, whilst, high above, their branches mingled and formed a tunnel for the water to flow under. Here the trout would leap; here the water-rat would sneak from its earthy chamber and break the tide into thin ripples as it noiselessly made for the opposite shore; here the sunshine would fall in threads through the leaves and gild the black long-legged insects on the surface of the water.

Ten o'clock was striking when Holdsworth was driven into Hanwitch by the landlord of the South-bourne inn, who was rich enough to own a horse and gig. The drive had been a very short one, and in the landlord's opinion seven-and-sixpence had never been more easily earned. The gig was stopped at the door of the "Hanwitch Arms," and Holdsworth got out. Then came a porter, who nodded pleasantly to the owner of the gig, and hoisted the portmanteau on his shoulder.

"My respecks to the governor, Joe. How is he?"

"Pretty middlin'! How's yourself?"

"Why, I can't say as I'm quite the thing. The weather's been rayther agin my rheumatiz.—Wish you good mornin', sir."

And with this farewell to Holdsworth, the landlord drove himself away.

Holdsworth's plans had been fully settled by him the night before; and one part of them was that he should put up at some inn at Hanwitch, while he made inquiries of deep interest to himself, and obtained a lodging. Having followed the porter into the bar and ordered a bed for the night, he re-entered the street.

His emotions, as he first began to walk, were conflicting and painful. He was now in the town where his wife lived; any moment might bring them face to face, and the wildest anxiety to see her was mixed up with a sensation of shrinking fear of the encounter. He stared eagerly at the people, and now and again, when a little child passed, his heart beat rapidly, and he felt his blood leave his face. But he mastered himself soon, repeatedly muttering, as a reassuring argument, that, were they to meet, Dolly would not know him.

He was in the main street, walking slowly, and helping his step with a stick, not more from habit than from necessity, for he was frequently seized with a weakness in the legs which would sometimes oblige him to stop, or seat himself if a seat were at hand. His object now was to find out where Dolly lived, a question he would not ask the landlady at Southbourne, lest, added to the inquiries he had already made, it should excite her suspicion and set her surmising.

He noticed a small chemist's shop opposite, and, his mind establishing a friendly connection between drugs and dentistry, he crossed and entered. A bald-headed man in spectacles received him with a bow.

"Can you tell me where Mr. Conway, the dentist, lives?"

The chemist, who knew perfectly well, scratched his ear and seemed to reflect. He drew teeth himself, and was not disposed to furnish a rival with a patient if he could help it.

"I know the name, sir, and——might I ask if you want anything done to your teeth."

"No, I merely wish to know where Mr. Conway lives."

"It's not for me to speak ill of a brother practitioner, and as I shan't mention names, no harm can be done," said the chemist, with his eye on Holdsworth's mouth; "but I do say that it's a pity people should start in a business, requiring as much skill as the highest branches of surgery, without knowing the difference between an eye and a wisdom tooth, and drinking to that degree that their hands tremble like the windows of a coach in full tear."

"Does Mr. Conway drink?"

"I name no names," replied the chemist, assuming an injured expression of face. "I should be sorry to take away any man's character, not to speak of the bread out of his mouth, though there are some people not quite so particular as me in that matter, and will start lies which should make 'em afraid to go to bed. All that I say is, that if I had a toothache, and wanted to get my jaw broke and my gum tore out, I'd go to a certain person livin' not a day's walk from this shop, and ask him to look at my tooth."

Saying which he nodded vigorously, and, taking up a bottle, began to mould a piece of blue paper over the cork.

"Where does this Mr. Conway live?" inquired Holdsworth, who judged that there might be a good deal more of professional animus than truth in the chemist's observations.

"I believe," replied the chemist, sulkily vouchsafing the information which he could scarcely longer evade, "that the party you refer to lives in the Ellesmere Road. He did yesterday; but some persons in this world are so dependent on their landlords that there's no tellin' what's going to happen to 'em to-morrow."

Thanking this very good-natured and remarkably ingenuous chemist for his direction, Holdsworth quitted the shop and walked up the street. He asked a butcher-boy the way to Ellesmere Road, and was told to keep straight on, until he came to a "Methody's Chapel, ven he'd see a turnin', vich 'ud be the road he ast for."

The Methodist Chapel was a good distance off, and as Holdsworth's pace was slow, he had plenty of leisure for reflection, which was bitter enough; for, strive as

he might to waive the chemist's gossip as mere trade
scandal and jealousy, his mind persisted in fastening on
it, and turning it about, and coining deep anxiety out
of it.

If this Mr. Conway *were* the drunkard the chemist
affirmed him to be, and the pauper too—for the sarcasm
about "persons being dependent on their landlords" had
not been lost—what kind of life was Dolly and *his* child
leading? He frowned, and felt his hand tighten on the
handle of his stick; but a milder persuasion grew in
him, and he forced his mind away from the subject.

So bright a morning as it was would bring forth many
people; and the High Street was tolerably well filled
with pedestrians, and old people in bath-chairs, wheeled
along the gutters for fear of the horses, and nurses
dragging children by the hand, and waggons, and tradesmen's traps. The early coach from Canterbury came
thundering along the street, the guard blowing his horn
and causing house-windows to fly open, and heads to
protrude, and a handkerchief, or, maybe, a duster here
and there, to be waved in coy recognition of the hand-
kissing of certain spruce and finely-attired gentlemen
on the top of the vehicle.

But, varied and cheerful as the scene was, Holdsworth had no eyes but for the women and children he
met, at whom he darted quick eager glances, which must
have sent some of the women tripping along with a
sincere conviction that they had met with one admirer,
at all events, that morning.

He passed the market-place with its stalls loaded
with garden produce, and clean little shops submitting
a tempting array of plump fowls, geese, sides of bacon,
legs of pork, and strings of sausages; and in about

twenty minutes' time reached the Methodist Chapel, and turned into the Ellesmere Road.

A short broad road, with the sun-lighted country beyond; on either side, small newly-built villas, with now and again a house presenting a more venerable aspect. There was grass in the roadway, and one or two of the villas had placards in their windows. In the front garden of one of the nearer houses an old gentleman, with an inflamed face, and a white hankerchief over his head, was plying a rake. No other person was visible; but, when Holdsworth had advanced a few steps, a woman came out of a gate and approached him. His heart came into his throat, and he stood stock still. She drew near, but she was not Dolly. She glanced at him as she passed, struck, maybe, by his pale face, and the singular mixture of old age and youth which his appearance and figure suggested.

He breathed deeply and walked forward, glancing to right and left of him.

The last house but one on the left was the house he wanted. A brass plate inscribed with Conway's name and calling was fixed to the iron railings, and over the door was a lamp furnished with blue and red glass.

Holdsworth dared scarcely glance at it. When his eye encountered the name he turned cold, and felt the damp perspiration suffusing his forehead.

He came back hurriedly, with the bare impression on his mind of a small house with the upper blinds drawn, and with an untended garden in the front.

He returned to the main entrance of the road, stopped, looked back, and then slowly retraced his steps.

There was a house of an older fashion than any of the others on the right-hand side, about midway; one

that had evidently taken root there many years before
the little villas had gathered themselves together to
intercept its view and violate its pastoral solitude.   Its
doorway was sheltered by a roomy porch, with creepers
clambering up its trellised supporters ; its darkling windows had the burnished glitter upon them that is peculiar
to old glass ; its eaves were capacious enough to accommodate a whole colony of swallows, and it had a fair
piece of ground stretching away at its back.   The bright
brass knocker on the green door, the white doorsteps,
the purity of the window glass, and the spotlessness of
the window drapery, afforded an excellent guarantee
of the housewifely qualities of the inmates.   In one of
the windows hung a card.   Holdsworth opened the gate
and knocked.

"I should like to see your apartments," he said to
the cheerful-faced, middle-aged woman who had promptly
replied to his summons.

"Certainly, sir ; please to walk in."

She threw open the door of a long sitting-room, smelling of lavender and mignonette, and furnished with worked
chairs, old china, a tall wooden clock with a febrile tick,
a hearth-rug decorated with blue and yellow roses in
wool, and a sour squeezed-looking bookcase which
seemed to hold sundry folios under protest, and to
threaten the instant ejection of a number of small books
on the top shelves, which leaned one against another,
some of them gaping apparently in the last extremity of
terror.

"For yourself, sir ?   Or might there be children ?"

"For myself."

"Why, then, sir," exclaimed the woman, with great
alacrity, "I think I can accommodate you.   You can

have this room, and a bed-room just over it, and the use of the pianner in the next room when you see company, for fourteen shillings a week."

"That will do," said Holdsworth.

The woman, smiling like clockwork, proceeded to inform him that she was a widow, and had nobody else in the house but her mother, who was very aged and silly-like, and only left her room, which was upstairs, once a week for a turn in the garden; that anything more peaceful than her house was never known, and that if the gentleman was studious, he would never be interrupted with noises.

She then led him upstairs to the bedroom, which was as comfortable as any man could wish.

On their return to the sitting-room, Holdsworth, who was tired, asked permission to rest himself, and sat down near the window which overlooked the road, where he could just obtain a glimpse of Mr. Conway's house.

He broke away from the overpowering thoughts which the sense of the near presence of his wife and child forced upon him, and steadying his voice, turned to the woman who stood at the door, and asked her if she knew any of the people living around.

"Why, sir, I know most of my neighbours by name, though I can't say as e'er a one of 'em are friends of mine."

"I noticed a dentist's house just now, over the way. What sort of business can he do in such a road as this?"

"Oh, you're speaking of Mr. Conway!" she exclaimed, with a shake of the head. "It's his own fault if he don't do a good business, for I hear that he's pretty clever at making teeth and drawing of them, and the likes of that; but he don't seem to have no patients, and I know why; but it's not for me to meddle in other folks' concerns."

"Why?"

"I suppose you're no friend of his, sir?" she said.

"I never saw the gentleman in my life."

"Well, then, to speak plainly, he drinks; and it's pretty well known; and so there's no wonder gentle-folks won't go near him."

Holdsworth forced a look of unconcern into his face as he asked:

"Is he married?"

"Oh yes, sir; and a sweet dear creature his wife is; Mrs. Holdsworth as was. Hers is a sad history. She lived at a place called Southbourne—maybe you know it—it's an hour's walk from here; and I was told her story by Mrs. Campion, as used to keep a greengrocer's shop in that village, and served most of the gentry about. She—I'm speaking of Mrs. Conway—lost her husband at sea, and married the present gentleman two or three years afterwards. Mrs. Campion said she was driven to it by want o' the bare necessaries of life," added the woman in a subdued voice.

Holdsworth was silent.

"I don't think," continued the woman, "that she leads a very happy life. We sometimes has a chat to-gether when we meet out o' doors, and she's the civilest, sweetest young thing I ever knew. But," she exclaimed, catching herself up, "all this is no business of mine; and I hope, sir, you'll think none the worse of me for gossiping about strangers' affairs. I was strivin' to answer your questions, sir."

"Thank you," said Holdsworth, rising, but keeping his back to the window. "Can you receive me to-morrow?"

" Oh yes, sir ; at any time you're pleased to come."

" My name is Hampden. I shall sleep to-night at the 'Hanwitch Arms.' Here are a couple of sovereigns, which will serve you as a security for my taking your rooms. I leave myself in your hands, and have no doubt I shall be comfortable."

The woman took the money with a courtesy, thinking to herself that she had never met with a more polite and considerate gentleman. Holdsworth left the house. He cast a swift glance at the villa with the plate upon the railing, and then hurried towards the town.

CHAPTER XXV.

HOLDSWORTH spent the greater part of the evening in writing a letter to Mr. Sherman. At twelve o'clock next day he was an inmate of Mrs. Parrot's house in the Ellesmere Road.

In his walk to the lodgings he had met only strange faces, one or two of which looked after him, struck, perhaps, by his keen fugitive glance, his slow pace that stole along the ground, and his depressed head, as though there were a shame in his heart that made the daylight painful.

Mrs. Parrot fussed about him for some time, and tired him with an account of the articles she had purchased for him. Her memory was slow, and her capacity of reckoning very indifferent; hence it took her twenty minutes to account for the expenditure of twelve shillings. Happily, it was her mother's day for walking in the garden, and Holdsworth could see the old lady—a mere wisp of a figure, in ancient black satin reaching to her ankles and clinging to her legs, a nose like the Duke of Wellington's, and a chin like Punch's—hobbling along a gravel walk, looking with afflicting agitation around her, and coughing like a rattle, as a signal to her daughter, who, when she had done with her accounts, hurried out.

The control Holdsworth had kept upon himself, while Mrs. Parrot remained in the room, he could now put aside; indeed, the suffering caused him by his pent-up agitation imperatively demanded that the emotion should have play. Now he would walk hastily to and fro the room, and then fling himself into a chair, clasping his hands tightly, and then rise and stand before the window and send glances passionate and shrinking at the house occupied by the Conways.

Now that he was close to his wife, now that any moment might reveal her walking past his window with his child, perchance, at her side, he dreaded lest the unparalleled situation he had forced himself into would prove too heavily charged with cruel conditions for him to bear. Never once then, never once afterwards, did the vaguest impulse possess him to go forth and declare himself and claim her. No! A sense of honour that was inexorable, since it prohibited the faintest echo of the soul's secret passionate yearning to make itself audible, had decreed his silence and enforced the obedience of inclination.

The only concession granted was the enjoyment of such ghostly and barren pleasure as his heart could find in the knowledge of the close neighbourhood of the two who were so dear to him. Oh! bitter waking of memory, to recall him from the sunny vision of the old times when his joy was complete, and love a permanent possession to enrich his nature with all gracious and generous emotions, to thrust him into the gray and bleak twilight of a loveless and desolate life, which the recovered power could only embitter by recurrence to the things that were lost!

His eyes wandered ceaselessly and restlessly towards

the window. From time to time people went by with
the slow, aimless step of persons who walk for no other
end than exercise. An old gentleman, with a white
moustache and a dark skin, stopped, with another old
gentleman, in high shirt-collars and a tail-coat, opposite
Holdsworth's window, and argued, with many galvanic
flourishes of the arms and grimaces of the face. There
was much political excitement abroad at that time, owing
to the Reform Bill of the Grey Administration, to which
the royal assent had been given; and the dark-skinned
old gentleman — whose age, warmth, and intemperate
flourishes were as demonstrative of his politics as his
language — bade his companion take notice that, before
five years were passed, England would be a tenth-rate
power, governed by a mob, with a Jesuit seated on every
hearth, a Nuncio preaching at St. Paul's, not a Bible to
be found in the country, and the gallows groaning under
strings of honest patriots. The old gentleman in the
high shirt-collars, who clearly shared his friend's opinions,
nodded savagely, asked with his shoulders, "What would
you have?" and then moved on a dozen paces, to be
stopped again by the other old gentleman with pro-
phecies, maybe, more blood-chilling and awful than those
he had already declaimed.

Presently Holdsworth, scarcely conscious of what he
was about, left the window and approached the bookcase. He pulled out a volume, which proved to be an
old copy of Gulliver's Travels, "adorn'd with sculp-
tures;" and his eye lighting on that passage in which
Gulliver closes his account of his second voyage,[1] his
thoughts trooped off to his old sea-faring life, the book

[1] "In a little time I and my family and friends came to a right
understanding: but my wife protested 'I should never go to sea

closed upon his fingers, and he sank in deep meditation.

The restoration of his memory was comparatively so recent, that he had found no leisure to recall those frightful experiences of his which could not recur without overwhelming him with an unspeakable horror of the sea. He now understood that it should have been his duty to call upon the owners of the " Meteor," and acquaint them with the circumstances of the wreck of their vessel, and the deaths of the persons who were in his boat, all whom he clearly remembered. There were friends, doubtless, both in England and America, who could wish to receive tidings of the fate of these people, though the long interval of five years should tell as plain a story as Holdsworth could relate. He knew not whether the inmates of the other boats had been saved, and he would have given much to ascertain this; but he understood that any communication he made to the shipowners would be almost sure to appear in print, by which his wife would learn that he was alive. "No! let the world think me dead!" he exclaimed bitterly. He had only to live for the past now—for that memory which had betrayed him and ruined his life. His future was bare and barren, and there was nothing in all the world that could kindle one ray of comfort in his hopeless heart but the bleak privilege of dwelling near his wife and child.

He restored the book to its place and returned to the window.

In the roadway, a few yards to the right, a little girl was standing, holding a doll. She was a very little

any more;' although my evil destiny so ordered, that she had not the power to hinder me."

creature, with bright yellow hair down her back, and she held the doll in motherly fashion on her arm, and caressed it with her hand.

Her back was towards Holdsworth, whose eyes were rooted upon her.

She turned presently and looked down the road, and Holdsworth saw a little face upon which God had graven a sign that made the poor father clutch at the wall to steady himself. For there was his own face in miniature —the face that Dolly had loved before the sufferings of the mind, and the anguish of hunger and thirst, had twisted from it all resemblance it had ever borne to what was manly and beautiful in the human countenance.

He pressed his hands to his eyes and gazed again, then ran to the bell-rope and pulled it. But when he had done this he wished it undone. For would not his agitation excite Mrs. Parrot's suspicions? What was there in a stranger's child that should so interest him?

He bit his lip and controlled himself with desperate will; and, when Mrs. Parrot opened the door, he said to her in a steady voice and with a forced smile:

"I am sorry to trouble you. I am very fond of little children. Pray can you tell me who that child is, there?"

Mrs. Parrot drew to the window, evidently finding nothing odd in the question, and said:

"Why, that's little Nelly Holdsworth, Mrs. Conway's daughter."

"Ah!" exclaimed Holdsworth.

"She *is* a dear!" continued Mrs. Parrot. "I am very fond of that child, Mr. Hampden. She's the only child i' the road I allow to come into my garden, for children are so wilful, there's no tellin' what they'll do the moment your eyes are off 'em. See what a little lady she looks, and how prettily she holds her doll! She's waiting for her mamma, I suppose."

Mrs. Parrot rapped with her nails on the window. The child looked round, and Holdsworth shrank away. Mrs. Parrot beckoned. Holdsworth would have stopped her, but could find no words.

"She's coming, Mr. Hampden. I'll bring her to you, sir, if you'll wait a moment."

And out she went.

In a few seconds she returned, leading by the hand the child, who hung back when she caught sight of the white-faced, bearded man.

"There, Mr. Hampden, this is my pretty young friend, little Nelly!" exclaimed Mrs. Parrot, stooping to give the child a kiss. "Go and shake hands with the gentleman, my dear, and show him your nice doll. I'll tell you when I see your mamma."

"Come, dear, come to me," said Holdsworth in a low voice.

The child approached him slowly, stopping now and again, and looking shyly at Mrs. Parrot.

"Tut! tut!' exclaimed that lady. "What are you afraid of, Miss Nelly? Go and shake hands with the gentleman, like a little lady."

Holdsworth put out his hand; the child advanced a step nearer; he fell upon one knee and drew her to him.

For some moments he could not speak; he could only look at her—look with eyes of all-devouring love absorbing all the sweetness of that young face, feeling a pang of exquisite joy, but shivering quickly as his fingers locked themselves upon her tiny hand.

He longed to press the little creature to his heart, to fasten his lips upon her mouth, to weep over her.

"Tell me your name, little one!"

"Nelly," replied the child, keeping at arm's length from him, and staring into his face.

"Nelly what?"

"Nelly Ho'dwor't."

His own name, thus lisped by her, thrilled through him; he caught his breath, and said:

"May I kiss you?"

She put up her mouth, and he kissed her.

"How pretty your hair is!" he murmured, in a voice of exquisite tenderness, which made Mrs. Parrot turn suddenly and look at him. He met her glance with a smile, and said:

"I am very fond of children. Will this little girl come and see me here sometimes?"

"Ay, that she will, sir. Won't you, Nelly?"

"Det."

"How old are you, Nelly?"

"Four."

"Who gave you that doll?"

"Mamma."

"You will bring dolly to see me, and we will have tea, all three of us. What have I got here? A bright shilling! That will buy dolly a parasol!"

No words can describe the tone his voice took as he spoke.

"What do you say to the gentleman for this beautiful present?" cried Mrs. Parrot.

"Tanks," said the child, putting the doll on the floor to examine the money with both hands.

"Oh, here comes your mamma!" said Mrs. Parrot.

"Make your reverence to the gentleman . . . there's a dear; pick up dolly . . . that's right."

She took Nelly's hand and ran with her out of the room.

The mother, standing at her gate on the other side of the road, looking up and down the road, caught sight of Mrs. Parrot and the child, and crossed over to them.

They remained opposite Holdsworth's window talking, while he, shrinking against the wall, peered at them through the muslin curtain.

The five years which had passed since he had seen his wife had worked but a very little change in her. There was more womanly fulness in her form; and this was about all those five years had done for her. Her face was still as youthful as when Holdsworth had last looked on it, her eyes still possessed their deep and delicate tint, the hair its richness and lustre, the mouth its sweetness, the whole face that almost infantine expression, conveyed by soft shadowy lines and the archness of the pencilled eyebrows, which made it beautiful in repose, more beautiful yet in sorrow. But, young and fair as she seemed, there was a deep-rooted care in her face which, without qualifying its freshness, yet mingled in her smile, and lived in her eyes, and fixed a wistful look on her, such as would be seen in one who lingers long, long waiting for the summons to depart which no day brings. Her dress was shabby, her gloves old; but her beauty made even her faded apparel, cut after the unbecoming fashion then in vogue, picturesque. She wore a white crape handkerchief over her bare shoulders, and a bonnet-shaped hat, ornamented with a dark feather, which, drooping over her back, imparted a peculiar vividness to the light, sheeny gold of her hair.

Strained as his ears were, Holdsworth could not hear her voice, though Mrs. Parrot's kindly cackle was audible enough. It was manifest that they exchanged mere commonplace civilities; and presently Mrs. Parrot dropped a courtesy, and the mother and child walked slowly away.

Holdsworth watched them with just such a look in his eyes as had been in them when, racked with torture in the open boat, he had cast glances full of passionate despair round the horizon for the ship that was to rescue him. He saw the little girl hold up her shilling, whereupon the mother stopped and looked back, then continued her walk and passed out of sight.

CHAPTER XXVI.

IT was natural, after the first liveliness of the emotion which had been excited in Mrs. Parrot's breast by the installation of a lodger worth fourteen shillings a week to her, had in some degree subsided, that she should begin to wonder who that lodger was.

She had been particularly struck and greatly taken by his behaviour to the little girl, and inferred, of course, that he was a humane and tender-hearted man, a conjecture which, although it was true, did no credit to her sagacity, considering the circumstance on which it was based; since it is a notorious fact, that great rascals will admire, pet, and "tip" little children, whose parents they would not scruple to rob of their very last farthing.

But though Mrs. Parrot had no doubt as to her lodger's humanity of character after what she had seen, she could not by any means feel so sure as to the position he held either in or out of society, the calling he had followed, if ever he *had* followed a calling, or the part of the world he came from. His name was Hampden. That was English. But had he a Christian name? No initial stood between the Mr. and the Hampden, on the card affixed to his portmanteau. *Was* he a Christian?

She hoped he was.   She was no judge of other religions ;
but she must say, when she let her lodgings to people,
that she liked to *feel* that they were Christians.

He had ordered dinner at two o'clock ; and when
she came in to lay the cloth, for she kept no servant,
she found him still at the window, staring into the
empty road as earnestly as if it were filled with a very
beautiful and novel procession.   But she could only
suppose that he looked out of the window because he
was new to the place.

He smiled softly when he met her glance, but did
not speak, nor would she hazard any remarks herself,
for fear of being thought intrusive.   All that he said
during dinner was to express himself well pleased with
her cooking ; but she noticed, in removing the dishes,
that, pleasantly as he had praised the piece of roast
mutton, he had scarcely tasted it, and that of the four
potatoes she had put into the dish, three and a half
remained.

Whilst in the kitchen she heard him leave the house,
and, when her task was done, she went upstairs to her
mother's room, whither she had conducted the old lady
soon after little Nelly's visit.

"If the gentleman don't eat more every day than
he's just had for dinner," said she, throwing herself back
in a chair and fanning her hot face with the corner of
her apron, "I reckon we shall have a funeral here
before long."

"A what!" gasped the old woman, who sat upright
in a cane chair, near the open window, with an
immense Bible on her right hand and her spectacles on
the top of it.

"He's no more than skin an' bone as he is," con-

tinued Mrs. Parrot, " but it was a picter to see him
with the child. I never see a man more soft with a
child before."

" He ain't likely to make strange nises o' nights, is
he, Sairey ?" exclaimed the old woman, earnestly regard-
ing her daughter with a pair of eyes from which all
expression and light seemed literally washed out, leaving
nothing but two circles of weak, dim blue.

" I don't think so. He seems to me quiet enough.
He's fond o' staring into the road. One might think
he's trying to find out where he is. I niver see a
stranger face. He don't look English-like, and yet he
talks uncommon well. I can tell by his boots—which
is square as square at the toes, and his clothes, which
have an odd twist somehows—that he's not from these
parts. Maybe, he's from Ireland."

" I hope not, Sairey," ejaculated the old woman,
bending forward with the profoundly confidential air of
old age. " I was once fellow-sarvint with a Ayrish
futman as was allus talkin' of burnin' down houses, an'
his speech ran on so it were niver to be trusted, for
niver was such lies as he used to tell. You'd best gi'
him notice, Sairey. You can say I gi' yer more trouble
nor you can well get through, and recommend Burton's
lodgin's to him. Burton's a strong man, and kapes
dogs."

" Tut! I'm not afeard!" said Mrs. Parrot, tossing
up her hands and giving her cap a pull. " There's no
more harm in the man than there is in you, for didn't
I tell yer how he gave the girl a shillin' and spoke that
soft to it, it made me feel as if I could ha' cried. Give
him notice, and him not here a day yit! Fourteen
shillin' is fourteen shillin' in these scarce times, to say

nothin' of his being as well-spoken a man as iver you listened to in your life ; an' as for his face, it is but as God made it, an' beauty is but skin deep, as t' parson says, an' I'm for lettin' well alone."

"If he ain't Ayrish," said the old woman, stroking the back of her lean hand, " he may be very well. But sitch talk of invasions from that nashun as I used to hear when I was a gal, an' the drink an' shootin' as goes on there, is enough to wet your hair with perspiration . . ."

"*I* didn't say he was Irish. *I* don't know what he is. He was askin' about Mrs. Conway, though she's unbeknown to him, as any one might tell who heerd him questionin'. He wants Miss Nelly to bear him company at tea, and I don't see why the child can't come, if the mother 'ull let it. I won't take it upon myself to bring the child in. I'll speak to the mother when I see her. I like Mrs. Conway. She's a nice-spoken lady, but seems to know a deal of grief, poor thing. It 'ud be a mussy if that husband of hers 'ud take it into his head to pull out all his own teeth. The cook at Mrs. Short's was tellin' me he's grown that wicious there's no wishin' him a civil good mornin'. An' drink ! Didn't I see him pass here yesterday evenin', staggerin' on his legs like a doll which a child tries to teach walkin' to ?"

"The 'pothecaries used to draw teeth in my day ; now they must be all gentlefolks as looks into your mouth," said the old woman, who had been three minutes searching in her pocket for the snuff-box that lay open, with some of its sand-coloured contents spilt, in her lap.

"Pretty gentlefolks !" exclaimed Mrs. Parrot, pull-

ing up the old woman's dress and tilting the spilt snuff
into the box. "If they're all like Mr. Conway, I'd rather
carry a toothache to my grave than have it stopped wi'
the lockjaw, which they tell me he gave to Mr. Timpson ;
for drink had taken away the use of his mind, and he
pushed the wrong instrayment into the man's mouth
and nearly choked him, he did, and then took out two
wrong teeth after all ; beautiful teeth they wos, for Mr.
Timpson showed them to me hisself, with the tears
standin' in his eyes, wropped up in silver paper."

"Thank God ! he can't draw none o' my teeth !"
mumbled the old woman, talking through her nose in
rapt enjoyment of the flavour of the snuff. They're
all gone."

"I noticed Mrs. Conway's gownd to-day. If I was
her husband, I'd scorn to let her appear in sitch a rag.
And there was darns in the knees o' that child's stockings as made 'em look forty year old. They're always
i' the same dresses, both of 'em. There's a silk she puts
on o' Sundays, all wore thin over the buzzum, and I
remember the bonnet she had on to-day iver since I've
known her. Sitch a pretty face as she has, too ! I expect he must ha' told her some fine lies to get her to
marry him. They say he niver did well, even when he
was in the High Street, wi' that show-box of his stuck
up, filled wi' gaping gums an' naked teeth as turned the
stomach to see. He must ha' sold that piece of ugliness,
for I don't see it nowheres outside his house, which is a
mussy, for I'd as lief see a skiliton on a pole for a sign !
Fancy a doctor settin' up a death's-head to show his
trade !"

She jumped from her chair with a face and gesture
of disgust, and throwing some knitting with the pins

through it into her mother's lap, adjusted her cap before
the glass, and left the room.

There is always some truth in gossip: and there was
a great deal in what Mrs. Parrot had said of Mr. Conway, who, as we have seen, held no place at all in her
opinion. But then sympathy for Dolly was to be expected from a woman who, if she did not know what it
was to live with a drunkard, had known what it was to
live with a surly man, whose eye was evil, and whose
voice was thick, and whose characteristic method of expressing discontent was by holding his clenched fist
under his wife's nose.

Mr. Conway is passing Mrs. Parrot's door at the very
moment that Mrs. Parrot is leaving her mother's bed-
room ; we shall not have an opportunity of seeing much
of him, having the fortunes of a better kind of hero to
deal with ; so, while Holdsworth is away from his lodgings, we'll step into the road and have a look at the
dentist, and follow him into his house.

He is a man with sandy whiskers and light hair, but
by no means ill-looking. On the contrary, there are
materials in his face out of which a very pleasing countenance could be made; a well-shaped nose, a well-shaped
forehead, a good chin, a facial outline clearly defined and
perfectly symmetrical.

But there never was a better illustration than this
man's face of the truth, that good features make but a
very small portion of beauty.

I want a word to express that middle quality of
aspect which is contrived by the mingling of comely
lineaments with bad passions. Possibly the effect is no
more than a neutralisation of nature's good intentions,

wherein we behold a handsome countenance sunk into
a species of physical negation, by moral qualities tugging
it hard in the direction of repellent ugliness.

A most unstriking face at which you would barely
glance, and pass on absolutely unimpressed. His thin
lips might mark both cruelty and selfishness; his eyes
are made heavy by their drooping lids, and the irids
are pale and unintelligent. He is dressed in the style
of the times, of course; pantaloons strapped over his
boots, a frock-coat gaping in a circle round a great
quantity of black satin stock (in which are two pins and
a chain). But the pantaloons are frayed at the heels
and bagged at the knees; and the coat is suspiciously
polished at the elbows and the rim of the collar. He
walks with a quick, uneasy step, his hat slightly cocked,
and his hands in his breeches pockets, and arriving at
the gate of his house, opens it by giving it a kick with
his foot.

He entered the sitting-room with his hat on, and
found the cloth laid for dinner, but nobody in the room,
which was a soiled and dingy apartment, although the
house was a new one, and the paper fresh and the ceiling white. But no paper and whitewash could qualify
the sordid suggestions of the old drugget imperfectly
nailed over the floor, the old leather sofa and the old
leather arm-chair, the mantelpiece decorated by a pair
of plated candlesticks marked with indents, the dingy
red curtains, the *papier mâché* table in the window, with
the mother-of-pearl dropping out of it.

The subtle magic of feminine fingers which extracts
from rubbish itself what hidden capabilities it may possess of comforting the eye with some faintest aspect of
taste, seemed either never to have been exercised upon

U

this room, or to have found itself powerless to deal with it. The only feminine sign was a small bundle of child's stockings on the top of an old work-basket on the sofa.

Mr. Conway put his head out of the door and called, "Are you there, wife?"

"Yes," replied Dolly's voice from downstairs.

"How long will dinner be?"

"Five minutes!"

He threw his hat down and walked into the "surgery," a room at the end of the passage, furnished with a chest of drawers, a toilet-table and a looking-glass, an arm-chair, an ugly circular box with a basin let into it, standing beside the arm-chair; on the toilet-table, some small hand-glasses, a pair of forceps, and three unfinished false teeth. Through the window was to be seen a slip of garden of the breadth of the house, and about fifty feet long—its neglected state, its few pining shrubs, and a flag-pole with a vane a-top that croaked to every passage of the wind, showing up very squalidly against the neighbouring garden, which was richly stocked with wall-fruit and ferns and green plants.

Little Nelly was in this piece of ground with her doll, seated on the grass, and at that moment making such a picture as a painter would stop to study and receive into his mind; her round dark-blue eyes following the swallows which chased each other high in the air, her mouth pouted into an expression of exquisite infantine wonder, her bright hair about her shoulders, and looking, as the breeze stirred the sunshine upon it, like a falling shower of fine gold.

Mr. Conway stared at the child for a moment, and then turned away and sauntered towards the door, but came back to open one of the drawers in the chest and extract a leather-covered bottle, which he shook at his ear, and put to his mouth.

O God! what contrasts there are in life, lying so close together that the devil, though his worship be no bigger than a man, might measure the space between with outstretched hands! Look at Purity and Innocence in the garden, with its eyes raised to heaven; and the skulking fellow in the dingy room swallowing brandy as a man steals money; and in the room below—a darksome, scantily-furnished kitchen—a sweet-faced woman doing servant's work, and urging the slattern by her side into quicker movements, that the gentleman upstairs shall have no occasion to use bad language.

She comes upstairs presently, this Dolly, her face flushed, and breathing quickly from the hurry of her movements, and bears with her own hands a dish that will furnish but a poor repast, though she has done her best to make what little there is palatable. The slattern, with wisps of red hair about her forehead, and loose shoes, which beat a double knock at each step upon the uncarpeted staircase, follows, armed with a jug and a loaf of bread. Behind comes little Nelly, whom the mother has summoned before leaving the kitchen, and who has climbed the staircase with more labour than Mont Blanc is scaled by the Alpine tourist.

No word is spoken. Nelly is lifted into a chair by her mother, and Mr. Conway seats himself before the dish and fills a glass from the jug of ale, taking care—a true connoisseur in such matters—to let the liquor fall from a height, to secure a froth, into which he dips his mouth and nose.

The slattern leaves the room; and Dolly cuts up

some meat and bread for the little one, with a whisper in her ear to say grace.

"Did you get the money, Robert?" she asks presently, eating little herself, and noticing how Robert bribes his appetite with sups of ale.

"No.   Davis was out."

"What shall we do?   I have only five and three-pence left, and this meat is not paid for."

Pence make a sordid enumeration; but we talk of pence, reader, when we have only pence to spend.

"We must sell something, that's all," says Mr. Conway, with a kind of defiant recklessness in his manner.

She gives him a quick glance, looks at her child, and then closes the knife and fork upon her plate.

He does not notice that she has eaten about as much as would serve a bird for a meal; neither does he appear to remark that she drinks water. *He*, at all events, keeps the beer-jug at his elbow, from which, in a very short time, he pours out the last glass.

The child alone continues eating.

"*I* don't know what's to be done!" he exclaims in a voice of suppressed anger, pushing his chair from the table. "The people have dropped me for that French quack, in Mornington Street.   I saw three carriages at his door when I passed just now.   I ought never to have left the old shop.   I did well there."

"You would do well here if you gave yourself a chance," says Dolly.   "The lady who called yesterday evening came again this morning.   Martha told me she looked annoyed when she heard you were out.   She will go to some one else, I suppose, now."

"Let her!" he calls out.   "How am I to know that people are coming to me after dark?   Week after week passes, and they don't come, and—am I going to hang about here a whole night, in the hope of a patient turning up ? Why didn't she leave word at what hour she meant to call to-day ? I went out to collect some money, and you know it, though I can guess what is in your thoughts. But it's false—there's my hand on it !"

He let his hand fall heavily on the table, and stared at his wife. She slightly turned from him, and looked through the window. He left the table and began to pace the room. The child, having emptied her plate and wanting something to play with, had taken the shilling Holdsworth had given her from her pocket, and tried to make it spin on the cloth.

" What's that Nelly has got there ?" said Mr. Conway.

" A shilling," answered Dolly.

" Did you give it her ? . . . Look at our dinner ! . . . You would pamper that child if we were starving. Talk to me of your five and threepence when you can give your baby a shilling !"

" I did not give it to her."

" Who then ?"

" A gentleman."

" What gentleman ?"

" A gentleman lodging at Mrs. Parrot's."

He looked at her with irritable suspicion, and then said :

" Did you see him give it ? Did he take you and the child for beggars ? . . . Confound his impudence ! . . . Send Martha over to him with it."

He turned to ring the bell.

" Stop !" said Dolly, quietly. " Nelly tells me that Mrs. Parrot tapped on the window to speak to her, and when she went in, she saw the gentleman, who kissed her, and gave her the shilling to buy her doll a parasol. No insult could have been intended by this."

"Oh, that was it!" exclaimed Mr. Conway, "Well, and why do you let the child keep the money? She'll lose it. Take it from her."

"It belongs to her. She will not lose it."

"Yes, she will. Nelly, give that money to your mamma."

But Nelly doubled her fist over it, and hid her hand under the table.

"Do you hear what I say?" cried Mr. Conway.

"Why will you not let her keep it?" asked Dolly.

"Am I master here or not?" shouted Mr. Conway. "Give that money to your mother, child!"

Nelly began to whimper, terrified by the man's voice, but loath to surrender her little treasure. He stepped up to her, whipped the little hand from under the cloth, and forcing the shilling from it, put it into his pocket.

"Though I'm a beggar by my own folly," he exclaimed, walking to the door, "I'll not be insulted and defied by the beggars I have brought about me."

His fingers were in his pocket, and it seemed as though he would pull the money out and fling it on the table. But second thoughts prevailed; he jerked his hat on his head, and marched out of the house, banging the door after him.

Dolly watched to see if he would step across to Mrs. Parrot's; but he walked straight on.

"Hush, my darling, hush!" she exclaimed, catching up the sobbing child. "Dolly shall have her parasol; I will buy it myself. Hush, my pet! Nelly's tears break poor mamma's heart. . . . Oh, John! oh, hus-

band!" she murmured; "why did God take you from
me? Why did He lead me and my little one into this
misery?"

Truly, it was misery, of a forlorn and hopeless kind.
But you have seen the man Dolly had married at his
worst. The most brutal husband is not always brutal.
The drunkard is not always drunk. More colours than
black and white go to the painting of a man off the
stage, where corked eyebrows strike no horror, and
blood-boltered cheeks prove nothing more than a neglect
of soap.

Mr. Conway had his soft hours, when he would shed
tears, smite his breast, and call himself a fiend—having
reference, by this flattering title, to nothing but his
behaviour to Dolly.

He was undoubtedly in love with her when he
married her; and the sweet face which had made him
haunt Southbourne, to the neglect of his patients, would
still, even after two years, have too much potency not
to occasionally soften and give movement to the human-
ities which lay in him, hardened and drowned in drink.
Though he had always, as long as people could remember him in Hanwitch, been what they called a dissipated
man, he had managed somehow or other to get a living,
to keep his landlord civil and wear good clothes. Ladies
were not wanting who called him handsome. His manner, when sober, was courteous; his language correct;
his fingers dexterous in pulling teeth out or putting
teeth in. Those who knew anything of him knew that
he never saved a penny; that were he to make ten
thousand a year he would never save a penny; but they
always said that, if he would only take a deep-rooted
dislike to beer and brandy, go to bed at ten and rise at

seven, attend to his business and give up smoking pipes
in the streets, he might obtain enough money to enable
him to keep a carriage and live in good style.

How he met Dolly matters little. She was living in
one room at Southbourne at that time, trying to obtain
a livelihood by taking in needlework. She was miser-
ably poor, with a little baby at her breast. Old Mr.
Newcome, the rector, did his best for her, and allowed
her what little he could afford out of his slender income,
which enabled her to pay her rent. But she had to
clothe and feed her child and herself, and the work she
procured was scanty and poorly paid for. God knows
how she managed to struggle through those days! Mr.
Conway asked her to marry him, but she answered "No,"
bitterly, for her love for Holdsworth was a passion.
Then her only friend, Mr. Newcome, died; her health
broke down; she was absolutely destitute; and so, for
her baby's sake—but shrinking from the marriage as
one shrinks from the commission of an evil deed, and
with a heart in her so heavy that nothing but her love
for her child seemed to keep her alive—she gave her
hand to Mr. Conway, and went to live with him at
Hanwitch.

She had no affection for the man. Her marriage
was a bitter necessity, and she hated it and herself for
that. She had no knowledge of Conway's habits, though
she had had penetration enough to miss certain moral
qualifications which are to be felt and cannot be explained. Now she discovered that he was an intemperate, improvident man, hasty in his temper, selfish, and
at the same time neglectful of his own interests.

He was some way ahead in his downward career
when he married her. The addition his marriage made

to his expenses quickened his pace, as an object, rolling slowly at first, improves its velocity in proportion to the increase of its distance from the starting-point. One by one his patients deserted him. He insulted his landlord, to whom he owed money, who gave him notice to quit. He then hired the little house in which we have found him, and was now illustrating one of the great mysteries of social life—the mystery of living without money, of keeping a house over his head without a shilling in his pocket, of wearing boots and coats without the means in his purse to pay off the milkman's sixpenny score.

How is this done? There are people doing it every day. They are doing more: they are keeping men-servants, renting big houses, wearing fine dresses, frequenting fashionable haunts, on nothing a year. How Thackeray puzzled over this problem! How Dickens tried to explain it and failed: for he is always driven to a last moment, when some good genius steps forward to help. Imagination can't deal with a feat which makes nothing do the work of a great deal.

There is no doubt something aggressive, even to good nature, in the brooding melancholy that goes about its duties lifelessly, which gives spiritless attention to matters of moment and significance, which looks complaint without speaking it, and addresses itself to every task of life with an air of reproachful endurance.

A man possessed of such an inflammable temper as Conway would be constantly taking fire in the presence of such a melancholy; and it must be confessed that Dolly embodied the part with some degree of completeness. Silent and mournful submission to fate was the wrong attitude to assume towards a man in whom was a good deal of the fool. A powerful virago, with muscular arms and a venomous tongue, would have kept him to his work and out of the taverns by the irresistible influence of words supported by finger-nails.

Dolly, whose heart was never with him, soon learned to despise him. It is true that she endeavoured, at the beginning of their married life, to win him from his extravagant and reckless courses by entreaties and the mild persuasion of caresses; but she soon ceased her appeals on finding that they took no effect, and only rarely alluded to his habits, which, having plunged them into poverty, were keeping them there, and sinking them lower and lower each day.

With an inconsistency not very uncommon, he resented her silence at the same time that he knew the expression of her thoughts would enrage him. He was still sufficiently under the control of her beauty to feel jealous of her love, which he very well knew was with the man they both thought dead. That truth had leaked out long ago. He once heard her teaching her child to pray; and presently lift up her own voice in a prayer which had no name in it but John's, whom she cried aloud to, bidding his spirit take witness of the sufferings which had driven her into an act that made her hateful to herself. Once, when her gentle sweetness was stirred into passion by him, she declared that she had never loved him; that she had married him for her child's sake; that if God took her babe from her she would kill herself, for her husband was in heaven, and his voice spoke in her conscience, eternally reproaching her for forgetting the vow they had made — *that though death should sunder them, the survivor would be true to love and memory, and live alone.*

But his petulance, his churlishness, his occasional brutality, indeed, was not owing to this. She had merely put his own knowledge of her into language; and since he had married her, fully persuaded that the gift of her hand had been dictated by pure necessity only, he could scarcely find himself alienated by the confession of her motive. Poverty and drink were the two demons that mastered him. And poverty without drink would have done the work; for his happened to be one of those boneless natures which give under a very small weight; one of those weak characters who, if they find themselves in a gutter, are satisfied to lie there and roll there, and moisten the mud with which they bedaub those about them with tears, and make their settlements gross with oaths, and shrieks, and reproaches.

CHAPTER XXVII.

ALL next morning Holdsworth kept watch for Dolly and his child, but did not see them. But Mr. Conway had passed when Mrs. Parrot happened to be in the room laying the cloth for dinner, and the woman had directed Holdsworth's attention to him. The glimpse he obtained, however, was very brief. All that he saw was a sandy-whiskered gentleman, with a tilted hat, aim with rather uncertain legs for the gate with the brass plate upon it, and vanish with an alacrity that was painfully suggestive of a disordered vision.

"There he goes! Drunk as usual!" exclaimed Mrs. Parrot, disgustfully, giving the table-cloth an angry twitch.

"How does he live? I have seen nobody call at his house yet!"

"No, sir; and I don't think you're likely to. Persons as can't get served at the other tooth-drawers are too sensible to walk all this way to get their jaws broke."

"Are they *very* poor, do you think?"

"Why, sir, I suppose he must pay his rent somehow, but I don't know as he does anything more. I'm told that they owe money all over the town, but the trades-people make no fuss, because, as Mr. Jairing the butcher says to me, 'It's all very fine, Mrs. Parrot,' he says, 'talkin' of hexecutions, but what's the use o' going to the expense of a distress when there's nothing to seize ?' There's a deal in that, sir."

"God help them !" muttered Holdsworth to himself. Then looking up he said, "Do you think Mrs. Conway would let her little girl come and have tea with me this afternoon ?"

"I should think she would, sir, and feel honoured by the askin'."

"I have not seen the child to-day."

"No, sir ! Mrs. Conway don't often come out. She kapes a bit of a wench as does her arrands, and I've told the slut times out o' mind to put her bonnet on, an' not go flyin' down the road as though a orficer was arter her, disgracin' of our neighbourhood, and frightening away any respectable person as might be comin' wi' a bad tooth. I don't think of *him*, sir. If I could put a sixpence in his way I would, for the sake of his wife an' the little one."

"How shall I invite little Nelly if I do not see her ?"

"I'll run across, if you like, when I've got your dinner ready, and ask Mrs. Conway if she'll let the child come. Perhaps you'll just watch, sir, and tell me when the husband leaves the house. I don't want to meet him if I can help it."

An hour elapsed before Holdsworth saw Mr. Conway pass on his way to the High Street, on which he rang the bell and informed Mrs. Parrot that she might now call on Mrs. Conway in safety.

His anxiety to have the child impressed his landlady as a very odd thing. She could understand his admiration of Nelly ; she could also understand his calling her in and giving her a kiss and a present. No man's heart, she considered, could fail to be warmed by the sight of so pretty a little girl. But she could not understand him posting himself at the window, and looking troubled because he did not see the child, and showing himself as anxious to have her to tea as if she was a grown woman, and he was courting her.

She sailed across the road (watched by Holdsworth), her cap-strings streaming over her shoulders, and walked up to the door of the Conways' house, and gave a single knock. She was kept waiting so long, that when the door was at last opened by the "bit of a slut," who, to judge by her complexion, appeared to have been devoting the last hour or two to black-leading her face, Mrs. Parrot, instead of asking for Mrs. Conway, began storming at her for "kaping respectable folks on the doorsteps while she sat readin' ha'porths o' bad fiction by the kitchen fire."

"I wasn't readin'. I didn't hear yer. Who do you want—missus?" said the girl sulkily.

"Why, Mrs. Conway, of course. Show me in, and go an' tell her at once that I'm here," replied Mrs. Parrot, not waiting to be shown in, but pushing into the middle of the passage.

The girl shambled off, and presently Mrs. Conway came up the kitchen stairs. The skirt of her dress was pinned up at the waist, and her arm-sleeves wore above her elbows, displaying the whiteness and fineness of the skin, though the arms were very thin.

"How do you do, Mrs. Parrot? You will excuse my wretched untidy appearance. I am doing a little washing downstairs, and would not keep you waiting whilst I made myself presentable."

"Niver mention it, ma'am," answered Mrs. Parrot, looking with pleasure, mingled with pain, at the sweet face, in which, now that there was no hat to shadow it. the sorrow and care were clearly seen. Her prettiness was but enhanced by the looped-up skirt, showing the little feet and small firm ankles. Her bright hair was in disorder, and there was the little flush of recent exertion on her cheeks.

"I've called wi' a message from my gentleman lodger. He wants Miss Nelly to drink tea with him, and sent me across to ask you to let her come."

"The same gentleman who gave Nelly a shilling yesterday?" asked Dolly, looking half surprised and half pleased.

"Yes, ma'am. He's a very nice person, and seems uncommon partial to children. He's been all the morning on the look-out for your little gal, and I hope you'll let her come, ma'am, and bring her doll wi' her, for I think he'll take it to heart if you refuse."

"Oh, I will certainly send her. Will half-past three do? I shall have to dress her. Pray give my compliments to the gentleman, and thank him for his kindness. You have not told me his name."

"Hampden, ma'am; Mr. Hampden."

"I have not yet seen him. Is he an old man? Few young men care for children."

"To tell you the truth, ma'am, I've got no more idea of his age, than I have of the age of my house. He's got a deal o' gray hair on his head, and yet he isn't an old man either, although to see him walk, leanin' on his stick, you'd take him to be sixty. I think he means to make friends wi' your little gal, if you'll let him, just for want o' company. He don't seem to know anybody

in Hanwitch, nor to follow any callin' like. I doubt he's
a bit rich ; but you see, ma'am, he only took my lodgin's
the day before yesterday, and I've not had time to make
him quite out yit."

Saying this, Mrs. Parrot dropped a courtesy, and
turned to depart, taking a quick comprehensive glance
at the dingy little parlour as she passed, and mentally
comparing it with her own rooms.

Holdsworth was at the window when she returned,
and she could hardly forbear laughing, so tickled was
she by his expectant face.

" Mrs. Conway's compliments, sir, and she says that
her little gal will be with you at half-past three,
thankin' you for your kindness," said she, her eyes
twinkling with her suppressed but perfectly good-
natured mirth.

" Thank you, Mrs. Parrot, for taking so much
trouble," exclaimed Holdsworth gleefully. " What
time is it now ? A quarter to three. I shall just have
time to walk into the High Street and buy a cake.
She will like a cake—a plum-cake I think ; and shall I
get some marmalade ? Yes, she will enjoy marmalade
—and what else ? Tell me, Mrs. Parrot ; what do
little children like ?"

" Why, mostly sweet things, sir. I guess the marmalade 'll take Miss Nelly's fancy. But don't you trouble,
sir ; I can run out and buy you what you want."

" No—I am obliged to you. There are other things
she might like which I shouldn't be able to remember
without seeing them. We will have tea at four, Mrs.
Parrot. I shall be back in twenty minutes."

Mrs. Parrot watched him leave the house and walk
down the road as swiftly as he could, leaning on his

stick. "Well, if iver I saw the like of this!" she exclaimed aloud. "I'll not tell mother; it might scare her. There's something downright sing'ler in the notion of a stranger takin' all this trouble, and goin' almost wild-like all along of a little gal he never saw before yisterday. Some folks 'ud call it alarmin'."

Her nerves, however, were equal to the occasion; for whilst Holdsworth was away, she journeyed upstairs and unlocked a little glass-fronted cupboard, screwed into a corner of her bedroom, from which she took a teapot, a cream-jug, and two cups and saucers of brilliantly-coloured china; likewise from an open box under her bed a tray magnificently decorated with mother-of-pearl birds of paradise seated on pink trees, and surrounded by a prospect not to be paralleled on this side the moon.

She returned to the kitchen with these things, and then entered the garden and picked a bouquet of sweet-scented flowers, with which she furnished the tray. Then she set to work upon a loaf of bread, and produced in no time a number of thin and appetising slices; which done, and the tray being arranged, she fell back a step to admire the effect.

At a quarter-past three Holdsworth returned, followed by a boy with his arms full of bags. He called to Mrs. Parrot, who came out and took the bags from the boy, and placed them upon the dining-room table. More things than edibles had been purchased; though of these there was enough to give an evening party upon —fruit, cakes, pots of jam, gingerbread-nuts, sweetmeats, tarts; there was a doll; there was also a horse and cart; and there was an immense box of bricks.

Mrs. Parrot turned pale, and was much too astonished

to speak, as Holdsworth thrust the bags and pots, the buns and the tarts, into her arms, and requested her to take them at once into the kitchen, and display them on plates to the very best advantage, ready for the little one when the bell should ring for tea. He then hid the toys in a closet, and stationed himself at the window to watch for Nelly.

Punctual to the moment, she came out of the house, led by the hand by the servant, who looked horribly grimy. Holdsworth ran to the door and opened it, and when the child came timidly up to him, snatched her up in his arms, and hastened with her into the sitting-room, kissing her all the way.

" There's a good little pet," he said sitting down and keeping her on his knee. " Let me take off your hat. Nelly mustn't be afraid of me."

" My own ! my own !" he murmured, as his lingering fingers caressed her soft hair, and he gazed with passionate love at her big eyes, roving with a half-scared expression from his face around the room.

" Me dot dolly," she said, producing the old toy from under her cloak.

" Ay, that's right ; and dolly shall have a slice of cake all to herself. Here she is !" he exclaimed, seeing Mrs. Parrot peeping in at the door. " Will you take her hat and this little cape ?"

" How do you do, dear ?" said Mrs. Parrot, giving the child a kiss.

" Look at my frock !" exclaimed Nelly, holding up her dress, which had a little embroidery work upon it, and which bore marks of much patient mending and darning.

" Beautiful ! beautiful !" cried Mrs. Parrot. " I've

set the kettle on to bile, sir, and tea 'll be ready whin-
iver you're pleased to want it."

So saying, she dropped a courtesy, being greatly impressed by Mr. Hampden's undoubted wealth, illustrated
by his prodigal purchases, and withdrew.

Father and child! A lonely man, gentle, honourable, faithful, as any whom God in His wisdom has
chosen to afflict, opening his heart to receive and fold
up the sweetness and innocence of his own little baby!

Ah! I think even Mrs. Parrot might have guessed
the strange mystery of this man's desire for the child,
had she but watched him from some secret hiding-place
when the door had closed upon her.

He surrendered himself to his emotion when he felt
himself alone with the little girl, and for many moments
could not speak to her, could do no more than look at
her, searching her fairy lineaments with something
almost of a woman's ecstasy, reading his brief history of
hopeful, beautiful love in her fresh deep eyes, and drinking in greedily the memories of the days that were no
more, which thronged from the face that mirrored his
as it was when Dolly knew him, as the dew-drop
mirrors the sun.

But he was recalled to himself by the gathering expression of fear in Nelly. Indeed, there was something
alarming enough to her in the concentrated passion, all
soft and holy as it was, that shone in his fixed regard.

Such abandonment to feeling would not do, if the
part he was to play was to be complete.

He placed her gently on the floor, and, going to the
cupboard, brought out the doll.

"See, Nelly! here is a little lady I invited expressly
to drink tea with you. She told me that she had often

seen you pass her shop in the High Street, and that she
wanted to live with you. You must take her home
when you leave me, will you?"

Nelly stood for a moment transfixed by the spectacle
of this gorgeously-dressed creature, resplendent in blue
gauze, bronzed boots, gilt sash, and flowing red feather.
Then—so permanent is human affection—she threw
down her old doll and ran forward, with outstretched
arms, to welcome and hug the stranger.

But the sum of her amazement was not yet made out.
Once more Holdsworth dived into the mysterious cupboard and produced the horse and cart, which, he told
Nelly, was the chariot that had brought the young lady
to his house, and without which she never condescended
to take the air, being much too fine a lady to walk.
The box of bricks followed; and presently Nelly was
on the floor, taking up the three toys one after the other
in quick succession, her avariciousness of enjoyment
perplexed by the number of the objects that ministered
to it.

Holdsworth knelt by her side and watched her face.

A man need not be a father to find something elevat-
ing and purifying in the contemplation of a child's
countenance, varied by tiny innocent emotions, reflecting the little play of her small passions, as her eyes
reflect the objects that surround her. But that subtle
and sacred bond, which unites a child's life to a parent's
heart, creates an impulse to such contemplation which
makes the pleasure sweeter than any other kind of
pleasure, by the infusion of an exquisite pathos, mingled
with the only kind of pride to which vanity seems to
contribute nothing.

The natural bitterness which Holdsworth felt in

thinking that his little girl did not know him, that misfortune had thrust his love out of the sphere of her own and his wife's life, was converted into tender melancholy by the emotions Nelly's presence excited, and left his pleasure unalloyed by pain. Here was a little being who was his at least; his by a right no sin, no folly, no error could challenge; indisputably his, to survive, if God permitted, into his future, when the time should come for him to call himself aloud by the name of Father, and ask her love as some recompense for that present sacrifice of his which was enforced by grand obedience to the high laws of morality.

How hard it was to be thus true to himself, thus true to his wife, thus true to the little one who must needs share some portion of that obligation of shame which would befall them all, were he to confess himself —Judge! for you see him kneeling by his child's side; you may behold his love in his eyes; you may know that no upturned luminous glance of hers but thrills along the chords of his passion, and makes his heart gush forth its overfull tenderness, even until his sight grows humid, and he turns his thoughts in a piteous aside to God for courage and will, so to sustain this strange, pathetic happiness, that no sorrow shall follow it.

"Nelly, we will have tea now," he says; and he rings the bell, and then comes up to the child again, and turns her face up, kisses her suddenly, and seats himself at a distance with his chin upon his hand.

Then Mrs. Parrot came in, armed with the tray, which she placed upon the table, while she challenged her lodger's admiration by lightly lifting her gray eyes and smirking.

Yes, it was very beautiful. The bouquet made the room odoriferous at once; the birds of paradise looked splendid; the cups were elegant enough to induce one to go on drinking tea with stubborn disregard of the nervous system, for hours and hours together, if only for an excuse to handle them and have them under the eye. In order to bring little Nelly's head a little above the level of the table, Holdsworth piled three or four of the folios on a chair, on which he seated her; and that the two dolls might be seen to advantage, he very ingeniously tied them together, and set them on a chair, leaning against the table, with a plate and a slice of bread-and-butter before them; whereat Nelly laughed rapturously, clapping her hands and filling the room with sweet sounds.

It was all Fairyland, these cups and toys and cakes and what not, to the little girl, whose tea at home was often no more than a slice of dry bread, when her step-father had drunk away the money he should have given to his wife, and left her without the means to purchase an ounce of butter. The sun was at the back of the house, and its rules of yellow light flooded the floor at the extremity of the apartment, and flung a golden haze over that portion of the room where the table stood. There was something so charming in the scene thus delicately lighted, that Mrs. Parrot, who had been struggling with her modesty for some minutes, while she fidgeted over the plates and dishes, suddenly exclaimed:

"I humbly beg parding for the liberty, sir, but would you mind mother just takin' one peep? She came into the kitchen while I was dressin' the tray, an' I told her what was goin' forward, an' I think it 'ud do her heart good to see this beautiful show."

"Let her come by all means," replied Holdsworth, touched and diverted by the perfect simplicity of these people.

Presently fell a respectful knock, and Mrs. Parrot re-entered, followed by a Roman nose that came and vanished like an optical delusion near the handle of the door.

"Come in, mother; the gentleman's kind enough to say you may," said Mrs. Parrot; and in faltered the old woman, dropping an aged courtesy, and making her spectacles chatter in their wooden case as she strove to withdraw them.

"Ain't this a picter, mother?"

"Niver see anything to aquil it," replied the old lady, putting on her spectacles and gazing around her with many a convulsive motion of the head. "Why, Sairey, them's our best cups!"

"Yes, I told you I was usin' them. Don't you see the little gal, mother?"

"See her? Yes,—of course I do. But she don't want an old 'ooman like me to kiss her, eh, my pretty? I'm very much obleeged, sir," dropping a creaking courtesy, "for the sight o' this table."

"Would your mother like one of these cakes for her tea?" said Holdsworth.

"Oh, sir, you're very good.—Mother, the gentleman wants to know if you'll accept of one of these cakes for your tea?"

"Thank ye, sir. I relish a bit o' somethin' sweet now and agin," replied the old lady, dropping another courtesy as she received the cake. "I was cook to Squire Harrowden, lar' bless yer! I dessay it were years afore you was born, and they did say as there niver was my aquil i' the makin' o' pie-crust. I've cooked for as many as a hundred and tin persons, ay, that I have," with intense earnestness, "as Sairey 'll bear me witness, for she's heerd the story from her own father, as was gamekeeper to the Squire, an' a more likely man you niver see, sir. His name was Cramp, which he was a Croydon man, as you may happen to know the name if you was iver in them parts."

"Come, mother, we have stopped long enough," exclaimed Mrs. Parrot, putting her hand upon the old lady's arm.

They both courtesied; and then the old woman let fall the cake, which rolled under the table. Holdsworth recovered it for her, which act of condescension was so overwhelming that she let the cake fall again; on which Mrs. Parrot lost her temper, and hurried the old dame through the door at a velocity to which her legs were quite unused, and possibly quite unequal. She might be heard feebly remonstrating in a voice similar to the sound a key makes when turned in a rusty lock; and then the door was closed, and Holdsworth and Nelly were left alone.

*   *   *   *   *

If Mrs. Parrot had dared, she would have been glad to advise Holdsworth "not to let the little gal eat too much, there bein' nothing worse nor sweetstuff for young stomachs, which finds milk-and-water sometimes too much for 'em." But, happily, Nelly was not a glutton; besides, the majority of human beings at her age eat only as much as they want, and no more; we wait until our judgment is matured, until life is precious, until we have experienced most of the distempers which arise from an overloaded stomach, before making ourselves thoroughly ill with over-feeding !

By this time the child was perfectly at home with Holdsworth, and enjoying herself immensely, varying a bite at a slice of cake with a bite at some bread covered with jam, sipping the good milk Holdsworth had obtained for her with great gravity, and staring at the dolls, and then bending to make sure that her bricks had not taken to their heels while she was looking at the horse and cart, and that the horse had not bolted with the cart while she was looking at her bricks.

Holdsworth scarcely removed his eyes from her face. When he spoke to her there was a softness in his voice that melted like music on the ear.

At last she pushed her plate away, and Holdsworth rang the bell, and giving Mrs. Parrot private instructions to make up a parcel of the remainder of the cakes, etc., ready for Nelly to take home with her, he clasped the child's hand and went with her into the garden, she holding the new doll, he dragging the horse and cart after him.

There was a square of grass in this garden, and a bench on it ; and here Holdsworth sat, while Nelly played with her toys.

It was a roomy, old-fashioned garden, with aged walls, full of rusty nails and rotten ligatures, and a few tall pear-tears sheltering a small circumference of ground at their feet; and many fruit-trees sprawling wildly against the walls. The moss was like a carpet on the flint walk, and the box at the side of the bed was high and thick ; and at the top of the garden was an old hencoop, hedged about with wirework, behind which some dozen hens scratched the soil for worms, and made the air drowsy with their odd, half-suppressed mutterings.

Moods possess us, sometimes, which such a scene as this will affect more pleasurably than a garden bursting with exotics, and tended with the highest artistic judgment. There is something very calming in homely shrubs, and old fruit-trees with their roots hidden by the long, vivid grass, and uncouth weeds thrusting their rude shapes among violet beds; and the solemn chatter of barn-door hens sunning themselves in hot spaces, or lying like dead things with a wing half-buried in sand and dirt, will sometimes impart a more agreeable tranquillity to the mind than the choicest songs of nightingales warbled in groves under a full moon.

Holdsworth suffered the child to have her full sportive will for some time, and then, thinking her tired, called her to him.

She ran to him at once, and he perched her on his knee.

" Is Nelly afraid of me now ?"

" No.   Nelly dot afraid.   Nelly loves 'oo."

In proof whereof she put her mouth up for a kiss.

" Will Nelly come to see me every day ?"

" Det."

" Does Nelly's papa love her ?"

He believed that she had been taught to regard Mr. Conway as her papa.   It was a sore tax upon the gentle mood then on him to put the question in that form, but he wished to learn if his child were well treated by her step-father.

The question puzzled her.   Indeed, she was a very little thing, and backward in her speech.   It was delicious to see her knit her tiny brows, and gaze with her full, deep, earnest eyes on Holdsworth, with a half-intelligence in her face, and all the rest child-sweetness.

Like all children, who cannot answer a question, she remained silent ; a hint parents would sometimes do well to take.

"Does Nelly get plenty to eat ?"

" Det."

This was not quite true ; but then Holdsworth, who knew nothing of children, was ignorant that little infants will borrow their answers from your voice or face, so that to get an affirmative from them you have only to speak or look affirmatively.

" Does mamma teach Nelly to pray ?"

" Det. Nelly pray."

And, to prove how well she could pray, she put her two hands together, hung down her head, and whispered:

" Dod bless dear mamma and Nelly. Dod bless little Nelly's dear papa."

She looked up coyly, as though ashamed.

Dear reader, smile not at these simple words, nor think them puerile. When we behold a little child praying, we know how the angels worship God.

A sob broke from Holdsworth as she ceased. Who was little Nelly's dear papa but he ? His wife's love had dictated that prayer, and it was their child who told him of her love. Ah ! God had deigned to hear that prayer, whispered by a wife's heart through the lips of her infant, and had blessed him with this knowledge of her devotion, and had brought him from afar to know it.

No ; not want of love had made her faithless to his memory. Faithless she was not—she could not be if her heart nightly spoke to God of him through her child.

Let him look at the little girl now ; let him feel the

fulness of the love she inspired in him; let him imagine that he was desolate and friendless, and in want, and that this frail flower, this tender little lamb, pined and grew wan and ragged for food and raiment; let him mingle with his own emotion the pain and torment which a mother's heart would feel in the presence of this baby's sufferings · and then let him condemn his wife, if he could, for sacrificing her memories and accepting food and shelter from any hand that offered them under any honourable conditions.

He could not speak again for some time; and Nelly, growing tired of sitting, slipped from his knee, and betook herself to her toys.

Then his eyes kindled anew, and he watched her eagerly. He longed to ask her questions—to hear her lisp him sweet assurances of his Dolly's love—to learn from her little lips that her mother was his, had been, would always be his, though separated from him by a barrier as formidable as death. But there was no question he could put which the child might not repeat again; for, backward as she was in speech, her small imperfect language would be intelligible enough to the mother. His curiosity would be too unnatural in a stranger not to excite Dolly's suspicions; and if they should not even lead to the discovery of his secret, they might be the means of breaking off all intercourse between him and his child.

And so he remained silent; and presently, as he sat watching the little creature pushing her doll to and fro in the cart and talking to herself, a calm came upon his heart—a sense of exquisite repose and security. You would have said, to look upon him and remark the placid sweetness that reigned in his face, that the child's prayer had veritably done its office—that God had blessed him indeed.

A long hour passed. The garden was fresh and cool; the declining sun mellowed the gray walls and kindled many little suns in the vine-draped windows; the sparrows flitted quickly with short chirrups from tree to tree; and the crooning of the hens added completeness to the peace and tenderness that breathed in the air.

Once again Nelly was on Holdsworth's knee, fetching vague replies from her struggling perceptions for his questions, when Mrs. Parrot came out of the house and said that Mrs. Conway was in the sitting-room, waiting to take her little girl home.

Holdsworth glanced quickly at the window of the room, but did not see her. He put the child down hurriedly, and said:

"There, my little pet, run along with Mrs. Parrot."

"Won't you come and speak to Mrs. Conway, sir?" asked Mrs. Parrot. "She wants to thank you for your kindness."

"No—no—pray don't let her call it kindness," stammered Holdsworth, who was very pale.

"I'm sure she'll take it unkind if you won't let her thank you, sir," said Mrs. Parrot earnestly. "She's been watching you both through the window for the last five minutes, an' I couldn't help tellin' her what a fine treat you have given Miss Nelly. Besides, she's seen them toys," she added, looking at Nelly's presents.

A whole lifetime of nervous pain was in that moment's pause. Could he meet her, speak to her, and remain unknown? His desire was to hide. It seemed inconceivable that in five years such a change should be wrought in him as to render him unrecognisable by his wife.

But the pressing necessity of immediate action was too sudden to give his imagination time to alarm his judgment. He must dare the encounter, since it was not to be obviated by any means which might not prove more productive of suspicion than bold confrontment.

He laid the utmost tyranny of his will upon his feelings, and saying:

"Perhaps you are right, Mrs. Parrot. Mrs. Conway will think me rude if I do not see her," took Nelly's hand and walked with her to the house.

Dolly was seated in an arm-chair near the fireplace, leaning her cheek on her hand. Her attitude showed that she had been watching the group in the garden.

She stood up when Holdsworth entered and bowed to him.

Nelly ran to her, holding up her doll.

"Look, mamma!"

The action was timely; it enabled Holdsworth to walk to the side of the window, where the shadow lay darkest, and there he stood.

This he had sense enough to do; but for a moment or two the room swam round him, and he grasped the back of a chair.

Would she know him?

That thought swept like a galvanic shock through him, and made his blood tingle.

It brought hope with it and fear; a wild paradoxical emotion of yearning love and the blighting sense of the sorrow and dishonour recognition would involve.

"I have to thank you very much, Mr. Hampden, for

your attention to my little girl," she said in a low sweet voice—how remembered !

"Her society gives me great happiness," he replied, with the faintest tremor in his tone.

It might have been that sign of agitation which made her look at 'him suddenly.

His gaze sank. But he felt her eyes upon his face, and the eager, restless scrutiny that filled them.

But if ever a memory of something infinitely beloved to her had been renewed by his reply, it melted upon her conviction of the death of him whom Holdsworth's voice had recalled to her, as snow upon water.

Could it have been otherwise?

Not five years—not twenty years—not a lifetime, maybe, of ordinary sufferings could have so transformed his face but that her love could have pierced the mask.

But the unnatural misery of those ten days in the open boat—the hunger that had wasted, the agonising thirst that had twisted his face out of all likeness to what it had been, the growth of beard and moustache that hid the lower part of the countenance, the gray hair, the bare forehead, the deformed eyebrows, the rugged indent between the brows, the stooped form !—

Here was a transformation that would have defied a mother's instincts— that would have offered an impenetrable front to perception barbed into keenness by the profoundest love that ever warmed the heart.

And yet, looking at this woman attentively—looking at her gazing at yonder man, cowering, it might almost seem, in the friendly shadow of the wall—there was something in her eyes, something in her face, something in her whole manner, that would have quickened your pulse with a moment of breathless suspense.

In such matters, as in the loss of memory, we must recognise the existence of a deep spiritual insight having no reference to the revelations of the mind. There are convictions which do not satisfy, though cemented by logic and acted on by their possessor with sincere conscience. Against such convictions instincts will surge as waves break upon a shore. Echoes are awakened, but are thought purposeless. And the conviction is still maintained, while the secret truth rolls at its base.

The voice of Holdsworth, but not his face, had set Dolly's instincts in motion.

But then her conviction that Holdsworth was dead was a permanent one ; and under it her instincts subsided into uneasy sleep, though there was a shadow of melancholy on her face when she removed her eyes, which had not been there before Holdsworth spoke.

"I hope Nelly has been good, Mr. Hampden."

"Very good, indeed."

He seemed to know that the crisis was passed, for he breathed more freely, looked at her, and removed his hand from the chair.

"These toys are very beautiful. I really feel unable to express my gratitude to you."

"You owe me no thanks. My gratitude is due to you for allowing your sweet little girl to come and see me."

"Mrs. Parrot tells me you are very fond of children ?"

"Very. I hope little Nelly will often be here. I am quite alone, and she cheers me with her pretty prattle."

She glanced at him quickly and sympathetically, as he said he was alone, and sighed.

Holdsworth noticed that her dress was very shabby ;

but her beauty lost nothing by her apparel. He thought her looking sweeter than when he had left her five years before. Her riper charms were made touching by an under colouring of sadness, and there was languor in her movements and speech—sign of heart-weariness.

"It is time for us to get home, Nelly," she said, looking uneasily towards the window. "Go and give Mr. Hampden a kiss, and thank him prettily for his beautiful presents."

The child approached Holdsworth, who kissed her gently, repressing the passionate emotion that, had he been alone, would have prompted him to raise her in his arms and press her to his breast.

"Here are some little cakes," he said, taking the parcel Mrs. Parrot had prepared, and giving them to the child, but addressing Dolly, "which will amuse her to play with. When may she come again, Mrs. Conway?"

"Oh, she must not intrude . . ."

"No, no! she cannot come too often. Pray let me make a companion of her. She has completely won my heart. May she not walk with me sometimes? I promise to take as much care of her as if she were my own child."

He had advanced a step and spoke eagerly, bending forward; but meeting her full eyes fixed on him with a little frown of mingled fear and amazement, he turned pale, fell back a step, and forcing a smile, said hurriedly:

"I am sometimes—sometimes laughed at for—for my love of children."

She did not answer him for some moments, but stood watching him with a startled expression, suggesting both fascination and terror. Then she averted her eyes slowly, the colour went out of her cheeks, and she murmured something under her breath.

"You remind me of one who was very dear to me . . . I beg your pardon . . . there is often a strange resemblance in the tones of voices."

She took the child's hand, and was mechanically walking to the door.

"Me want dolly and horse," said Nelly, holding back.

Holdsworth picked up the toys, and went into the passage to open the door. They bowed to each other, and Holdsworth returned to the sitting-room.

The moment he had dreaded had come and was gone. He had met his wife, spoken with her, and she did not know him.

He had noticed the sudden surprise and fear that had come into her face; he had noticed the deeply thoughtful mood in which she had quitted the house. But these things proved no more than this: that a note, familiar to her ear, still lived in the tones of his voice, and had aroused for awhile the memory which rarely disturbed her now, save in dreams at night.

Well! what he wished had happened. Suffering had deformed him, time had changed him, to some purpose. He could play the game of life anew, as one freshly come upon the stage. His paradise was closed to him, but he could stand at the gate and be a looker-on at the sphere in which his most sacred interests played their parts; he could respect and uphold, by his withdrawal and secrecy, her, whose vows to him his imagined death had cancelled; he could have his child for a playmate, and sow in her heart those seeds of love, which, if God should ever suffer her to know her father, would, in the fulness of time, bless him with an abundant harvest of happiness.

But, though he would not, for the worth of his life, have had things otherwise than they were, yet, as he stood in the room from which the light had departed with his child's sweet face, the tears rose to his eyes and sobs convulsed him.

Oh, it was hard to look back upon his sufferings, and feel that nothing but suffering yet remained ; hard and bitter to behold those whom he loved, those whose love would spring to meet him were he to make but one little sign, and to know that he was as dead to them as if the great desolate sea rolled over his body.

But here was a noble self-sacrificing heart that could not long mourn its own afflictions.   High virtues are always pregnant with high consolations, and a good man's grief for himself is short because he carries many tender ministers to it in his bosom.   There was no triumph now to complete, for his conquest over impulse had been achieved at Southbourne.   He drew to the open window at the back, where the air was fragrant with the smell of hay from the meadows beyond, and the cool evening perfumes of flowers hidden amid the shrubbery in the garden, and watched the sun sinking, whilst his thoughts followed it to the distant deep, whose breast it overhung, and on whose lonely surface he had watched it rising and setting with a despair the memory of which filled him with thoughts too deep for tears.

CHAPTER XXVIII.

THREE days passed before Holdsworth saw Nelly again. He then, from his window, beheld her playing on the pavement opposite with the horse and cart he had given her.

He called, and she came running over to him gleefully at once.

Mrs. Parrot was despatched to request Mrs. Conway's leave that Nelly might stop to tea with Mr. Hampden, and returned to say that "the little gal might, with the greatest of pleasure."

Again and again Nelly was summoned out of the road by Holdsworth, sometimes of a morning, sometimes of an afternoon, when he could see her. The little creature soon learnt to resist all her mother's suggestions that she should play in the back garden; she liked the pavement in the road, especially the pavement opposite Holdsworth's lodgings, and with an air of inscrutable mystery would keep a sharp look-out for Holdsworth, while she feigned to be absorbed in her toy. Ah, the artfulness of some little girls! But then there were always gingerbread and cakes for her in the miraculous cupboard in the corner of Holdsworth's room; and the temptation to obtain these luxuries, and to evade the

slice of bread and cup of thin milk and water which
formed her evening meal at home, was sometimes powerful enough to send her toddling out of the back garden,
where her mother placed her, into the road, actually
unobserved by mamma, who, imagining that she still
played in the garden, would be astonished by Mrs.
Parrot coming across and saying that Miss Nelly was
with Mr. Hampden, and please might she stop to tea.

Often, if Holdsworth had the good fortune to see his
little girl in the morning, or early in the afternoon, he
would put on his hat, and leaving word with Mrs. Parrot
to tell Mrs. Conway, should she ask, that he had taken
Nelly for a walk, clasp the child's hand and stroll with
her into the town.

Nelly enjoyed these rambles hugely. Their two
figures contrasted strangely, and many a woman's eyes
would follow them, because the measured step, the
thoughtful brow, the sunken face of the man, and the
golden-haired child at his side, with her bright young
face and big eyes drinking in the sights and processions
of the streets, and little twinkling feet, tripping so fleetly
and dancingly along, that one would say she held his
hand to prevent herself flying away, formed a picture
which a woman's heart would love to contemplate for
its prettiness.

They would sometimes turn out of the hot streets,
when Nelly's listless glance would show her weary at
last of the splendours of the toy-shops (before which
they regularly stopped) and wander to the river's side;
and there, in the shadow of trees, Holdsworth would
rest himself, while Nelly cleared the space around her
of all the daisies and buttercups she could find.

These were hours of deep and calm enjoyment to

Holdsworth, who, until the chimes of the town clocks
warned him to rise, would lie, with his head supported
on his elbow, that his face might be close to Nelly's
that he might catch every fluctuating expression that
made her eyes an endless series of sweet signs, that he
might hear every faltering syllable that fell from her
lips.

Soft and cool were the sounds the river made, as its
gentle tide gurgled a secret music among the high rushes,
or rippled round stumps of trees or projections of stone
lodged in the bank. Winged insects flashed many-
coloured lights upon the eye as they swept from shadow
to shadow, parted by a rivulet of sunshine falling through
the openings in the trees. Now and again a trout leaped
with a pleasant and lazy splash. From the shores
opposite, behind the trees, came the smell of the warm
red clover, mingled with the multitudinous hum of bees.
Afar, at a bend of the stream, an angler might stand
watching his quill, with his head and shoulders mirrored
in the clear water—so exquisite the counterfeit that one
might easily make a parable out of it, and sermonise
slumberously, as befitted the drowsy influence of the hot
day, on those illusions of life which mock the heart they
mislead in its search after truth.

Once, when Holdsworth was taking Nelly home, after
a long rest on the river's edge, he met Mr. Conway, who
stared very hard, but passed on without addressing the
child. Nelly drew close to Holdsworth when she saw
the man.

Holdsworth knew Conway perfectly well by sight
now. The dentist had repeatedly passed the window
at which Holdsworth stationed himself on the look-out
for Nelly; and of late, it might have been noticed, he

would glance with no unfriendly expression towards Mrs. Parrot's old-fashioned house.

His walk, when he did not actually reel, as he very often did, might have been studied with some disgust as an illustration of character. It was a species of gliding movement, such as a man might be supposed to adopt, whose self-abasement he himself holds irrevocable, and who has made up his mind no longer to walk, but to sneak through life. The influence of importunate creditors might be marked in the quick, furtive glancing of the eye, that wandered from side to side and challenged every individual it rested upon. One half-dulled perception of his social obligations might yet linger; or perhaps it was an innate love of dress which, from being a vice in prosperity, would degenerate into a kind of sickly virtue in poverty, that gave him an indescribable air of seedy jauntiness, tilting his soiled hat, swathing his neck in a bright kerchief, and furnishing his body with a small-waisted frock-coat.

It was very natural that Mrs. Parrot's lodger should be somewhat of a mystery to him. Having no liking for children himself, but, on the contrary, a rather decided aversion to them, he could not understand what this Mr. Hampden saw in Nelly to make him so prodigal in his gifts, so eager for her society.

Who *was* he? As Mrs. Parrot made a point of avoiding him, he could not very well question her about her lodger; but since she was the only person in Hanwitch who was likely to know anything about him, he got one of her tradesmen to cross-examine her. But this *ruse* resulted in little. All that Mrs. Parrot could tell was, that her lodger's name was Hampden, that he was a

gentleman with rather queer habits, and that he seemed
to have lots of money.

It was something to find out that he had lots of money.

On the strength of this Mr. Conway suddenly discovered Nelly to be a very interesting child, and never
seemed more pleased than when she was over the way
at Mrs. Parrot's.

The fact was, the dentist had an idea. It was a
small, contemptible, tricky idea, such as poverty and
drink would beget between them.   He kept it to himself and waited.

Dolly, of course, was deeply gratified by Mr. Hampden's affection for her child.   At first her curiosity had
been morbidly excited by this stranger.   Something
there had been in his voice which stirred memory to its
centre: and the strange, baffling, elusive thoughts it
had induced kept her spiritless and nervous for some
days after the interview between them.   Twice she
dreamed of the husband she believed dead.   The dream,
in both instances, was perplexed, and left no determin-
able impression; but its iteration increased her melancholy, and made memory painful and importunate.

She accounted for her feelings by referring them to
the recollections which had been abruptly renewed—
dragged, so to say, from the grave in which they lay
hidden; and this clue being put into her hand, left her
easy as to the *raison d'être* of her depression.

Indeed, no suspicion of this stranger's identity with
Holdsworth could have entered her mind without being
instantly followed by conviction.   The thought never
occurred to her: how *could* it?   She believed him dead,
and the permanent habit of this belief took the quality
of established proof of his death.

But even if she had doubted his death ; if ever she had cherished the hope that he would one day return to her—a hope that she had held to passionately for awhile, but which had dropped dead out of her heart when she gave her hand to Mr. Conway—no memory that she had of him would admit the possibility of the change that had been wrought in him.

There was a sign to be made—a look, a smile, a whisper—which would flash perception into her, knit into compact form the thoughts which his voice had troubled, and confess him her HUSBAND, though hollow-faced and wan ; though stricken as with age ; though presenting the ineffaceable memorials of grievous torture.

But, until this sign should be made, he must be a stranger to her ; a puzzle, perhaps ; a man of eccentric habits, and of an odd and striking aspect—but not her husband.

Nor, strange as his suddenly-acquired affection for Nelly might seem to others, could it come to her as a surprise. The mother's vanity would easily account for the pleasure her little daughter gave to the lonely man.

Once, when Mrs. Parrot, meeting her in the road, said that "It did seem strange that a man an' a child, as had niver set eyes on each other before, should love each other in the way Mr. Hampden and Miss Nelly did : " Dolly answered, "Yes ; but though I am her mother, yet I must say that Nelly is a pretty and very winning child, and there is nothing uncommon in strangers taking a fancy to children."

No ; that was quite true, Mrs. Parrot answered ; and told a story of a rich lady admiring a little beggar girl in the street ; and how the rich lady took the wench into her carrich, and got the parients' leaf to adopt her ;

and how the beggar girl came into the rich lady's fortin, and grew up into a stately an' 'aughty woman, an' married a lord, she did, as was beknown to many.

"It 'ud be a comfortin' thing to you, ma'am, don't you think, if Mr. Hampden was to adopt your little gal. It 'ud be a relief to your feelings, wouldn't it?" Mrs. Parrot said.

If some half-formed thought, bearing a resemblance to Mrs. Parrot's view, had flitted across Dolly's mind, let us not marvel. Never was her mood sadder, never was her secret grief sharper, than when her child's future formed the subject of her thoughts. Who would give Nelly a home if she died? Who would love the little thing; rear her in the knowledge of God, of her broken-hearted mother, of her poor drowned father?

"I could not part with her, Mrs. Parrot; she is the only link that binds me to bygone happy days. I could not spare her. My life would be *too* lonely for me to support it. But I often pray to God that she may find a friend—such a friend as I am sure Mr. Hampden would make her—when I am dead."

This hope—that Mr. Hampden *would* prove that friend—was the real source of the comfort that filled her heart each time she saw her little girl trip across to Mrs. Parrot's house.

She seldom saw Holdsworth. Sometimes she thought he avoided her. Twice, when she was leaving or returning to her house, she saw him in the porch, and each time he hastily withdrew, when she would have crossed over to speak to him. On rare occasions she met him coming from the town. Once he raised his hat and passed on : once she went up to him to thank him for his kindness to Nelly. He answered her hurriedly, speaking with an effort, and terminated the interview almost abruptly by bowing and leaving her. Then, again, his voice affected her powerfully. She stopped and looked after him ; and went on her way, brooding, with a little frown of anxious, painful thought.

On his part, the weight of his secret, when they thus met, face to face, was insupportable. The wild rush of impulse combated by inflexible resolution, created a conflict in his breast beyond his capacity of endurance. He could not have prolonged a conversation with her. It was shocking to feel himself unknown ; it was shocking to feel that he might betray himself. But he could watch her from his window. He knew now her hours of going and coming, and would station himself behind the curtain, and follow her with exquisite tenderness in his eyes, and sadness, crueller than words can tell, in his heart.

How was this all to end ?

Here was the thought that now tormented him. Six weeks had passed since he came to Hanwitch. He was living frugally, indeed ; and of the money he had brought with him from Australia a large portion still remained. But his few hundred pounds made a very slender capital ; and when they were spent what then ?

He knew very well that he could return to Sydney, that Mr. Sherman would welcome him back, and reinstate him in his old post. But the mere thought of leaving England was misery to him. Suppose, under any plea, he obtained Dolly's leave to take Nelly with him, could he part from Dolly ? He might never see her again. Then let him think of her companion ; of the sordid, hungry life he *knew* she was leading—knew, though he could devise no expedient for relieving her, that might not be resented as an affront and lose him Nelly's companionship.

He would rather have her in her grave than leave her as she was.

If urgent distress should ever come upon her, he would be at hand to succour and support her. And that such urgent distress *must* come sooner or later— that the day sooner or later *must* arrive when she and her child would be without a home, he had but to watch the maundering man who passed his windows backwards and forwards day after day, aimless, sodden, and growing shabbier and shabbier every week in his appearance, to know.

CHAPTER XXIX.

A VISIT.

How was Holdsworth to get a living? For what was he fit? He was a good clerk; Mr. Sherman had called him so, at least; Hanwitch was a tolerably large place, and he ought to find no difficulty in obtaining employment. At any rate, he must try.

One morning he put on his hat and walked into the town.

When he reached the High Street, he stopped and considered.

There was a bank; he could apply there. Then there was a brewery. If these failed, there remained an insurance office.

These represented polite avocations.

There were shops in abundance, where men, better looking than he, smiled over counters, and carried parcels, and stood bare-headed on the pavement at carriage-doors. But Holdsworth was still too much the sailor at heart to tolerate the notion of shop-serving. He would start a little school rather than do that. And indeed school-keeping seemed more feasible than anything else. Mrs. Parrot's lodgings would serve him there; boys would assemble by degrees; and he could set and hear lessons, and teach writing and mathematics, as well as any university man.

Meanwhile, let him try the bank.

It faced the market-place in the High Street, had a well-worn door-step and stout, noisy swinging doors. Holdsworth entered, and found himself in a badly-lighted office, with a counter across it, behind which were three or four clerks. A man who looked a fourth-rate farmer was paying money in, and whilst he counted a great accumulation of greasy silver, which he had discharged in company with a number of soiled, infragrant cheques out of a leather bag, he paused at every twenty to submit an observation of a rural nature to the intelligence of an elderly personage with long whiskers, and a somewhat Hebraical cast of visage, behind the counter.

The manager, for so the long-whiskered man was, observing Holdsworth to be a stranger, politely asked him his business.

" Can I speak to the manager ?"

" Certainly, sir; *I* am the manager. Walk this way, please."

Saying which, the manager bustled importantly into a back room, and threw open a side door for Holdsworth to enter.

" Pray be seated, sir. Nice weather."

And the manager drew a chair to a desk, clasped his hands on a volume of interest-tables, and fixed his eyes on Holdsworth.

" I have called to inquire if you are in want of a clerk," said Holdsworth.

" I beg your pardon ?" exclaimed the manager.

Holdsworth repeated his remark, adding that he was in want of a situation, and would be glad to fill any vacancy there might be in the staff of the bank clerks.

The manager, who had expected something very

different from this, got up instantly; his business-smile vanished, he thrust his hands into his breeches pockets, and exclaimed:

"Clerk, sir! Who told you we wanted a clerk?"

"Nobody. I have called here at my own suggestion."

"God bless my heart! You are quite out of order, sir! Really, these intrusions upon my time . . . . you should have explained your wish at the counter. When we want a clerk, we know where to find one, backed, sir, with first-class securities and influential recommendations."

"Then I have made a mistake, that's all," said Holdsworth, surveying the manager with great disgust; and paying no further heed to the protests with which the other followed him to the door, he walked into the High Street.

This summary treatment was enough to last him one day. His indignation yielded to depression, and he returned slowly and moodily to his lodgings.

This was the first time in his life he had ever made an application for employment; and his reception, which was really genteel and civil compared to the receptions experienced by men, old and young, every day, in search of work, at the hands of employers, wounded his sensibility and filled him with a sense of degradation.

He regained his lodgings, and endeavoured to console himself with philosophy.

But philosophy, says Rochefoucauld, triumphs over future and past ills; but present ills triumph over philosophy.

His sensibility did not smart the less because he reflected that hundreds of better men than himself had been insulted by rejections as offensive as that with which his inquiry had been encountered.

Thoughts of something tender and innocent will often quell the stubbornest warmth. Holdsworth grew mild in a moment when his mind went to little Nelly.

" I'll try the brewery to-morrow," he said to himself; " and if that fails me, I'll advertise for a situation ; and if nothing comes of that, I'll start a school."

Thus thinking he walked to the window, hoping to see his child in the road.

Nobody was visible but the old politician with the inflamed face, who was pacing slowly along the pavement, his hands locked behind him, his eyes bent downwards, and his brow frowning grimly. Presently, Holdsworth knew, the other old politician, who lived at the corner house, would come out, and there would be much gesticulation, and violent declamation, and frequent pauses, and moppings of the forehead with red silk pocket-handkerchiefs. Rain had fallen in the night, and cleansed the little gardens in front of the villas of the three weeks' accumulation of dust that had settled upon them, and freshened up the leaves and grass. In the bit of ground before Mrs. Parrot's house the flowers had withered on their stalks, but the shrubs still wore the bright greenness of summer ; the soil was dark and rich with the grateful moisture, and breathed a fragrance of its own upon the morning air.

Holdsworth was about to quit the window when he caught sight of Mr. Conway coming out of his gate. He fell a step back, and watched the man from behind the curtain. Mr. Conway advanced a few yards along his own side of the road, and then crossed, with his eyes fixed on Holdsworth's window.

Was he coming to the house? He moved softly and furtively, and when he was abreast of Mrs. Parrot's gate, threw a glance behind him, pushed the gate open, and knocked.

As Holdsworth did not know the man to speak to, he did not for a moment suppose that this visit was meant for him. Much was he surprised, and even agitated, when Mrs. Parrot came in and said that Mr. Conway was in the passage, and would like to see him.

The first idea that rushed into Holdsworth's head was, "I am known!" But conjectures were out of the question, for the man was waiting. "Pray show Mr. Conway in," he said; and in Mr. Conway came.

Holdsworth bowed, and so did the other, with a kind of spasmodic grace—a good bow spoiled by nervousness. He had dressed himself with care; he was cleanly shaved; his hair was carefully brushed; his shirt collars were white; and his boots shone.

Holdsworth had never before seen him so close. The light from the window fell upon his face and showed the cobweb of veins in his eyes, the puffy whiteness of his skin, the blueness of his lips, the tinge of gleaming purple about his nostrils, and all the other signals which the alcoholic fiend stamps upon the countenances of his votaries, so that, let them go where they will, they may be known and loathed by honest men as his adopted children.

But he was sober now; as sober as a man can be who has drunk but a glass of ale since he left his bed, but whose flesh is soaked with the abomination of the taverns, and whose brain can never be steady for the fumes that rise incessantly into it.

"Mr. Hampden, I believe?" he exclaimed in a

creamy voice, standing near the door, which Mrs. Parrot
had shut behind him, and twisting his hat in his hands.

"Yes; pray be seated," replied Holdsworth, looking
at him steadily, certain now that the object of this visit
was not what he had imagined it.

Mr. Conway sat down, and put his hat on the floor.
His embarrassment, when his business should come to
be known, might show a possibility of redemption, or at
least satisfy us that most of the bad qualities he was
accredited with might have been absorbed into his
nature with the drink he swallowed. No thoroughly
bad man could feel the nervousness that disturbed
him.

"I have called, Mr. Hampden, to thank you for your
kindness to my little step-daughter. Indeed, sir, both
my wife and myself thoroughly appreciate your goodness. Believe us, we do."

"Pray do not trouble to thank me. She is a sweet
child, and it makes me happy to have her," answered
Holdsworth, now at his ease, and studying his visitor
with curiosity and surprise.

"Ah! she is indeed a sweet child. A perfect treasure to her mother, and quite a little sunbeam in my
house—darkened, I regret to say, by misfortunes beyond
my control to repair."

"I am sorry to hear that."

"I never can sufficiently deplore having adopted so
ungrateful a vocation as dentistry. I was born to better
things, Mr. Hampden. My father had an influential
position under Government; but he died in poverty,
and I was apprenticed by an uncle . . pray forgive
me. These matters cannot interest you. Privations
press heavily upon a man at my time of life. Dentistry

seems to fail me ; and yet, when I look around, I find no other calling which I am qualified to espouse."

He sighed, and pulled out a pocket-handkerchief, with which he wiped his mouth.

Holdsworth was silent.

"Poverty I could endure, were I alone in the world," continued Mr. Conway ; " but it is unendurable to me to witness the best of women and the dearest of little children in want. My poor wife does not complain ; but I witness her secret sufferings in her wasting form and irrepressible tears, and it goes to my heart, sir, to see her, and feel my miserable incapacity to relieve her."

"Do you mean to say that she is actually in want?" exclaimed Holdsworth in a low voice.

"Yes, sir ; we all are. As I hope to be saved, I haven't more than two shillings in the wide world !"

"Have you no source of income outside your profession?"

"No. I did well in the High Street; but I had many rivals and enemies, who spread lying reports about me, and lost me my best patients. Give a dog a bad name ! I left my establishment in the heart of the town, and came into this road because rent was cheap here ; and God knows if I can tell how I have lived since," he cried passionately, his natural bad temper breaking through his affectation of suffering and ill-treatment. " The pawnbroker has been my only friend ! Am I to sell the bed from under me? Oh, sir, I think of my wife, of my poor little child—for my child she is, if love can make her so—and the thought is death to me !"

He flourished his handkerchief and looked piteously at Holdsworth.

" How can I serve you ?"

" Ah, sir !" exclaimed Mr. Conway, sinking his voice
into a yet more whining note, the while a gleam entered
into his eyes ; " what right have I to trespass upon the
benevolence of a stranger ? of a gentleman who has
already placed me under a thousand obligations by his
kindness to my little daughter ?   I feel myself a wretch,
sir, when I reflect upon the unfortunate position I have
placed my poor wife in.   I was flourishing in those days;
I could have given—I *did* give her and her baby a good
home.   But what position is so secure that it can stand
against the lies of rivalry and jealousy ? the slanderous
reports of ruffians who make capital for themselves out
of a neighbour's trifling errors, and—and—oh ! damn
them !"

" How can I serve you ?" said Holdsworth, coming
quietly back to the point.

" If I dare name my wants to you, sir—if I dare
presume upon that benevolence which you have so sig-
nally illustrated in your behaviour to little Nelly, I—
I——"

" I am a poor man," said Holdsworth, as the other
paused ; " and can afford but little.   But that little is
cheerfully at the service of your wife and child, who
must not be allowed to want."

He spoke emphatically, to let the man understand
the purpose to which he intended his gift or loan should
be applied.

" But for that wife and child, sir," answered Mr.
Conway, apparently struggling with his emotion, " *could*
I place myself in this position ?   Is there any personal
necessity, however imperative, that would force me to
lose sight of the pride which renders starvation prefer-

able to alms-seeking, to the gentleman born? No, sir," he continued, with an air of injured dignity; "poor as I am, I can still recognise the claims of my birth upon my actions; and I repeat, that were it not for my wife and her little one, no affliction, however unsupportable, should oblige me to intrude even upon *your* benevolence."

He paused, and seeing Holdsworth look impatient, exclaimed hurriedly:

"If ten pounds——" and stopped.

"You wish to borrow ten pounds?"

"Ah, sir, if I dare——"

"Of what service will so small a sum be to you?"

The man looked struck; Holdsworth had expected to hear a larger sum named, he thought.

"Ten pounds—to a poor man—to a poor family, sir, ten pounds is a great deal of money."

"I will lend you ten pounds willingly, on condition that you spend it on your wife and Nelly."

"Certainly, certainly," replied Mr. Conway meekly. "You may depend upon being repaid, if I have to pawn the shirt off my back to get the money."

I suppose that this kind of security (generally offered by men who have not the least idea of repaying a loan) must be figurative—a poetical figure of debt. How far would the shirt off a man's back help the redemption of the debts borrowed on the strength of it?

Holdsworth gave Mr. Conway two five-pound notes. The man took them eagerly, and whilst he buried them in his trousers' pocket, poured forth a profusion of thanks.

"Does Mrs. Conway know of this visit?" asked Holdsworth, stopping his noise.

"No, sir; but believe me, I shall not fail to acquaint

her with your kindness," he answered, taking his hat
and rising.

Holdsworth's impulse was to request him not to speak
to her of this gift—for loan it would be ridiculous to
call it. But he checked himself with the consideration
that, were Mr. Conway to break his word, Dolly would
find food for dangerous questioning in the request.

He said, instead, " You will not forget the purpose for
which I have lent you this money ?"

" Trust me, sir; trust me," murmured Mr. Conway,
pressing his hat to his heart. " If you will give me ink
and paper I will make you out an I O U at once."

" Never mind that. Nelly is a growing child, and
requires nourishing food: devote the money to her and
her mother, and you will make me grateful."

He walked into the passage, and Mr. Conway, bowing
humbly, passed into the porch, where he stood a moment
or two peeping at his house; then, with another bow,
hurried into the road, and vanished in the direction of
the town.

The poverty of the Conways, then, was unquestion-
able. Holdsworth had often speculated upon their
position, but had never reached nearer to the mark than
supposing that they lived from hand to mouth, and just
made shift to support the day that was passing over
them. That they were actually in want, actually
destitute indeed, it had never entered his mind to imagine. He believed Conway's story. And it was very
certain that, if the man had no private means of his
own, he must be hopelessly poor, for he made nothing
by his profession. In all the six weeks that Holdsworth
had been in Hanwitch he had not seen as many people

call at Conway's house; and of these, supposing them to be patients, half of them had come away after speaking with the servant, doubtless informed that master was out.

But even guessing so much, Holdsworth guessed only half the truth : and it was well, perhaps, that he did not know all, for grief must have mastered his judgment, and forced him into the confession which he prayed, night and morning, for will to restrain. It was after dark always when Dolly, closely veiled, would creep down the road, with some little bundle under her shawl, for the pawnbroker, that she might obtain a trifle in order to furnish her child with a meal on the morrow. It was in the privacy of her own home that she laboured, as no menial ever *will* labour ; sitting up late night after night, over the endless task of darning and mending her own and her child's shabby apparel ; often going supperless to bed, and waking to a day even more hopeless than the one that had preceded it.

The devoted man, who would have given his life to win her happiness, knew nothing of all this. Even his little child's dress told him no story, though a woman might have read a full and pathetic narrative of toil and poverty in the frock, turned and re-turned, mended and patched, and darned again and again.

Holdsworth seldom saw her now : yet, if ever she caught sight of him at his window, she had always a kindly smile, a grateful nod : and what with the shadow of her hat over her face, and the distance which softened the lines of care, grief, and weariness into the sweet and delicate effect of her beauty, he was ignorant of the serious and withering change that had taken place in her, even during the short time that had elapsed since they had last met and spoken in the High Street.

Nelly came over to him at one o'clock, and he kept her to dinner. The child was hungry, and as he watched her eating, he thought of Dolly.

"Has mamma got a good dinner to-day, darling?"

The little thing looked puzzled; but upon Holdsworth repeating the question, answered "Noo."

He thought she was mistaken, since, after what Conway had told him, the man's first action, he believed, now that he had money in his pocket, would be to attend to his wife's necessities. But though he repeated his question in different shapes, the child invariably answered, "Noo, mamma got no din-din."

"No dinner at all! Are you sure, my pet?"

Yes, the child was sure, as sure as a child could be.

Holdsworth sprang up and rang the bell, and entered the passage to await Mrs. Parrot. She came out of her kitchen, and Holdsworth exclaimed, mastering his agitation:

"I want to confer with you, Mrs. Parrot. Nelly tells me that her mamma has no dinner to-day. Is this likely—is this possible, do you think?"

"Indeed, sir, since you ask me, I do then, and God forgi' me for thinkin' the worst," answered Mrs. Parrot.

"But," cried Holdsworth, "I gave Mr. Conway ten pounds this morning, stipulating that he should spend it on his wife and child!"

"He!" exclaimed Mrs. Parrot, almost savagely. "The wretch! ten pounds! he'll spend it all i' liquor! Oh, sir, why didn't you give it to the poor lady?"

"Yes—I ought to have done so," replied Holdsworth clasping his hands. "But how could I—what excuse *could* I have found for sending it to her? Oh, Mrs. Parrot! something must be done. I can't bear to think of the poor lady actually dinnerless. What can we contrive? Remember—she is a lady—we must be careful."

"To think of your lending ten pounds to that villin!" cried Mrs. Parrot, whose mind was staggered by the munificence of the sum and the artfulness of the man in obtaining it. "I niver heerd of such a thing! And was that his reason for callin'? If I'd ha' only known his object, I'd ha' sent him packin' with his blarney, wouldn't I?"

"What do you advise?" said Holdsworth, eagerly.

"Well, sir, I'm sure I don't know what to say. She *is* a lady, and it wouldn't do to send her butchers' meat across, would it? I'll tell you what we *could* do, sir; I could kill one o' my fowls and leave it with my compliments, pretending I had killed some yesterday, and wished her, as a neighbour, to taste my fattening."

"That will do! But, instead of killing your fowls, take this half-sovereign and run at once to the poulterer's, and buy a couple of pullets. You can then take them across, and she will suppose they are your own rearing. Will you do this?"

"With the greatest of pleasure, sir; and I'm sure you must have a very kind heart to take so much interest in poor folks."

And Mrs. Parrot ran off for her bonnet, and was presently hurrying down the road with a market-basket on her arm, and her untied bonnet-strings streaming over her shoulders.

Holdsworth waited impatiently for her return, whilst Nelly, who had finished dinner, toddled about the room, gazing with round earnest eyes into the recesses, and the cupboards, and at the shepherds on the mantelpiece, and the yellow roses on the mat.

In ten minutes' time Mrs. Parrot came back with her face flushed with the heat and exercise, and darted into the house as though she had swept half a jeweller's shop into her basket and was flying for dear life.

"There, sir, what do you think of these?" she exclaimed, dragging a pair of handsomely-floured pullets out of the basket and holding them at arm's length, as though they were a pair of ear-rings. "Aren't they beauties, sir?"

"How can I send them across? Will you take them?"

"Oh yes. I can jest leave 'em at the door wi' Mrs. Parrot's compliments. She'll be sure to guess that they're my rearin', and save me from an untruth, though my religion is none so fine, thank God, that I should be afeard to tell a kind o' white lie to help any poor creature as wanted."

She then examined the pullets attentively, to make sure that there were no trade-marks upon them in the shape of tickets, adjusted her bonnet, wiped her face, and walked across the road.

Holdsworth waited in the passage until she returned. She was absent a few minutes, and then came back smiling, with the lid of the basket raised to let Holdsworth see that it was empty.

"Did you see Mrs. Conway?"

"No, sir, I wouldn't ask for her," replied Mrs. Parrot, wiping her feet on the door-mat. "I jest says to the gal, 'Give this here to your missis with my compliments, and tell her that they're ready for cookin' at once, as they're been killed long enough.' I niver see any gal look like that wench did when she took the pullets. I thought she'd ha' fainted. She turned as pale as pale, and then she grinned slow-like, and then laughed wi' a sound for all the world like the squeak of a dog that's smotherin' under a cushion. Here's your change, sir. Pullets, six shillin', and one is seven, and two is nine, and two sixpences makes it right. Will you please to count it?"

Holdsworth thanked her, and returned to the sitting-room with a relieved mind. But scarcely was he seated when Mrs. Parrot knocked on the door, and mysteriously beckoned him into the passage.

"I forgot to say, sir, that I ast the gal before coming away if her master was in, and she said 'No.' I says, 'When will he be in?' She says, 'I don't know, missis; he went out this mornin', an' he's not been back since.' Mark what I say, sir!" added Mrs. Parrot, raising an emphatic forefinger, "he'll not give a penny o' that money to his poor wife, but jest keep away from her till he's drunk it all out."

Accompanying which prophecy with many indignant nods, she walked defiantly towards the kitchen.

The idea of Dolly's miserable position, never before impressed upon him as it had been that day, made Holdsworth wretched. He seated himself at the window and stared gloomily and sadly into the road. Nelly came to him and tried to coax him to play with her, but he had no heart even to meet the little creature's sweet entreating eyes with a smile. He caught her up, pressed her to him, and kissed her again and again, while the hot tears rolled down his thin face.

Never before was his impulse to tell Dolly who he was and snatch her from the misery, the unmeet sorrow that encompassed her, so powerful. Love and pity strove with the dread of dishonouring her by the revelation. Could he endure to think that this delicate, gentle girl was linked to a man who neglected her, who might even ill-treat her, who at that moment might be squandering the money that had been given him on his own gross appetites, without thought of the wife and child wanting bread at home? What must be the issue of such a life if it were permitted to endure? Sooner or later Holdsworth must avow himself to save her and his child from that uttermost degree of ruin and misery to which Conway was dragging them.

He had hoped to devote his life to them. His dream had been that Conway's character was not irretrievably bad, that kindly entreaty, cordial advice, and pecuniary help might bring him to a knowledge of his folly and set him once more on the high-road to respectability. Such a redemption would have been Holdsworth's sacrifice ; but his own happiness was as nothing in his eyes compared to Dolly's. Faithfully would he have performed his duty to her, nobly would he have vindicated his own most honourable, most exalted devotion, could he have reclaimed this erring man and taught him to give his wife as much happiness as it was possible for a heart that ceaselessly mourned a dead love, to know. Thus he could have been his Dolly's good angel, and whilst God permitted him, have kept watch over her and her child, dead to her belief, but active as the holiest love could make life in his helpful secret guardianship.

He perceived the vanity of that hope now, and yet despairingly clung to it, because, if he surrendered it, he felt that he must confess himself, and from this he shrank as from a deed that would inflict a deeper degradation upon her, while Conway lived, than any she could suffer from her husband's behaviour.

One must either entirely sympathise with his profound susceptibility of the obligation his supposed death had forced upon him to fulfil, or ridicule him as a man absurdly fantastical in his views of morality. There seems no middle standpoint to judge him from.

But unless there be too much austerity in his virtue to make it admirable, then, to properly appreciate it, we must remember the extraordinary tenderness of his nature, his exquisite sensibility, which shrank from the mere thought of tarnishing the pure honour of the woman he loved.

That he believed her honour would be tarnished were he to proclaim himself in the lifetime of her present husband, was enough; and whether he was right or wrong; whether he was correct in holding the obligations of the marriage-service holy, binding, and to be disturbed only at the risk of God's wrath, when incurred with a spotless conscience, when entered upon in innocence and good faith; or whether he should have regarded the marriage-service as a mere civil convention which made his wife his property, claimable by him on the common ground of the law of priority, without reference to any action she might have committed in honest belief that he was dead; one thing we must allow him—an unparalleled quality of unselfishness, the existence of which, while it attested the sincerity of his views (since he had his heart's deepest affections to lose and nothing to gain by retaining them), elevated his conduct to the highest point of heroism.

Nelly had never before found him unwilling to romp with her; when he raised his head she watched his face with a strange, wistful look, and putting her finger to his cheek, said :

"Why do 'oo cry?"

He forced a smile for answer, caressed her, and then placed her on the ground, thinking she was weary of sitting.   But she climbed upon his knee again, and repeated her question with great earnestness:

"Why do 'oo cry?"

"Because I am silly and weak, my little one.   I am forgetting that there is a good and just God over me, who will hear my prayers and help me, as He before did, when I was alone on the wide sea."

He said this aloud, but spoke rather to himself than to the child.

"Dod loves Nelly," said the little thing, "and Nelly loves 'oo.   Nelly kiss 'oo."

That was all the comfort she could give him; but it fell tenderly on his ear.   He kissed her gratefully, rocking her gently to and fro in his arms with his eyes on her face.   She soon, however, rebelled against an attitude which crippled her limbs, and slipped on to the floor, and to amuse her he gave her a book with pictures in it, which she examined gravely, talking to herself as little children and aged people do.

In this manner the afternoon passed; but never was Holdsworth more depressed, more restless, filled with more nameless anxieties and misgivings.

Apart from all moral considerations, his future was terribly uncertain.

Suppose the Conways left the town?   He must follow them, for he could not bear the separation; and what would they think of his pursuit?   Suppose all his efforts to obtain a living failed, what should he do?

At five o'clock Mrs. Parrot came in to put on Nelly's

hat : that was the regular hour at which the little girl was sent home by Holdsworth.

"My apron is dirty," said the worthy woman, "so I'll not go across with you, my dear. But I'll watch from the porch until I see you safe in."

So, receiving a kiss and a piece of gingerbread from Holdsworth, the child toddled into the road, and when she was inside the gate, where her mother would see her, Mrs. Parrot closed the door and went back to her ironing in the kitchen.

CHAPTER XXX.

THE KNOT IS CUT.

A STORM broke over Hanwitch that night, and left behind
it a strong wind which swept up great masses of clouds;
and the morning sunshine streamed and darkened in
quick alternations, and made the air lively with the
movement of shadow.

Holdsworth, deeply disturbed by conflicting anxieties,
had slept but little, and at eight o'clock left his bed and
started for a walk before breakfast, hoping that the
breeze which thundered about the house would freshen
and inspirit him.

Gaining the High Street, he turned to the left and
walked along a narrow pathway that took him through
the fields to Maldon Heights, as the hill that overlooked
Hanwitch was called. He climbed the grassy slope and
stood awhile on the summit, drinking in the hooting
wind and watching the fluctuating scene that ran from
his feet to the horizon. The oats and barley in many
fields were not yet cut; and it was a sight to see them
breaking into wide spaces of delicate gold under the sun,
and growing gray again as the cloud-shadows sailed over
them. When the sunshine lingered awhile, these fields
seemed to reflect the shadows which had passed, for the
wind rushed like a dark arm along them, and pressed

the graceful grain into the likeness of a wave, which swept forwards with swiftness, making the fields dark where it ran. The farther trees appeared to hold steady under the breeze; but there were nearer trees which swayed their branches in wild gesticulations of entreaty, and flogged the wind as it roared among them, bearing away trophies of green leaves and broken twigs. The birds breasted the gale with short flights, or turned and yielded to the invisible power with small cries. Every object the eye rested on appeared in motion, so lively was the effect of the cloud shadows upon the houses and the weight of the wind upon the surrounding country.

It was a morning to clear the most hypochondriacal mind of despondency, and Holdsworth felt its cheerful influence as he stood exposed to the swinging rush of warm air, and watched nature dancing to the tunes sung by the wind as it swept through the sky.

He had made up his mind to call at the brewery that morning, and he took a look at it as he passed the street in which it stood on his way home. The gaol-like building, with the steam about its windows resembling rich London fog, which refused either to stop in or go away, was scarcely calculated to improve his hopes. Big beef-faced men in aprons rolled huge casks out of a courtyard into a cellar filled with sawdust, damp, and gloom; the throb of the engine could be heard distinctly, and the wind that blew out of the street came in agitated, disordered puffs, as though the smell of the beer had made it rather drunk.

Holdsworth shook his head as he passed on. It struck him that there would be little chance of his getting employment in that steaming, panting, perspiring quarter; and that he would be acting more wisely if, instead of challenging rudeness by personal inquiries at places where nobody wanted him, he spent a few shillings in advertising for a situation.

Determining to do this, he made what haste he could back to his lodgings, meaning there and then to manufacture an advertisement.

He entered his sitting-room, rang the bell to let Mrs. Parrot know he had returned, and sat himself down to consider the terms in which he should make his wants known.

" What would you like for breakfast, sir ? " said Mrs. Parrot, opening the door.

" Oh, anything you please. A new-laid egg if you can find me one."

" Yes, sir. I took four beauties out just now. Have you heard the news, sir ?"

" No. What news ?"

" Well, sir, it's what I allus thought must happen ; and day after day I've bin expectin' it, as mother 'll bear me out. They've got the brokers in at the Conways."

"The brokers!" exclaimed Holdsworth, turning round in his chair quickly.

" Yes, sir. Their gal told the milkman just now, as giv' me the news. And what's wuss—leastways some might call it wuss, though I should consider it a good job myself if I was his wife—Mr. Conway hasn't been home all night !"

" The villain !" exclaimed Holdsworth through his teeth. And then he jumped up and began to pace the room excitedly.

" Stop !" he cried, observing that Mrs. Parrot was about to withdraw. " Are you sure this news is true ?"

" Oh, I've no doubt of it, sir. When the milkman

told me, I was jest goin' to run across and see the poor lady, and then I says to myself, 'What use can I be to her ?'"

"I may be of some use, though," interrupted Holdsworth. "Never mind about my breakfast just yet. When did the man enter the house to take possession ?"

"Last night, sir, the gal told the milkman."

"Great heaven ! And has she been alone all night ?" He stopped short, seized his hat, and, brushing past Mrs. Parrot, went quickly out of the house.

Mrs. Parrot watched him from the porch, lost in amazement.

He pushed open the gate, marched up to the door, and knocked loudly. His mood was one of deep excitement. The sense of the crushing misery that had fallen upon Dolly had given a poignancy to feeling that set all self-control at defiance.

The door was opened by the servant, and out with her came a smell of strong tobacco smoke.

"Is Mr. Conway in ?"

"No, sir, he ain't," answered the girl, looking behind her and then at Holdsworth, with a scared face.

"Where's your mistress ?"

"In the parlour, sir."

"I should like to see her."

"She's not wisible. She's in grief, and ain't to be seen."

"Go and tell her that Mr. Hampden has called and would like to say a word to her."

"I don't think——"

"Do what I tell you !" exclaimed Holdsworth.

The girl slouched backwards and pushed her head into the parlour-door.

"She ain't here. She's gone upstairs," said she, and upstairs she went, slapping the staircase with her shoes as she went.

An individual with a round red face, a white hat, a spotted shawl, a coat nearly to his ankles, a long waist-coat, and a black clay pipe in his mouth, lounged elegantly out of the room which Mr. Conway had called his "Surgery" at the end of the passage, and leaning collectedly against the door, nodded familiarly to Holds-worth, took his pipe from his mouth, expectorated, and said "Morning."

"Good morning. Are you the man in possession?" replied Holdsworth.

The individual nodded and replaced his pipe.

"When did you come?"

"Last night," answered the man in a thick voice. "And a werry queer look-out it is. Blowed if they've got any butter in this house!"

"What is the amount of the debt?"

"Twenty-three pun four and sevenpence," said the man, removing his pipe to expectorate again. "Are you a creditor?"

"No," answered Holdsworth, listening for Dolly's footsteps.

"Then if you vent on your bended knees for grati-tood you vouldn't be overdoin' it," said the man, giving Holdsworth a sagacious nod. "There ain't above ten pound in the house, and not that. Cast yer eye into that parler. The best of the goods is there, and if you can make three pound out of 'em, I'll swaller my pipe."

And then an idea smiting him:

"You ain't come to have a tooth drawed, have yer?"

"No."

" Vot's your opinion of tooth-drawin'?" inquired the man confidentially, retiring and reappearing again, holding up a pair of forceps. " Ain't it rayther a queer go, don't you think? I knew a barber as drawed teeth. He never used nothing of this kind. Vot do you think he did? Bust me if he doesn't set you in a chair, fastens a bit o' vire to the tooth as is to come out, and ties t'other end of the vire to the leg of a table. Ven all's ready, 'Mind yer eye' he sings out, ups with a razor, rushes at yer makin' horrible mouths, up jumps you, avays you run, and leaves your tooth behind yer!"

He gargled an asthmatical laugh, adding: "That's vot I call a sensible vay of drawin' a tooth; no bits of cold iron shoved into yer mouth as if yer tongue vas hair and vanted curling."

"Please, sir, will you step into the parlour and sit down," said the girl, thrusting her head over the banisters and calling to Holdsworth. " Missis 'll be with yer in a minute."

He entered the wretched little parlour, while the " man in possession " retreated to the surgery arm-chair, and sat severely contemplating some unfinished teeth on the table in front of him.

· In a few moments Holdsworth heard footsteps outside, and Dolly came in, holding Nelly's hand. She was terribly pale, with a look of terror and exhaustion on her face painful to see. There was an unnatural sleepless brilliancy in her eyes that heightened her worn, hopeless expression. She had thrown an old shawl over her shoulders, and through the portion of the fair skin of the neck that was exposed the veins showed dark. The hand she gave to Holdsworth was like a stone.

He was so overcome by the sight of her misery, that

for some moments he could not speak.   The child came
up to him and rubbed her cheek against his hand.

"This is kind, very kind of you, Mr. Hampden," she
exclaimed in a low, faint voice, sinking upon the sofa
and shivering as she hugged the shawl about her
shoulders.

"You are in great distress, I fear.   I only heard the
news just now.   I came over to you at once," he
answered tremulously, the fierce beating of his heart
sounding an echo through his voice.

"It is what I have been daily expecting for many
months—for many bitter, cruel months!" she exclaimed.
"It has come at last.   We are homeless now.   And my
husband, who ought to be at my side, has left me.   He
was away all day yesterday and last night.   O God!
what a night it has been!" she moaned, rocking herself
to and fro.

"Don't say you are homeless," he cried; "you have
a friend.   Let me be your friend.   Mrs. Parrot shall
give you a home for the present . . if you will accept
it."

She looked at him with stupefied eyes as one who
doubts her senses, then said : "We have no claim upon
you.   Oh! how noble-hearted!   Nelly, Nelly, come to
me, come to me!"

The child ran to her mother, and, being frightened
by the passionate despair in her voice, hid her face in
her lap and burst into tears.   But Dolly's eyes remained
dry—lost nothing of their wild brilliancy.   She dragged
her child to her, and swayed to and fro with tearless
sobs that shook and convulsed her.

"I have deserved this," she presently moaned.   "I
was faithless to the truest love God ever blessed a

woman with. Why was he taken from me? My child was starving, and the sight of her wasted body drove me mad with grief. I never loved Mr. Conway—he knew it . . . He has left me! Oh! he is a coward to leave me! What am I to do? I am a lonely woman —I have this child to feed and clothe—I have not a relative to turn to—and now we are homeless! O God! this is too much, too much!"

She hid her face in her child's hair.

Nothing but the dread that the truth, at that moment, might kill her to hear, prevented him, as he listened to her heart-broken words, from kneeling to her and calling her wife. He watched her with a strange steadfastness of gaze, and with a face more bloodless than hers. The impulse to avow himself had recoiled and driven the blood to his heart; a faintness overcame him, but he battled with the deadly weakness, and the better to do so, rose and strode across the room and stood near his wife and child, looking down upon them.

"I will help you to the utmost of my power," he said, speaking slowly, and with a difficulty that presently passed. "Whilst I live, neither you nor your child will be friendless. Trust me, and make me happy by knowing me to be your friend."

She raised her feverishly-lighted eyes, and said in a quick, febrile whisper: "You cannot take the burden of the three of us upon yourself."

"No! I would not raise a finger to serve your husband now. He has money, but he left you in want all day yesterday, and you have been alone through the night. . . But I will befriend you and your child. Whatever I can do shall be done. I am not rich—I would to God I were, for your sake. Were I to pay this debt, I should only delay the loss of your furniture for a few days; others would come, and I should not have the money to deal with them."

"What am I to do?" she wailed, clinging to her child.

"Mrs. Parrot's house will be your home for the present. We must wait until we get news of Mr. Conway."

"Oh, Mr. Hampden, is he not cruel to have left me in this position! No one knows but God what I have endured during the last year! When I was battling with poverty alone I was happier and richer. My memories were fresh and pure, my conscience was clear, but I sacrificed them for Nelly's sake, and now I am deserted and the most miserable woman in the whole world!"

She broke into a long piteous cry, but no tears came into her eyes.

"Let me take you at once from this wretched home. Come!"

He went to the door and held it open. Dolly stared around her like a sleeper suddenly aroused, and then rose with the child in her arms. Holdsworth called to the servant and told her to fetch her mistress's hat. The "man in possession" lounged out of the back room and stared with a dry smile.

"Goin'?" he asked.

Holdsworth did not answer him. The weight of the child was too great for the half-fainting mother, who tottered as she stood. Holdsworth took Nelly from her and placed her on the ground.

"You ain't a goin', missis," are yer?" said the servant, handing Dolly the hat, and whimpering.

"Yes," replied Holdsworth; "and if Mr. Conway should call, tell him that his wife is at Mrs. Parrot's."

"Oh, mum, I don't like to be left alone with that man!" cried the servant, looking down the passage.

"Vy not?" said the man.   "If you're all goin', who's to cook my wittles, I should like to know?"

"*I*'ll not stop!" exclaimed the girl.   "I wouldn't trust myself anear him."

"You're free to stop or go, as you please," said Holdsworth, giving her some money.

"Then I ain't to be paid out arter all?" exclaimed the man, striking a match, and holding it flaming in one hand and his pipe in the other.

"Not by me," answered Holdsworth, opening the hall-door.

He took Nelly's hand and gave Dolly his arm. She drew a long quivering sob as she passed through the garden; and then, seeing some inquisitive faces staring over the wire-blinds in the opposite house, hung her head and stepped out quickly.

Mrs. Parrot, hearing them come in, ran out of the kitchen, and stood looking from one to the other of them in mute astonishment.

"Mrs. Conway will make a temporary home of your house, Mrs. Parrot," said Holdsworth. "You will kindly prepare a bed-room for her and Miss Nelly, and place your drawing-room at her disposal."

Dolly had sunk into a chair. He poured out some wine and held it to her, but she waved it away, striving to suppress her sobs.

"Oh, ma'am, pray don't take on so," cried Mrs. Parrot, going up to her.   "Things 'll come right, ma'am. You'll be heasy an' comfortable here."

Holdsworth knelt on a chair beside her, holding the wine. Oh, it was hard that he could not take her to his heart and whisper the word that would change all her anguish into joy. But if ever the barrier that was raised between them had been felt, it was felt by him then. Her honour now, more than ever it had been, was become peculiarly his care. The sense of her being another's, that his own claims were as naught in the presence of her belief that she was Conway's wife, was never before so sharply felt. Her misery had given her in his eyes a sanctity that made his yearning love sacrilegious. Humility conquered emotion, and he crept away from her side, and stood looking at her from a distance, holding Nelly's hand.

Meanwhile, Mrs. Parrot's fingers were busy with Dolly's hat strings and the shawl over her shoulders, and she murmured incessantly all manner of kindly sentences, of which their extreme triteness as consolatory axioms was greatly qualified by her motherly manner.

"There, my dear," she exclaimed, laying the hat upon the table, "drink a little wine : you'll be better presently. Life's full o' troubles, God knows! and there are husbands in this world as is enough to make a woman forget her sect and strike 'em. But a friend, ma'am, is as good as sunshine to a frost-bitten man, and I'm sure you've got a good and kind one in Mr. Hampden."

"It's my husband's desertion," cried Dolly, "that I think of. I don't mind the loss of my home. But to think of *his* deserting me and my little one when he *could* not know that I had a friend—when I married him for Nelly's sake, to get her bread. Yes, Mrs. Parrot, to save her from starving. And to feel that I defied my conscience only to be brought so low—*so* low !"

" God forbid, my dear, that iver *I* should set husband an' wife agin' each other," replied Mrs. Parrot, glancing at Holdsworth, to see how he might relish her remark ; " but I *must* say that, if Mr. Conway's left yer, it's a good thing, an' the last thing on this airth as would trouble me if I was you. You've gone through a deal o' sufferin' for him, an' if he's desairted you, you can't come to worse harm nor was he to have stood by his home like a man, which he niver was ; and there's not one o' your neighbours as don't know that you've had more trouble than any Christian woman i' this world ought to have. And it may sound a hard sayin', but if he's gone," she exclaimed, looking defiantly at Holdsworth, " I hope and pray it's for good an' all."

It often happens in real life, as in books, that a closing remark will take a weird appropriateness by the sudden confrontment of the fact of which it is only the shadow. Mrs. Parrot had barely shut her mouth when the passage echoed with the clattering of the knocker on the house-door. Never was such a delirious knocking. Mrs. Parrot turned pale, persuaded that Mr. Conway had come home drunk, and had reeled across to her house to demand his wife and create a horrible " scene."

Dolly raised her head, and it was plain that the same idea had occurred to her, by the indescribable expression of mingled hate, fear, and loathing that entered her face.

Mrs. Parrot giving her moral organisation a twist, ran out. Scarcely had she opened the door when in burst Martha, the servant from over the way.

" Oh, missis ! oh, missis !" she screeched, " what do you think ? Master's drowned ! O Lord ! Where's Mrs. Conway ? He's dead an' gone ! Here's the gent as brought the noos. Oh, sir, please tell the missis here !"

She turned, and in her excitement caught hold of the sleeve of a little stout man who stood behind, and literally dragged him forward.

"Let go, you fool! What are you a doing of? Are you Mrs. Conway?" he asked of Mrs. Parrot, who stood staring with wide-open eyes, grasping her dress as if she were only waiting to take a deep breath before tearing herself in two.

"No, she ain't! This ain't Mrs. Conway!" cried the excited Martha.

"You told me she was here!" exclaimed the man.

"So she is; ain't she, missis?"

"Great 'iven! what a clatterin'!" cried Mrs. Parrot, recovering her tongue. "What is it you've got to say, sir?"

"Why, this," answered the little man, who was evidently a very irritable little man—"Mr. Conway's body was found in the river this morning at a quarter before seven, and he's lying now in the Town Hall, and I've come to give the news; and curse me if ever I'll undertake such a job again, if I am to be mauled about by such a fool as this when I'm out of breath, and fit to drop with perspiration."

"Mrs. Parrot! Mrs. Parrot!" called Holdsworth.

The half-distracted woman ran into the sitting-room, where the first thing she saw was Dolly in a dead faint, lying upon the sofa, with Holdsworth kneeling by her side.

"She overheard your voices!" he exclaimed, turning up a face as white as death. "Pray God the shock may not kill her. Look to her, Mrs. Parrot, I *must* speak to the man outside."

He jumped up and left the room, and found the little irritable man in the act of walking away.

"I beg your pardon. One moment!" he cried, running out after him. "Pray excuse my agitation—you have brought shocking news. Is it *indeed* true?"

The little man turned and took in Holdsworth from head to foot, and answered: "It is true, sir. I've seen the body myself. It's in the Town Hall. He's been in the water all night, the doctor says."

"All night?"

"He was found by a man named Williamson. They all knew who he was when they saw him. He must have been drunk when he fell into the water, for the path was wide enough for a horse and cart. Dr. Tanner asked me to step round with the news as he heard I was coming this way. Good morning."

The little man nodded and walked away. Had Dolly been a rich man's wife, a sympathetic deputation, introduced by the churchwardens, might have made a procession to her house to break the news gently, but how can you expect sympathy for the wife of a man who dies owing everybody money?

Holdsworth was stunned, and stood for some moments staring idly from the porch. He then returned hastily to Dolly's side.

"She's comin' to, sir," said Mrs. Parrot, slapping the poor girl's hand, and expending what breath she had upon the cold white forehead. "What awful noos, sir! . . . Conway dead! I can't believe it. And drowned, too! Oh, poor wretch!"

"Hush!" exclaimed Holdsworth.

Dolly had opened her eyes, and was staring blindly at him. He moistened his handkerchief with water on the sideboard and pressed it to her head. Nelly stood at the window gazing at her mother with a look of wist-

ful fear in her face.   At the door was Martha's countenance, seamed with lines of perspiration, her mouth
open, and her hair hanging like a string of young carrots
over her forehead.

"I feel very weak," muttered Dolly, striving to sit
upright, but falling back.

"Something terrible has happened.   Ah! Robert
is dead!"

The memory rushed upon her like a spasm, and she
spoke in a cry.

"Come, my dear, don't try to speak yet," said Mrs.
Parrot.

"Where is Nelly?"

Holdsworth led the child to the sofa.   The mother
looked at her little girl, opened her arms, and burst
into tears.

"Thank God for that!" said Holdsworth, turning
away.   Watching her face as her consciousness had
dawned, he had felt that, if tears did not relieve her,
her heart would break.

CHAPTER XXXI.

HUSBAND AND WIFE.

THE little irritable man had brought true news. The report was all over the town : everybody was talking of Conway's death. A woman living in the road called upon Mrs. Parrot to give her the story, not knowing that Mrs. Conway was within. Her husband had met Williamson, the man who found Conway, and had got the account from him clear of all exaggeration.

It was just this : Williamson was a carpenter, and was walking to Thorrold Marsh to execute a repairing job at a house there. He was this side of Hanwitch, just by the bridge facing Squire Markwell's place, when he saw a human hand sticking out of the water. He peered and saw a man lying on his back, the water half a foot above his face, showing the drowned figure as plainly as if it were under glass. Williamson pulls off his coat, tucks up his shirt-sleeves, catches hold of the hand, and up comes the body like a cork. The moment he had the body ashore he knew who it was; left his bag of tools on the bank, and ran as hard as his legs would carry him into the town to give the alarm. The inspector and two constables, and a couple of men with a stretcher belonging to the Town Hall, start out of the High Street and are conducted by Williamson to the body. A crowd gathers about the tail of the procession, the body is put on the stretcher, covered up, and carried to the Town Hall in the sight of a multitude large enough to diffuse the news through the length and breadth of Hanwitch in ten minutes.

So dead Mr. Conway was, if ever a man was dead in this world; and now, the woman told Mrs. Parrot, people were only waiting for the coroner's inquest, to learn how he came by his death.

But the verdict, however it might run, would be inconclusive, since there were no witnesses to show how Conway fell into the water. But this much was known; that yesterday Conway had called at the "Three Stars" and ordered a fine dinner to be got ready for him, with champagne and the best of wines; and to let the landlord understand that he meant what he said, he pulled out a handful of sovereigns and let them fall into his pocket again, chink! chink! When dinner was done, he left the house intoxicated, and what became of him the "Three Stars" didn't know; but the "Pine Apple" did, for he came there in the afternoon and squeezed himself behind the bar, made love to the barmaid, drank some tumblers of rum, and got into an abusive argument with an ostler, whose eye he threatened to blacken if he contradicted him again. On which he was turned out.

That was his day's history, so far as it was recorded in human knowledge. The rest could be guessed; and the public were not slow in explaining their theories. Of course he was drunk, had rolled into the water, and was too senseless to get out again, though the water where he lay was not above two and a half feet deep.

Nobody cared twopence about his death. It gave the shop-people something to talk about until customers dropped in, and then it was, "What's the next article?" and Conway was forgotten. When a bubble explodes upon the surface of a stream, nothing mourns. The tide rolls on just the same, with sunshine or darkness in its breast, as the case may be ; the pikes lose no jot of their voracity, and gudgeons swim into their maws ; the minnows jump at the flies. Shall law, commerce, or anything else stop because a drunkard is drowned? Cover him up ; let him hide his face until the pale jury come to take a peep ; then pop him out of sight in a hole, and get back as fast as we may to dinner.

But there were two persons on whose destiny this man's death was to exercise an influence as wonderful, and gracious, and beneficial, as though, instead of a dead drunkard, he was a good spirit—an angel charged with a mission of love, sent by God Himself to work out and complete the happiness of the man who had been heavily tried, but who, in his bitterest trial, had never been found wanting.

And I truly think that for such men—men who in their sorrow reverentially bow their heads and say, "God knows, I believe in Him ; He shall lead me as a little child"—who murmur not, but, praising their Heavenly Father always, make their actions a profound heroism by obeying His voice in all seasons, not more faithfully in moments of joy than in moments of anguish —for such men we shall seldom err in prophesying a time in their lives when the heat of the day shall be shaded from them, and their burden and their conflict removed. "O man, greatly beloved, go thou thy way till the end ; for thou shalt rest, and stand in thy lot at the end of thy days."

Dolly had asked to be left alone with her child.

Deeming Holdsworth a stranger, she had felt the restraint of his presence upon her, deeply as she was moved by his goodness. Her heart ached: misery had mastered her. The mere sense of having found a friend in this her time of piteous need could not suffice her. More was imperative: communion with God, communion with the husband who, she believed, looked down upon her from Heaven. To no mortal eyes could she lay bare the exquisite grief that lacerated her heart; and though she should find no comfort even in the Heaven she turned to, yet her full and poignant misery demanded escape in words and tears, and she asked to be left alone.

Holdsworth entered the room facing his own apartment. This was Mrs. Parrot's drawing-room. Here she had a piano; here she had some wonderful stuffed birds under glass shades; here she herself sat on Sundays with her mother, when her house was unoccupied.

He struggled to calm himself, that he might master and appreciate all the significance of the position in which he was placed by the sudden death of Conway. But his moods were wild and hurrying; the play of emotion was quick and painful. He saw his wife in her grief; he saw her wrestling, with no eye but her child's upon her, with the anguish that filled her; he felt her loneliness: he felt the cruel hopelessness that weighed in her heart as lead; he felt, above all, the dreadful sense of degradation which must attend her reflections upon the death of her husband, Conway; upon the wretched, miserable life she had led with him; upon the complete and bitter reversal of the sole end for which she had married him.

The barrier that divided them was gone. Could

there be any scruple now to hold him back from her? If there yet lingered one feeling of delicacy to prompt him to delay his confession for a little, until the dead was buried, until something of the horror of the sudden death had yielded to time, should it not be removed by the knowledge of her misery, which he had it in his power to dissipate and turn to gladness? Why should she weep? Why should she feel one instant of pain, when he could change her tears to smiles, her grief to joy?

He stole to the door of the room she was in and listened. He heard her sobbing, and that sound vanquished his last hesitation.

He turned the handle gently and entered. She was on her knees beside the sofa, her arms twined about Nelly, her face buried in the child's lap. She started, looked at him, and rose slowly to her feet. He approached and stood before her.

"Will you not trust me as a friend?" he said, in a voice a little above a whisper.

She tried to answer him, but her sobs choked her voice. He seated himself and took Nelly on his knee, and, whilst he smoothed the child's hair, continued: "There *is* hope, there *is* comfort for you and this little one. Check your sobs and listen to me. I can give you comfort, for I have known what it is to lose one that is dearer to me than my heart's blood, to lose her and to find her again. She was my wife, and I left her to go to sea. The ship I sailed in was wrecked, and for many days I lay consumed with hunger and thirst in an open boat, seeing miserable creatures like myself dying around me one by one. And when I was rescued my memory was gone; I could not remember my own name, my home, the wife I had left, the country I had sailed from. But the voice of God one day directed me to leave Australia and go to England. I reached London, and there a man spoke to me of Hanwitch, a name familiar and dear to me for my wife's sake. And when I came to Southbourne, the beloved old village gave me back my memory. I knew whom I had come to seek, and what I had lost. They told me that my wife thought me dead, and was married and lived with my child here—in this road—in that house yonder! O Dolly! O wife!"

Her sweet sad face, as he continued speaking, had been slowly upturning to his, and, when their eyes met, he put the little child upon the floor and stretched out his arms, crying, " O Dolly! O wife!"

But she!

There was a look of petrifaction, stranger and more awful even than death, upon her face; her eyes glared, her lips were parted: and to have seen her thus stirless, thus white, thus staring, thus breathless, you would have said that she was dead, even as she sat there.

Then the life leaped into her, she started from the sofa with a loud hysterical laugh, and flung herself on her knees before him, crying, "John! John!"

"Dolly!"

"John! John!" she repeated; and she brought his hand to her eyes, and stared at it; and then grasped his knees and raised her face to his, talking to herself in hurried, inaudible whispers, and fixing a piercing gaze upon him.

"John! John!" she cried out again.

He put his arms around her, and would have pressed her to his heart, but she kept herself away with her hand against his breast, preserving that keen, unwinking, steadfast, wonderful gaze.

"Do you not know me, Dolly?" he cried.   "Look at me closely; hear my voice! hear me tell you of the old dear times! We were to meet in the summer, do you remember, Dolly? and we were never more to part; and you were to keep a calendar and mark off the days. O God! what weary days—what endless days to both of us! And do you remember the walks we took the day before we parted, down by the river, where I sat and cried in your arms because the sight of your sorrow broke me down and I had no more comfort to give you?"

But still she would not let him clasp her.   Still she kept her hand pressed against him, and her eyes, now growing wild and unreal with fear, upon his face.

"O God!" he cried in his agony.   "Will she not know me?   Has my secret come upon her too suddenly? Darling! darling! I could not see your tears, I could not hear your sobs, I could not feel the desolation and misery that was breaking your heart, and still keep myself hidden from you.   Oh, bitter has the trial been to watch you—to know you to be mine—to see my little child—and to be as a stranger to you!   Call me John! Call me husband!   Speak to me, Dolly!   Tell me that no change that pain and suffering have made in me can disguise me from your love!"

She released herself from his arms and sprang a yard away from him; and there, as she stood transfixed, watching him with large, steady eyes, her dishevelled hair about her forehead, her hands clenched, and her head inclined forward, she looked like a marble figure of madness, her habiliments carven to the life.

She had thought him dead.   For many, many months

she had prayed to him as one in Heaven. Did she
know him now? Yes, but as a dead man might be
known—with unspeakable fear and unspeakable love;
with the horror of superstition and the passion of deep
affection.

Thus they stood for awhile, their eyes fixed on each
other: then a heavy sigh broke from him; he turned
to his child.

"Nelly, my little one, come to me! I am thy
father!"

He extended his arms. The action and words broke
the spell. With an indescribable cry Dolly fled to him.

"John! John!" she murmured. "My husband—
my very own! Come back to me from the dead!
Come back to me after all this cruel waiting!"

And then she broke from him again, and watched
him yet again from a distance, then ran and flung her
arms around his neck, crying, "John! John! Why
did you not come to me before? why did you not come
to me before?"

The hot tears were streaming down his cheeks now:
he held her tightly, saying, in broken tones:

"We are together—never more to part. I am thy
very husband! I have loved thee always! Oh, God
be praised, the merciful God be praised for this!"

"Nelly, Nelly!" she cried; and she ran from him
and seized her child, and held her up.

"She is ours, John! our little one! We have found
papa, Nelly! There he is! There is Nelly's papa!
God has given him back to us—we were broken-hearted
just now . . . O husband! . . . husband!"

She broke down; a dangerous excitement had up to
this moment sustained her. She sank into a weeping,

sobbing, fainting woman in a moment; but his arms received her, his breast pillowed her, and there she rested for many minutes, with no sound to break the holy silence that filled the room but his deep quivering sobs.

When we peep at them again, a half-hour has passed, and the wife is seated near the husband with her arm around him; and the child is on her father's knee. The fear that threw a film upon the exquisite emotions of the girl has passed; she is listening to his story, interrupting him often with quick exclamations of distress, then fondling him and listening again, vibrating with eagerness, with love, with amazement, which makes her pale face kaleidoscopic with expression. He is telling her of his sufferings in the boat, of his rescue, of his friends in Australia, of his return to England, of his arrival at Southbourne; and as she hears him tell the story of his noble unselfishness—how, to save her from the sorrow and the shame that must have attended his disclosure, if made while Conway lived, he held his secret, but could not keep his love from going forth to his child— she knows that he has brought back to her the same grand heart he took with him five years ago; the same magnanimous qualities; the same pure impulses; the same heroical capacity of self-sacrifice.

And then she tells him her story; and now it is for him to soothe her with the love that has transformed his face and made it beautiful with a deeper and subtler beauty than it had ever before worn. For, as she recurs to those piteous times of her distress, her tears gush forth afresh and her eyes grow wild, as though she did not believe in the happiness that had come to her at last.

I see them sitting in that room while the bright
morning sunshine pours upon the window and floods
the floor with its radiance; I hear the birds singing
merrily in the garden, and the cosy chucking of the
hens and the sound of the fresh sweet wind as it sweeps
through the pear-trees and sends the red-edged leaves
rustling to the ground.

I see the child's large deep eyes wandering from
father to mother, from mother to father, with the small
face busy with the unformed consciousness that struggles
in it.

I see the mother careworn and pale, but with the
light of rapture on her face that discloses all its secret
sweetness, watching, ever watching, with soft eyes
shining with happy tears, the dear one whose arm is
around her.

I see Holdsworth with the patches of gray upon his
hair, his sunken cheeks and bowed figure symbolising
while his life shall hold the unspeakable sufferings of
mind and body he has known since we first beheld him.
I see him, with the calmness of perfect joy mellowing
his eyes, and enriching his face with a colour that owes
its lustre to the spirit, so that it shall be there in darkness and in sunshine, holding his wife to his heart, often
pressing his lips to his child, often glancing upwards
with looks of ineffable gratitude; and I think of those
two lines which Goldsmith says are worth a million:

"*I have been young, and now am old: yet never saw
I the righteous man forsaken, nor his seed begging their
bread.*"

*   *   *   *

A knock falls upon the door; the door is opened,

and enter Mrs. Parrot. Does she start dramatically? I promise you there is more genuine astonishment conveyed by the little jump she gives, as she falls back a step and then stands staring, than in any movement designed to express wonderment you will see performed on the stage.

So the mystery is solved, is it? So her lodger isn't a gentleman after all, but an insidious man who, under pretence of liking Nelly's company, has been paying attention to mamma! and now, with Conway's body lying in the Town Hall, dead only a few hours, is actually caressing the widow in Mrs. Parrot's respectable house!

Holdsworth and Dolly exchange glances, and Dolly hangs her head with a look of confusion on her face (and well she may, thinks Mrs. Parrot) as Holdsworth puts Nelly down and rises.

"I am really sorry to introod," says Mrs. Parrot haughtily, "but my motive for knockin', sir, was to inquire when you would like your breakfast sarved?"

"We'll talk of that in a moment," answers Holdsworth. "I have something to say to you. This lady is my wife!"

"I beg your parding," says Mrs. Parrot, growing very pale.

"My wife, Mrs. Parrot. You have heard of Mr. Holdsworth who went to sea and was drowned? He was not drowned. I am Mr. Holdsworth!"

"You!"

She tottered, ran forward, grasped the table, and shrieked, "You!"

"Yes, Mrs. Parrot," exclaimed Dolly, "this is John —my own darling husband, who I thought was dead."

"And do you mean to say, sir," gasped Mrs. Parrot hysterically, "that you knew who you was yourself all the time ?"

"All the time that I have lodged with you."

"An' you've seen your lawful wife day arter day without speakin' of it, or sayin' who you was ?"

"Yes."

"Because," stammered Mrs. Parrot, still clinging to the table, "because you says that a wife can't have two husbands, and so you hid yourself that you might spare her feelin's ?"

"Yes, that is why, Mrs. Parrot," cried Dolly.

Mrs. Parrot took a deep breath, and then, to the amazement of the others, burst into tears.

"Oh, sir, I can't help it," she sobbed. "I niver did hear in all my life of such beautiful conduct. Niver . . And is this your child ? . . . Why, of course it is ! Oh dear ! who'd ha' thought that any mortal man could ha' acted so nobly ! Oh, sir, let me shake your hand."

She not only shook his hand, but actually fell against him and kissed him ; and then, overwhelmed with her effrontery and her feelings, was rushing out of the room, when Holdsworth stopped her.

"One moment, dear Mrs. Parrot. You are the only person in Hanwitch—in the world I may say—who knows our secret. Will you keep it ? We have many reasons for not wishing it known."

"I will, sir, I promise you," blubbered the honest woman, "since you ask me ; but if it wasn't for that I'd go and spread the noos everywhere, I would, for I niver heerd of such beautiful conduct before, niver, in sarmons or anywheers else ; and it 'ud be the makin' of many a man to be told of it. God bless you both,

I'm sure. God bless you, little gal. You've found a good father—a rare good father!"

And out she ran choking.

So the curtain falls, for the end has come. No need to raise it again, for you who have sat so kindly and patiently through this little drama must know as well as I what will become of the two chief characters and their little one when they have made their bow and withdrawn. Australia is before them, with generous friends to welcome them to their new home, and listen with interest and tenderness to their strange story of bitter separation, and sweet and sacred reunion.

Enough has been written; the quill that has driven these creations to this point is but a stump; the hand that holds it is tired; the companionship of the shadows which have kept me company is broken. What fitter time, then, than now to say good-bye?

POSTSCRIPT.

I MUST claim the reader's indulgence while I speak for a moment of that portion of the foregoing narrative which refers to the hero's loss of memory.

That loss of memory has been brought about by trials and sufferings such as I have attempted to depict in the early chapters of this narrative, is too certain to make it necessary that I should adduce instances (which are very readily procured) as proof. That such loss has lasted, not for months only, but for years, will be seen by the following anecdote, which suggested this story, and which I extract from the *Noon Gazette* of July, 1772 :—

" Last Sunday died at Winchelsea a character of whom a correspondent, a gentleman distinguished both by his parts and benevolence, has obligingly furnished us with the following account : That his name was *William Stephens*, and that he was a mariner, who, many years since, was pressed from his home to serve on board His Majesty's ship of war *The Vapour ;* that he was then married but two weeks ; that whilst cruising off the Portugal coast *The Vapour* was wrecked, and *Stephens*, with some others, saved his life by clinging to a portion of the wreck, in which condition they languished near three days, and were then rescued by a French merchantman, who carried them into *Bordeau* (*sic*): that on *Stephens* being questioned, he was found to have lost his memory, on which he was sent into England, and was hired as porter by *Mr. Hudson*, of the *York Inn*, in or near to *Folkestone*, in *Kent*, where he remained for two years in entire ignorance of his past, until, his memory returning, he set off for Winchelsea on foot, and arrived to find his wife married to one *Eel*, a cobbler, whose life Stephens threatened if he did not restore him his *Nancy*. This the cobbler did, and so the matter ended. It occasioned much gossip, and to the end of his days Mr. Stephens (who settled down as a carpenter, having lost all relish for the sea) was regarded with curiosity, and had to the houses of the neighbouring gentry, whom his singular story never failed to divert."

There are on record many instances of loss of memory, occasioned by various means. In some cases the deprivation has been complete, and the restoration sudden, and resembling an abrupt revelation. In other instances it has been accompanied by faint, glimmering, haunting reminiscences, creating indescribable anxiety, but growing up suddenly into a sound and permanent recovery.

Printed by R. & R. CLARK, *Edinburgh.*